T0089847

WATCH

SIXTH WATCH

Book Six

SERGEI LUKYANENKO

TRANSLATED BY ANDREW BROMFIELD

HARPER

NEW YORK • LONDON • TORONTO • SYDNEY

HARPER

HarperCollins books may be purchased for educational, business, or sales promotional use. For information, please email the Special Markets Department at SPsales@harper collins.com.

Originally published as Шестой дозор in Russia in 2015 by AST.

English translation © Andrew Bromfield 2016.

First Harper Paperbacks edition published 2016.

FIRST EDITION

Designed by Sunil Manchikanti

Library of Congress Cataloging-in-Publication Data has been applied for.

ISBN 978-0-06-242844-8 (pbk.)

16 17 18 19 20 DIX/RRD 10 9 8 7 6 5 4 3 2

This text is mandatory reading for the forces of Light.

—THE NIGHT WATCH

This text is mandatory reading for the forces of Darkness.

—THE DAY WATCH

SIXTH
WATCH

PROLOGUE

FIFTEEN YEARS IS A LONG STRETCH.

In fifteen years a man can be born, learn to walk, talk, and use a computer; learn to read, count, and use the toilet as well; and then, a lot later, learn to fight and fall in love. And sometimes, to round things off, he brings new people into the world or dispatches old ones into the darkness.

Over the course of fifteen years spent in prisons for especially dangerous criminals, murderers pass through all the circles of hell, and then go free. Sometimes without an iota of darkness in their souls. Sometimes without an iota of light.

In fifteen years even the most ordinary man radically changes his life several times. He leaves his family and starts a new one. He changes his job maybe three or four times. He makes a fortune and is reduced to poverty. He visits the Congo, where he smuggles diamonds, or settles down in a deserted little village in the Pskov Region and starts breeding goats. He takes to drink, acquires a second degree, becomes a Buddhist, starts taking drugs, learns to fly a plane, and goes to the Maidan in Kiev, where he gets a smack across the forehead with a truncheon, after which he enters a monastery.

Basically, lots of things can happen in fifteen years.

If you're a man.

. . . But if you happen to be a fifteen-year-old girl, you know for absolute certain that nothing interesting has ever happened to you.

Well, almost nothing.

If anyone could have had a heart-to-heart talk with Olya Yalova (five years ago her mother could have done it and three years ago her granny could have—but now no one could), she would have told that person three interesting things about herself.

First—how much she hated the stupid sound of her own name!

Olya Yalova!

You couldn't make it up.

When she was a kid, they teased her and called her Olya-Yalo, like the twin girls in that ancient children's film *The Kingdom of Crooked Mirrors*. But that wasn't too bad. After all, it was a good film (in seven-year-old Olya's opinion), and she even looked a bit like those twins. Olya-Yalo? So fine.

But then in fourth year at school, when she was ten, a certain classmate of hers . . . Yeah, right, "a certain classmate . . ." It's great when at that age you're already blond, handsome, and top of the class, with rich parents who adore you and your surname is Sokolov (from *sokol,* meaning "falcon") . . . well then, this "certain classmate" of hers decided to look up what the other pupils' names meant on the Internet . . .

And then you discover that "Yalova" means nothing more than a cow with no calf. A barren cow. And so "barren cow" becomes your nickname from ten to thirteen. Sometimes it's abbreviated to just "cow," sometimes even to "B.C." The humiliation of it and all the tears you cry make you start staying at home, reading books and guzzling tea with biscuits—until your figure really does look like a cow's . . .

The second supremely important thing to have happened in the life of Olya Yalova (or Olya-Yalo, as even she thought of herself) was ice hockey. Genuine ice hockey with a puck. Women's ice hockey— well, girls'. She joined the class entirely by chance, when one day she happened to have a dream about that villain Sokolov: For some reason she was standing there absolutely naked in front of him, and the handsome devil (at the age of thirteen Sokolov had developed into a tall and quite obscenely attractive boy) was wincing, covering his eyes with his hand and hissing through his teeth: "cow . . ."

Either simply her time had come, or ice hockey was precisely what was needed, but all the excess fat drained off Olya in six months, and a year later—at fourteen—she was the star of Russia's national youth team.

And suddenly it turned out that all this time, hiding under those plump cheeks and fat thighs was a tall (at fifteen Olya had outgrown everyone in her class and her trainer looked her up and down somberly and said: "I won't let you switch to basketball!"), strong (they were just joking and this stupid quarrel started up . . . Olya herself didn't even notice when she knocked down two of her male classmates—and they just sat there on the floor, gazing at her fearfully, afraid to get up) girl (very definitely a girl—when Olya walked out of the shower she cast a glance at herself in the mirror and smiled, because she knew that every single poor fool whose name she didn't even want to know would narrow his eyes in lustful delight at the sight of her.

And the third supremely important thing in Olya's life was only just about to happen. With her hands stuffed into her pockets (it was frosty, but she didn't feel like wearing gloves), Olya walked past the Olympic Stadium, with the still-incomplete minarets of the main municipal mosque towering up behind it, and then past a small Orthodox church. It was early evening, the streetlamps were all glowing brightly, but there weren't very many people out on the streets, even though this was the city center. Moscow wasn't used to genuinely frosty Russian weather anymore—a mere minus fifteen Celsius was enough to make everyone go running off home or huddle up in their cars.

And now she went across the narrow little street and down into the pedestrian underpass to the other side of Peace Avenue. Then she was intending to go down a side street with trams clattering along their rails and into the high-rise apartment block set on a massive platform with a colonnade—a "stylobate" (three years of compulsive reading had not gone to waste; it had left Olya's head crammed with a whole slew of random words and haphazard bits and pieces of knowledge). This was the house where the villain Sokolov lived. The handsome devil Sokolov. No longer Oleg Sokolov now, but "Olezhka"—who was hers and hers alone!

They'd been dating for six months already. Only no one knew about it. Neither at school nor at her ice hockey class. And her mother and granny didn't know either.

The feud between Olya Yalova and Oleg Sokolov had gone on for far too long. But now . . . no, not right now, but starting from tomorrow, Olya wasn't going to hide anything any longer. Tomorrow she and Oleg would arrive at school together.

Because today she was going to spend the night at his place. Oleg's parents were away. Olya's granny and mum thought she was going to stay overnight with a girlfriend after training.

But she was going to stay at Oleg's place.

They had already decided everything. Before this the most they had done was kiss . . . well . . . that evening in the back row of the cinema didn't really count, even though Oleg had let his hands roam free . . .

Now it was all going to be serious. They were fifteen already, it was shameful to admit they hadn't had sex yet. They'd be mocked to death! So maybe the girls on the team weren't having it, but they simply didn't have the time, and they were too tired. And then there were so many classes at school now . . . But in general, at the age of fifteen there were hardly any virgins left, boys or girls.

Olya knew that, because she'd read about it on the Internet, and the result of three years of obsessive reading is not merely superfluous knowledge, but also excessive confidence in the printed word.

Somewhere in the depths of Olya's soul (which was probably skulking in her stomach right now), there was a faint, cold pulse of fear. Or even doubt.

She liked Olezhka. Kissing with him was great. And hugging too. And . . . and she wanted more. She knew perfectly well how it all happened . . . how it was supposed to be . . . well, after all, it was on the Internet . . .

And basically, Olya wanted that.

Only she couldn't understand if she wanted it now or later. With Oleg or with someone else.

But she'd already promised to go. And Olya Yalova didn't like to break her promises.

The side street greeted her with a cold wind blowing from the direction of the Three Stations on Komsomol Square, and with a sudden, surprising darkness. Surprising because the streetlamps were on, the windows in the apartment blocks and the shop signs were glowing, but for some reason their glow failed to dispel the gloom—the tiny spots of light were suspended in the night, bright but powerless, like the distant stars in the sky.

Olya even stopped for a moment. She glanced around behind her.

What sort of nonsense was this? She'd be there in three minutes. One minute, if she ran. She was five feet nine inches tall and had better muscles than lots of young guys. She was in the center of Moscow, it was seven o'clock in the evening, and there were plenty of people around on their way back home.

What was she afraid of?

It was just that she was afraid of going to Oleg's!

She couldn't even keep her promise. She'd promised too much, and now she'd gotten scared just like a little girl. But she was a grown woman . . . almost a grown-up already . . . almost a woman . . .

Olya adjusted her woolly hat with the pompom, arranged the sports bag on her shoulder more comfortably (towel, clean panties, and a pack of panty liners—Olya suspected that she would need them tomorrow), and quickened her stride.

Junior Police Lieutenant Dmitry Pastukhov wasn't on duty. He wasn't even in uniform when he raised his arm to stop a car on the corner of Protopopov Lane and Astrakhan Lane. The reasons Dima Pastukhov was here at this hour of the day might upset his wife, so

SERGEI LUKYANENKO

we won't go into the details. All that can be said in Dima's defense is that he was holding a plastic bag containing a box of Rafaello chocolates and a bouquet of flowers, both bought from a vending machine nearby, in the Billa supermarket.

Dima didn't give his wife flowers and chocolates very often, only once or twice a year. Which in this particular case, strangely enough, is a mitigating factor.

"What do you mean, five hundred?" Dima haggled feistily. "Three hundred's the top price at the outside!"

"Have you any idea how much gas costs?" the dusky southern driver asked just as feistily from behind the wheel of his battered Ford. Despite his nonlocal appearance, he spoke perfect, cultured Russian. "Call an official taxi—no one will take you for less."

"That's why I flagged down a private car," Dima explained. In his own mind he was basically prepared to pay five hundred—it was quite a distance—but force of habit made him haggle anyway.

"Four hundred," the southerner declared.

"Let's go," said Dima, and glanced around the street for no particular reason before ducking into the car. The girl was standing only five steps away. Swaying and looking at Dima.

She was, after all, a tall girl with a curvaceous figure, and in the semidarkness she would have passed for a grown woman, but right now the light from the streetlamp was falling straight onto her face—and it was the face of a child.

The girl had no cap on her head, and her hair was tousled. Tears were pouring out of her eyes. Her neck was bloody. Her nylon ski jacket was clean, but there were streaks of blood on her light-blue jeans.

Dima put the plastic bag and the bouquet on the car seat and dashed over to the girl. Behind him the driver swore a convoluted oath when he spotted the girl.

"What's wrong?" Pastukhov exclaimed, grabbing the girl by the shoulders. "Are you okay? Where is he?"

Somehow Pastukhov was quite sure the girl would tell him immediately where "he" was, and Pastukhov would overtake the scumbag and detain "him" and, if Pastukhov got lucky, some part of "him" would get smashed or broken in the process of arrest.

But the girl spoke in a quiet voice.

"Are you a policeman, then?"

Pastukhov, not really fully aware that he wasn't in uniform, nodded.

"Yes. Yes, of course! Where is he?"

"Take me away from here," the girl said plaintively. "I'm cold, please take me away."

The rapist was nowhere nearby. The driver clambered out from behind the steering wheel, took a baseball bat out from somewhere (everyone knows that almost no one in Russia plays baseball, but bat sales are comparable with the USA). A married couple strolling along Astrakhan Lane saw the girl, Pastukhov, and the driver—and ducked into the supermarket. But a kid with a school satchel, moving along Protopopov Lane in the opposite direction, stopped and whooped in delight, so joyfully that Pastukhov promptly recalled the Bible's eulogy of corporal punishment in the raising of children.

"You can't leave the scene of the incident right now . . ." Pastukhov began.

Then he stopped short.

He saw where the blood was coming from.

Two tiny holes in the girl's neck.

Two bite marks.

"Let's go," he declared, and tugged the girl toward the car. She didn't resist, as if once she'd decided to trust him, she'd stopped thinking about anything at all.

"Hey, she needs to go to the police," said the driver. "Or the hospital. Hey, the Sklifosovsky's not far, hang on."

"I *am* the police," said Pastukhov, pulling his ID out of his pocket and sticking it under the driver's nose. "No Sklif. Sokol Metro station, and step on it."

"Why Sokol?" the driver asked in amazement.

"That's where the Night Watch office is," said Pastukhov, laying the girl in the backseat and thrusting her sports bag under her head. He put the girl's feet on his knees. Dirty melting snow dripped off her "winter" sneakers. But that way her neck didn't bleed on him. It was a good thing a vampire's saliva stopped the blood flowing after feeding.

The bad thing was that vampires didn't always stop in time.

"What Night Watch?" the driver asked, puzzled. "I've lived in Moscow for twenty years, and I don't remember anything like that."

And you won't remember afterward either, thought Pastukhov, but he didn't say it out loud. After all, when he himself first paid a visit to the Others, he wasn't completely certain they would leave him his memories either.

But never say never.

"If you drive fast," he suggested, "I'll give you a thousand."

The driver eloquently explained where Pastukhov could stick his thousand and stepped on the gas.

The girl lay with her eyes closed. Either she had fainted or she was in shock. Pastukhov cast a sideways glance at the driver—he had his eyes glued to the road. Then, feeling like a rapist and a pervert, Pastukhov cautiously parted the girl's legs.

The crotch of the jeans was clean, not stained. At least no one had raped her.

Although, to be blunt, from Pastukhov's point of view, sexual rape would have been the lesser evil by far. It would be more normal.

PART ONE

MANDATORY ACTIONS

CHAPTER 1

"YOU'VE BEEN STUCK THERE TOO LONG," SAID GESAR.

"Where?" I inquired.

"Not 'where,' but 'on what,'" the boss said without looking up from his papers. "On your backside."

If the boss started getting rude for no good reason, it meant he was seriously perplexed about something. He wasn't in a temper— that always made him exquisitely polite. He wasn't frightened—that always made him sad and lyrical. So he was preoccupied and perplexed.

"What's happened, Boris Ignatievich?" I asked.

"Anton Gorodetsky," the boss continued, still not looking up. "You've been in the training and education section ten years—a bit too long, don't you think?"

I started pondering.

This conversation reminded me of something.

"Are there any complaints?" I asked. "I reckon I do a pretty good job . . . and I don't avoid work in the field."

"That is apart from saving the world every now and then, raising a daughter who's an Absolute Enchantress, and getting along well with your wife, who's a Great Enchantress . . ." the boss said sourly.

"I also tolerate my boss, a Great Magician," I replied in the same tone.

Gesar finally condescended to look up. He nodded.

"Yes, you tolerate me. And you'll go on tolerating me. Right, then, Anton Gorodetsky. There are unregistered vampires operating in the city. Seven attacks in a week."

"Oho," I said. "They gorge themselves every day, the perverts. What about our field operatives?"

Gesar seemed not to have heard me. He sorted through his papers.

"The first victim . . . Alexander Borisov. Twenty-three years of age. A salesman in a boutique . . . unmarried . . . blah-blah-blah . . . attacked in broad daylight in the Taganka district. The second victim, the next day. Nikolai Evgeniev. Forty-seven years of age. An engineer. The Preobrazhenka district. The third, Tatyana Rumiantseva. Nineteen years of age. A student at Moscow State University. Chertanovo district. The fourth, Oxana Elizeeva, fifty-two years of age. A cleaning woman. Mitino district. The fifth, Nina Andronnikova, a schoolgirl, ten years of age . . ."

"What a scumbag," I blurted out.

"In broad daylight, Matveevsky district."

"He's switched to women," I said. "He's sampled them. And now he's started experimenting with age."

"The sixth victim, Gennady Davydov. Sixty years old. A retiree."

"Is there a pair of them carrying out the attacks, then?" I suggested.

"Maybe it is a pair," said Gesar. "But there's definitely a female involved."

"Where's the information from? Did someone survive and tell us?" I asked.

Gesar ignored my question.

"The seventh and, for the time being, the last victim: Olya Yalova, a schoolgirl, fifteen years old. By the way, say thank you to your old acquaintance Dmitry Pastukhov. He found her and delivered her to us quickly . . . which was very helpful."

Gesar gathered all his papers together, straightened up the edges with the palm of his hand, and put them in a folder.

"So, one of the victims survived?" I asked hopefully.

"Yes." Gesar paused for a second, looking into my eyes. "They all survived."

"All of them?" I exclaimed, baffled. "But then . . . were they turned?"

"No. Someone just fed on them. A little bit. They sucked on the last girl pretty seriously; the doctor says she lost at least a quart of blood. But that's easily explained—the girl was on her way to see her boyfriend, and apparently they planned to have . . . er . . . intercourse . . . for the first time."

Strangely enough, Gesar got embarrassed when he mentioned it. And his embarrassment was clear in any case from the formal term that he used instead of "sex."

"I get it," I said with a nod. "The girl was full of endorphins and hormones. The vampire, whatever gender it was, got drunk. It's lucky he or she pulled away at all. I've got the whole picture, boss. I'll put a team together straightaway and send them—"

"It's your case." Gesar pushed the folder across the desk. "You're the one who's going to hunt this vampiress . . . or these vampires."

"Why?" I asked, astonished.

"Because that's the way she or they want it."

"Have they made any kind of demands? Passed on any message via the victims?"

An impish smile appeared on Gesar's face.

"You could say that. Take the case and go. If you decide to work in classic style, you can get the blood from the stockroom. Oh yes . . . and give me a call when you figure it out."

"And you'll tell me something smart," I said morosely, getting up and taking the folder.

"No, I simply had a bet with Olga on how long it would take you to solve it, Anton Gorodetsky. She said an hour, I said a quarter of an hour. See how much faith I have in you?"

I walked out of Gesar's office without saying goodbye.

Half an hour later, after I had glanced through the documents, laid them out on my desk, and gazed at the lines of print for a while, I gave him a call.

"Well?" Gesar asked.

"Alexander. Nikolai. Tatyana. Oxana. Nina. Gennady. Olya. The next victim would be called Roman, for instance, or Rimma."

"I was closer to the truth, after all," Gesar said smugly. "Half an hour."

"They're certainly ingenious," I remarked.

"They?"

"Yes, I think so. There are two of them, a guy and a girl."

"You're probably right," Gesar agreed. "But ingenious or not . . . it would be better if we didn't let things get as far as the 'T.'"

I didn't say anything. But Gesar didn't hang up.

And neither did I.

"Something you want to ask?" Gesar said.

"That vampire girl . . . fifteen years ago . . . the one who attacked the boy Egor. Was she definitely executed?"

"She was laid to rest," Gesar said frostily. "Yes. Quite definitely. For certain. I checked myself."

"When?"

"This morning. It was the first thing that occurred to me too. Check out everything we have on whether the pseudorevitalization of vampires is possible."

And then Gesar hung up. Which meant that he'd told me everything.

Everything I needed to know, of course. But not everything that might come in useful, or everything that he knew himself.

Great Ones never tell you everything.

And I've learned to do that myself. I hadn't told Gesar everything either.

Our hospital ward was located in the semibasement, on the same level as the guest rooms. Below that were the repositories, the jail cells, and other high-risk areas that needed to be guarded.

No one ever formally stands guard over the hospital. In the first place, it's usually empty. If a member of the Watch is injured, a healer will heal him in two or three hours. If the healer can't heal him, then most likely the patient is already dead.

And then, in the second place, any healer is also a highly qualified killer. Basically, all it takes is to apply a healing spell "backward," and the result will be fatal. Our doctors don't need to be protected, they can protect anyone you like themselves. What was it that belligerent, drunk doctor said in the old Soviet comedy movie? "I'm a doctor. I can fix it, and I can break it."

Now, however, when there was a patient in the hospital, and that patient was a human being who had been attacked by a Dark One, they'd put a guard on the door. Arkady, who had only recently started working in the Watch, used to be a schoolteacher. And, exactly as his new colleagues expected, he claimed that hunting vampires was far easier than teaching physics in tenth grade. I knew him, of course, just as I knew everyone who had trained in the Night Watch in recent years. And he certainly knew me.

But I halted at the entrance to the hospital suite, as regulations required. Following some ideas Arkady had about the correct dress code for a security guard, he was wearing a formal blue suit (which is logical enough, in principle). He got up from behind his table (fortunately for the guards here, our paranoia hasn't yet gone so far as to require them to stand in position, spells at the ready), looked me over in the ordinary world and in the Twilight, and only then did he open the door.

All according to instructions. I would have acted the same way five years ago.

"Who's in there with the girl?" I asked

"Ivan. As usual."

I liked Ivan. He wasn't just a healer, he was a doctor as well. In general, the human professions of Others and their magical vocations don't often coincide. For instance, military men almost never become battle magicians. But healers, as I know from my own wife, are mostly doctors too.

And he was a good doctor. He started as a rural district doctor in the late nineteenth century, working somewhere in the province of Smolensk. He was initiated there too, and became a Light One, but he never abandoned his profession as a doctor. He had been in the Smolensk Watch, and the Perm Watch, and the Magadan Watch—life had jerked him about a bit. After World War II, he ended up in Austria and lived there for ten years—also working as a doctor—and after that he lived in Zaire (now the DRC), New Zealand, and Canada. Then he came back to Russia and joined the Moscow Watch.

Basically he had a huge amount of experience—of life in general and of work as a doctor. And he looked the way a doctor is supposed to look—thickset, about forty-five or fifty, graying a bit, with a short little beard, always in a white coat (even in his Twilight form) and a stethoscope dangling on his chest. When children saw him they shouted out gleefully, "Dr. Doolittle!" and grown-ups started reciting their medical history frankly, holding nothing back.

The one thing he didn't like was to be addressed formally by his name and patronymic. Maybe because he'd gotten used to responding simply to "Ivan" when he was abroad—or maybe there was some other reason.

"Glad to see you, Anton," the healer greeted me, emerging from his room at the entrance to the ward. "Have you been given the case?"

"Yes, Ivan," I replied, with the fleeting thought that our conversation was somehow very formal, as if it were a scene from a bad novel or some abominable TV series. Now I had to ask how the girl was feeling . . .

"How's the girl feeling?"

"Not too bad." Ivan sighed. "Why don't we go in and have a glass of tea? She's sleeping at the moment."

I glanced in through the door. The girl really was lying there under the blanket with her eyes closed, either sleeping or pretending to sleep. It didn't seem right to check—not even using magic, so she wouldn't notice.

"Okay," I said.

Ivan loved to drink tea, and in its most mundane form—black with sugar, only occasionally with a slice of lemon. But it was always delicious tea, the most unusual and unfamiliar varieties, only without any of the herbs that elderly people so often like to sprinkle into their beverage.

"I once met a man who mixed geranium petals into his tea," said Ivan, pouring the strong brew before diluting it with hot water. He wasn't reading my thoughts, he was simply old enough and experienced enough to realize what I was thinking about. "It was disgusting muck. And what's more, those petals were slowly poisoning him."

"So how did it end?" I asked.

"He died," the healer said with a shrug. "Knocked down by a car. Did you want to ask me about the girl?"

"Yes, how is she?"

"She's fine now. The situation wasn't critical; they got her here in time. She's a young girl, strong. So I didn't go for a blood transfusion. I stimulated her hemoplasty, gave her a glucose drip, applied a calming spell, and gave her some valerian with motherwort."

"Why both?"

"Well, she had had a very bad fright," said Ivan, permitting himself a smile. "For your information, most people vampires feed on get frightened . . . But the basic danger was the loss of blood, the shock, and the frosty weather. She could have lost consciousness, collapsed in some dark entranceway, and frozen to death. It's fortunate that she came out to find someone. And it's fortunate she was brought to us—less mopping-up work to do. But anyway, she's a strong, healthy girl."

"Be polite with the polizei," I told him. "He's our polizei. A good guy!"

"I know. I wiped the driver's memory clean."

"The driver's a different matter . . ."

For a couple of minutes we just focused on drinking our tea. Then Ivan asked, "What's bothering you? It's an ordinary enough incident. A vampire's gone off the rails. But at least he isn't killing anyone."

"There's one thing about it that's strange," I said evasively. "Without going into details—I have reason to believe that this is a vampire I know."

Ivan frowned.

Then he asked: "Would that be Konstantin Saushkin?"

I shuddered.

Well, of course . . . . That business with the female vampire was a long time ago, and it didn't create much of a sensation. Svetlana, the Higher Enchantress, had eclipsed that hapless pair of vampires and the young kid they almost devoured.

But every Other knew about Konstantin—my friend Kostya— who became a Higher Vampire and almost turned everyone in the world into Others.

"No, Ivan. Kostya was killed. He burned up. This is a completely different story. A different vampire . . . a vampiress. Tell me, have you ever heard of vampires coming back to life?"

"Vampires are just corpses who've come back to life anyway."

"Well yes. To a certain extent. But I mean when a vampire was laid to rest—but then came back to life."

Ivan thought. "I think I have heard something about that," he admitted reluctantly. "Ask a few questions in the archive, maybe something like that has happened in the past . . . And talking about the past. I've been watching this series about a colleague of mine. Mishka."

"Which Mishka?" I asked.

"Why, Bulgakov, of course!" Ivan said in a tone of voice that made it clear he was talking about someone he was very proud to have known.

But I hadn't known that Ivan was close to the famous writer.

Maybe he'd been responsible for Bulgakov starting to write all sorts of mystical and sci-fi stuff?

"A good likeness?"

"Yes, it definitely has something," Ivan said, taking me by surprise. "It's quite enthralling, I never expected anything like that from the Brits. He was played by a young guy, a newcomer probably. But he gave it his best shot. I got a real kick out of remembering Mishka! And then I took a look at this other series too . . ."

He was in a mood to talk—and not about vampires. He obviously found his job boring.

Of course, there are all sorts of Other illnesses—from Twilight tonsillitis (don't laugh, it really is very cold in there!) to postincantational depression (caused by abrupt swings in an Other's magical energy level).

And then there are the ordinary human illnesses that he also treated.

But even so, in our office there isn't all that much work for a second-level healer. And we don't visit the doctor very often of our own free will.

"Sorry, got to go and pay the girl a visit," I said, getting up. "Thanks for the tea . . . So can I discharge her?"

"Of course," Ivan said with a nod. "I'll wipe her memory clean if you like."

That was a friendly suggestion. A tremendous suggestion. Wiping someone's memory clean, especially a young girl's, is a shameful kind of business. Even if it's for her own sake. After all, we basically kill something in the person with a purge like that.

"Thanks, Ivan," I said, nodding. "But I'll probably do it myself. I won't shift the burden onto you . . ."

He nodded.

He understood everything.

I left Ivan in his office (or what do they call what doctors have? A reception area? A duty room?) and walked into the ward.

The girl, Olya Yalova, wasn't asleep. She was sitting cross-legged on the bed and watching the door, as if waiting to see who would come in. It looked so much like clairvoyant prescience that I felt wary and took a look at her aura.

No. Unfortunately not! A human being. Not even the slightest Other potential.

"Hello, Olya," I said, pulling up a chair and sitting down in front of her.

"Hello," she said politely. I could tell that she was tense, but trying to look as calm as she could.

In principle, nothing looks more disarming than a young girl dressed in pajamas that are a little bit too big.

Right, let's repeat mentally to ourselves that she's fifteen years old . . .

"I'm a friend," I told her. "You've got nothing at all to worry about. In half an hour I'll put you in a taxi and send you home."

"I'm not worried," the girl said, relaxing. She was only a year older than Nadiushka, at the most, but it was the year that transforms a child into an adult.

Well, okay, not into an adult. Into a nonchild.

"Do you remember anything about yesterday evening?" I asked.

The girl thought for a moment. Then she nodded.

"Yes. I was going"—the pause was almost imperceptible—"to visit someone. And suddenly I heard . . . this sound. Kind of like a song . . ." Her eyes misted over slightly. "I went . . . there's a narrow little street there, with a shop on one side and a yard behind a fence on the other . . . and standing there . . . she was standing there . . ."

"A girl?" I prompted.

Usually a vampire victim who has survived remembers the attack itself, but has absolutely no memory of the attacker. Not even the attacker's sex. It's some kind of defense mechanism the bloodsuckers have developed in thousands of years of hunting people.

But in Olya's case there was a special nuance—the vampire (vampiress, if I was right) had fed for too long. In that condition vampires tend to lose control of themselves.

The girl paused for a moment and then nodded.

"Yes. A girl . . . I don't remember the face clearly. It was thin, with high cheekbones . . . I think she was young. With short, dark hair and sunken eyes. I walked up to her as if I was dreaming. She waved her hand and I took off my scarf. Then she"—Olya gulped—"she was right there beside me. All of a sudden. And . . ."

She stopped talking. But I kept on asking questions. I wanted to know the details.

The devil is in the details, everyone knows that.

"She bit me on the neck and started drinking my blood," said Olya. "She drank for a long time. She kept twitching and groaning . . . and . . ." The girl hesitated for a moment. "And pawing my breasts. Not like a boy . . . but even more disgusting. A girlfriend and I fooled around once at training camp . . . Well, I even quite liked it. I'm not a lesbo, don't think that. We were just fooling around. But this was really repulsive. She's not a woman, and not a man. She's not a human being at all, a vampire . . ."

The little-girl/young-woman Olya looked into my eyes very seriously.

"She's dead, right?"

"Yes," I said, nodding. "It's a special kind of death. Not final. Don't be upset, you won't turn into a vampire."

"The doctor told me that yesterday," Olya said with a nod. "Now will you make me forget it all?"

I didn't lie to her. I nodded.

"I suppose I could ask you to let me keep my memory," Olya said pensively. "But . . . but I won't. In the first place, you're not likely to agree. And in the second place, I don't want to remember this. I don't want to know there are vampires in the world."

"And there are others who catch them too," I said.

"That's good," the girl said with a nod. "But all the same, I don't want to remember this. I can't become one of you, can I?"

I shook my head.

"Then it's better if I forget everything," the girl decided. "Let me think I spent the time at my girlfriend's place."

"Just let me ask one more question," I said. "Was the girl vampire definitely alone? Or was there a male vampire there with her? Maybe he didn't attack, just stood somewhere nearby . . ."

She shook her head.

"Thank you, you've been really helpful," I said. "All right. Now tell me the way everything should be."

"I was going to see a boy, you see," Olya continued. "We were supposed to have sex. The first time. He came out to meet me. And he found me. And when I started walking toward the vampire, he walked beside me and kept asking what I was doing, where I was going . . . And then . . . when he saw her . . . She smiled at Olezhka, and her fangs glinted. And he turned around. And ran away."

Her frankness was simply astounding. The kind you sometimes see in a train, when total strangers who have been brought together for a day or two on their journey get absolutely plastered, knowing that they'll never see each other again. And people are equally frank when they know they don't have long left to live.

But strictly speaking, that was how things stood here too. The present Olya Yalova would disappear forever—after all, twelve hours of her life would be wiped out. And a new Olya Yalova would appear. Version 1.1. Updated and debugged.

I didn't say anything. It was a good thing the girl had told me about the boy. That meant I would have to . . .

"Don't forget to wipe his memory clean," the girl went on. "Make him forget we had feelings for each other. And I want to forget that too."

"Aren't you being a bit too harsh?" I asked.

"He ran away. Do you understand that? He abandoned me! Left me to that monster!"

"Olya," I said, taking hold of her hand and hoping the gesture looked friendly, or fatherly, and not flirtatious. "A vampire's call, and its glance and smell, affect everybody, even the very strongest person. You couldn't help going to her. Your friend couldn't help running away. She ordered him to run—and he ran. To be quite honest, I don't think this is the love of your life, but don't be too hard on the boy."

The girl thought for a minute and then sighed, but apparently in relief.

"All right. Then let him think he was frightened away by a gang of hooligans. And let me think the same thing. That we both ran off, only in different directions. Let him feel ashamed anyway, and let me be a bit angry with him. Say just for a week or two . . ."

"What guileful creatures you women really are!" I couldn't help exclaiming. "More cunning than any vampire!"

Olya finally relaxed completely and smiled a broad, open smile.

"Yes, that's the way we are!"

"Now sleep," I said.

And, of course, she fell asleep.

I left Olya, snuffling peacefully on the bed, to Ivan's care. He could tidy her up, dress her, put her in a taxi, and send her home. He was a doctor, after all. I also told him about young Oleg, whom Olya was on her way to meet—the authority of a Fourth-Level Other was adequate to dispatch a patrol to find the boy and wipe his memory clean.

And I went to the archives.

A huge section of our documents and the information accumulated by the Watch has been transferred to electronic form. Of course, it can only be accessed on the internal computer network; there's not even an inkling of any access to the Internet.

But by far the greater part of the documents and information remains in paper form.

As well as on papyrus and parchment, and even just a smidgen on clay.

Gesar once told me this is a matter of security—it's far simpler to put protective spells on physical items than on—how can I put it?—gigabytes and terabytes of information. But I think that's just double-talk.

Most of this information couldn't be transferred into electronic form anyway. Or at least it would be incredibly difficult to do.

Take, for instance, the Witches' Spell Book. Written in children's blood on pages made from the skin of virgins. A revolting thing, I quite agree. But you have to know your enemy . . .

The children's blood, we discovered, can be replaced by old people's blood. Or adults' blood. Or pigs' blood. It makes no difference.

But if you write the spells in the blood of an Other, they stop working when you read them. And the same thing happens with dogs' or cows' blood too.

But chickens' blood and cats' blood are okay!

And what's more, the skin of virgins is not necessary at all; it can be replaced by any kind of skin, any kind of parchment, or any kind of paper. Even toilet paper or emery paper. Witches have so many recipes with blood, skin, tears, and parts of virgins' bodies because most witches are old and hideous. Rejuvenating spells don't work on them; only the camouflaging ones do. That's why witches hate beautiful young girls and do abominable things to them whenever they get a chance. Hang-ups . . .

But blood really is necessary. How and why is something scientists haven't completely figured out yet. But uploading a book like that onto a computer is pointless, it won't work. You can't learn any spells from it.

Or take the healers' recipes. Light magic, no horror involved . . . as a general rule. Looking at the popular recipe for a migraine elixir, we discover that five of the seven ingredients are not written down, but are denoted by smells! That is, you have to sniff the pages of the book!

And yes, you're quite right, if you write in "vanilla," "chestnut honey," or "rye bread" instead of including the smells, the elixir won't work.

The healer has to sniff the ingredients as he makes up the recipe, even "powdered chalk," which doesn't smell of anything much. Even "spring water," which doesn't have any kind of odor at all.

And by the way, on this point the scientists are almost unanimous: The smell stimulates the Others' hippocampus and the cortex of the temporal regions, and this influences the spell in some way.

But in what way?

And what can we say about magical objects? Or the methods that require tactile contact? They can be described, of course, but the value of the description will only be approximate at best.

So on the computer (which, of course, was where I started) there was only a brief information bar:

VAMPIRES, REANIMATION (incorrect; the correct term is RENEWED PSEUDOVITALIZATION)—the process of restoring the pseudovital functions of vampires after ultimate dispersal (see DISPERSAL), final laying to rest (see LAYING TO REST), or total physical destruction.

Described by Csaba Orosz (C. Orosz, 1732–1867), index no. 097635249843; Amanda Randy Grew Kaspersen (A. R. G. Kaspersen, born 1881), index no. 325768653166.

I took this printout and went down to the sixth floor, where, after passing the security post (a bit more serious than the security for the infirmary—two Others), I was finally allowed into the premises of the archive.

Helen Killoran was Irish—a rare thing for the Moscow Night Watch. Of course we have heaps and heaps of immigrants from all the republics of the former Soviet Union. We also have a Pole. And a Korean. And the interns on work-experience programs come from all over the place. But they don't stay here for long.

One day, about ten years ago, Killoran came to Moscow too. Black haired, easygoing, punctual, bashful, a nondrinker—basically, she was nothing at all like an Irish woman as popular culture portrays them. She was a Fifth-Level Other, which didn't embarrass or bother her in the least. Her passion was the past and ancient times. If she hadn't been an Other, she still would have spent her whole life in archives, and to her mind magic was merely the icing on the cake of old documents and artifacts.

Helen Killoran adored systematizing. And for her, Moscow became a paradise that had long ago become unattainable in Europe.

Yes, we have good archives. Nothing there disappears. Everything lies there safe and sound.

For centuries.

I vaguely recalled that before Killoran the archive was supervised by a jolly, affable man who had one shortcoming—he couldn't find anything. Except by accident. And so the most a visitor could count on was an open door and a powerful flashlight, because the wiring was always on the blink and you could be left in total darkness in the center of a huge hall at any moment.

Helen had spent one year putting the archive in order—or rather, in what we were willing to acknowledge as order. Then she had catalogued and classified everything, including the unsorted materials—which turned out to be about ninety percent. After that she informed Gesar that there was enough work here for forty or fifty years, so she would take Russian citizenship and sign a contract with the Night Watch. Gesar gaped at her and said that as a bonus the Night Watch would buy her an apartment near the office. Helen was embarrassed and said there was no need to buy anything, just paying the rent would be enough. Gesar reasonably explained that over fifty years the cost of renting would be enough for several apartments, after which he attached me to Helen—to help her clear all the bureaucratic hurdles.

In my opinion, Helen shouldn't have bothered with any of the formalities, neither the citizenship nor the apartment. She practically lived in our archive anyway, only getting out once or twice a week—the archive had been thoughtfully equipped with a small studio apartment. But I dutifully helped her deal with the Moscow bureaucracy, after which we became friends (as far as it was possible to be a friend of Helen's, if you weren't an ancient manuscript).

I opened the door of the archive and walked into a huge, dark hall lined with shelving all the way from the floor right up to the immensely high ceiling. There were several dozen halls like this in the basement, but Helen always worked in the first hall; even she felt lonely down here. Clearing my throat to announce my presence, I moved through the semidarkness toward a blinding cone of light at the center of the hall. Helen was sitting at a desk that had an immense cardboard box from an old Horizon-112 TV set towering above it, and she was sorting through the school exercise books packed into the box. A single powerful lamp in a metal shade was burning above the archivist's head. Helen was wearing worn jeans and a warm knitted jacket—the heating system couldn't cope with the immense basement.

Helen was genuinely delighted to see me. I was offered tea (and politely refused it—which, however, made no difference) and any help I required. By way of reciprocal politeness, I chatted with Helen about the work of Constable and Turner (my entire contribution to the minilecture was attentive listening and encouraging noises) and I drank half a mug of tea.

I made a mental note that we should arrange archive and infirmary duty for our colleagues. They could call in occasionally with their questions and their work concerns to visit their colleagues who were dug in so deep in their lairs. There were probably others, apart from the doctor and the archivist. The scientists in the science section. The armorers . . . although no, colleagues called in to see them frequently and quite willingly. But I hadn't visited Killoran for heaven only knew how long, it could have been a year, or even longer . . .

We really ought to send the young people to visit our hermits.

It would brighten things up for them and be good for the novice Others.

"Why do you want such rare information, Anton?" Helen asked, glancing through my request, then immediately checked herself. "If it's not a secret, of course."

My level and position in the Watch allowed me, in principle, to request any information at all without any kind of explanation. But I couldn't see anything wrong with consulting Helen on things.

"There's been a series of attacks on people," I said. "The victims are all alive."

"And how many are there?"

"Seven," I said. And I repeated: "All alive."

Helen raised one eyebrow, looking at me.

"Alexander Borisov," I said, starting to list them. "Nikolai Evgeniev. Tatyana Rumiantseva. Oxana Elizeeva. Nina Andronnikova. Gennady Davydov. Olya Yalova."

"You've given me the first names and surnames," Helen said thoughtfully. "You haven't given me their age, what they do, the circumstances of the attack. That's the first strange thing. The victims include men and women, although the bloodsuckers usually specialize . . . There's a strong sexual side to vampirism. That's the second strange thing. All the victims are alive, which means the vampire has good self-control. But in that case, how did the Watch find out about the attacks? It's easy enough to conceal the crime, if the victim is still alive. Simply wipe someone's memory clean, and they'll think up some explanation for the weakness . . . flu . . . And that's the third strange thing."

I nodded. I was genuinely enjoying the conversation.

Of course, Helen wasn't a field operative and never had been.

But didn't I already tell you that she likes systematizing things?

"And the fourth strange thing is why you've told me all this," Helen concluded. "You are apparently seeking either confirmation of your own conjectures, or my advice . . . which is also strange, of course . . . Oh no! There's a fifth strange thing too. Why on earth have you, a Higher Magician who trains novice Others, taken on this case anyway?"

"Bravo!" I said.

"Theory number one," Helen continued. "You have decided . . . or Gesar has decided . . . that I've been stuck in the archives for too long. You yourself were once dragged out of the computer center and dispatched to patrol the streets. I don't like this theory; I'm very fond of this archive of yours."

"Helen," I said, pressing my hand to my chest. "I swear that I have no intention of dragging you out of your cozy archive into the noisy streets of Moscow."

"Then the second theory. You are expecting advice." Helen took a scuffed notebook and a stump of pencil out of a pocket of her jeans. She jotted something down quickly on a clean page.

Then she nodded.

"Aha. There was a reason why you gave me the names. Alexander, Nikolai, Tatyana, Oxana, Nina, Gennady, Olya. Let's take the first letters: A-N-T-O-N-G-O . . . Anton Gorodetsky. The vampire was hinting that it's you he wants. The vampire only attacked, he didn't kill, because he wanted the Watch to find out about the attacks. The vampire couldn't give a damn about who he bit—a little girl or a retiree—as long as the letters matched. Obviously, Gesar understood all this too—and that's why he assigned the investigation to you. This vampire is a vampire out of your past—right?"

"Yes, that's the way it is," I said. "Only the vampire is female."

"Did someone remember her?" Helen asked in surprise.

"The latest victim, Olya. The vampiress gave her a severe sucking and didn't wipe her memory clean. But even that's not the point."

Helen didn't speak for a few seconds. Then she looked into her notepad again.

"Why yes," she said. "Of course. Borisov, Evgeniev, Rumiant-seva, Elizeeva, Andronnikova, Davydov, Yalova: B-E-R-E-A-D-Y. Be ready."

"Intriguing," I said.

"Intriguing, you say . . ." Helen said with a nod, studying the notepad. "Be ready . . . Maybe she was trying to frighten you? Interesting. What was she going to write at the end, with these bites? Did Gesar spot it?"

"Who knows? The boss is probably no more stupid than I am."

"But what do you want from me, that's the riddle," Helen muttered. She started chewing on her nails, without the slightest sign of self-consciousness. "I'll find you all the materials in any case. Advice. Well, I'm flattered, if that's it . . ."

"Advice," I confirmed. "You have a cast of mind that's . . . original. If you've set this shambles in order, you can do the same with this data."

"It's some vampiress out of your past," said Helen. "Judging from the information you requested, you laid her to rest . . . but you fancy that she has come back."

"I didn't lay her to rest. The Inquisition did. But she really was laid to rest. Gesar checked that. She's the only female vampire who could have a bone to pick with me . . . although vampires don't pick bones, do they? It's logical to assume that somehow she has risen from the dead."

"I'll find all the documents," Helen murmured. "But how else can I help . . . you're no fool, you spotted everything yourself."

"Just think about it a bit, Helen," I asked her. "I don't want to make this business a matter of public discussion."

"But what is there to think about here?" Helen closed her notepad. "You've already got everything you can out of these surnames, first names, and patronymics, haven't you?"

We stared at each other.

Then Helen chuckled.

"You! A Russian! You Russians have that unique middle name—the patronymic. And you never even thought that if the first name and surname have a meaning, you ought to check . . ."

I was no longer listening to her. I closed my eyes and remembered. In my young days, when I used to study for exams, I was certain I had a poor memory, but the abilities of an Other can work wonders . . .

"Alexander Igorevich, Nikolai Timofeevich, Tatyana Sergeevna, Oxana Yurievich, Nina Orestovna, Gennady Ustinovich, Olya Robertovna."

"I-T-S-Y-O-U-R," said Helen, telling me what I'd already realized for myself. I wasn't sure what I'd been expecting to hear.

"Be ready . . ." I said, stating the message of the first letters of the patronymics.

"It's your . . . Your what?" Helen continued.

"Anton Gorodetsky, be ready, it's your . . ." I concluded. "So that foul slime bag has something in store for me, does she? Maybe she's decided to take revenge?"

"Calm down," Helen said gently. "She hasn't mentioned your daughter or your wife, has she?"

My rapid heartbeat slowed down again.

"Yes. You're right, it could have been worse," I said. "Thanks, Helen, you really did see something that I missed."

"That's because I'm not Russian and I'm looking in from the outside," the Irishwoman said didactically. "Anton, you're a Higher Other. And so is your wife. And your daughter's an Absolute Other. What can one vampiress do against you? Even if she has come back to life? Even if she's become a Higher Vampire?"

I didn't answer. All this was right . . . only the blatant audacity of the attacks, this challenge thrown down so openly—it all seemed to cry out: "It's not that simple!"

"It's not all that straightforward," I said.

"Stay here, Anton." Helen sighed. She picked up my printout and took a huge flashlight out of the desk drawer. "I'm going to get your documents."

"Why do you walk around the archive with a flashlight?" I asked.

"Some of the documents don't like the light," Helen replied. "They can take fright and disappear for a few days . . . or years."

She stepped out of the cone of light and disappeared. A moment later her voice reached me from a distance—she was walking across the hall without switching on the flashlight.

"And, it's less frightening here in the dark, Anton. It means you don't see lots of things . . ."

CHAPTER 2

EARLY IN THE MORNING, AT A QUARTER PAST SEVEN, I WAS standing in the kitchen whisking up an omelette in a little old enamel saucepan with a fork. The skill I had acquired a long, long time ago, in a little one-room apartment, allowed me to do this practically without a sound; I only clattered the fork against the bottom of the little saucepan once.

As I whisked the omelette I tried to recall where this saucepan came from, with the enamel cracked off in places and the cheerful little yellow duckling on the side. After all, it wasn't part of Svetlana's dowry. I used to cook with this saucepan back in my student days. And it wasn't new then either; my mum gave it to me when I rented my first apartment . . .

Yes, it's at least fifty years old . . . If not more. This little saucepan remembers the USSR and Comrade Brezhnev. Now that's something I don't remember, but it definitely does. And maybe even Khrushchev? And the Cuban Missile Crisis? And the Great Fatherland War . . .

No, that's going a bit too far. That's not possible.

I couldn't resist it any longer though. I looked at the little saucepan through the Twilight.

The contents glinted with a reproachful yellowish shimmer, reminding me that eggs and milk are foodstuffs of animal origin.

Well, I'm sorry, all you unhatched chicks and calves deprived of milk, but we humans are predators.

I moved on from the aura of the food and tried to read the saucepan's aura. That's a difficult trick, probably impossible in principle for a Second- or Third-Level Other.

But I managed it—by compensating for my lack of experience with force and zapping as much energy into the memory of the metal as I sometimes expended in a week.

People had eaten out of this saucepan. Good food and plenty of it, as they say. For some reason (maybe because of the jolly duckling on the side?) a lot of food for children had been cooked in it. Including for me.

It wasn't made during the war years of course, but right at the beginning of the fifties. And the remelted metal included the iron of smashed tanks; even now there was still something black and orange blazing, something smoky roaring and shuddering, melting and groaning . . .

It's a good thing the aura of objects is invisible not only to humans but to most Others . . .

"Dad?"

I looked up. Nadya was standing in the doorway of the kitchen, watching me curiously. To judge from the school uniform (she goes to a lycée, and they're strict about that there), she was all set to go to her lessons.

"What, my love?" I asked, and tried to keep mixing the omelette, but for some reason the fork was stuck.

"What are you doing? There was such a bright flash, I thought you were opening a portal."

"I'm cooking an omelette," I said.

Nadya demonstratively sniffed at the air.

"I think you've already cooked it. And it got burned."

I looked into the little saucepan.

"Yes, looks like it."

My daughter smiled for a few moments, looking at me. Then she turned serious.

"Dad, has something happened?"

"No. I wanted to read the saucepan's history. I overdid the Power a bit."

"But apart from that, everything's all right?"

I sighed. Trying to hide something from Nadya was pointless. Ever since she was about seven, I suppose.

"Well, not absolutely. I'm concerned about this vampiress . . . Stop, where are you going?"

"To school. Is that okay?"

"Mum's still in the shower. Wait!"

Nadya started getting nervous.

"Oh, Dad! I only have to go through three courtyards! I'm fifteen years old!"

"Not three, but four. Not fifteen, but fourteen. And a little bit."

"I'm rounding up!"

"That's the wrong direction."

Nadya stamped her foot.

"Dad, stop that, I'm an Absolute . . ."

"An absolute who?" I asked.

"Enchantress," Nadya growled. Naturally, she realized there was no way she could win this argument.

"That's good then, an enchantress, and not a fool. You might be boundlessly powerful, but an ordinary rock, if they hit you from behind . . ."

"Dad!"

"Or an ordinary vampire call, when you're not prepared for it . . ."

Nadya walked over without saying a word and took the saucepan from me. She sat down at the table and started eating with the fork that had been used for beating the eggs.

"Nadya, I'm not a tyrant," I said. "Wait for Mum. Or let's go now, I'll take you."

"Dad, when I walk along the street, three Others keep an eye on me."

"Two," I corrected her. "From the Night Watch and the Day Watch."

"And a third one from the Inquisition. He has a powerful artifact, you don't notice him."

So that's how it is . . .

"Well, are they going to let a demented vampiress attack their beloved Absolute Enchantress?"

"I know about all that," I agreed.

"Dad, I wear seven amulets. Three of them are specially targeted against vampires."

"I know."

Nadya sighed and started poking at the omelette and muttering.

"There's not enough salt."

"Salt's bad for your health."

"And it's burned."

"Activated charcoal is very good for your health."

Nadya spluttered in laughter and put the saucepan down.

"All right, I surrender. Mum can take me, only she mustn't let anyone see her. If my class sees that my parents bring me to school . . ."

"You're worried about what they think?" I asked, taking out a frying pan. I didn't feel like messing about with an omelette any more. "I'll make fried eggs . . ."

"Yes!"

"That's good," I said. "Lots of Others who realize who they are as children very quickly stop paying any attention to ordinary people. It's good that you're not like that."

"Dad, that girl, the last one who was bitten . . ."

"Well?"

"Did she ask to have her memory wiped clean herself?"

I nodded and broke an egg over the frying pan.

"Yes, she did. Smart girl. Even if she had persuaded us to leave her the memories, it would have been hard for her to live with them."

"I suppose so," Nadya agreed. "But I couldn't have done that. It's like killing yourself."

"What a clever daughter I have."

"She takes after your wife," Svetlana said, walking in. "Not quarreling in here, are you?"

"No," Nadya and I chorused.

"Some kind of . . . residual energies." Svetlana gestured vaguely with her hand.

"Dad was cooking an omelette," Nadya said, and giggled.

Naturally, I'd told my girls everything the day before. About the attacks. And about the riddles. And about the contents of the cardboard box from a Note 202 reel-to-reel stereophonic tape recorder, which Helen had kindly packed to the hilt with the documents that I needed.

Unfortunately, my story hadn't provoked even the slightest unease. And if it had only been Nadya—I understand that youth is heedless and foolish . . .

But Sveta also took a skeptical view of my story.

She accepted that a message to me was encoded in the names of the victims. But at the same time, she flatly refused to take the threat seriously. "Those who truly wish to do evil do not inform others of their plans."

And Sveta rejected my hypothesis that the people had been attacked by a vampiress who had once been laid to rest following our encounter. First, although I don't work the streets all the time, I had managed to offend quite a few vampires and vampiresses. Second, the ones I had offended could have friends, "sisters in blood"—that's quite a serious business with vampires, though not as serious as in the Hollywood fantasies. And third, in most cases bloodsuckers don't bear grudges for years and years, they don't take revenge in the style of the Count of Monte Cristo. They're rather earthbound creatures. Practical.

Otherwise, with their mode of life—or more precisely, afterlife—they couldn't exist for long.

All in all, my unease of the previous day had been put down to "the caveman mentality of the household patriarch." I took offense at such blatant feminism, went to the kitchen, and sat down to go through the documents. Then Sveta and Nadya, having watched some soap opera or other of theirs, came to the kitchen to drink tea, and I moved to the "study." Unfortunately, spacious as our apartment is, it's not spacious enough for me to have a separate room for working at home, so I'd set up a study for myself in the glassed-in loggia. And everything would have been fine—it was warm in there and there was plenty of space—but it turned out that I can't really work properly with a view of the courtyard, and the people, and the cars. I can't concentrate—I keep turning my head toward the glass wall, like a lethargic schoolboy in a boring lesson.

Nonetheless, I dutifully sat through the remainder of the evening with the documents and sorted them out into several groups. Then I used a laborious and complicated spell to force myself to understand Hungarian and Danish—although I wouldn't exactly say the result was that I "learned" them. I sorted out the documents again and read Amanda Kaspersen's article "On the Resilience of Vampires and Its Limits." I realized that either when it was written the Day Watch in Denmark was very weak, or in the early twentieth century moral attitudes were far simpler. Miss Kaspersen crudely tortured the vampires who were taken prisoner by the Night Watch, subjecting them to vivisection (if that term can be applied to the living dead, of course) and keeping scrupulous minutes of the whole procedure. Even I, with my total lack of affection for bloodsuckers, started feeling queasy.

Burning, freezing, cutting into pieces, removal of organs, poisoning . . . even radiation, which was still so exotic in those times—Amanda stuffed radium into the captive vampires in massive doses!

I looked into the biographical note on Miss Kaspersen and discovered that she worked in the Night Watch from the age of fifteen, that is, from the end of the nineteenth century. That was all it said, but possibly she had personal reasons to hate vampires?

Anyway, after everything I had read, I didn't feel like working anymore and I went to bed.

But today, after sending my daughter off to school, accompanied by my wife, I calmly went back to my documents. Everything that clearly had nothing to do with the case or had already been read I put back into the box that once held an ancient tape recorder (how on earth had those boxes survived in our archive? Did someone put a spell on them, or what?).

Unfortunately, Amanda Kaspersen's documents, for all their exhaustive savagery, had not given me any help at all. The assiduous young Danish woman had ascertained that vampires are very, very, very durable, that killing them is hard, and they repair any injuries quickly. Amanda considered the most reliable means (not counting magical laying to rest) to be severing the head and burying it at least two and half yards away from the body (I didn't even try to figure out how the distance was chosen), or total and complete incineration ("to ashes"), with the ashes being scattered to the wind and "immersion in a barrel of vodka, gin, homebrew liquor, or other alcoholic beverage of sufficient strength to support combustion."

Well, even children know that vampires can't tolerate alcohol.

I gathered all of Amanda's documents and put them into the box (by the way, there weren't just copies, but even some originals— how did they find their way in there?) and crossed her name off the printout. Amanda had convincingly demonstrated that if you take a vampire and torture it good and hard, it will die conclusively and not bother anyone again. I had discovered lots of new things about the female character and Danish national customs, and I now realized why the Danes cut that poor little giraffe, Marius, to pieces in front of children. And I suspected that I would never be able to look at Legos in the same way again.

But there wasn't anything I needed in the documents.

Well, there was still Csaba Orosz.

Hungary has never been renowned as a place where vampirism is especially rampant. The legendary Count Dracula, who, as it happens, was not a vampire but simply a cruel human being, lived next door, in Rumania. The Hungarians themselves, on the whole a good-natured people who are fond of wine, meat, and scrumptious sweet stuff, have always been rather intolerant of vampires eating them. And in addition, unlike the English and the Americans, they have always been uncivilized enough to believe in vampires.

So in Hungarian territory vampires have always dragged out a miserable and secretive existence.

Even without the intervention of the Night Watch.

After the young maiden's entertaining notes on vivisecting vampires, I didn't immediately understand the tone of Csaba Orosz's text.

But a fact is a fact—Csaba Orosz was an enthusiastic admirer of vampires!

I looked up the biographical note on Orosz. He was a Light One, Seventh Level. He was initiated rather late, at the age of sixty. Orosz, who was working as a provincial apothecary at the time, was delighted at the prospects that had opened up to him—he traveled around the world, even getting as far as Australia and Central America. Then he settled in Budapest and started working in the Night Watch, in some minor office position.

A Light One, no doubt about that. But a vampire lover!

After reading all of Orosz's articles and several later publications about him (the funny thing is that it was mostly Dark Ones who wrote about Orosz), I thought I understood his motives.

He became an Other too late. You can't wind back age—he could give himself the appearance of a young man, he could boost his health, he could look forward to many decades, or even centuries, of fulfilling life. But youth—genuine youth—had already gone forever.

And he wanted youth.

Vampires and witches—these are two extremes. Vampires are

always young, even if it is the youth of the undead. Witches are always old, although not many folk are as full of life as witches are.

Orosz admired the youthfulness of vampires. Their polish. Their manners. All the false brilliance and glamour that vampires have developed as camouflage, as a way of luring their victims. And the former apothecary from the town of Székesfehérvár apparently understood all about this—but he admired it.

Well, there's no accounting for taste.

Csaba Orosz, of course, didn't drink blood, and he didn't try to whitewash vampires. He understood their nature perfectly well. But his admiration for the physical capabilities of vampires, their strength and stamina, their magic that was so different from the magic of other kinds of Others—all this soon turned him into a very strange person. Although he was a Light One who worked in the Night Watch, Orosz constantly wrote about vampires, collected information about them, and studied them. Apparently the vampires were flattered by this. He spent time with them (well, and why shouldn't a law-abiding vampire who observed the provisions of the Great Treaty consort with a law-abiding Light Other?). They told him about themselves, they even allowed him to perform experiments of some kind (far gentler than the Danish girl's, of course).

Everyone likes to be the focus of attention. They say that the most spine-chilling psychos, when they are finally caught, are absolutely delighted to start reciting the story of their atrocities. Vampires are no exception.

Basically, Csaba Orosz became a collector of vampire folklore. He was awarded some kind of "Badge of the Guild of Vampires" and set off to travel around the world with it. This was the first thing that astonished me, for I knew of several attempts that vampires had made to set up a unifying structure, but they had never really come to anything—vampires are individualists, they only acknowledge . . . hmm . . . blood kinship. Either family ties, or the ties of initiation . . .

But with his Guild Badge, Orosz gathered folklore everywhere. He roamed the world again. Came back to Budapest. And, book by book, he published a five-volume encyclopedia called *Everything About the Others Known as Vampires*.

This was when everything went askew (you couldn't call it a scandal, there were too many belly laughs).

Others—both Light Ones and Dark Ones—read the encyclopedia and discovered that it was chock-full of balderdash. A number of well-known facts were embedded in a string of wild yarns preposterous enough to make the paper blush in shame.

Csaba Orosz wrote in all seriousness that vampires were the very first Others, who later gave rise to the werewolves and other shape-shifters ("corrupted vampires" in his terminology) and the Light and Dark magicians.

Orosz painted a vivid picture of how, long, long ago at the dawn of mankind, the Two-in-One—the God of Light and Darkness—appeared to the first Other (a vampire, naturally) and allowed him to taste of his divine blood, thereby bestowing upon him the powers of the Twilight.

Csaba Orosz related the biblical legend of the flood, except that in his version the flood occurred because in their pride the vampires decided to turn all the people in the world into vampires (Csaba didn't pass over the delicate question of how, meaning on whom they would feed—in his legend the vampires decided to drink the blood of animals and of their own children, that is, first feed on them, and then transform them into vampires—a kind of waste-free cycle). And it was for this pride that the God of Light and Darkness punished the vampires with the flood, and only Noah and his family were saved . . . and one vampire, a little infant whose vampire parents had put him in a wooden box and launched him upon the waters, and then the box was picked up by Noah's wife . . . Well, now do you see what can be made out of the Bible if you have no inhibitions, but you do have a distinctive sense of humor and an urge to explain everything from the vampire point of view?

Csaba Orosz also retold the stories of a whole slew of other events, presenting them in a new light. Joan of Arc, Thor Heyerdahl, Émile Zola, and Thomas Edison were all vampires. And Tesla was a vampire too, of course. He was turned into a vampire by President Roosevelt's wife, Eleanor (who had been turned into a vampire by Roosevelt himself).

All famous people were vampires. Or at least they sympathized with them.

When I learned, after a cursory glance through Orosz's encyclopedia, that Joseph Stalin was also a vampire, it very nearly brought tears to my eyes. What a shame that Russia's liberal media hadn't read this encyclopedia! They could have cited it. If you ask me, the liberal media are where all the most genuine vampires are to be found.

I put down the fifth and final volume. And sighed.

Poor, unlucky Orosz had fallen foul of his own guiding light. As I understood things, he had fallen in with a company of vampire jokers (it does happen, they do exist) who had led him down the garden path with their stories about vampire customs and world history from their perspective.

Among the mass of fantasies, jokes, and hoaxes that he gullibly noted down and passed on, there were probably some grains of sound sense. If I only knew how to identify them.

Probably the only thing relating to the possibility of revitalizing vampires was the story of the Eternal Vampire, a very liberal reworking of the story of the Eternal Jew. Of course, it wasn't Christ whom the Eternal Vampire offended, it was Merlin, but the consequences were similar. Henceforth he was condemned to wander eternally, but he couldn't drink blood—it burned him like fire—so he suffered unimaginable torment and fed mostly on wine (which was extremely odd and inconsistent, in view of vampires' intolerance of alcohol).

But then it suddenly occurred to me that all the advice I'd read recommended dousing vampires with strong spirits. Maybe they were able to drink wine?

Ah, phooey, it was all raving nonsense.

It was also mentioned that the most valiant (oh, what a word the Hungarian had chosen!) and intrepid of the vampires could be reanimated by the God of Light and Darkness after being laid to rest. But on this point even Orosz didn't let his fantasy off the leash.

Glancing through the final document, I discovered how Orosz's life ended. No, he wasn't drunk by a vampire, and he wasn't shot by Soviet soldiers—which I had been vaguely afraid of on seeing the date of his death. He couldn't give a damn about politics, and the vampires didn't touch him. Orosz caught a cold while strolling through a park in autumn, came down with meningitis, failed to consult a healer in time, and the human doctor made a mess of things.

An absurd death!

I packed all the documents into the box, went to the kitchen, and brewed some tea. And just then Svetlana got back—with two plastic bags of positively monstrous dimensions.

"You could have warned me," I reproached her. "We could have gone to the supermarket together."

"I got carried away," said Svetlana. "I wasn't planning to get so weighed down. I saw Nadya off to school, and then I thought I'd just drop into Ashan . . ."

"You took a pretty long time," I said, glancing at the clock as I unpacked a bag crammed with vegetables. "Did it take you four hours to choose a salad?"

"I circled around the school for a while first," Svetlana confessed unhesitatingly. "You're panicking for no good reason, of course. But I just took a look at how things are there anyway."

"And?" I asked, finishing with the first bag and starting on the second one.

"They're guarding her." Svetlana chuckled. "One of ours, two from the Day Watch, and a gray one, from the Inquisition."

"Gray?" I asked in surprise.

"He's a Light One originally," said Svetlana. "But all of them have that grayish shade."

I snorted. I'd never spotted any details like that in the Inquisitors' auras. Although I had sensed that they had a certain common quality about them.

But then my thoughts took a rapid turn in a different direction.

"One Light One, two Dark Ones, and an Inquisitor?" I asked.

"Yes," Svetlana replied, tensing up immediately at my tone of voice.

"That can't be right. It violates the rule of parity. Either two of ours, or one Dark One."

"They could have counted the Inquisitor . . . as a Light One," Svetlana said, bewildered. She was trying to justify herself now, knowing she ought to have realized immediately that the imbalance was impossible. But the Light Inquisitor had thrown her off. She had added him to "our side" and decided everything was all right.

"No one knew about the Inquisitor," I said, slamming the fridge door and looking into Svetlana's eyes. "Only Nadya noticed him. I didn't. And the Watches didn't know about him. Nadya mentioned one Light One and one Dark One."

A second later we were already in the stairwell, running down the steps. We probably didn't need to hurry—if nothing had happened in four hours, the chances were that nothing was going to happen. But we ran. Opening a portal would have taken longer. Even getting into a car and driving would have taken longer. The school was blocked off in the Twilight and opening up a way through would have taken quite a lot of time too. The run through the courtyards was just two minutes.

And we ran, knowing that either we didn't need to hurry at all, or we were already way too late.

In a modern city you don't often come across anyone running. People often plod slowly past the shop windows. When they walk, it's always fast. But running . . . There are two scenarios for that:

a short sprint to the bus stop, hoping to catch a bus that's already leaving, and the daily spurt of some enthusiastic follower of a healthy lifestyle—somewhere in a park or close to one—wearing a natty tracksuit with headphones jammed into their ears.

Anyone running, who isn't running to a bus stop or wearing a tracksuit, automatically arouses suspicion.

Who is he running away from?

Who is he chasing?

Perhaps he's a burglar who's been spooked by an alarm system? Or a rapist who has attacked a woman in an elevator? Citizens feel a desperate desire to join in the hunt and participate in the most ancient of human amusements.

But there were no shouts of "Stop thief!" or "Grab that villain!" A man and a woman, just running along—but they looked as if they'd be only too glad to give someone a poke in the eye.

And the egotism of city life won out. The citizens looked away—let them run if they want, there must be some reason for it. Only the frost-proof old grannies, out strolling with their grandchildren or freezing solid on the benches, reached furtively for the cell phones their grandchildren had given them, in order to capture the runners in a blurry snapshot. What if the polizais come and start looking for witnesses? And here, I've already got a photo!

As long as there are grannies in Russia, no courtyard need ever feel unsafe.

People watched us with lively interest, and some of them, either the most curious or the most empathetic, shouted to us: "What's happened?" We didn't answer, and they didn't try to detain us.

We hurtled through three courtyards and came out by the school fence.

Well yes, three. Nadya was right, and I was wrong. But they were big yards, especially the third one, so I had every right to say that the school was four courtyards away.

By the wall we both stopped.

And exchanged glances.

"Everything seems quiet," I said. I looked through the Twilight—inside the building I saw the blurred yellow and green patches of auras. Schoolkids, not frightened by anything, not hurt. On the first level of the Twilight the school was thickly overgrown, just as it should be, with blue moss, the parasitical plant that is the only representative of flora and fauna in the Twilight world.

Svetlana relaxed too. We looked at each other, smiling.

And then turned toward the school again.

"Too quiet," said Svetlana.

After all, a school is more than just pupils from year one with white bows in their hair, little poems recited at the morning assembly, and a forest of hands raised by little kiddies who are dying to answer a question.

It's also bad marks and insulting nicknames, scoldings from the headmaster and entries in the register in red ink; it's star-crossed love and pokes in the teeth from some hooligan; it's defeat in a game of volleyball and a stolen smartphone.

It's a huge, great mass of emotions! It's a seething cauldron with Power splashing out of it. That's why schools get overgrown with moss; it consumes human emotions.

And children in school never have uniformly tranquil auras like this.

"Let's go," said Svetlana. She made a peculiar kind of movement with her left hand and I spotted a flurry of tiny little sparks glittering in the air, outlining an invisible oval. Some kind of local defense, something like the Magician's Shield, but activated in advance, in "standby mode." I thought perfunctorily that I ought to check out how she did that.

"Gesar . . ." I called, following after Svetlana. We didn't even discuss if we needed to call for backup and who we would call. "Gesar . . ."

I put a little more Power into my voice.

"Anton?"

"Emergency at Nadya's school."

"Code?"

I was about to say "six," which signifies "critical situation in a location with a large gathering of people, possible casualties," but then
Svetlana stopped and grabbed me by the arm.

"Two," I said. "Code two—gray."

A two is a critical situation in a location with a large gathering of
people, with proven casualties. Gray meant the victim was a member
of the Inquisition.

He was lying between the sports field, which was fenced off with
metal mesh, and the main entrance to the school building. His pose
suggested that he'd been running toward the school . . . a really young-
looking guy with the fading aura of a Light Other (and this time I did
spot the tone that Sveta had called gray—as if the general light tone
had been dusted with dark speckles). The level, of course, was already
blurred, but it was at least third, maybe closer to second . . .

The young man was completely and irreversibly dead. And what's
more, he'd been killed in a way that was so unusual I'd never even
heard about it before.

The left half of the Inquisitor's body was charred. The clothing
had been partly burned away and partly transformed into brittle
black flakes. The wind was mercifully blowing away from us, but the
nauseating smell of roasted flesh still reached us.

The right half of the Inquisitor's body was frozen. To be more
precise, frozen solid—when he fell, his arm had snapped off at the
elbow. The ice still covered his body in a thin crust; it had only
melted on the snapped-off arm, which was lying in a red puddle.

I blinked and sent Gesar a mental image of the dead Inquisitor.

The boss swore. A very vile and convoluted oath. No, I'd never
doubted that his knowledge of Russian was thorough. But this was
really very intricate.

And even so, it was inadequate to express what we had seen.

"Wait," Gesar told me. "Don't go sticking your neck out. Do not
enter the building!"

I assume he wasn't even hoping that we would obey him, but at least he had said what he thought necessary.

"Gesar, what level was he?" I asked, looking away from the dead body.

"About seventy years ago, when we first met, he was Second Level. Probably First now."

"He was First Level," I told Svetlana as we set off toward the doors of the school, skirting around the dead Other on the upwind side.

Sveta didn't answer. Everything was clear anyway—to kill a First-Level Other—and an Inquisitor in the bargain, with their special spells and cunning amulets—was a very difficult proposition. Even for a Higher Other it meant at the very least an intense and danger-ous battle with an unpredictable outcome.

But the Inquisitor had been disposed of instantly and conclusively. And he had also been left near the entrance, as a warning.

I flexed my hands and shook my fingers, "hanging" spells on them. And as I did it, I realized I was involuntarily biasing them toward defense.

Well, we'd see about that.

Two Higher Others is a different prospect from one First-Level Other.

We walked into the school.

I saw the first bodies in the entrance hall, beside the cloakroom—two little boys, about ten years old. It looked as if the attack had taken place during lessons; there were hardly any children in the corridors.

Svetlana leaned down over one, I took the other.

"He's asleep," my wife said.

"Out like a light," I confirmed. "Morpheus?"

"Nadya's bracelet was triggered," Svetlana said. "Didn't you realize that?"

And then it hit me too.

Apart from constantly being followed around by two Other guards—no, three, as it turned out—ever since she was little, Nadya had worn protective amulets. Gesar had tried to foist some of his own on her as soon as she was born, but Svetlana had responded by giving him such an earful that he had kept his mouth shut ever since.

The amulets were chosen and charged by Svetlana. Most of them had disappeared when Nadya's infancy came to an end (I don't remember what she charged the trinkets with, but they had protective magic in them), to be replaced by enchanted toys (if you only knew what Nadya's teddy bear was capable of doing to a grown man, your hair would stand up on end).

Now the amulets were Nadya's jewelry—the way it has always been for women.

My contribution to my daughter's safety wasn't very great. Working with artifacts is more a female kind of magic; it's no accident that witches are so fond of it. But even so, the ring in her left ear had been charged by me—if Nadya was the subject of unwanted attention, she generated a field of inattention so powerful that any human being, animal, or Other, even if he was a werewolf dying of hunger, completely lost all interest in her.

Nadya was very suspicious about this earring. She believed that it occasionally "went on the blink" and frightened off inoffensive admirers. The two of us had even had a serious conversation about that. I explained to Nadya how offended I was by her lack of trust, and she apologized.

It's a good thing that for all her power, my daughter doesn't know how to work with subtle energies yet. Well, of course the earring went on the blink. Just a tiny little bit . . . When Nadya turns eighteen, it will stop doing it—and don't you even think of reproaching me if you don't have a teenage daughter of your own!

I also charged the chain that Nadya used for her pendant. Svetlana worked on the pendant, but I fixed the chain, and I hung the

Gray Prayer on it—a spell against the undead, primarily, that is, against vampires. Well, and I charged one of the trinkets on the silver bracelet—a little book with the title *Fairy Tales*.

(Now do you understand why witchcraft and artifact magic are mostly women's work? They have things to record the spells on. We men only have our watches and cuff links—and that's clearly not enough.)

The spell that I crammed into the silver book of fairy tales was the "Wolfhound"—a powerful spell targeted at werewolves and shape-shifters. It frightened them off, and if they attacked anyway, it could kill them. The Wolfhound also frightened off vampires, although it was less effective on them. One of its shortcomings was low selectivity—shape-shifting Light Magicians took the full hit, just like werewolves.

The bracelet with nine trinkets on it (little orbs, figures, goblets, and books) was Nadya's primary line of defense. I basically knew how it was arranged, and now I could roughly picture what had happened.

"Everything's all right," I said. "Everything must be all right, Sveta. The artifacts worked as planned."

The protective spells were supposed to come awake first, like the one in that earring, the Sphere of Inattention, which altered the appearance of the "veil," and several other spells that were intended to distract an aggressor and divert his interest. If they didn't work, then a magical SOS signal was sent (I didn't put much faith in that though—all signals of that kind can be jammed, and there hadn't been any SOS signals today), and then the attacking spells were triggered—against human beings, against Others, and especially against vampires and shape-shifters.

And Morpheus was one of the links in the final line of defense. If it had already been triggered, plunging everyone around into a magical sleep, that meant the situation was critical. The enemy could not be frightened away or destroyed.

Nadya had to be defended with minimal damage to anyone nearby. And what's the safest thing for human beings if Others start settling scores somewhere close by?

That's right—sleep.

We moved farther into the school, advancing cautiously, as if through enemy-held territory. I walked slightly ahead, prepared to attack or counterattack. Svetlana was slightly behind me and to my left.

But there wasn't any enemy.

There was another young lad sleeping—a bit older than Nadya, probably. He was clutching a pack of cigarettes in his hand. The brat had been on his way out of school for a smoke!

And then we saw the guard who was usually on duty between the spacious entrance hall with the cloakroom and the main school building. He had a desk and a chair there, and on the desk was a register in which he was supposed to record any visitors, but I couldn't remember him ever doing that. Guards-cum-janitors of this kind usually spent their time watching TV or reading cheap, trashy magazines. But this man didn't watch TV, because he didn't have one, and he didn't read anything, for lack of interest. When there were no children or adults at his post, he took out a basic cell phone and played Tetris on it. He'd been playing Tetris for the whole four years that Nadya had been coming to this school, and I don't think he even suspected that any other games existed.

He was basically a simple guy, with an uncluttered mind—after serving his time in the army, he had kept working in it under contract for another five years, and then he was discharged. For the army changes as the country does, which means there are fewer and fewer jobs in it for simple guys like him.

You'd like to know how I know all this?

Well, I could give you a detailed biographical note on every single one of Nadya's teachers.

So right now this clueless, ugly, dimwitted guy, with whom I had absolutely nothing in common, was lying by the wall, having smashed into it with such great force that the plaster had fallen off in places. The school is an old building, soundly built to last, no plasterboard or plywood here—if the century-old plaster does break off, it takes part of a brick with it.

The guard had been flung with such great force that the brickwork had cracked. And so had his skull—there was a small puddle of dark blood under his head. If vampires don't bite or use spells, they prefer the simplest resolution to all conflicts—brute force.

"He's alive," Svetlana said. She made a short magical pass with her hand—sending some spell in the poor wretch's direction. "It looks worse than it really is. Even the spine is undamaged."

Although Svetlana walked behind, she directed me with either her movements or subtle mental instructions. The Twilight inside the school was absolutely pure, no traces of a battle and no auras of Others, including our daughter. Only the auras of sleeping children and teachers, as well as the dim, barely visible aura of the unconscious guard.

It wasn't the right moment to reflect on all this. But nonetheless, it occurred to me that this unattractive and rather stupid man hadn't stepped aside for the infuriated vampire who had just killed the Inquisitor. How many intelligent, beautiful, strong individuals would be capable of that? I didn't know.

But at that very moment the quiet, spiteful little voice that sometimes speaks in our souls to muffle the voice of our conscience whispered: "So perhaps the reason he didn't step aside is that he's a fool?"

I nodded to the voice.

Yes, maybe that's exactly right. Since I hear this voice in my soul, it means I've become a genuine Other. But I still don't agree with this voice—after all, I am a Light One.

CHAPTER 3

EVEN AS A CHILD, LEAVING THE CLASSROOM IN THE MIDDLE OF a lesson, you sense that special school atmosphere. It's not really all that alarming. It's more that you feel out of place—how come everyone else is in the classroom, and here you are, walking along the corridor? It's just not right!

When you grow up, this feeling only gets stronger.

"Third floor," Sveta said quietly behind me.

"I can't sense her," I complained as I walked up the steps.

"Neither can I." My wife's voice was perfectly calm. Too calm for this situation, and that meant serious unpleasantness ahead for someone. But I did remember Nadya's timetable: math in room 306 and English in 308.

The third-floor corridor was completely deserted. I glanced bleakly out the window, wondering if Night Watch operatives (or even Day Watch operatives, for that matter) had cordoned off the school, if Gesar the Great and Terrible was stalking around in the yard.

No.

Nothing there.

Except for the Inquisitor's body.

And incidentally, where was the bodyguard from the Night Watch and the bodyguard from the Day Watch?

Most likely they were dead and we simply hadn't come across them yet.

First we glanced into room 306. The math teacher, Lyubov Yegorovna, was asleep at her desk. A red-haired boy was sleeping beside the blackboard with his head slumped against it. The rest of the class was asleep at their desks too. All of them were tranquil, obviously having good dreams. Only this was the wrong class, either a parallel one or a year younger.

Svetlana quietly closed the door and we moved on along the corridor to room 308. Dead silence filled the air; even the city seemed to have frozen all around us. I suddenly thought that the silence was far too deep . . . maybe some kind of magical noise reducer had been used?

But even if the enemy had done that for reasons of his own, it was to our advantage now.

We reached the door. Exchanged glances. Svetlana nodded, and I opened the door smoothly—I wasn't exactly expecting to run into an ambush, simply playing it safe. You can burst into a room by kicking down the door. Or you can try to ease your way in slowly, opening the door inch by inch.

But the effect is just as good if you simply open the door calmly and confidently, like someone who has a perfect right to do it.

I opened the door—and my wife and I breathed a joint sigh of relief when we spotted Nadya.

The "final line of defense" consisted of three spells that were all activated at exactly the same moment.

The first visited "Morpheus" on everyone in the vicinity. With luck, it could snare attackers too, but its primary purpose was to get people out of harm's way.

The second spell sent an alarm signal to the offices of the Watches and to Svetlana and me. I hadn't really been counting on this particular spell and, as it turned out, the signal hadn't got through.

And the third spell—that imposed a "Freeze" on Nadya herself.

The Freeze had always been regarded as a mild attacking spell. It halted time—and the enemy froze like a fly in amber, giving you time to think over what to do with him and what spell to serve up for him next.

But there were certain disadvantages to a Freeze. First, an Other could defend himself or herself against it quite easily, so it was mostly used against ordinary people or animals. Second, while the opponent was under the influence of the Freeze, it was impossible to do anything to him—absolutely anything at all—because for our world he had ceased to exist. A target hit with a temporal freeze was clearly visible, he was surrounded by a faint blue glow, and if you touched him, it felt like he was wrapped in a tight, elastic membrane. But nothing could tear through this membrane; it was impossible, no magical or material means could do it. As the scientists explained: "although the object appears accessible to our sense organs, in reality we are observing a mere projection, and the object itself does not exist in our time." Third, a Freeze required a long setup time: it either had to be there "on your fingertips" in advance or else inscribed on an artifact.

In our case all the disadvantages had been converted into advantages. The Freeze applied to Nadya had put her completely out of her enemies' reach.

Nadya had frozen at the window, and judging from her pose, she'd been running, intending to jump out. Straight through the glass. From the third floor.

For an Absolute Enchantress already capable of controlling her powers, this wasn't very typical. I took a second to examine Nadya's silhouette, enveloped in that bluish radiance, and decided that she wasn't running away, but chasing after someone.

I didn't like the alternative.

And then my mind took in the whole picture and I relaxed completely.

Denis was there, standing beside Nadya. He was a Light Battle Magician from somewhere in Siberia, either Tomsk or Omsk—as a typical Muscovite, I was always getting them confused, which brought a grin to Denis's face. He was a young lad, very promising.

I didn't know he was guarding Nadya, but I thought it was a very good choice.

I'd never met the Dark Magician from the Day Watch. But it looked like he was another ambitious young guy who'd been glad to accept the job of security guard for "the Absolute girl." If anything, he was rather too young and good-looking for me to view him without feeling suspicious. The young schoolgirls walking around here were all so naive, later on in life they'd start falling in love with Dark Ones. I hate all these human stupidities, like the cult of vampires and all sorts of other evil. It starts off with a couple of stupid jokes, tittering and snickering, "Draco Malfoy's such a sweetie," "Edward's a real dreamboat," and then they start strangling kittens in basements and reciting prayers backward . . .

"I haven't used this spell very often," said Denis—he and the Dark One hadn't noticed our presence yet. "The Freeze, it stops time. There's no way to break through it, unless you know the code. And then, there might not be any code, and we'll have to wait for it to dissipate on its own."

"There's no time," the Dark One said anxiously. "Can we shift her?"

He set one hand firmly against the back of Nadya's head and the other against her waist and pushed with all his might. I realized that nothing would happen to my daughter, that they were simply trying to evacuate her quickly to somewhere safe, but I found his offhand manner offensive. These Dark Ones!

"Can we lift her?" Denis asked, and tried to hoist Nadya up by her backside. With the same result.

"She has to be attached to some kind of anchor points," the Dark One reasoned. "Something's coming back to me . . . The center of the earth, maybe?"

"A Freeze is attached to arbitrary spatial vectors, you dunce," Svetlana said behind me with surprising venom.

The Watchmen swung around.

"What went down here, guys?" I asked as amiably as I could,

trying to smooth over my wife's severity. "There's a dead Inquisitor in the yard . . ."

Without even glancing at each other, the Watchmen threw their hands out toward me. Denis flung out his left hand and the Dark Magician flung out his right. With their free hands they grabbed hold of each other.

Suddenly it dawned on me.

It wasn't the female vampire who had killed the Inquisitor, wounded the guard, and frightened Nadya so badly that she'd tried to jump out the window.

It was the two Watchmen!

The Light One and the Dark One.

The Watchmen were traitors!

I could see their auras, and Denis was Light, absolutely, immaculately Light, and the young guy from the Day Watch was Dark, but they were standing there holding hands like a couple in love, all set to zap us with the same spell that had killed the Inquisitor . . .

A surge of hellfire and a blast of cosmic cold shattered against the Shield put up by Svetlana. It was definitely a Magician's Shield, but some version of it that I didn't know.

The Shield held.

Well, that's only natural; a Magician's Shield pumped full of energy can withstand anything at all. I've tested that myself.

And it's only natural for a Shield constructed by a Great Enchantress to withstand a blow from two ordinary, rank-and-file Others.

But this blow was so powerful that for an instant I thought the Shield was going to burst.

The door frame on my right didn't just catch fire, it simply crumbled into ashes, and part of the wall collapsed into dust. A deep black trench ran across the floor—as if a stream of lava had flowed over it. The heat started baking my feet through the soles of my shoes.

On Svetlana's left the wall gave out a shrill, sad ringing note and started splitting into pieces. I don't know if it had been chilled down to absolute zero or not, but the builders clearly hadn't anticipated a temperature drop like this.

The Watchmen slowly lowered their hands. Apparently they hadn't expected us still to be alive. They weren't the only ones—I hadn't expected that either.

"I think," Svetlana said in a quiet voice, "that for safety's sake I'll have to kill one of you. And then the other one can tell us what happened here. The only thing you can do if you want to survive is surrender immediately."

What she said was good, those were the right words. And what's more, entirely sincere—I could sense that Svetlana really felt like killing someone right now. In the wayward Watchmen's place, I'd have surrendered.

The Light Watchman and the Dark Watchman looked at each other.

And then I realized—no, they weren't going to surrender.

Apparently, dumbfounded as they were by our resilience, they weren't frightened in the least. They didn't think they'd really given it their best shot yet.

They were all set to continue.

But where was Gesar?

I struck out at both of them together. To hell with Denis being one of ours—this was no time for trying to figure out if he was a traitor or under some kind of spell.

A whole series of small spells tore into the Watchmen. The spells' main virtue was their variety—battle-magic classics: the Fireball; the Triple Blade, as old as the hills—it chops into a man like an axe into firewood; the White Spear, a stream of energy; Opium—even though Morpheus hadn't worked; and the Grater, which I kept because it was so nonstandard. Opponents don't usually expect an attack with everyday magic, and after the Grater has rasped over their skin, they don't usually feel up to working magic anymore.

My calculation was simple: The diverse range of attacks would overload the Watchmen's defenses, which would give us time for a proper attack. Not many Others who don't belong to the Higher level are capable of attacking with a cascade of four or five spells simultaneously. And repelling an attack like that is no piece of cake either.

I was expecting anything at all.

Maybe success—in that case our opponents would collapse, pierced through by invisible blades, scorched by a jet of fire, enveloped in flames, with their skin scraped off, and sound asleep.

That's right—a truly appalling sight!

Or maybe failure—our colleagues were no fools, they had to have a Magician's Shield around them, and some kind of protective amulet, all ready to set up a Crystal Sphere or a Sphere of Negation.

That's the way it usually goes in a battle, to be honest. The first attacks fizzle out in Shields. Then the energy of the protective spells runs out and the enemy . . .

Usually the enemy surrenders.

But I could never, ever have imagined what did happen.

All the spells hit the target.

I saw Denis's jacket split apart as three invisible blades sank into it; I saw the Dark One's coat burst into flames as it was pierced by the White Spear and he staggered from the blow. I saw them both engulfed in flames and the Grater scraping over them.

It meant nothing to them.

Denis started brushing flames, mingled with blood, off his face (a good fireball sticks to the skin, like napalm). He took no notice of his wounds at all. And the Dark One started weaving some spell of his own.

Logic had let me down.

There was only one way what I had seen could have happened—if both Denis and the Dark Magician were already dead. Either transformed into vampires, or raised from the dead.

Then they wouldn't give a damn about the flames and the wounds.

So I put all the power I had available to me right then into the

Gray Prayer, the simplest, most reliable, fail-safe spell against the undead.

The only thing that determines if the Gray Prayer will work is the Power behind the spell.

I struck so hard that it would have disembodied any vampires within twenty inches or twenty miles in the direction of the spell. I'd only ever struck that hard once before, in Saratov, when I tried to destroy my friend and enemy Kostya. No, to be honest, I struck even harder that time—I'd been pumped full of Power by Gesar and Zabulon. On that occasion I think I really did disembody several perfectly law-abiding vampires.

But I was much less experienced then. This time I didn't splash the Gray Prayer out in all directions; I compressed it into a beam, directed at the Watchmen, and angled it slightly upward, so that the spell would rise as it traveled over the ground, moving up into the sky.

If there were any vampires flying by in a plane at that moment, I wasn't to blame.

When you use the Gray Prayer, the world seems to turn colorless—that's the Twilight showing through into our reality. Undead creatures can't take that, I was told once—they all exist by virtue of the difference in magical potential between our world and the Twilight.

This time too, the world turned as colorless as an old cinefilm and a gray tide flooded over the Watchmen. They seemed to notice it and exchanged glances.

But they had no intention of crumbling into dust.

They stood there, bloodied, pierced through and through, and on fire. They couldn't be alive. But they couldn't be dead.

So what was going on here?

And that was when Svetlana made her mistake. A perfectly understandable mistake. As Sherlock Holmes said: "When you have eliminated the impossible, whatever remains, however improbable, must be the truth." She saw everything that I did. And she drew the logical conclusion—the Watchmen were alive, but they were under the influence of a "Dominant," a spell of unconditional obedience. That was why they'd killed the Inquisitor. And that was why they'd attacked us. And that was why wounds and pain didn't bother them.

Svetlana cast three spells on them at once, and what's more, they were spells that hadn't been prepared in advance. "Remoralization"— the Watchmen were supposed to be liberated from any imposed behavioral paradigm and return to their primary morality. "Barrier of Will"—if they were being controlled directly, like marionettes, the contact should have been broken. And "Sphere of Calm"—a reliable spell of reason and rationality.

If the Watchmen were obeying some powerful Other, they would recover their wits now.

But they laughed! That was the most offensive thing—they understood Svetlana's attack and their response to it was merry laughter. They stood there with blood pouring out of them, their clothes blazing like bonfires—and they laughed, laughed heartily, even with a kind of benevolent condescension—like grown-ups showing their appreciation for children's attempts to recite poems and dance at a kindergarten matinee performance.

And at that moment I felt afraid. Apparently we Higher Magicians didn't frighten these guys one little bit.

And the next moment they started tearing into us.

The Watchmen didn't try anything fancy—they used the "Press" and tried to crush us with sheer power. Knowing Svetlana, I was sure her shield was charged to the hilt, but it held for about three seconds, and that was all. In that time Svetlana had managed to put up another Shield and I poured everything that I still had left into it—but even this Shield only lasted for a couple of seconds too.

Then we were swept through the classroom, through the burned and frozen doorway, out into the corridor, and into a central heating radiator that was set at just the wrong spot under a window. It's a good job it wasn't the old ribbed, cast-iron kind, but even the modern duralumin didn't exactly feel soft. The blow knocked the breath out of me and for a moment everything went black. A second later I came around and caught Svetlana's glance.

It was a long time since she'd given me a look like that—confused and pitiful.

"I'm sorry," she whispered. "I miscalculated somewhere . . ."

The Watchmen walked toward us, leaving Nadya in the Freeze for the time being. They weren't hurrying, but they weren't wasting any time either. The flames on them had gone out. The Dark Other was brushing flakes of soot off his coat as he walked.

"Denis," I said, struggling to my feet. "Denis, come to your senses. I'm Anton Gorodetsky. We work in the same Watch. We're . . . friends."

"How can we be friends, we've only seen each other maybe three times," Denis replied with a smile.

And again this was so crazy, so bizarre that I felt like screaming. He was acting normal!

I stepped back, pressing against the wall, and my spine nuzzled against a hot central-heating pipe. I reached for the reserves of Power that I had come to think of as inexhaustible since I became a Higher Other. Ah but no! They'd been wiped out, totally exhausted. In a minute, or maybe two, the Power would start accumulating in me again—but I didn't have those minutes.

The two Watchmen took each other by the hand again. Was that essential or did it just make the magic easier for them?

In despair, I reached out, trying to draw Power from Nadya's classmates, but they were in an enchanted sleep, and in that state people are very poor donors. Nadya was right there—a genuinely inexhaustible source of Power—but she was sealed off by the Freeze.

"Here," Svetlana whispered, and I caught the little scrap of energy she sent me. An absolutely tiny little scrap. Worthy of some Seventh-Level Other, not a Higher Light Enchantress. Svetlana smiled helplessly, as if apologizing to me.

The hot central-heating pipe was burning me painfully from ankle to shoulder blade. A thick, strong pipe.

I swung around and the final scrap of Power that Svetlana had poured into me sliced through the pipe at the floor and the ceiling. I tore the pipe out—two jets spurted upward and downward out of the stumps, dousing me with scalding hot water. I could only be thankful that steam central-heating systems are forbidden in schools.

Taking a swing across the entire width of the corridor, I smashed that three-yard pipe into the Light Magician Denis's neck. Something crunched, he gave a muffled sort of bark, and his head slumped over at an angle that you never see in anyone who's alive, no matter if they're people or Others.

But Denis had no intention of dying. He started spinning along the corridor, holding his head up with his hands as if he was trying to straighten it out. As if his skull had slipped off some bearing on his spine, and he could simply set it back in place.

The Dark One struck out anyway, but he had been put off his aim. The hot water gushing out of the stumps of the pipe instantly froze into an icy stalactite and stalagmite. But there was no time to admire the sight—I jabbed the Dark One in the stomach and heaved with a furious howl, driving him back and smashing him against the wall of the corridor. The pipe slid across the Dark One's stomach, slipping into the hole left by the White Spear. I even heard the crash as the pipe hit the wall . . .

There was a short, awkward pause—behind me ice crunched as Svetlana tried uncertainly to get to her feet. The Light Magician Denis was careering around the corridor, trying to hoist his head back up into place. The Dark One gazed at me with huge round eyes, stuck to the wall by the pipe like a beetle impaled on a pin.

Then things took another bad turn.

Svetlana fell. Apparently she'd taken a really hard hit. The Dark One grabbed hold of the pipe and started walking toward me, moving hand over hand and feeding the pipe through himself. And Denis's head snapped into place with a crunch. I cast a sideways glance at him—the Light Watchman was giving me a very bad look. An offended kind of look.

"Sveta, run!" I shouted, realizing that she wasn't going to run anywhere if she couldn't even get up. I would have shouted: "Jump out the window!"—but that reminded me too much of Nadya's unsuccessful attempt to escape.

"You're finished!" said Denis. The tone of his voice had changed; it sounded as if my blow had damaged his vocal cords. "I'm going to turn you inside out . . ."

I don't think it was just a figure of speech. I myself could have come up with two or three spells that produced the very same unappetizing effect.

But at that very moment everything changed again.

A shadow came hurtling out of absolutely nowhere, from out of the shade and patches of light. I couldn't make out the face, or even the figure, the vampire was moving so fast. I only saw the dark aura of the undead.

The vampire broke Denis's neck again—actually broke it. I heard that terrible crunch that's impossible to forget. And then hurled him along the full length of the corridor—the Light Other went tumbling head over heels almost as far as the stairs. The next moment the pipe was torn out of my hands; it wrapped itself twice around the Dark One and pierced him through again. The Dark One yelled—probably more out of indignation than out of pain—and set off toward the stairwell after Denis.

I was expecting the deranged Watchmen to attack again. But nothing of the sort. The Dark One helped Denis up and they both disappeared into the stairwell.

I took a step toward Svetlana and sat down beside her on the floor. My hands were shaking, and my legs too. Most likely a psychological reaction—I felt naked stripped of my Power.

The vampire was gone.

"There," Svetlana said, and ran her tongue over her lips. "And you were afraid. She wasn't hunting you . . . or Nadya . . . She was protecting us."

"She?" I asked. "Did you get a good look at her?"

"No. But that powerful emotional drive. Absolutely feminine. Don't you think so?"

I took hold of her hand.

"How are you?"

"I could really, really do with some magic right now," said Svetlana. "Preferably in the next two or three minutes."

"Why, what's wrong with you?"

"A broken rib," she said with a smile. "And it's bad. My heart's punctured."

"Hell . . ." I gasped, moving toward the classroom on my knees. "Hell and damnation . . . hang on . . . Just don't do anything stupid!"

"A couple of minutes. I promise," Svetlana said in a faint voice.

I ran to our frozen Nadya just as I was, on my knees. And then I got up and reached out with my lips to my daughter's forehead.

Left on its own the Freeze would have dispersed toward evening.

But with a kiss, it instantaneously melted away.

I had to hang on to Nadya with all the weight of my body, to stop her from leaping out of the window. For her nothing had happened—she was dashing toward the window, then suddenly her wet, disheveled, crazy-looking father appeared out of nowhere and almost knocked her down onto the floor.

"Nadya . . . your mother's in the corridor, hurry!" I growled, collapsing onto the nearest chair. A girl who looked like the class egghead was sitting beside me, snoring. I felt like switching off and going to sleep too, as if all the adrenaline in my blood had turned to valerian drops.

But Nadya was already in the corridor. I sensed a flash of Power out there—first Nadya did something to herself, then she poured energy into Svetlana. And all without a single sound, without any tears or wailing. My girls are fighters!

Then I felt a charge of energy as strong as if I'd downed an entire pot of coffee in a single gulp. I got up and shouted: "Thanks, sweetheart."

I looked around.

The battlefield was certainly impressive. Especially the door that had been blasted out with fire and ice.

The clean-up squad would have a job on their hands . . . but where were they?

And where was the boss?

"Gesar, I invoke you!" I yelled out the formula, as ancient as the Twilight itself, for summoning a teacher. "Gesar, I invoke you! Gesar . . ."

"Stop yelling, will you?" a voice said right beside my ear.

I swung around.

The Most Radiant Gesar, aka Gesser, aka Djoru the Snotty, aka Boris Ignatievich, aka Berl Glaichgevicht (this wasn't very well known, but I had found it out by chance in the course of a cordial wine-sampling session with a certain Jewish Battle Magician), aka Boris Presianovich (which I had discovered in a really amazing fashion and had kept quiet about), anyway—the Most Radiant Gesar, Higher Magician and Magician Beyond Classification, Light Other, Conqueror of Demons and Son of Heaven, Hero of Tibet and Mongolia, central character of the national epic the Gesariada, venerated by the Kalmyks and honored with a huge equestrian statue in Buryatia, head of the Night Watch of Moscow and therefore, de facto, of the whole of Russia, was standing behind me.

Or rather, not exactly standing. He was unsticking himself from the wall and the floor, acquiring human form, gathering himself together like the liquid terminator-robot in that film. I watched this process for a few seconds, totally dazed. I think part of Gesar was actually transparent, spread out across the floor like glass.

"Have you been here long, boss?" I asked. I looked at his hands— they were shaking.

"Long enough," he replied evasively.

And then the air beside him darkened, started sparkling, and condensed into a figure in dark clothes: Zabulon.

"That's impossible," I said, looking at him. For some reason his appearance finally threw me for a loop. "I can think of two . . . even three ways of hiding like the boss . . ." I began.

"There are at least six," Gesar replied. "And I wasn't hiding, I camouflaged myself."

"But concealing yourself in the Twilight," I continued, ignoring what my boss had said. "That's impossible. I was fighting here, as you probably noticed. I looked through the Twilight. Through all the levels. I'm still looking through it now. You weren't there."

"A portal?" Zabulon suggested in reply.

I shook my head.

Zabulon sighed. He ran a keen glance around the classroom, then sighed again and sat down at the desk, casually elbowing aside the class intellectual.

"All right, I'll give you a hint. I was between the levels of the Twilight. You don't know how to look there. And I'm not going to teach you, so forget it."

"But . . ." I said, as if the way Zabulon had hidden was more important than anything else just at that moment—including the reason the Great Dark One was hiding at all. "Okay then. I'll think it over when I have a moment."

Then Nadya came back into the classroom, together with Svetlana. While my daughter was clearly agitated, Svetlana gave no impression at all of a woman who had just fought a duel to the death and lost it, and only a moment ago was dying.

"Gesar," she said. "Zabulon. Why am I not surprised?"

"Because you sensed us?" Zabulon inquired. He ran his finger across the school desk, licked the finger, and nodded, as if he were tasting a rare wine.

"Because I know you," said Svetlana, looking at Gesar. It was a hostile kind of look. Inappropriate for a Light Healer. Gesar jerked his head nervously.

"Svetlana, this is all very, very serious. In a situation like this, it's much more important to observe and gather information than it is to launch a magical Armageddon . . ."

I suddenly started trembling nervously.

"If you were using Nadya as bait . . ." I whispered, looking at Gesar.

"Stop!" the boss roared. "Come to your senses, Gorodetsky! And think twice before you make an accusation like that!"

He raised his hands, showing me his open palms and simultaneously lowering his defenses. Now I could see all the spells he had on his fingertips.

I gulped. Six of them were battle spells that I knew, but these versions had distinctive features . . . extremely interesting ones. Four others had obviously been set up in a hurry. Three portals—attuned to me, Svetlana, and Nadya. And the "sarcophagus of time."

Everything indicated that Gesar had been prepared to evacuate us and depart into eternal limbo with our attackers.

"Sorry, Gesar," I said.

"Do you really think that a threat to your daughter that her own mother and father—Higher Others—couldn't handle is a trivial matter?" Gesar asked. "Do you seriously think that I could have beaten those"—he hesitated for a moment—"traitors, if the two of you couldn't manage it? With your absolute coordination?"

"We were observing," Zabulon said amicably. He gave me a smile that was astonishingly, blindingly white, like a Hollywood actor's. In the case of an actor, or any other ordinary person, everything would have been clear—he'd had his real teeth pulled out and implants put in.

But Zabulon, of course, had simply grown them. Although it wasn't really clear why he was suddenly concerned about his appearance. His teeth always used to be just normal teeth.

"I already realize that," I snarled.

"We were prepared to intervene," Zabulon went on. "Both of us. Believe me, Anton, I don't like it when members of my staff are abused . . . and transformed into puppets!"

"How could it possibly have happened?" I began.

"Gentlemen and comrades," Gesar said abruptly. "The Inquisition's cleanup squad and specialists have arrived. Everyone here has another thirty-five minutes to sleep, during which the area will be tidied up and false memories will be implanted. I suggest we proceed—"

"—to my office," Zabulon added rapidly, chuckling. "We can discuss the situation there. I find it awkward, dear Gesar, that I'm always coming to your place and never have a chance to show any hospitality of my own."

"You know what you need to do," Gesar replied halfheartedly.

"I have no power over you," said Zabulon, smiling again and spreading his hands wide. "I invite you as guests without malicious intent or design. I guarantee your protection and safety, freedom of entry and exit, and immunity from harm both physical and mental."

He raised his palm—a tiny little bundle of darkness was spinning on it.

"All right," I said. "Right . . . thirty-five minutes . . ." I looked at my watch. "Nadya, you can stay here. Your class still has sport and choir."

"Dad!" Nadya shouted indignantly. "Stop it, Dad, you're joking!"

"School is no joke," I said, stealing a glance at the others.

Zabulon was frankly merry. Svetlana was smiling faintly. Nadya . . . Nadya was fuming. Gesar was serious; only the corners of his mouth quivered slightly.

"You're absolutely right, Anton," said the boss. "But . . . we'll have to listen to your daughter's story of what happened. So I excuse her from her lessons."

"Thank you, Uncle Gesar!" said Nadya, delighted. And she pulled a face at me.

Zabulon got up and stretched. As the girl he'd been sitting beside started slipping over sideways, he held her up and said, "Quite a pretty little girl, really . . . take off the glasses and style her hair properly, and she'll be a beauty. What's her name . . . Nadya?"

"Her name is you-go-to-hell!" Nadya exclaimed indignantly.

"Zabulon, the girl's only about fourteen," Svetlana remarked.

"Well for me that's much the same as Astakhova," Zabulon chuckled. "For my age, fourteen or ninety-four—that's no age at all . . . Now don't worry, don't worry, I'm not going to seduce these little schoolgirls. Their kind are five kopecks a dozen, if you really want them."

No way could I seriously believe that Zabulon had suddenly been overwhelmed by desire, and seriously enough for him to to start discussing the sex appeal of Nadya's classmates.

That meant he was playing the fool. Either trying to provoke someone or trying to distract them from something.

Unfortunately, there was no way to figure that out right now.

"Please, after you," said Zabulon, waving his hand to open a portal—a really swanky one: it opened immediately after the wave of his hand and looked like a dark, silvery mirror with sparks glinting inside it.

"Your love of cheap effects will be the death of you," Gesar muttered, walking into the portal first.

"If only they were cheap." Zabulon sighed, gesturing for us to go in. "Ah, if only . . ."

The Night Watch office used to be on Tverskaya Street, not far from the Kremlin. In our Watch we used to joke about them "feeding off the negative energy."

I don't think the amount of negative energy in the center of Moscow had declined at all, but a couple of years earlier the Dark Ones had moved to the Moscow City business district, buying three floors in one of the office skyscrapers. Naturally, I had never been in either of the Dark Ones' offices.

I assume that in his physical form Gesar had never been there either.

In any case, when we found ourselves at the main hub of the Dark Ones of Moscow, Gesar stood there and gaped, looking around with an expression of obvious perplexity.

The Moscow Day Watch was housed in an immense, brightly lit hall, with low partitions at chest height. Sitting in the cubbyholes formed by this labyrinth were young sorceresses and elderly witches, morose vampires and frolicsome werewolves, battle magicians and female healers.

"Well, well," said Gesar. "Zabulon, you really do keep abreast of the times. Maybe even a step or two ahead of them."

"In the twenty-first century you can't behave the same way as you did in the fifteenth," said Zabulon, appearing behind us. "Or even in the twentieth. If you like, I can put you in touch with the owner of the building."

None of the Dark Ones reacted at all when we appeared; they seemed to have been forewarned. Well, they squinted sideways at us, of course. And some of the cheekiest ones tried to view us through the Twilight. But on the whole there was a vigorous, upbeat working atmosphere in the hall, the kind that's typical for a publishing house or a firm producing almost any kind of item. "I'm quite satisfied with our building," said Gesar.

"Of course, a remarkable underground dungeon, storerooms, an archive . . . everything the way it should be for the Light Ones," Zabulon murmured. He was still in the same agitated mood. "This way to the conference room, please. As you can see, we have an open-plan concept, open space. It's good for team spirit, encourages friendly competition on the job. But right now we have to talk in private . . ."

No, of course I hadn't been expecting to see them brewing up philters in human skulls and carving up virgins on black-marble tables in the Day Watch office.

At our place no one goes around with saintly expressions, discussing highly moral topics in sickly sweet voices.

But this . . . this was so much like a business!

Now what kind of bee had flown into Zabulon's bonnet?

The conference room in the Day Watch offices was splendid: a minimalist interior with walls of dark-gray tropical wood. The immense window-wall with a view of the Moscow River had red velvet curtains. The table was an antique, at least a hundred years old, covered with green baize fabric that had faded with age. The chairs were also "vintage."

"You got it from the Kremlin," said Gesar, sitting at the head of the table without asking if he could. It was a statement, not a question.

"Of course," Zabulon admitted, sitting down opposite him.

Our family somehow naturally found itself between them. I sat closer to Zabulon and Svetlana was closer to Gesar. Nadya ended up between us.

"Tell us what happened, Anton," said Gesar.

I sighed.

"Can I count on you answering questions frankly? Both of you?"

"Yes," Zabulon said immediately. "You can. I'll tell you everything I know about what's going on."

Gesar frowned, but he nodded.

"At breakfast, Nadya told me she had three bodyguards. From both of the Watches and the Inquisition. Only, my wife and I couldn't spot the Inquisitor," I said. "And when Svetlana was accompanying Nadya to school, she noticed two Dark Ones and a Light One."

"You decided it was that female vampire," said Gesar.

"Yes, that's what we decided," said Svetlana, nodding.

"After that it's all very simple," I went on. "We dashed to the school . . ."

"Why didn't you open a portal?" Zabulon asked.

"Portals are blocked on the territory of the school," Gesar said morosely. "They're allowed on the way out, but not going in. I personally removed the block for you and me, Zabulon."

"But why didn't you run through the Twilight?" asked Zabulon, continuing his interrogation. "You would have saved time."

"Entry via the Twilight is closed off too," I said. "The most we could have done was run as far as the school fence. Which is like switching on a siren as you pull up."

"Fair enough," Zabulon agreed.

"The Inquisitor was lying dead in the yard. We thought the vampire had done it."

"How could a vampire have inflicted wounds like that . . ." Gesar muttered. Fortunately, it wasn't a question. He'd probably decided to put our stupidity down to parental panic.

"We ran into the school, saw the wounded guard and the sleeping children . . . And dashed upstairs."

"That's enough, we saw everything from then on," Zabulon said politely.

What a creep. Our desperate battle had been fought out right in front of his eyes.

"Nadya, what do you remember?" asked Gesar.

Nadya sighed.

"Almost nothing. The lesson was going on. And then . . . there was a burst of Power out in the yard. A very powerful one. I even decided to take cover in a Sphere of Inattention and go out to take a look . . . Oh, Mum, what's wrong with that? It was a special situation . . ."

"Carry on," said Gesar.

"But this . . . wave ran through the Twilight," Nadya said after thinking for a moment. "A wave. Something was moving closer. I couldn't see it, I only sensed danger. I set up the Sphere, got up, and dashed for the window. I thought I ought to jump out and levitate . . . And that's all. The next moment Dad woke me up and shouted that Mum needed help."

"We're simply wallowing in information," Zabulon declared gleefully. "We should celebrate. Does anyone object to coffee? Cigars? Perhaps some cognac?"

Silence hung in the air for a few seconds. And then Gesar asked:

"Zabulon, when I called, you weren't abusing any psychedelic substances, were you?"

"What?" Zabulon exclaimed, outraged.

"You weren't drinking whisky at a tasting in London? Guzzling pills at a party in Thailand? Or sniffing cocaine in Las Vegas?"

"I was working on some papers," the Dark One said resentfully. "I'm snowed under with bureaucratic red tape. I'm simply happy to have escaped from that miserable paper shuffling . . . I'm sorry, Gesar, but you're insulting me!"

The heads of the Night and Day Watches stared daggers at each other. Both of them were leaving something unsaid. Both of them were being cunning. Both of them were playing the fool—only each in his own way.

The usual thing, basically.

"And now I want to hear what you have to say," I said. "And if I get the impression that you . . . it doesn't matter which one of you . . . isn't telling us everything, I'll take my wife and daughter and clear out of here."

"Where to?" Zabulon asked.

I gave him a broad smile.

"A place where no one will find us," Svetlana said in a cool voice. "We've had enough, Great Ones. You've been toying with us, keeping us in the dark for a long time . . . both of you. Now you're going to switch on the lights—or we'll handle our own problems for ourselves."

"What happened to the bodyguards?" I asked. "Who is that vampire and why did she come to our rescue? Why were you Great and Wise Ones afraid to show your faces?"

Gesar and Zabulon looked at each other.

"Go ahead," said Gesar. "You're better at telling the truth."

Zabulon nodded. He rested his gaze on Nadya for an instant—as if he was hesitating whether to speak in front of her. But he didn't try to send her out.

"We have a crisis, Anton. The most serious crisis for the last two . . . the most serious crisis I can remember, and I can remember a lot of things."

"More serious than the Tiger?" I asked doubtfully.

"An hour ago all the Prophets and all the Higher Seers proclaimed exactly the same prophecy," said Zabulon.

"Which Prophets and Seers?" I asked abruptly. "The Dark Ones?"

"The Dark Ones. The Light Ones. What difference does that make, anyway?" Zabulon asked with an ironic smile.

"That's exactly when I called for help . . ." I said, suddenly catching on.

"No. Slightly earlier. Exactly when the bloody battle began around the school attended by the Absolute Enchantress."

"I see," I said with a nod. "That means when I made my appeal for help, the Light Ones were already trying to make sense of the prophecy. And the Dark Ones too. And the operational HQs were probably working on their own, while Gesar and Zabulon discussed what was happening in private . . . ah, but no. Gesar asked Zabulon where he was . . . What's the extent of the prophecy? Moscow? The district? The region?" I asked, suddenly transfixed by an ominous presentiment.

"You weren't listening properly," Gesar said abruptly. "And I've told you more than once before—forget about that human geography."

"All of them, Anton," said Zabulon. "All the Other Prophets and all the Higher Other Seers. Every single one in the world. It's a good thing there aren't many of them."

I licked my dry lips. All of us have some prophetic ability. In the crudest form, it's "calculating a probability," when even a weak Other (sometimes uninitiated) knows where there's going to be a traffic jam on the road, or which plane he shouldn't get on.

For Higher Others—including even me—it becomes possible to foresee the probability of a certain event. The important thing here is to understand in advance what events have any probability of occurring at all . . .

Seers see the future constantly. Even when they're not consciously aware of it. Their world is a shimmering mishmash of the probabilities of human history. In this mishmash Ukraine fights Russia for the Crimea, President Obama converts to Islam, the pope comes out of the closet, and the Netherlands legalizes cannibalism for medical purposes.

And even far less likely events are also real for Seers.

The only thing the Seers can't perceive is the fate of Others. All of us who walk in the Twilight are hidden from them. Our lives and our actions are not so easy to read.

It's the Prophets who see us.

They see absolutely everything. Fortunately not all the time and usually not deliberately. You can't ask a Prophet to see something specific—the Prophet himself decides (or maybe the Twilight decides for him) what he will see and how he will inform the world.

"What is foretold?" I asked, not even surprised by the old-fashioned phrase that had flown off my tongue. At that moment it was appropriate.

"It was not spilled in vain, nor burned to no purpose. The first time has come. The Two shall arise in the flesh and open the doors—" Zabulon suddenly broke off. He looked at me, and in his glance, the glance of an old, pitiless, relentless enemy, I read . . . well, all right, not pity. Commiseration. But a weary kind of commiseration, and for himself too. It was the way the first violin might have looked at the second trombone, standing on the deck of the *Titanic* as it went down.

"Three victims, the fourth time . . ." Gesar said dryly, looking at us.

"Five days are left to the Others," said Zabulon.

I sensed Svetlana put her arms around our daughter and hug her close. I didn't stir a muscle. Somehow I'd lost my fondness for beautiful gestures in recent years. And beautiful words too. And prophecies are always inordinately beautiful.

"Six days are left to people," said Gesar.

"To those who stand in the way, nothing will be left," Zabulon added.

And suddenly he smiled his blinding-white smile.

"The Sixth Watch is dead," Gesar continued. "The Fifth Power has disappeared. The Fourth has not come in time."

"The Third Power does not believe, the Second Power is afraid, the First Power is exhausted," Zabulon concluded.

There was silence for several seconds.

And then Nadya asked: "Did you rehearse that?"

"What?" Gesar asked, as if he hadn't heard.

"You did it so smoothly. One finished and the other started."

"It's a Prophecy, little girl," said Gesar. "A Prophecy that has just been proclaimed by all the Prophets on earth. I believe your lives are in danger. Yours, your father's, and your mother's. You are the three for whom the two have come."

"I understood that," said Nadya. "It's almost open text . . . for a Prophecy. They're coming to kill our family. In five days the Others will die. And a day after that—all people will die. Are the days counted from the Prophecy or from when we die?"

"We haven't managed to work that out yet," Zabulon said in an apologetic tone. "Perhaps the countdown has already started, perhaps it was broken off when you survived. All Prophecies are deliberately vague . . ."

"And that's why, the moment we started shouting for help, you showed up to observe—but not to help," Svetlana said in an icy voice. "Wonderful. Gesar, at least *you* know what I think of you, don't you?"

Gesar squirmed on his wide, comfortable chair, looking as if he wanted to start apologizing and roar out some harsh response at the same time.

"Sveta, stop it," I told her. "All right. Gesar, Zabulon, we've heard you. I accept that there were good reasons for your caution. We're all going to die, I understand that. Now I'd like to know what you gleaned from observing what was happening, what help you're prepared to give us, and if there are any materials at all on this subject in the archives of the Watches and the Inquisition."

Gesar looked at Zabulon. Zabulon looked at Gesar.

"Damn and blast . . ." Zabulon suddenly swore, which was completely out of character for him. "Why, you coached him, I'm sure you did . . ."

"Don't try to wriggle out of it," said Gesar.

Zabulon lowered his hand under the tabletop and brought it back out holding something. His palm was clasped around an old, smoke-blackened pipe, carved of stone or perhaps wood that had long ago turned as hard as stone.

"Let's have it, Dark One," said Gesar.

Zabulon handed him the pipe without saying a word.

"So you still say Merlin himself smoked it?" asked Gesar, clearly savoring his moment of triumph. "There wasn't any tobacco in Europe back then."

"You'd be too squeamish to hold it in your hands if I told you what he did smoke," Zabulon muttered.

Gesar chuckled and put the pipe into his jacket pocket.

"So this whole business was just a charade?" Svetlana asked in a tense voice.

"No," Gesar answered. "It's the honest truth. But I still took the risk of placing a bet that neither Anton nor you nor Nadya would panic. Merlin's own pipe is just too desirable a prize. Even if there are only five days left to own it."

CHAPTER 4

THE WORST THING OF ALL WAS THAT NEITHER GESAR NOR Zabulon had noticed anything special about the Other traitors.

It was definitely them—the Light Magician Denis and the Dark Magician Alexei. At least, their auras had remained the same. And even the level of their Power hadn't changed—to a casual outside observer. Third Level for Denis and Fourth Level for Alexei.

But nonetheless the energy they wielded was so immense that the Great Ones had preferred to avoid giving battle.

"I would class them as Higher Others," said Gesar. "Not from their auras, but from the power of their spells."

"And the spells themselves are most unusual," Zabulon added. "I've never come across anything like them before."

"Maybe they camouflaged themselves?" Svetlana suggested.

Gesar gave her a heavy, querulous look.

"Perhaps. Only you see, Sveta . . . You couldn't camouflage yourself from me. Just as I couldn't camouflage myself from you. Nadenka, now—she could. Camouflage can only work for a more powerful Other."

"So are they 'Zero' Others then?" Nadya asked. "Like me?"

"Well, what did you feel?" Gesar asked her.

"I couldn't make out who they were at all," Nadya confessed. "Just power coming closer. And a sense of danger. Like a tsunami."

"Like the Tiger?" Zabulon suddenly asked.

Nadya shook her head vigorously.

"No, I could hardly even see the Tiger. Only . . . a kind of rippling . . ." She wiggled her fingers in the air. "If I looked really hard."

(That's the trouble with these descriptions of the indescribable. Nadya was only three years old when she baffled me by saying: "The second layer of the Twilight is salty!")

"Then it's not the Twilight," said Zabulon. "Well, most likely not."

"Someone unknown to us wants to kill us for reasons also unknown to us," I said. "Wonderful. And the greatest magicians in Russia can't understand a thing. And what about the vampire?"

"Vampiress," Gesar corrected me. "Unfortunately, Anton, it was a Higher Vampiress in attack mode. Trying to get a good look at her is like trying to count the beats of a hummingbird's wings as it hovers over a flower bud."

Zabulon turned toward Gesar in surprise. He took a cigar (already lit) out of his jacket pocket, took a draw on it, and then said, "My dear enemy. Today is an amazing day. Tell me, have you never thought of writing poetry?"

"What are you talking about?" Gesar asked in astonishment. "Small hummingbirds flap their wings up to a hundred times a second, which exceeds the physiological capacity of human vision to follow. A vampire in attack mode reaches a speed of a hundred and fifty to a hundred and eighty miles an hour, which over short distances makes him impossible to see clearly. I think I defined the situation very precisely and appropriately."

"Ah," said Zabulon. "I see. Let it go, I was imagining things . . . Yes, Anton, your boss is right. It was a Higher Vampiress. It wasn't feasible to get a good look at her."

"There's no proof of it, but applying Occam's Razor, it's obviously the same one," Gesar added.

"What do you mean the 'same one'?" Zabulon said.

"It's not that important," Gesar said dismissively. "A few days ago we had a series of . . . incidents. Anton was handling it."

"A series of incidents with a vampire?" said Zabulon, raising an eyebrow. "And you didn't register a protest? Curious."

"It's not important, not important," Gesar repeated in a voice so false that a child wouldn't have believed him. "Apparently the vampiress has decided to defend Anton, hoping for leniency . . . I'll make sure to keep you informed."

Zabulon chuckled. I had no doubt that now the entire Day Watch would go dashing out to search for the vampiress. And it looked as if that was exactly what Gesar had been trying to achieve.

"So, all the Prophets in the world have conspired and they're foretelling the end of the world," I said. "My family has been attacked by a deranged Dark One and a deranged Light One, and what's more, they command powers so great that the two Highest Magicians in Russia chose to observe, but not interfere in what was happening. And these deranged traitors were driven off by the Higher Vampiress whose incidents I was investigating. Simply magnificent. What do you advise, Great Ones?"

"Anton, I have no fondness for you at all," Zabulon said quite sincerely. "But your daughter is very important. It's vexing that she's a Light One, but that's the way it turned out—so let her be a Light One. Therefore I am inclined to protect you and your family. And again, I am certain that your lives are in some way connected with the lives of all Others . . . and of all people too, come to that. And so . . . I offer you asylum and protection within the walls of the Day Watch."

I chortled.

"Zabulon, dear fellow, believe me, I am quite capable of ensuring the safety of my own colleagues," said Gesar. "Although, of course, I should be glad to see your vampires . . . in the outer circle of the defenses. It seems as if our deranged colleagues are helpless against vampires. A very strange, but interesting situation. Let's work together!"

I looked at Svetlana. She gave a faint nod. I took hold of Nadya's hand and pressed hard twice on her little finger.

"All right, Dad," my daughter said.

Blue panels of crackling light started fluttering around us. The table came apart where the panels pierced through the wood. The patterned parquet flooring of Karelian birch started smoking under our feet. Cracks ran across the ceiling.

"Stop that!" Zabulon barked, jumping up off his seat.

"The sand and the pendulum, Dad," Nadya suddenly said.

I looked at her for a moment, then I thought I understood. And I replied.

"In the morning the blue moon rises."

Gesar frowned. He continued sitting there quietly, looking at us, but he clearly didn't understand these last two phrases, and that infuriated him.

The dark, empty gap of a portal opened up in front of us. We stood up, I kicked my chair away, and it flew into a wall of blue light and shattered into splinters.

"I'm sorry, Great Ones," I said. "But in view of the circumstances, I am obliged to take the safety of my family into my own hands."

Svetlana stepped into the portal first, keeping hold of our daughter's hand. Nadya followed her and I went after Nadya, still clutching her hand. If I had let go of her for even a split second, the portal would have ground me into mincemeat.

"I told you, Dark One," I heard my boss's voice say. "Merlin's tobacco pouch, if you please!"

Unfortunately, I then passed through the portal, which closed behind me, and I didn't hear Zabulon's reply to Gesar.

It was dark all around us. I raised my free hand and waved it through the air. No effect. Then I ignited the Firefly spell on the tips of my fingers—probably the very simplest spell of all.

The large room was filled with an even, white light.

Apparently the motion sensor on the wall had broken down. After all, I hadn't been here for two years. I walked over to the wall and clicked the switch. There was power—the chandelier on the high ceiling lit up. An old, ugly chandelier made of bent brass tubes and matte-white glass horns. No doubt made some time in the middle of the twentieth century.

"What was the blue moon about, Dad?" Nadya asked.

"What were the sand and the pendulum about?"

"Well . . . I thought that if I blurted out some kind of nonsense," said Nadya, "then the Great Ones would try to find the hidden meaning in it. And they'd be less likely to trace the portal."

"I got that. And I decided to back you up."

Meanwhile Svetlana walked around the room. There was nothing interesting in it. Old furniture—a Yugoslavian suite from the times when Yugoslavia was still a big country and not a bundle of territories all at each others' throats. Two sofa beds. A window covered by heavy, dusty curtains. Svetlana pulled one curtain back—there was a brick wall behind it. The only relatively modern thing was a flat-screen television set, but a cheap and plain one.

"What town is this?" Svetlana asked.

"I told you. St. Petersburg."

"That's right," she said with nod. "I can't get any sense of the surrounding aura at all."

"We tried really hard," Nadya announced delightedly.

I'd bought this apartment in the center of St. Petersburg three years earlier and then spent a long time camouflaging it in secret. I was attracted to it because it was located in an old nineteenth-century building that had been remodeled and restructured numerous times, and the spacious old "aristocratic" apartments had been broken up into communal apartments and separate rooms. Some time in the fifties this strange apartment had appeared, with its window bricked in (the window used to look out into a narrow enclosed yard before then in any case) and its tiny bathroom (a cast-iron, sit-in bath with a toilet standing flush up against it). There was no kitchen as such, only a wide, deep closet space that accommodated an electric stove and a tiny table.

An ancient granny who came from a rich merchant family used

to live here. I think the previous generation had owned the entire building, or at least a couple floors of it. The old lady had survived the revolution, the civil war, and the blockade of Leningrad. She taught French and translated some books and spent her life entirely alone, all the while generously showering her neighbors' children with sweets and toys. Living in one room with no window and no kitchen didn't bother her in the least.

And later on, in the sixties, she had somehow managed to get permission to leave and move to Paris, where she lived for another quarter of a century, even marrying two Frenchmen and then getting divorced from them with a scandalous brouhaha. Before she left she had registered some distant relative as resident in her apartment. An interesting life altogether, no denying that.

The relative tried to live in the apartment. He furnished it in a more contemporary style and took out the bricks, opening up the window into the yard. Six months later he couldn't stand it anymore and filled the window back in. Six months after that he took to drink. Then he swapped the apartment, where it seems that only the old woman ever felt at ease, for an apartment in the suburbs.

The new owner wisely didn't attempt to live in the room. Instead, now that he had a foothold in this expensive and beautiful building, he tried to buy up the rooms next to it and combine them into a single apartment. But nothing came of his efforts. The apartment had served as a rendezvous for dates, as security for loans, a present for newlyweds, and a storeroom for all sorts of junk.

And maybe for shadier business too—I didn't check.

And then I bought it—through a front man. And in one month I had erased all traces of the apartment's existence from the surrounding world. That is, it was still listed in the municipal records, I paid for the power and water (or rather, the money disappeared of its own accord from an anonymous digital currency account that was set up), and one of the doors on the stairway landing was still the old wooden door leading into this unusual apartment.

Only now multilayered drapes of protective and camouflaging spells concealed the apartment from everyone—Others and ordinary people alike.

Svetlana had never even shown her face here. Yes, on the whole she approved of my idea—a totally secure place that not even Gesar knew about. Ever since people used to live in caves, every woman has felt the need to have a safe burrow of her own. But Svetlana left the arrangement and furnishing of the refuge entirely up to me, as the organizer, and to Nadya, as an infinite source of Power.

"The telephone works," I said, picking up the receiver of the old landline phone. I walked into the "bathroom." "Water . . . there is water . . . only it needs to be run for a while," I admitted, looking at the rusty liquid flowing out of the tap.

"The television," Nadya said proudly. "I made Dad put in a television. There was an old Horizon in here. This big!" She spread her hands to demonstrate. "It worked, but it wasn't even color!"

"We have to flush the toilet plenty of times," I said. "It has oil in it as a hydraulic seal. So does the shower. There are provisions in the cupboard in the kitchen—canned food and soup, rusks, sugar, tea, coffee."

"I don't like where you're going with this," said Svetlana.

"There's also a bottle of cognac and a few bottles of wine," I told her.

"I still don't like it."

"Sveta, whatever might have happened to those guards—first and foremost they were hunting Nadya," I said. "No one knows about this place, and it's protected as securely as possible. I think it's safer than the Watch offices."

"Dad, what's on the disk?" asked Nadya, picking up an external hard drive off the TV stand.

"Films. Everything you used to love three years ago. Cartoons and fairy tales."

"Oh, Dad," Nadya exclaimed indignantly.

"Sorry, I didn't think of updating the video library," I said. "Or I would have filled the disk with anime and fantasy movies."

Nadya pouted resentfully.

"I agree that Nadya ought to stay here," Svetlana said thoughtfully. "But why on earth should I—"

"So that our daughter doesn't do anything stupid," I explained. "Sorry, Nadya. But I wouldn't like you to leave this place because of some bad premonition or sheer boredom and run into those two . . . You stay here, girls. I'll come to get you in a day or two. But please hide in the meantime."

Svetlana nodded. Reluctantly and crankily, but she accepted my logic.

"What are you going to do?"

"The same as usual," I said. "Look for the bad guys and protect the good guys."

"You need a Prophet," Nadya said.

"Yes, my darling daughter, and we have one."

Nadya nodded.

"You need combat support even more," said Svetlana. "Sorry, but . . . you won't be able to cope on your own."

"I have some ideas about that too," I said. "Don't worry."

"Contact?"

"Absolutely none," I said. "Everything can be traced. I'll drop in to see you in twenty-four hours. You make some coffee, okay?"

Svetlana nodded. Then she hugged me impulsively. Nadya snorted and turned away, examining the hard disk drive, as if she could view the contents just by looking at it.

Although I wouldn't swear to it that she couldn't.

The portal that Nadya opened at my request led me back out into the conference room.

Nothing there had changed—only the chair that was shattered after it caught a kick from my foot in the heat of the moment had been cleared away.

Apart from that, Zabulon was sitting there, slavering his cigar with his lips, and Gesar was painstakingly filling his pipe with the contents of Merlin's tobacco pouch—whatever it was.

"Back again," Gesar said without even looking at me. "Well, I can't blame you. Sooner or later every one of us realizes that a secret hideaway is a useful thing."

"You didn't bet on whether I'd come back?" I asked.

"No," said Zabulon. "I was certain you'd come back. I just hadn't expected you to have the wits to hide your family."

By his standards this was a serious compliment.

"I'm ready to keep listening," I said, sitting down.

"There's nothing more to listen to," Gesar replied.

"How's that? What happened to our guys? What happened to the vampiress?"

"All the analysts are already at work," said Gesar. "But so far we know no more than you do. You can hook up with them, or you can work independently. I can let you have a few men."

"I'm ready to help as well," said Zabulon. "You can hook up with my analysts too."

He didn't seem to be joking.

"Gesar, I request permission to conduct an independent investigation, the right to bring in any members of the Night Watch, use the archive and the special vault, and have the scientists deal with my requests as a first priority."

"You are granted that right," said Gesar. He held his hand out toward Zabulon and opened it.

"What?" Zabulon asked in bewilderment. "You want to swear by the Light and the Darkness?"

"Give me the matches."

"Ah . . ." Zabulon took a box of matches out of his jacket. "Take them, you aesthete."

Without saying a word, Gesar struck a match, held it for a moment to allow the head to burn off, then began fastidiously lighting his pipe.

"You definitely don't want to know what it is you're smoking?" Zabulon asked.

"No, it's enough for me that Merlin smoked it."

Zabulon shrugged.

"Dark One, I have a request to put to you."

"Put it."

"I need a car," I said. "I'm going to go to the school now, to examine the evidence at the scene and have a word with our people who are working there."

Zabulon took out his keys and tossed them across the table to me.

"Take it. And no need to return it, I'm fed up with it already."

"Thank you," I said with a nod. "The second thing—I need your analysts and archivists to respond to my requests."

Zabulon thought for a moment.

"All right. But they'll only respond to requests that concern what's going on now."

"That's reasonable," I agreed. "The third thing . . ."

Zabulon laughed.

"You've matured, Anton. Fifteen years ago you wouldn't have accepted anything from me. But now it's 'I want health, money, and sexual potency—that's in the first place . . .'"

"No, there are only three points," I reassured him. I squinted at Gesar—the smoke coming from his pipe had an unpleasant, acrid odor. But Gesar was smoking it with a stony, imperturbable face. "A car. Information . . . At least some information; I realize you'll keep part of it back. And the third thing is—I need to talk to the very oldest vampire of all."

Zabulon frowned.

"That's curious. Perhaps the Master of the Vampires of Moscow would suit you? Or the head of the European organization?"

"Master Yekaterina is too young," I said. "She's not even two hundred yet, is she? Master Pyotr is a bit older, but he hasn't been actively involved in things for a long time and they say he never gets out of his coffin. I don't necessarily need the highest-ranking one, just one who's as old as possible."

"I'm impressed," Zabulon admitted. "But I can tell you in secret that it's a very good thing Pyotr went batty about abstinence and spends most of the time sleeping in his vault. Fewer problems for everyone . . . All right, Anton, I have a good idea of who you need to see and how I can persuade that person to come to you. But you have to get that person to talk frankly yourself, I'm powerless when it comes to that."

I nodded.

"Be at home this evening," said Zabulon. "I'll give you a call if there's any kind of hitch. But I expect everything will be fine and you'll get a visit."

"You're taking a risk," said Gesar, looking at me.

"With my boss's permission, I'll take that risk," I said, getting up. "Call, write, send telegrams. And don't forget the food parcels."

"Good luck, Anton," I heard the boss's voice say when I reached the door. Gesar continued beside Zabulon—it looked as if their conversation would only begin in earnest after I was gone. Then Gesar started coughing.

"Just what is this shit?" he asked.

"Well, I did give you a hint," Zabulon replied snidely.

I hadn't asked for the car because I didn't have one of my own or I couldn't requisition any car that took my fancy.

I wanted to see just how far Zabulon was prepared to go. Well, and in case things went awry—which I wasn't particularly expecting—so that I could show any Dark Ones that I was well in with their boss.

Zabulon drove a Volvo family car—at least it was a normal sedan, not some kind of overhyped SUV. A good car, but without any excessive swank to it. And inside it everything was neat and tidy, lived in, just slightly rearranged to suit the owner's taste—and yet at the same time absolutely sterile. Not a single hint at the owner's personality. A pack of tissues and some napkins in the glove compartment, a dash cam on the windshield.

Well, what was I expecting?

Skulls with incense burning in them?

A log recording the day's atrocities?

And it was also amusing that all the spells had disappeared from the car. They had been here; I could still sense a faint trace. Protective, camouflaging, servicing . . . But while I was walking down from the office, while I was looking for the car in the parking lot, it had become absolutely ordinary and human.

Well, that was exactly what I should have expected.

I cast a light veil against traffic cops over the car. I didn't even bother to protect myself against security cameras—Zabulon had removed the protection, they could send the fines to him.

And I set off to Nadya's school.

The schoolyard was clean, the remains of the dead Inquisitor had been removed. Sitting at the entrance was a guard who looked very much like the one who had been hurt, only he was a part-time member of the Day Watch, an Other and—if all the details are important—a vampire.

I nodded to him and he got up and bowed politely.

The corridors were empty; there were lessons going on. Only on the third floor did I come across a boy walking along the corridor. The boy's eyes were blank and sleepy.

"What are you doing?" I asked. "Where are you going?"

"I have to do my lessons. I'm going to the toilet," the boy replied. "I said I needed to go to the toilet. I really need to pee. But I said that about the toilet, because I wanted to smoke in the toilet. But I have to do my lessons!"

The boy was twelve or thirteen; at that age they don't use the word "pee," especially to grown-up strangers. They might say "piss," or "take a leak," if the child is highly cultured.

I glanced at him through the Twilight. Aha, clear enough. Like everyone in the school, he was under a light concentration spell.

Right now, perhaps for the first time in the history of universal education, all the children in a school really were studying.

Only in this youngster the pull of nicotine (it's a very, very powerful drug) was battling against the inner attraction to knowledge.

"You will take a leak and go back to class," I said. "You really, really want to study. And you don't want to smoke anymore; cigarettes disgust you."

"I want to study," the boy said, relaxing, and he walked on.

And I went to the classroom where the Other guards had caught up with Nadya.

Of course, there weren't any lessons taking place there right now. Repairs were in progress. Two men in overalls, a bucket of cement, bricks . . .

"Hello," I said. "Esan? Adrian?"

The guys turned to face me. Esan was Fifth Level. Adrian was Sixth. Both from the Night Watch reserve.

"Just leave out the wisecracks, Gorodetsky," said Esan.

He was over forty. A very cultured man, he used to teach in a university in his home country, and even wrote some kind of textbook. Then he left and came to Moscow to earn a bit of money from painting and decorating. He had been identified as an Other here—Semyon discovered him when he decided to redecorate his apartment.

"Okay, I will," I said.

Adrian, a young, dark-skinned guy, smiled cheerfully.

"What's the problem? Spells won't do the job for you here, this needs repairs. And all you Muscovites are useless. A Tajik and a Moldovanian—that's real power for you!"

"That's good," I agreed. "Power."

As far as I knew, these two guys, who had only recently acquired the full abilities of Others, were joint owners of a small construction firm. And why not? It's an excellent, Light kind of trade.

And in addition, it's handy for all the Others to have a builder they know. Not only can they get a dacha built, they can have a few spells put on it at the same time.

"Where are our boys?"

"They've moved up to the fourth floor," said Adrian.

I set off toward the stairs. Halfway up I was overtaken by the same boy, dashing back from the toilet to continue his pursuit of knowledge. What miraculous academic progress would be made in this school for the next few days!

On the stairs I met Las.

"Gorodetsky!" he exclaimed joyfully. "They told me you'd gone zooming off somewhere with the boss!"

"I'm back already."

Las turned serious, evidently remembering what had happened in the school less than two hours earlier.

"How's your daughter?"

"Everything's okay."

"And your wife?"

"Fine. We coped."

Las nodded.

"I'll be sure to light a candle for our patron saint . . ."

I had no problem with Las's religious enlightenment; in fact I rather liked it. But something here triggered my doubts.

"For whom?" I asked suspiciously.

"For Ilya. Ilya of Murom."

"Whose patron saint is he?"

"Well . . . Ours . . . the Others."

"Did the priest tell you that?"

"No, I figured it out for myself. A warrior. He fought against forces of evil. As a child he was paralyzed. But he was cured and initiated by three wayward militants."

"Wandering mendicants!"

"Right, sorry about that," said Las, totally unembarrassed. "But all the rest is right."

"Light your candle," I said with a nod. "No problem. What's happening here, in the school?"

"Well, we're gradually sorting everything out," Las said with modest pride. "I've been put in charge of the operation, by the way. Because this is the school where I—"

"You were a pupil here?"

"No, I used to teach singing. Only I didn't really teach anything, it was just a cover to give my friends a spot for their band to rehearse, so I know this place well. We're handling things. The kids are in their lessons, the teachers are teaching them, the Tajiks are doing their repairs, the healers are saving the wounded . . ."

"Wounded?"

"Oh yeah. That vampire went on a binge. Did he really save you?"

I nodded.

Las shook his head in wonder.

"Weird stuff. You know, he cut loose first. Wounded the guard. Then ran through the classrooms, sucking a bit of blood . . ."

"What?" At this point I was completely at a loss.

"Eight little kids! Just a little drop from each one, mind you. Maybe he was preparing for battle?"

"Maybe," I said pensively.

"Anyway, I don't understand these vampires." Las sighed. "Okay, back in the Middle Ages, if you wanted to suck a bit of fresh blood, without any syphilis or plague, and without any pockmarks or scars—then children were the only ones you should feed on. Not nice, of course, but logical. But now, in this day and age, why suck a kid's blood? It's laced with chemicals. All those low-alcohol cocktails! Nicotine! Burgers made with palm oil! A crazy amount of sugar from cola. Synthetic drugs. Dill and parsley smoking mixtures! Inoculations! Sheer poison!"

"And who would you recommend?" I asked. "You know, if I suddenly turn vampire?"

"I've been thinking about that myself," said Las, nodding with a perfectly serious expression. "Right now the best choice would be some thirty- to forty-five-year-old brainworker. That means he's already over his wild days, he can't afford to get up to too much mischief for his health's sake, and at the same time he's not old enough to have accumulated a whole load of toxins."

"I really don't know what to say to that," I confessed. "I think I'd better change the subject. I need classroom 7A."

"You mean you want Innokentii Tolkov?" Las chuckled. "We didn't put the spell on him, he's one of ours, an Other. He's on the first floor, in the first-aid room."

"What's wrong with that chump?" I asked, frowning.

Maybe I was being unfair to the lad, but I didn't like the way he'd been spending so much time with Nadya recently.

"Nothing's wrong with him. He's helping our doctor, as far as he can. It's practical experience for him, and it makes things a little bit easier for us."

Innokentii Tolkov really was assisting our doctor. He was draped in a white coat that was too big for him and focusing very seriously on what he was doing.

Ivan was just finishing treating the little wounds on the neck of a really small kid, barely even big enough for a first-year pupil. The boy was straight out of some children's book—he had big eyes, a long neck, and tousled blond hair, and he was sitting there quietly on the doctor's couch with his head leaning to one side, to make it easier for the doctor to inspect his neck. The very essence of cute sweetness. In reality, he was probably a quarrelsome, contentious troublemaker, an absolute nightmare for his parents and a headache for his teachers. But right now, under the spell, the boy sat there quietly, hardly even blinking as he listened to the doctor.

"And then you grabbed Lena by the neck and scratched her until she bled," Ivan was saying. "And then she grabbed you and scratched you too. And the teacher took you to the doctor's room. You made up. The teacher told you that if your parents complain, you'll both be expelled from the school, Lena and you. A plaster!"

Innokentii handed him the plaster. He saw me, started, and nodded.

Ivan deftly stuck the plaster over the boy's wounds and patted him on the back.

"Run back to class, Silvano. The teacher's waiting for you."

"Scratches?" I asked doubtfully as I shook Ivan's hand.

"The bites are all superficial," Ivan said with a shrug. "In fact I'd say that in most cases no arteries or veins were punctured at all, just a drop or two of capillary blood, nothing more . . . And I stretched the wounds out just a little bit; now they can be put down to a childish scuffle."

"So they weren't bitten for their blood," I said.

"Oh no. They were just bitten for the sake of the bite." Ivan sighed. "It's totally crazy . . . Is there anything I can do to help?"

"I need a list of everyone who was bitten," I said. "Name, patronymic, and surname. Preferably in the order in which they were bitten."

"Now you're complicating things," said Ivan, shaking his head. "Well . . . I'll try. Judging from the positions of the victims, the vampire moved in from the main door, going into classrooms every now and then and biting children. Give me half an hour or an hour."

I nodded.

"No problem. Text the list to my cell, okay? And another thing—I'll take Innokentii with me."

"If that's okay with him," said Ivan, glancing at the boy. "Thanks for the help."

"Thank you, Uncle Ivan," Innokentii replied, taking off the white coat. "It was interesting."

In the years since I first met Innokentii, or Kesha, Tolkov, he had changed dramatically. The first time I saw him, he was a terribly fat, astoundingly ugly, and hysterically weepy child. Well, you must admit there are some children like that.

Now Kesha was fourteen. He was almost the same age as Nadya, but he was one class behind her in school. He was still chubby, as he probably would be forever, but not so awfully fat as before—he had stretched and grown out of that. His ugliness hadn't gone away, but in some amazing fashion, it had been recast as what women refer to in embarrassed tones as "male beauty." That is, it was obvious he would never be handsome, but he would definitely catch any woman's eye. This is a strange thing that often happens to actors, especially Russian and French ones.

And that weepiness was long gone and forgotten. He was a very serious, composed young man, who spoke very judiciously.

A Prophet!

It was just a pity that Nadya and he had become such firm friends.

"I would," he said, walking over to me and holding out his hand.

"Would what?" I asked as I shook it.

"Like an ice cream. You were going to ask if I'd like an ice cream. Ice cream, in winter—of course I would!"

I laughed.

"Kesha! Common predictions aren't your professional profile. You're a Prophet."

"Yes, but a common Seer can't predict what a Higher Other is going to say," Kesha parried. "Let's go, Uncle Anton, I know a good little café near here."

"And why haven't you asked how Nadya's getting on?" I asked reproachfully as we walked across the schoolyard.

"What for? I know she's all right."

I got an ice cream and a coffee for myself as well. The café was a cozy place, not part of a chain; they even made their own ice cream here in the Italian style—soft, with fruit flavors. I didn't want anything sweet, so I chose the coffee flavor. Innokentii devoured a pistachio ice cream with obvious relish—it looked like he often treated himself to calorific indulgences like that in this place.

"Do you remember the prophecy yourself?" I asked.

"No," he said, frowning. This was clearly a sore point—Prophets rarely remember what they say. "But I listened to it afterward." Kesha licked his spoon and started reciting: " 'It was not spilled in vain, nor burned to no purpose. The first time has come. The Two shall arise in the flesh and open the doors. Three victims, the fourth time. Five days are left to the Others. Six days are left to people. To those who stand in the way, nothing will be left. The Sixth Watch is dead, the Fifth Power has disappeared. The Fourth has come too late. The Third Power does not believe, the Second Power is afraid, the First Power is exhausted.' "

"That's exactly right," I said. "Will you help me decipher it?"

"Why me, Uncle Anton?" Kesha asked, genuinely surprised. "I've got absolutely no experience. I might be a High-Level Other, but I'm still only learning."

"Because I trust you. Because you once proclaimed a very, very important prophecy indeed. Because we're friends. Because Nadya likes you."

Kesha was slightly embarrassed. But he didn't blush, he didn't look away, even though he was uncomfortable. And he answered with dignity.

"I like Nadya a lot, Uncle Anton. And I think she likes me too. We were going to talk to you about it. In a couple of years."

I gasped, feeling it was my turn to be embarrassed now . . . And hoping that I wouldn't blush.

"Let's say in . . . Er . . . Four or five years . . . Maybe six would be better."

"All right . . ." The young teenager didn't try to argue. "But really, why? You can call in any Seer or Prophet. Bring in Glyba, he's a clever man, he teaches our special course."

"Well, you see, Kesha, it seems to me that this case doesn't demand an awful lot of knowledge and cleverness. Although a solid grounding in the basics is essential. And you fit the bill perfectly, you get nothing but A's on the special course. Tell me how it all happened."

"I was sitting in class," Kesha replied. "And then it swept over me . . . I fell into a trance. I've got this thing now . . ." He stuck his hand in under his shirt and took out a little disk hanging on a chain, like a pendant. "It's a recording device. I came around and everyone was looking at me and giggling . . . 'He's flipped, jabbering gobbledygook.' You know, the usual thing . . . I put them all to sleep," Kesha said with a smile. "And wiped the last minute from their memories. Standard procedure for Prophets, all by the book, but it was the first time I'd done it. Then I listened to the recording. I called the Watch and transmitted the file. They told me well done, I'd done everything right, but it was a mass prophecy. Well, I waited for everyone to come around and stayed in the classroom, wondering what kind of heavy shit this was. And then it was like a shudder ran through the Twilight . . ." Kesha frowned. "There was a crash out in the yard. I tried to look through the Twilight, but I couldn't see anything, only blue moss scattering in all directions. And then I went out like a light, when Nadya's spell kicked in. When I woke up there was a Dark One standing over me. He gave me this miserable look, then spoke into the headset of his phone. 'I've got an Other here, First Level. A Light One.' Well, he helped me up. All perfectly polite and correct."

"And have you had time to think over the prophecy?" I asked, swirling the melted ice cream around with my spoon. It was warm in the café, the numerous plants and well-directed lighting giving the impression of a summer day. Only outside it was starting to get dark and it was gray and cold. Snow was just beginning to fall.

"Uncle Anton, I'm not a magician, I'm still studying."

"Understood. Tell me."

"Well, all these figures—they're just embellishment. They do mean something, of course. But they're mostly there for effect. A prophecy has to sound awesome and mysterious. Our Sergei Sergeevich is always telling us that."

"All right," I said, and nodded. "That is, we take them into account, but we don't get hung up on all these two-times-fours . . ."

"It was not spilled in vain, nor burned to no purpose," Kesha began. "I think it's a sacrificial offering. Blood has been spilled. Someone's been burned. Well, the beginning of a prophecy is usually fairly clear, and it usually talks about something bad . . ."

"I'd just once like to hear a prophecy about something good," I said.

"They do happen," Kesha said, consoling me. "What comes next? The first time has come. That's twiddle too."

Kesha had used this word already and I couldn't resist correcting him.

"Twaddle."

"No, twaddle is when someone just talks nonsense, but twiddle is when it's absolute gibberish and malicious too, or meant to distract your attention."

"I'm not well up with teenage slang," I admitted. "So it's twiddle, then?"

"Twiddle," Kesha said confidently. " 'The first time has come'—so what, it's come. And further on: 'The Two shall arise in the flesh and open the doors.' Well, that's twiddle as well. About those two Watchmen who flipped, right? Some valuable information that is. Then: 'Three victims the fourth time . . .' You probably think that's about you, don't you? Nadya, Nadya's mum, you . . . But it's not necessarily that. It could be anybody at all. It's not clearly attached to anything. If it said 'A Zero Enchantress and two Great Ones, her parents . . . '"

"It's never like that." I sighed. "All right, you've reassured me just a little bit. But only a tiny little bit. They came to Nadya's school, they attacked her, and when they saw us, they gleefully turned on us too. Nadya's definitely in that list of victims. And we probably are too."

"I did want to reassure you a bit," Kesha admitted. "Well yes, it probably is about you after all."

"Kesha, let's do without the reassurances. We're not children."

" 'Five days are left to the Others. Six days are left to people. For those who stand in the way, nothing will be left.' That's all clear, right?"

"Just one question. Five days beginning from when?"

"From the time of the fourth attempt to kill you," Kesha said in a quiet voice. "If they kill you."

"And then everyone will die? First the Others, then the people?"

"Yes," Kesha said after hesitating for a moment. "Although death isn't directly mentioned, the general tone and the use of series, especially the figures five and six . . ."

"Never mind the details, I believe you," I said.

" 'The Sixth Watch is dead,' " Kesha said, and started pondering. "Uncle Anton, that's really what's the most important thing. Definitely the most important. The Sixth Watch."

"Why?"

"Because here there's an asymptote at the point of inflexion, and that means—"

"I believe you!" I said, throwing my hands up in the air. "I believe you, Kesha."

"The Sixth Watch—what is that?" The boy asked curiously.

"Well, the Night Watch and the Day Watch are the first and the second," I said. "The Third Watch is the Inquisition. The Fourth Watch is the apparatus of the mass media. The Fifth Watch is like a fifth column, a secret organization within the Watches. The Sixth—oho, you're asking me about the Sixth Watch . . ."

Kesha's eyes turned big and round.

"I'm only joking," I said. "No one has ever called the Watches by numbers. There are a couple of stupid jokes, but that's all there is. The Sixth Watch is meaningless abracadabra."

"There has to be a meaning," Kesha said sternly. "Really and truly! Prophecy has laws!"

"All right. I'll think about it."

" 'The Fifth Power has disappeared, the Fourth has not come in time. The Third Power does not believe, the Second Power is afraid, the First Power is exhausted.' " Kesha spread his hands helplessly. "This part is totally incomprehensible, Uncle Anton. Perhaps there is a meaning. But it could be twaddle or twiddle. Just to make the prophecy sound mystical."

"So all we're left with is the Sixth Watch," I said. "One solitary little thread that we can cling to."

Kesha nodded guiltily.

"I'm sorry, Uncle Anton . . . I'll ask Glyba in our lesson tomorrow."

"Ask him," I said, getting up and putting the money on the table. The waitress, who had been looking at us in annoyance for a long time (we had two ice creams and two coffees, and had sat there for a whole hour), came toward us from the counter.

"Come on, I'll drive you home."

"I can go on my own, the metro . . ."

"No, Kesha. I'll feel more relaxed. There's nothing I have to do just now anyway. I have a meeting this evening, until then . . . Kesha?"

Innokentii was standing there, swaying and looking at me blankly. His pupils slowly dilated, turning his eyes into black gulfs glinting with red sparks. His face turned pale and little beads of sweat sprang out on it.

I froze.

You should never interfere with a Prophet who has fallen into a trance. Kesha would probably manage to stay on his feet.

Perhaps it would be a clarification of the prophecy? Such things had happened before. Or yet another prophecy?

Kesha's eyes suddenly narrowed and flooded with amber yellow. The pupils imploded and lengthened out vertically. I shuddered. The waitress, who had made such an ill-timed dash to get the money, squealed.

"Anton," said Kesha, looking at me. "First, take the boy with you. Second, hurry home. Third, it is not for you to decide. Fourth, I shall come again."

It wasn't like a prophecy. It looked as if someone had forced the Prophet to speak—and taken over the controls. The external forms, the structure of the phrases—that was from prophecy. The content . . . The content was something quite different.

"Exactly what sort of grotesque gibberish is that?" the waitress asked in a tearful voice. "It's unbecoming for decent people to behave in such a manner!"

"I do beg your pardon," I replied, fighting the urge to add "my lady." "But it is merely a childish prank. I beg your pardon, please accept this in recompense for your trouble . . ."

The waitress nodded stiffly, raked the money off the table, took the thousand-ruble note out of my hand, and walked away.

The urge to speak in an eloquent, old-fashioned manner—to the extent of a person's understanding of what is eloquent and what is old-fashioned—is a typical sign of a discharge of Power somewhere nearby. But what kind of discharge did it have to be to affect me, a Higher Other?

And why hadn't I identified it in any other way?

Kesha's gaze gradually cleared.

He shook his head and looked at me in amazement.

"Uncle Anton . . . Did I prophesy? Twice in the same day?"

"No, my boy, you driveled some absolute twiddle," I said. "Let's go."

"Home?" Kesha asked timidly.

"Home to my place. Let's say you'll be my guest. Call your mother."

"She's in Paris. With . . ." Kesha paused. "With her husband. My stepfather, kind of. He's called Grigorii Ilich."

"Kind of?" I asked, puzzled, taking my coat from the cloak-room attendant. And I cast a Sphere of Inattention over Kesha and myself—it wasn't a good idea for everyone to hear what we were saying, which really was very odd.

"It was I who brought them together," Kesha said awkwardly. "A year ago. I suddenly thought what an ungrateful swine I was and how my mum had never become really close to anyone, she was always with me, but she wasn't old yet, she could still find some happiness in life and even have a brother or sister for me. And Uncle Gosha is a good man. Conscientious and no fool, well to do. So he has taken my mother to Paris to celebrate their wedding anniversary. He invited me also, but I refused point blank, so that I would not be a hindrance to them."

Kesha pulled on his jacket, buttoned it up, and said sincerely:

"I probably am prepared to regard him as my father. In a certain, general human sense. Especially since he does genuinely try to take care of me . . . because he believes I need it, he tries to set me a laudable example as a man, one that I can follow later in life. That is noble, and he is worthy to be regarded as a father. But alas, it is too absurd, in view of the circumstances. Most regretfully, it was I who brought him and my mother together . . . Yuck! Why am I talking like this?"

"A strong discharge of Power. It affects the subconscious," I explained.

"Ah, I remember! They taught us that!" Kesha exclaimed, delighted.

We got into the car, I started the engine, and turned the heater up to maximum.

"Then what happened to me?" Kesha asked, sniffing. "If I wasn't prophesying . . ."

"Someone used you as a relay station," I explained. "They spoke to me through you."

"Who?" Kesha asked tensely.

"Who do you think?"

Kesha sighed.

"The Twilight."

"Yes. The Twilight. More precisely, the Tiger."

CHAPTER 5

INNOKENTII HAD OFTEN BEEN TO OUR HOME. THERE WAS A time when Nadya became his special patron, not so much in magical matters as in ordinary, human ones. At the time I felt this was a good thing. Especially since they didn't really become friends at all—Nadya was a year older than him, after all, and they were at the age when boys and girls feel embarrassed to be friends in the way that children are, and still don't know how to be friends like grown-ups.

But even so, Kesha sometimes came to our place to talk to Nadya. Then, at Nadya's request, we arranged for him to be transferred to the school that she attended. The Night Watch was wholeheartedly in favor; they couldn't have given a Prophet special protection—we don't have that much manpower—but they put him together with the Absolute Enchantress, and that was one less headache.

And Kesha started showing up at our home more and more often, either after school or on the weekends. Sometimes he invited Nadya to the cinema, which wasn't entirely a bad thing, but during the last year they had started going to clubs of some kind, which to my mind is completely excessive for teenagers.

And so Kesha hung up his jacket and took off his shoes in a perfectly habitual manner, and went to wash his hands. I went to the kitchen. Coffee is all very well, but we weren't in Italy. This was Russia, the "land of tea." Drink up your tea, or feeble you shall be . . .

"I'll have green!" Innokentii shouted from the bathroom, just one second before I was about to ask.

"That kind of trick is why no one likes you Prophets!" I replied. But I smiled. The boy was playing with his Power, checking it out, using a sledgehammer to crack nuts. What if all of a sudden he was able to control his abilities as a Prophet as freely as Seers could?

I brewed green tea for Kesha—the standard kind, with jasmine. And strong, nine-year-old pu-erh for myself.

Kesha came in and sat at the table facing me. He nodded gratefully as he took the cup.

"Uncle Anton, why did the Tiger want me to come to your place?"

"He probably wants to have a talk," I said with a shrug. "With you and me at the same time."

"Well, I'm not really important . . ."

"Okay, okay, no false modesty. Do you feel any premonitions?"

The boy shook his head. "No. You can't predict the Twilight."

"You manage to predict me all right."

"That's not really prediction," Kesha admitted. "It's just that I know you well. Whenever you want to talk, you always suggest going for an ice cream. And when you go to the kitchen, you ask who wants what kind of tea."

"So it's the deductive method, then."

"Well . . . And just a little bit of prophesy." Kesha suddenly smiled cunningly. "I do know I'll have a sore throat tomorrow. Which means I'm probably going to eat ice cream. I shouldn't eat it in winter at all; my throat's my weak spot. And just now, I knew I was going to drink green tea with jasmine. That meant you were going to make it. I can't predict your actions, but I can predict my own."

"That's a good trick," I said respectfully. "Well done!"

Kesha nodded, accepting the compliment without any false modesty. Then he asked:

"But who else are we expecting? Apart from the Tiger?"

"We? Sugar . . ." I said with a start. "Yes, that's right. Zabulon promised I'd get a visit from a . . . a certain Dark One."

"A vampire?" Kesha asked.

"Absolutely right. A very old vampire. So you can foresee after all?"

"No, I'm not foreseeing. Just seeing." Kesha pointed with his eyes to the window behind my back.

I turned around and barely managed to suppress a shudder.

A bat was hanging from the cornice outside the window. A huge, monstrous bat—its outspread wings were two yards across, its head was the size of a human head, and the body was brushing against the molding of the window frame.

"Ah, there's our guest now," I said in a low voice.

"How can they fly?" asked Kesha, also lowering his voice. "That weighs as much as I do."

"Sorcery, lad, sorcery," I said, getting up and going toward the window. The bat watched me with an unblinking gaze.

Only Higher Vampires are able to transform themselves into animals. But not even a Higher Vampire could have approached so close to my apartment, which was protected by absolutely every possible spell of the Light and the Darkness.

I looked at the bat through the Twilight. Through the first level, and the second, and the third.

At every level it looked like a huge bat, nothing more and nothing less. Yes, indeed . . .

I opened both panes of the window. The vampire just stayed there, looking at me.

"I admit you," I said. "Come into my home. I permit you to enter."

The three-times-repeated permission broke down some invisible barrier. Waddling heavily on its feet and the elbow joints of its wings, the bat clambered onto the windowsill. And froze there.

No one knows why vampires cannot enter a house uninvited. Human legends lie about almost everything—vampires *are* reflected in mirrors, vampires *can* eat garlic, they don't like sunlight, but they can tolerate it, they're *not* afraid of silver (but then, a silver bullet works just as well as a lead one), they're not afraid of crosses and holy water (unless, of course, the person trying to resist the vampire is a latent Other and believes in God sincerely and absolutely, in which case the cross will burn the vampire and the water will corrode his flesh). However, vodka or pure alcohol burn vampires even more fiercely, and they can be used by any atheist.

But the ban on entering someone else's home—that's true.

"Turn away," I told Kesha. "They don't like to change in front of strangers."

"No one likes it," the bat said in a hoarse voice after the boy turned away. This really was a very old and experienced vampire—he had even learned to talk when in animal form!

I didn't turn away. My home, my rules.

The vampire threw up its wings, wrapping them around itself, and stood up on the windowsill, with its head almost reaching the ceiling—then it started changing form.

He did this with extreme skill too. Very neatly. None of the splashes or loose scraps of flesh that inexperienced werewolves and vampires produce. A gigantic bat had been standing there in front of me—and now there was a person. An Other.

A female Other.

"Good evening," I said after a moment's hesitation and held out my hand.

"The evenings are always good to me," the vampiress said with a smile. She leaned elegantly on her hand and jumped down off the windowsill. "You can turn around now, boy."

Kesha immediately turned around with lively curiosity.

"Are you surprised by something?" the vampiress asked.

"Yes." To my amazement, Kesha wasn't even slightly diffident. "I thought you'd be naked. How do you manage to change form dressed?"

"Because I'm not a werewolf, but a vampire," the woman said. "Werewolves are naked when they change form, but we . . . We have our own cunning artifices. And what are you surprised at, Goro-detsky?"

"Zabulon promised that I would be visited by one of the oldest vampires of all."

The woman laughed.

"Anton, you didn't really expect to see an old woman, did you?"

"In principle, I was prepared for it. Especially knowing Zabulon's sense of humor."

"Ah, I understand. You were prepared to see an old woman with fangs. Or an old, portly male vampire. You imagined a touching, in-nocent little girl, who has lived for hundreds of years by sucking the life out of people—or a melancholy youth in the likeness of Dorian Gray. You wouldn't have been surprised by some sultry, passionate, brilliant beauty whom men would beg to sink her fangs into their throats . . . Or a tender, young blonde, the perfect embodiment of helplessness and guile."

"Yes," I said.

"And you saw an ordinary woman," said the vampiress. "A little bit worse for wear, with a backside that's a bit heavy, maybe, but on the whole, pretty ordinary."

"Bull's-eye," I said.

The vampire was a perfectly ordinary woman.

Middle-aged. Thirty-something.

Moderately good looking. That is, it could be fun flirting with someone like this, and some men would fall in love with her (well, if they thought of her as a normal human being), but nothing su-perattractive. Maybe her backside was "a bit heavy," but it looked perfectly fine to me.

And she was dressed in an ordinary way. Absolutely ordinary—jeans, a short, light coat (either she drove everywhere, or her home and job were right beside a metro station . . . or she flew everywhere as a bat).

And her face was in no way exceptional. No intense emotions. No blinding charm, no gloom, no stupidity, no wisdom.

"You're like Zabulon," I said. "You're . . . You're very ordinary."

The vampiress nodded.

"Yes, Anton. Someone who lives for thousands of years has to be ordinary."

"Oh wow!" Kesha exclaimed.

That word "thousands" shook me too.

"Even Master Pyotr . . ."

"A mediocre little vampire boy. He's not even six hundred yet. A mere suckling." The vampiress smiled: "Pardon the foolish pun."

"But he's the Master of the vampires of Europe!"

"So? Barack Obama is the president of the United States. What of it? That doesn't make him the cleverest man, or the richest, or the most influential."

I held my hands up.

"I surrender. Pardon my ignorance. We haven't been introduced."

"Eve."

"Anton."

"That can't be your real name, though," Kesha remarked, gazing at Eve with avid curiosity.

"No, of course not. But it's an ancient name, known to all the peoples of the world. I find it convenient."

A thought flashed through my mind, but I didn't even let it take shape. She was a very, very old and powerful vampire. And not even my Higher Other level made us equal.

If she wanted, she could tear Kesha and me to pieces.

"All right, Eve," I said. "I let you into my home, I repeated the invitation three times, I've introduced myself. I have an ancient right in accordance with an ancient law."

"The right to three questions?" Eve was obviously amused: the corners of her lips were twitching. "Ah, Light One, I invented that right myself . . . I can change it."

She sat down between us with a light, catlike movement. She looked at me. She looked at Kesha.

"All right, Anton, we'll play. You'll get three answers, but they won't be answers to the questions that are bothering you. They'll just be answers. We'll have a serious talk afterward, but this is just the warm-up."

"Who is the vampire who saved us and why did she do it?"

Eve laughed and wagged her finger at me.

"All right." I sighed. "A warm-up. What is the connection between you and Zabulon?"

Eva thought for moment. She licked her lips.

"Blood."

"That's not an answer."

"It is an answer, Anton Gorodetsky. You asked a question, I answered. It's an honest answer. If it didn't answer your question, the asker is to blame."

"All right," I said. "The second question. Csaba Orosz. How much truth is there in his book, and how much falsehood? Were the vampires simply making a fool of him, or are the legends that he tells genuine?"

Eve froze. She nodded.

"A good question. Most of what he says there is true."

"Can I ask something?" Kesha said.

"Let the boy ask," I said.

"How do you keep your clothes during transformation? It isn't magic, I would have felt it."

"An unexpected question," said the vampiress. "What an inquisitive little man! You see, this"—she adjusted the flaps of her coat and pulled up her jeans—"isn't clothing. I don't keep any clothes."

"It's all you," Kesha whispered. "You are . . ."

"I'm naked." Eve laughed. "But just how hard do you think it is to give your body the appearance of clothes, kid, if you can assume the form of a beast that flies? I am my own clothes. Any kind at all."

Eve's silhouette trembled, changing color and form. Now she was wearing a long white dress with a string of pearls around her neck and glittering shoes that looked as if they were made of crystal. Plump young breasts bulged up out of the plunging neckline.

"I'm not embarrassing you, am I boys?" she asked with a sly smile.

"No," I said. "Unfortunately, I know the true shape of your kind—so I can't be seduced by you in furs, or in silk, or naked. Sorry."

"Don't worry about it, Anton," Eve replied very seriously. "In my kind, sexual appetite passes after two or three hundred years. It's supplanted by the feeding instinct—that's more ancient, you know. Sex for me is drinking blood."

"I know," I said. "Well then, you've answered three questions that aren't important . . ."

"They are very important, even if you didn't realize it," said Eve. "But beside the point. What did you really want to ask me?"

"I wanted to ask you about the two who attacked us. And about the prophecy of universal death."

"I understand," Eve said with a nod. "But these are serious questions and they require a genuine price to be paid."

"What price?" I asked, already knowing the answer.

"The true price is always the same, Watchman. Blood."

I really didn't want to say this, especially in front of Kesha. But I'd been thinking about it for half a day.

"I'll give you permits," I said.

"What kind?" Eve inquired.

"For feeding."

Eva shrugged.

"Permits? For me? Anton, I have a whole heap of those permits. Some of them are on birch bark, and some are even on clay tablets. But after all, if I want to drink someone, surely you don't think that your Watchmen could catch me? You hunt newly turned vampires for weeks, and you don't catch all of them."

I didn't answer that. She was right—and I knew it perfectly well.

"But what if I want something a bit more interesting?" Eve suddenly asked. "To drink a pregnant woman? Or a three-year-old child? Some celebrity, a writer or a musician, one of those who sow the seeds of reason, goodness, the eternal values. I know you take people like that out of the vampire lottery."

"We don't take them out," I said firmly.

Eve laughed.

"But really? Will you give me a permit? On one side of the scales—the death of all mankind. Of Others, people, animals . . ."

"Thank you for the information," I said. "I didn't know about the animals."

For a while we just looked at each other. But my pitiful attempt to get a rise out of Eve was a failure. In fact, she suddenly gave me a sympathetic sort of look.

"Don't squirm, Watchman. I can just hear your banal clichés being rent asunder. I'm not interested in the blood of children and mothers, or of your musicians and writers either . . . After Dostoyevsky, everybody else's blood is rather thin, somehow."

"Such literary pretensions," I snarled.

"The fact that I am dead and I feed on human blood doesn't mean that I can't admire genuine literature," Eve replied. "I've read the fashionable ones, and the talented ones. No, relax, Anton, I don't want your intelligentsia, to put them in a frame and hang them on the wall."

"Then what do you want?" I asked.

"Blood. But it's a very long time since I've just drunk whatever comes along. I collect interesting bloods, Anton."

"Tell me what you want."

"The blood of a Higher Light One—for an answer to any question."

"And are you sure you can answer the question?" I asked.

"I'm sure."

"How much blood do you want?"

"Uncle Anton!" Kesha exclaimed. "Don't agree! What are you doing?"

"Shut up," I said. "And remember everything. You're the witness."

Kesha tried to jump up, but he sank back down again. His lips started trembling. He kept looking from me to Eve and back again.

"Don't try to stop him, boy," said Eve. "There's no coercion here, it's all voluntary. I don't intend to drink you dry, Anton. And I don't intend to turn you. Especially since that's very, very difficult with an Other, and virtually impossible with a Higher Light One. I'm not a killer." She smiled cunningly, and her eyes glinted as if they were alive. "Not just a killer. I'm a collector."

"How much?" I repeated.

"A swallow or two. Three at the very most, if it turns out that I like it."

"Drink," I said, rolling up my sleeve.

"No, no!" Eve exclaimed indignantly. "That's sacrilege. Pardon me, but I didn't just drop in for a quick tipple. Either the neck or the femoral artery. We won't embarrass the boy, will we? The neck."

"Get sucking, I didn't invite you here to make conversation."

"Ah, Anton, Anton!" Eve said and laughed again. "I really do like you! All that wonderful bravado and crudity, that disguised vulgarity . . ."

She got up and walked toward me, and I got up too. I caught her smell—fresh, sweet, and intoxicating all at once. Eve's eyes glittered, and a light half smile played on her lips. Right now she seemed genuinely beautiful.

"I see you haven't eaten for a long time," I said. "Your pheromone glands are full."

"If I wanted," Eve whispered, "all the men in this building would come running to me. And the boy would pass out from his lust. Don't you want to kiss me?"

"I do," I said, "but I know what I would really be kissing, so I'll abstain."

"I can do no more than ask," she purred, and set her head on my shoulder with a smooth, gliding movement.

I felt a prick on my neck.

Kesha gave a quiet shriek.

"Don't turn away," I said. "Count out loud. The bag of muscle on her neck will swell up with every suck."

My neck turned slightly numb. It didn't hurt anymore.

"One," said Kesha.

Eve raised her hand and stroked my head.

I didn't feel anything. No pain. No weakness. There was just a woman standing there . . . an attractive woman who had laid her head on my shoulder . . .

And was drinking my blood.

"Two," Kesha said in an anguished voice.

Eve straightened up with an equally smooth, elegant movement. She licked her mouth with her long, pink tongue. And wiped the remaining blood off her lips with the back of her hand.

"Kesha, give me a napkin," I said, holding out my hand. Kesha jumped up, almost knocking over his chair, and handed me a bundle of crumpled napkins—in bright cheerful colors, with a laughing Santa Claus on them. I pressed the napkins against my neck.

"It will clot on its own," said Eve. "I injected the enzyme, Light One."

"Thank you. And why only two swallows? Didn't you like it?"

"Alcohol and foul tobacco, the effluvia of the big city," said Eve. "I'm joking, Anton. It's very interesting blood. With a familiar after-taste, just as I expected, but interesting. I'll remember it. I wanted to put you in your place."

"Well, I don't object to that," I said.

"And remember for the future," said Eve. "In such . . . old ones as me, the sucking bag can hold up to one and a half or two quarts of blood. I could have killed you in two swallows. Or three. And it all would have been within the limits of what you permitted; the boy would have been a witness. Not drinking you dry, not turning you, three swallows. And if you couldn't live with one quart of blood in your veins, that would have been your problem, you fool."

She looked insistently into my eyes.

"A stupid fool," I agreed. "Thank you. I'll remember that."

"Now you can ask your question," said Eve. "Any question. If I can't give you any useful information . . . well, then you'll ask another one. Fair enough?"

"Fair enough," I said. "What happened to the Watchmen who were guarding Nadya, why did they attack the Inquisitor, why did they attack my family, where does their Power come from, and how can they be destroyed?"

"Why, you cheat!" Eve exclaimed, wagging her finger at me. "One question, remember? But I'm a kind vampire, Anton. I'll answer."

I sat down. Evidently the effect of the hormones that Eve had injected into my artery had worn off—I started feeling weak. Not a quart maybe. But she had sucked out half a quart of blood for sure. In two gulps. All the vampires I knew could suck in only three and a half or, at the most, five ounces at a time.

"The Watchmen were simply in the wrong place at the wrong time," said Eve, leaning down over me. "They don't exist anymore. An ancient god has manifested himself in their bodies."

"The vampire god."

"There weren't any other gods then, Light One. An ancient god. The Two-in-One. The God of Light and Darkness. The first one born of the Twilight, the first to acquire reason—and he made us, the vampires, his servants. Servants and priests, keepers of the great equilibrium."

"What equilibrium?"

"Don't interpret the boundaries of the question so widely, Watchman. The ancient god has incarnated himself, and that is very sad, Watchman, because we betrayed him. We vampires stopped doing what we were supposed to do. We changed, we took different paths. Many stopped drinking blood and started drinking life . . . directly."

I looked into the eyes of the one who called herself Eve, and saw a bottomless abyss. I saw the black sky of the childhood of human-kind. I saw warriors drinking the blood of their enemies, and sha-mans drinking the blood of warriors. I saw the Two-in-One emerge from the gloom and walk toward a campfire—and seal the most ancient of human covenants with blood . . .

"The Two-in-One is offended, the Two-in-One is insulted," Eve whispered. "People have forgotten him, people have betrayed him, they have taken other paths. And even vampires have accommodated themselves to the situation, become mired in depravity and gluttony; they have forgotten their duty to people. The Two-in-One will not forgive. The Two-in-One will destroy all of us. All the Others. For that he has to destroy the main danger: your daughter. And her parents. Because you won't hand her over for slaughter. The Inquisitor took his duty too seriously, he tried to stop them, although I think he knew what was happening. Well . . . perhaps he chose a quick and easy death? Who knows? But he couldn't stop the Two-in-One. Only the Sixth Watch is capable of destroying the Two-in-One. Only the Sixth Watch! But the Sixth Watch is dead."

"What is the Sixth Watch?" I whispered.

"That's a different question," Eve said with a smile.

"You'll die too, won't you?" I said. "Then why all these games? Answer me, just answer me! We have a common interest here."

"Perhaps I won't die," Eve said with a shrug. "I'm the last of those who remember the Covenant of Blood. I'm the last of those who saw the previous incarnation of the Two-in-One . . . I'm joking, Light One. I shall be killed too. But I accept it, this world is becoming too cruel."

"For vampires?

"No," said Eve, shaking her head. "Simply too cruel. And I don't like pointless cruelty, Gorodetsky."

"I need one more answer," I said. "Bite me again."

"But I don't need a double for the collection," Eve said in an offended tone. "No, Anton, for me you're spent material."

She paused.

"Although you do have something you could offer me."

"You're not getting Nadya," I said. "Don't even think about that."

"Yes, I know, I know. I didn't even bother to ask, to avoid provoking your aggression unnecessarily. But you have something to offer me apart from your daughter."

"All right," I said after a momentary hesitation. "I'm sure Svetlana will understand and agree . . ."

"I have the blood of a Higher Light Healer in my collection," said Eve. "Of course, Svetlana is the mother of an Absolute Enchantress, and that lends her a certain special piquancy, but . . . Probably, after all, no. I mean the boy."

"Why, you're out of your mind!" I said sincerely. I looked at Kesha and gestured to him reassuringly.

"By no means. A Higher Light Other, a Prophet—that's a great rarity."

"He's not a Higher Other, he's First Level."

"Oh! See, you've already started haggling!" Eve said contentedly. "He's First Level now, but he would have become a Higher One. It's a pity he won't have time now. But Prophets are such a rarity, especially Light ones. I'm willing to settle for him."

"Eve, he's a child."

"He's fourteen and a half; what kind of child is that?" Eve asked in surprise. "He has a passport. In a civil war he could command a regiment. Children are only excluded from the vampire lottery until the age of twelve. And I'm sorry, Light One, but he has the right to decide for himself!"

"I accept," Kesha said quickly.

"He does not accept," I growled.

"Why not?" Kesha asked with a shrug. He was pale, but didn't seem frightened at all. "We need the information, right? She won't kill me, she won't turn me into a vampire. So she'll drink a bit of my blood; what will I lose by that? It's all a bit perverted, of course, but at least she's a woman. Was a woman. Anyway, I regard donating blood as a useful activity, and we already know that twenty percent of donated blood goes to vampires anyway, don't we?"

Eve was openly reveling in this, shifting her gaze from me to Kesha and back.

I was thinking.

If it had all been sham bravado, if I could have seen that the boy was genuinely afraid . . .

But he wasn't afraid. Or rather, he wasn't any more afraid than I had been. He was feeling a bit disgusted. But he accepted the situation with absolute clarity.

And the stakes just happened to be the apocalypse.

"Not more than one and a half ounces a swallow," I said. "No more than three swallows."

"All right," Eve agreed. She walked over to Kesha, who jumped up and froze in front of her.

"And don't you smother him with your pheromones," I added.

"I won't," Eve agreed lightly. "What's this now, are you young people so careless about hygiene? Your neck's dirty."

"I'm fat, so I sweat easily," Kesha replied. "If you don't like it, take a towel and wipe it."

Eve clapped her hands.

"Bravo! Bravo! Anton, what a wonderful young fellow he is, don't you think? He takes his example from you."

She leaned her head over and nestled it against Kesha's neck.

I got up and walked around the table, moving closer to them.

She took a swallow—the bag of muscle on her neck swelled up. She paused for a moment and sighed deeply and passionately, staying glued to the boy. She swallowed a second time. Paused for a moment. Took a third swallow.

"Get off him," I said.

Eve stood there without stirring a muscle. She squinted at me with one eye—it was sinister, misted over . . .

"Get off him, Lilith," I whispered in her ear. "Or I'll disembowel your rotten paunch, I swear by the Light—"

The vampire who called herself Eve sprang away from Kesha and stared at me in hatred. It wasn't the threat that had frightened her, but the name.

"Close the wounds!" I ordered her. "We're playing fair here, remember?"

Lilith spat bloody saliva into her palm and ran her hand over

Kesha's neck. When she took her hand away, the blood had stopped flowing. Kesha sat down heavily on a chair. I gave him the rest of the napkins, and he pressed them against his wounds.

"I'll remember you," Lilith promised, staring daggers at me.

"You shouldn't take other people for fools, 'Eve,'" I said. "And now answer the question . . ."

"The boy gave the blood," said Lilith. "He's the one who should ask."

"Ask what the Sixth Watch is and how to organize it," I said.

"Is that your question?" Lilith asked Kesha.

Kesha didn't answer.

He shook his head.

"My question's a different one."

I ought to have yelled at him, stopped him. Explained that there wasn't any question more important than this right now. But I couldn't.

He had conquered his fear. He had given his blood.

This was the most ancient and most powerful magic in the world.

Kesha looked at me and I nodded.

"Tell me, what is the relationship between the Two-in-One, the Twilight, and the Tiger?" Kesha asked.

"That's quite a number of questions," said Lilith. "That's very many questions, you impudent little boy! And I won't—"

"It really is only one question, and you know it. The price was my blood, and you took what was given, you cannot return what you took, and I demand what was promised," said Kesha. "Speak."

"How do you know the words of the demand?" Lilith asked after a short pause.

"I'm a Prophet," said Kesha. "I simply knew that I would speak precisely those words to you."

"You won't like my answer," said Lilith. "I will tell you what you want, but not what you need, and you have nothing left to trade with me."

"Speak," I said. "You gave your promise."

"The Twilight is alive, but it has no reason, the Twilight only wants to live," said Lilith, spreading her hands as if she was amazed at her own words. "The Tiger is the Keeper of the Twilight, he is rational, but he has no will. The Tiger is powerful. But the Two-in-One has reason and will, and the Two-in-One is also a creation of the Twilight. If the Tiger stands in his way, he will sweep the Tiger aside. Everything living will be killed, because the Others are not only parasites, they are the guardians of life. If the Others die, every living thing will die. If all living things die, the Twilight will die. If the Twilight dies, the Tiger will die, the Two-in-One will die, and absolutely everything around this little lump of dirt will die. I have given my answer."

"You have not answered," I said. "Why are we the guardians of life? We Others are the same kind of parasites as you vampires. Why will people die after the Others?"

Lilith bared her teeth. Her fangs were not even withdrawn.

"You are being sly, and so am I. But you have been given an answer; no one promised to tell you all the details . . . Light One."

"All right," I said. "All right. We accept your answer. But we need to know what the Sixth Watch is."

Lilith shrugged.

"How can we pay for the answer?" I asked. I felt a bleak pain gradually constricting my chest. It was probably the way people feel just a moment before a heart attack. "Would the blood of my daughter . . ."

"No, Light One!" Lilith exclaimed, shaking her head. "The time for that price has passed. Her blood might burn me, I was prepared to take that risk—but not now! You don't have the price for another answer!"

I suddenly saw Kesha's eyes turn big and round, filling up with a mixture of amazement, hope, and fear—fear in the eyes of a boy who had just voluntarily offered his neck to a vampiress thousands of years old.

"Perhaps I have the price for any of your answers," a voice said behind me.

I turned around.

The Tiger was standing there, pouring himself a cup of coffee from a steaming pot. He was the same as before—a tall young man, dressed in a formal business suit. The Tiger lifted the cup to his face and took a sip. Then he slowly turned toward us.

"As you already remarked, I don't have a will of my own," said the Tiger. "But I do have blood. The blood of the Twilight, pardon the bad pun. You wish to round out your collection in a worthy manner before the end of time, don't you, you decrepit brute?"

The vampire's white dress turned pink, as if it was suddenly impregnated with blood. She shied away toward the wall, crashing into it, and white plaster dust sprinkled down onto her shoulders from the dull blow of the impact. Her legs buckled and she half squatted down, holding her hands out in front of her. The vampiress's fingers had turned into black claws.

"Well, what is your answer?" the Tiger asked.

"N-n-no!" the vampiress moaned. "No!"

She bounded away from the wall and darted toward the window, intending to either open it or jump through it, smashing the glass.

But the Tiger was already at the window, still holding the cup of coffee in his hand. Without making a single movement, the Tiger was there. He simply appeared at the spot to which the vampiress had jumped—and she was halted by his open hand.

"You didn't understand," he said. "You have no choice. I'll pay the price and you'll answer the question."

"I'll answer!" Lilith shouted. "I'll answer, I don't need any payment!"

"Rules are rules," said the Tiger.

He took a gulp from the cup and set it down on the window sill. Then he leaned his head over onto his right shoulder, presenting his neck.

"Bite me."

Lilith started trembling. Then she nodded, resigning herself.

"Yes . . . yes."

The vampiress's mouth touched the Tiger's neck for a moment—and instantly she recoiled. Her lips had turned crimson. Two tiny little bite marks had appeared on the Tiger's neck.

"You took the price and you will give the answer," said the Tiger. "What is the Sixth Watch?"

"The Six concluded a treaty with the Two-in-One," the vampiress whispered. "The Six can terminate the treaty."

"Who are they?" asked the Tiger.

"She who was born of the Light. He who was born of the Darkness. He who took another's Power. He who has no Power of his own. He who sees. He who senses."

"There must be three conditions," the Tiger said, "I know the rules."

Lilith nodded, gazing at him with hatred. Little clouds of steam were escaping from her mouth.

"Love, Hate, Nobility, Treachery, Strength, Weakness. This is the first condition."

The Tiger nodded.

Lilith raised her hands, looking at her fingers in amazement. Then she went on.

"The envoy of each of the Great Parties must be present. The leader of each Party must come or appoint an envoy. That is the second condition."

"What are the Great Parties?" I asked. "Light? Darkness?"

Lilith bared her teeth.

"I am obliged to name them, but not to explain them. Am I right, Tiger?"

The Tiger nodded, looking at her pensively.

"And the third condition," said Lilith, smiling sincerely now—I would almost say soulfully, but it was a very long time since she had had a soul. "The Six must be bound by the first and principal Power."

"The Twilight?" I couldn't stop myself from asking.

To my surprise, Lilith answered.

"No, Light One. The very first and principal Power. Blood."

"Perhaps you wish to say something else?" the Tiger asked.

"I hope you croak!" Lilith spat the words in his face. "I hope you all croak! And you, slave of the Twilight, too!"

"Well now, we'll soon find out. But you won't."

Lilith laughed.

"No, we'll see. We'll see. I've remained faithful to the Two-in-One, I welcome him . . ."

"Where you will go, there is nothing," said the Tiger, raising his hand.

Lilith started glowing with a blinding white light. Something was burning her from the inside. The white dress flooded with blood, then turned black—and the vampiress dwindled into a little mound of ash.

Kesha was dumbfounded. I took hold of his head and made him turn away.

"I'm sorry, I've made a mess," said the Tiger. "Do you have a dust-pan and brush?"

I looked at the remains of the vampiress for a while.

"No. Only a vacuum cleaner."

"That will do," said the Tiger. Without asking where to go, he walked out of the kitchen and came back with the vacuum cleaner. He examined the hose thoughtfully and lowered it to the floor. The vacuum cleaner started humming quietly. The Tiger held the brush to the dust, and the fine ash started flowing into the disposal bag in thin little rivulets.

He'd forgotten to plug the vacuum cleaner into the socket, but that didn't prevent it from working.

"Thanks for your help, I'll clean it up myself," I said. "I'd feel I was a poor host if I let you do my cleaning."

The Tiger gave a faint smile as he switched the vacuum cleaner off. Or did I imagine it? A smiling Tiger is a quite fantastic sight.

"Then one more thing and I'll be going," said the Tiger. "If you ask me if I understood what Lilith said, then no. I'm not the Twi-

light, I'm only a small part of it. You'll have to find the answer yourself."

"And what if I don't find it?" I asked.

The Tiger looked at me in surprise.

"Didn't you hear? We'll all die."

"How terrifying life is," Kesha said, turning and looking at the
heap of ash. And he yawned.

I looked at him.

"You go off to bed, Kesha. I won't take you home now, you can
spend the night in Nadya's room. Take some clean sheets, they're in
the chest of drawers . . ."

"In the bottom drawer," said Kesha, getting up. "I know."

"How?" I asked sharply. "How do you know that?"

Kesha gave me a surprised look.

"I am a Prophet after all . . . By the way, you do have a brush and
a dustpan—in the cupboard in the hallway."

I heard soft gurgling sounds close by. I turned and looked at the
Tiger.

He was chuckling quietly, pressing his hands over his mouth.

And then he dissolved into the air.

PART TWO

MANDATORY ALLIANCES

CHAPTER 1

THE ARCHIVE WAS AS COLD AND DARK AS EVER. BUT TODAY something had changed: There was music playing.

I wouldn't have been surprised to hear something classical, maybe Vivaldi or Bach. Or some foot-tapping Irish music, a jig or a reel.

But Helen Killoran was listening to a popular Russian bard.

Our verse is clear, shadows are we, twixt wakefulness and sleep
Living from hope to hope, from bivouac to cross.
Like molten magma, breathing sky, erupting from the deep,
It courses through our veins—the Haemoglobin Waltz.

I set off quietly, walking between the shadowy sets of shelves, with their slumbering lines of books, scrolls, printouts, punch cards, floppy disks, clay tablets, and laser disks.

How old we are, and which of us is which, we cannot understand.
Through little holes in dreams, this strange chord have we glimpsed,
    clear as an open hand,
So listen to it heedfully—perhaps it swirled above Japan
When the final kamikaze revved his engine high above the bones of his
    scalped land . . .

I walked up to the desk; a rather ancient radio/CD player was standing on it, with a memory stick protruding from its USB port. I pressed the stop button.

"Helen!"

"Yes, Anton?"

I shuddered and turned around. Killoran was standing behind me, clutching a fat tome in a leather binding.

"You frightened me," I said.

"I got a fright too," she replied. "I caught a glimpse of a flickering shadow. And I don't have a very full schedule here . . ."

She suddenly became embarrassed and put the book down on the table. Had she been intending to wallop me with that massive volume, then?

"That's a good song," I said. "I didn't know you liked the Russian bards."

"Not all of them," she said, wincing slightly. "But this is good . . . How's your case going? Have you caught the vampiress?"

"Our case is all very convoluted," I said. "Will you give me some tea? I feel like it today."

She smiled and switched on the kettle. I sat down at the desk, poured myself a cup when it was ready, and gave Helen a brief account of everything that she probably hadn't heard about down here in her basement. The only thing I left out was the Tiger's visit—it didn't matter if that meant Helen got the idea I was the one who laid Lilith to rest.

"Serious," she said, and thought for a moment. "Very serious. Is there something you want to find out?"

"Yes. I've sent a request to the Day Watch, and to our people too. But maybe you can come up with something here . . ."

"The Two-in-One?"

"And something else: the Sixth Watch. And the Great Parties."

"Is there anything on the computer?" Helen asked.

"No. Apart from the vampire legend of the Two-in-One from Orosc's book."

Helen nodded.

"There's something else too. I think you ought to know this . . ." I took out my smartphone and displayed the note I'd received from our doctor, Ivan, on the screen. "Another eight people bitten. In a single sequence. She bit them purely symbolically; it's no more than a signal. And the result is not what I was expecting."

Helen leaned down over the screen.

"The sequence of the bites?"

"This is it," I said with a nod.

"Roman, Oleg, Daniyar, Elena, Timofei, Silvano . . . Is that really a name?"

"It is. And what's more, the boy isn't even Italian, he's Russian. You can't imagine how strange some parents can be."

"Kurzhan, Yoachim. Really? Written with a 'Y'?"

"Absolutely right. I think the boy's Australian. Our kids probably call him Akim, but in the official documents his name's written as 'Yoachim.'"

". . . rodetsky," said Helen. "So she's finished your surname. Good for her."

"Uh-huh," I said, nodding. "That's clear enough and it's what we expected."

"Now the patronymics," Helen said. "What did we have there? 'It's your'?"

"Yes," I said. "No apostrophe, but she obviously couldn't find one of those."

"Denisovich, Evgenievich, Chinigizovna, Ivanovna, Stepanovich, Ibragimovich . . ." Helen glanced at me. "Ibragimovich—is that Silvano?"

"Yes," I said with a nod. "Silvano Ibragimovich. So? It has a fine, solemn ring to it."

"Olegovich . . . Nikolaevna . . ."

"That's right," I said. "'Decision.'"

"'It's your decision,'" Helen said with a nod. "More cheerful than 'it's your funeral.'"

"Yes. Although being asked for a decision in such an exotic way . . . that's a bit stressful too."

"Never mind, it won't be the first decision you've had to make," Helen reassured me. "And the conclusion. We had 'Be ready,' and now it's Hadrianov, Evgenieva, Abramova, Wolanski, Andriushin, Inozemtsev . . ."

Helen winced.

"Go ahead, ask," I said.

"Silvano Ibragimovich Inozemtsev?" Helen asked with a shudder. "Is that normal for Russia these days?"

"I don't have enough imagination to speculate on what might be considered abnormal for Russia these days."

"And what's he like, in general . . . this Silvano?" Helen asked queasily. "Did you see him?"

"I did, purely by chance. An absolutely wonderful child. Despite his first name-patronymic-surname combination."

Helen sighed and said, "Tokareva. Sukhanova."

"He awaits," I said with a nod.

"So in the end the meaning isn't what you were expecting at all," said Helen. "It isn't a threat. She hasn't come to get you. 'Anton Gorodetsky, be ready, he awaits, it's your decision.' "

"I wouldn't actually swear that there isn't any threat in that," I remarked.

"But she saved your daughter, didn't she, and you and your wife?"

"Perhaps she didn't want to share the prey? And we don't know who it is that awaits, do we?"

Helen shrugged.

"All right, Anton. I won't try guessing in the dark. What can I do to help you? In the first place. The Sixth Watch?"

"Better start with the Great Parties," I said. "They've already run through everything in the computer databases for me. The primordial powers—Light and Darkness—are sometimes called the Great Powers. But we're obviously dealing with something different here."

Helen sighed.

"Just a minute . . . So it's 'Parties' then."

She moved away again into the darkness, walked between the bookshelves, and stopped at one of them. A small pocket flashlight glinted feebly.

"Helen, why are you so fond of the dark?" I asked. "I understand a lot of the old tomes don't like the light. But it's awkward for you!"

"I have very good night vision," Helen replied, rustling documents. "And a very good memory."

"And catalogues," I said.

"Naturally. Catalogues too. Great . . . By the way, I'm amazed at how carelessly the previous archivist maintained the collection. Russia has a very fine traditional school of archivists, probably due to the custom of keeping so many documents secret from the people."

"Go on, mock away," I growled. "Bleak Russia, with its archives full of secrets, guarded by polar bears holding balalaikas at 'trail arms.' "

Helen snorted.

"Compared with the American, English, or French archives, yours aren't really all that secret. But that doesn't apply to the archives of the Watches, of course. They're entirely secret."

"Do you know something about the Day Watch archive then?"

"Of course. We have a certain amount of contact. We exchange duplicates and copies of documents, we consult with each other . . ."

"Well, I'll be damned," I said. "So much for the secrets of the Watch cellars. Is Gesar in the loop?"

"In general terms," Helen said evasively. "Hmm. The Great Parties. There is one reference. A treaty from the year 1215 'On Necessary and Unnecessary Measures.' Not the actual treaty, of course, a copy. It mentions the Great Parties."

"What is it about?"

Helen laughed.

"How should I know? You don't really think I've read everything in here, do you? Come on, let's go, I know where it's stored. Come on!"

I got up and walked toward the weak glimmer of the flashlight. Helen gripped my hand in her own firm, cold palm and drew me after her into the darkness. The pale, milky-white ray of light shone on the floor in front of us for a few seconds and then went out.

"Why?" I asked.

"It's better this way," Helen replied vaguely. "And my advice to you is not to look through the Twilight. In fact it's not even advice, but a very definite order."

"And why's that?" I asked, wincing involuntarily in anticipation of banging my forehead against some set of shelves as I stepped through the darkness. It was unbearable and I lifted my free hand to hold it out in front of me.

"It's best if you don't know why," said Helen. "Yes, shield yourself with your hand if you like, but don't switch on the light."

We walked about ten yards across the old, crunching linoleum that covered the floor in the first hall. Then, judging from the movement of the air, we entered the next hall, where it was either floorboards or old, dried-out parquet that creaked under our feet. At one point Helen tugged me abruptly toward her.

"Sorry," she said. "There was a bone jutting out from the shelf there, you would have crashed into it."

"What sort of bone?"

"Human. A shinbone."

"What's that doing in the archive?"

"There's a spell engraved on it."

"What spell?"

"No one knows, it's in an unknown language."

"But why is your archive in such a mess?" I asked, feeling the conversation starting to irritate me. "Bones jutting out across the aisles . . ."

"It only just jutted out," Helen explained. "As we were walking up to it."

I refrained from asking the stupid question of whether she was joking. She might not have been.

The wood under our feet came to an end. Now we were walking over stone slabs. They became uneven, as if they were swollen or bloated. Then they leveled out again.

And then Helen stopped and paused for a moment before speaking.

"We'll go around through hall eight, I think . . ."

"Have you seen the film *Stalker*?" I asked.

"Tarkovsky? Of course not. I read about it in an encyclopedia."

We walked across wood, then across stone again, and then over crudely laid cobblestones.

"Or the film *Buratino*?" I asked. "It's a Russian version of *Pinoc-chio*."

Helen laughed.

"What are you getting at?"

"Ah, Field, Field of Wonders . . ." I sang out of tune. "And the Fox Alice and the Cat Basilio take Buratino to the Field of Wonders. On a donkey. Riding around in circles. We've covered two hundred yards already. Our basements aren't that big."

Helen sighed. She switched on the little flashlight and brightened up our surroundings a bit. Dim though it was, the small ray of light illuminated the aisle between the shelves for about ten yards, after which everything was lost in darkness. Then she shone it in the opposite direction—the same thing. I tried to make out what was lying on the shelves, but she switched off the light.

"Not around in circles," said Helen. "Walking in a straight line isn't always the shortest route, but not around in circles."

We walked on for another three or four minutes. We walked through a puddle, with water dripping somewhere nearby.

"Helen, this is a total mess," I said in an attempt to reproach her.

"Yes, it has dried out a lot," she agreed. "I'll adjust the tap after this . . ."

I resigned myself to the situation, but in a final attempt to assert my own position I reached out my hand, trying to feel what was lying on the shelves. My hand ran into something warm and sticky that also seemed to be moving slowly . . . I jerked it back and hastily wiped it on my trousers.

Helen laughed in a way I found offensive

"Well, here we are . . . Just a moment, Anton."

And she suddenly let go of my hand.

"Helen?" I asked.

She didn't answer. I took one soundless step to the side, wanting very badly to switch on the light. I decided I would count to three and then do it.

"There it is," Helen said cheerfully. "Now we can have light!"

The little flashlight in her hand lit up with a bright, pure light, as if it had been switched into a different mode. Helen aimed it at a shelf, illuminating it from below, and looked at me with a smile.

"Just what did you expect to see, Great One? Me transforming into a vampire?"

"Why would you suddenly ask that?" I asked.

"Well, for starters, you have the Gray Prayer already half activated; even I can see that. Please don't use it, or you'll destroy loads of valuable documents."

"You came from a different country, ten years ago," I said. "You stay in here all the time, in the basement. You never stick your nose out into the light. And then you take me on this pleasant stroll . . ."

Helen laughed quietly.

"I'm sorry, Anton. But do you seriously think a vampire could disguise herself as a Light One so successfully and for so long? From Gesar? From Olga? From you? And then lure you into the darkness somewhere for bloody slaughter?"

"I didn't think anything!" I snapped. "And your hands are cold."

"Of course, with the temperature in here." Helen sighed. "I apologize again. I did pile it on a bit, I admit. Consider it a professional joke. But in here it really is best to follow indirect routes and not use any light."

"I'm sorry too, I was wrong," I admitted, furling up the half-extended spell on the tips of my fingers. The threads of Power poised to break loose receded into my skin.

"Okay, peace," Helen agreed. "Let's drop the stupid jokes. Look, that's your document."

For as far as the light allowed me to see, the shelves were crammed with plywood boxes. Some were flat and some were long, like packages of expensive bottles of wine. They were all protected by old-fashioned but functional spells of preservation. Some also had spells on them that were unfamiliar to me, but I didn't try to figure them out. At that point the shelves bore the code number LT-32 in big brass letters and numbers, screwed onto a shelf at eye level.

"It's a fairly old copy too," said Helen, taking down a flat box and opening it. "But it is paper already, not parchment. There doesn't seem to be anything magical about the item itself. Do you see anything?"

I looked at the thick sheet of heavy paper that she was holding and shook my head. It was hard to say without looking through the Twilight, but I didn't spot any magic.

"Do you know Old High German?" Helen asked.

"I don't even know plain, ordinary German."

"Then I'll give you an approximate translation. You'll have the official, checked translation by this evening."

Helen cleared her throat and peered at the calligraphic manuscript.

"Right . . . 'In the year one thousand two hundred and fifteen . . .' What's that year famous for?"

I thought for a moment.

"The Inquisition?"

"Right. The Holy See or, more precisely, Innocent III, founded the Inquisition."

"But all that . . ." I said with a shrug. "It's not serious. The Inquisition dealt with all sorts of nonsense. They drowned old women who healed with herbs, they persecuted Jews."

"Burned Giordano Bruno, persecuted Galileo . . ." Helen continued in the same tone of voice. "But you see, the Inquisition had potential. At that time everyone had faith, including Others. Most of the Light Ones believed that they had been endowed with a special gift by the Creator, and the Dark Ones were servants of"—she hesitated—"you know who. And if genuine Others had joined the Inquisition and added their abilities to the efforts of the Church . . ."

"We would probably have wiped out the Dark Ones," I said. "Completely."

"Not completely," said Helen. "New ones would have been born. And they would have been executed."

"Maybe the world would have been a better place," I suggested pensively.

"And all the ordinary people would know about Others, vampires, and werewolves. They would envy their Power, their longevity, their knowledge. And if they got a chance, the people would try to wipe out the Light Ones too, even though we devote our entire lives to protecting them."

"Something like that," I said. "Something like that . . ."

Helen sighed.

"Right, then . . . 'In the light of the establishment of the Inquisition and the corresponding Prophecies, following consultations and the corresponding guarantees . . .' It's not exactly 'guarantees' here, more like 'promises,' but 'guarantees' would probably be more accurate. 'The Six Great Parties gathered in the city of Rome.'"

"Bull's-eye," I said. "Helen, you're a star. You and your catalogue."

"'A report was presented by Elpis Hieraticus of Athens and Kurt Hesse of Cologne . . .' Strange, it doesn't even say if they were Light or Dark. And 'Hieraticus' sounds pretty much like a pseudonym. Okay, they suggested establishing contact with the Inquisition, essentially disclosing themselves to it and collaborating. 'They discussed . . . Argued . . . Objected . . . Declined . . . Accepted . . .'"

Helen sighed.

"I'm sorry, I can only understand the general sense. Anyway, the basic gist is this. They say they discussed the question of whether the Inquisition was dangerous for Others and whether they should have any dealings with it. In the end, 'It was considered dangerous, seductive, unpredictable, and harmful—unanimously. There must not be any relations between Others and the Inquisition, even if the Light Ones or the Dark Ones consider this useful for themselves or harmful for the other party. There must not be any open interference in the affairs of the Inquisition, even if the life of an Other is concerned.'"

"That sounds rather dubious." I chuckled. "I could trot out the names of several Dark Ones who were burned by the Inquisition, and not without a little help from the Watches."

"Giles de Rey," Helen said with a nod. "And his mistress too. And there were probably a few dozen genuine witches among the herbalist women. Simply from the law of large numbers. Of course, all laws get broken, but this one was basically observed. More or less."

"So who are these Great Parties?" I asked. "Never mind the damned Inquisition . . ."

"It doesn't say anything about that here," said Helen, puzzled. "Either it was common knowledge, which isn't likely—in that case any of our old men, like Gesar, would have answered your question about the Great Parties. Or it was so secret that whenever they were mentioned, there were no specifics."

"Dammit!" I said. "Dammit!"

"Wait," said Helen, peering hard at the piece of paper. "There are signatures here too, Anton."

"Well?"

"Without names," she said, moving the paper closer to me. "Apparently they didn't risk copying out the signatures. I wouldn't have risked it with some of them, to be quite honest. There are only the positions here."

"Well?"

"I don't know Old High German all that well," said Helen. "Why on earth were they using it in the thirteenth century, when it had already gone out of use? If only it was Middle High German or Early New High German. Ha! I used to be fluent in Early New High German."

"I'm astounded and I admit my own ignorance," I said. "But even so, could you give it a try? Or shall we look for a translator?"

"I can," Helen said. "Through the Twilight . . . Hang on."

She looked at the sheet of paper for a few moments, then sighed and set it aside.

"I've read it. Only I don't know if it will help. I can understand some things, but others . . . There are six signatures here. Obviously, they're the six Great Parties."

I didn't try to hurry her.

"Light," said Helen. "And Darkness. That's clear enough, right?"

"The Light Ones and the Dark Ones," I said. "I don't see any other options."

"I'd prefer to say the Night and Day Watches," said Helen, raising one finger like a strict teacher correcting a pupil. "These aren't Powers, they're Parties."

"Noted." I said. "After that will come the Inquisition."

"The Inquisition won't be there," said Helen. "The human, religious Inquisition was founded in 1215. Ours was founded—"

"In 1217," I said. "Right. Essentially, we borrowed the idea and the name. I'm forgetting the basic facts. All right, what comes next?"

"The Conclave."

"That's clear enough," I said with a feeling of relief. "I used to know . . . It's the Conclave of Witches. And it has always held itself apart. But . . . a Great Party?"

"Witches are only a part of the Day Watch now," said Helen. "Or the Night Watch, except that they prefer to be called enchantresses or healers."

"Helen!"

"Sorry, Anton, but there's no point in being sanctimonious about it. Healers and enchantresses are essentially witches. All women mostly use the devices of witches' magic."

"My wife is not a witch!"

"All right," said Helen. "I didn't mean at all that she fit the formal category. I was thinking of a certain essential nature."

"In their essential nature, all women are witches to some extent, even if they're not Others," I said. "But Svetlana can't be one of the Parties—I mean the Party that is the Conclave . . . She's never been a member of any witches' circles, she hasn't sworn loyalty to the Conclave, she's not a witch . . . de jure."

"Agreed," Helen said after a brief pause. "If you're worried by the idea that Svetlana might be needed in this Sixth Watch, then I agree—she doesn't fit the case. And I agree that you'll have to look for a genuine witch."

"What comes next?" I asked.

"The Master of Masters."

"I think that's simple enough," I said.

"Yes, it's logical. The Master of Vampires," Helen said, frowning. "But I've never heard of them having some kind of supreme leader. Vampires are bound by ties of blood; the line of authority is determined by who turned whom. But is there really a very top vampire?"

I didn't answer. I was thinking about Lilith.

Could she have been the first vampire in the world? The very, very first? Could the woman whom all the traditions and legends said was older than Eve have been transformed into a demonic, failed creation of God? That creature who had called herself Eve, either in a fit of pride or simply amusing herself with the simple riddle?

Anything was possible.

But then the Tiger had put an end to her. And vacuumed her up. Did that mean there was no more Master of Masters any longer? Or would someone else fill that position?

I made a mental note that I had a question for Zabulon—a very serious and important question.

"Apparently there is," I said to Helen. "And then again, I've never heard of anyone being the single most important member of the Night Watch. If we're talking on a global scale, that is. In Moscow,

Gesar's the most important, and in Russia too; it's not affirmed in any documents, but everyone knows it. But for the entire world . . . The very Lightest Light One. A great lord and sovereign . . . I haven't heard of that."

"Probably it's the same for us as for the vampires," Helen said sourly. "All based on geography."

We smiled knowingly at each other.

"The next Party is fairly clear too," Helen said, and pondered for a moment. "The Assumer of Appearance."

"Shape-shifters," I said with a nod.

"Have you ever heard anything at all about shape-shifters having some kind of leadership structure? A leader of the pack, or whatever?"

I shook my head.

"The Watches have local leadership," Helen said. "In Europe, for instance, the French and German Watches de facto run everything. The French Night Watch and the German Day Watch. Although the Dutch . . . Okay, I don't know, but Gesar can probably tell you who's in command there. The witches have the Conclave, that's clear-cut. The vampires have a Master, although no one has ever heard of a supreme Master for all vampires. But werewolves and shape-shifters?"

"A family structure," I said. "Those who have been bitten form a pride. But a pride is never very big, and there's just one leader—a male or a female."

"How harshly you talk about them," said Helen. "Like animals."

I ignored the reproach.

"And one pride never rules another," I said. "If a conflict arises, they fight. If the conflict becomes really nasty, the leaders fight. The defeated leader's pride is absorbed by the pride of the victor. But there isn't any kind of superpride."

"Ask Hena," said Helen. "He's the oldest shape-shifter there is, as far as I know. He transforms into a smilodon."

"I know," I said, rubbing the bridge of my nose. "The Assumer of

Appearances. Not even a hint at the name of a structure. Well, okay. I'll ask Hena. Read out who else is there."

"Now this has me puzzled," Helen confessed. "I could only translate it through the Twilight. The Basis."

"The Basis?"

"Cornerstone. Foundation. Mainstay. Basis. I don't know the word, I can only read its meaning. And it was the final signature. In documents like this, that's important."

"I know that, I'm not stupid," I said with a nod. "The authorizing signature, the binding decision. The Basis . . ."

"The Twilight?" Helen suggested.

"In person. It came and signed a document," I said with a shrug.

And I pictured the Tiger, vacuum-cleaning the floor in my apartment, with a cup of coffee in his free hand.

"Anything's possible," said Helen.

"Yes, it is," I agreed. "It's time to start asking the Great Ones questions."

Helen put the document back in its case, switched off the flashlight, and took me by the hand.

"Let's go back, Anton."

After the eternal, chilly damp of the basement, the corridors of the Watch seemed almost hot. Although judging from the sweaters that the Watch members I came across were wearing, something was wrong with our heating again. An old building is an old building.

I didn't go to the boss. I went to look for Olga. Her office was empty, and there was no one in the Internal Review Department, which she had been in charge of for the last few years. In any case, that department, jokingly known as "the Internal Inquisition," consisted of only two people—Olga herself and Alisher.

I found Olga in the Science Department, which was also almost empty—just recently some of its members had taken to "working from home," and right now the others were probably out beavering away "in the field," talking to Old Others and members of the re-

gional Watches, trying to dig up something that would clarify what
the Tiger had said.

It was surprising that no one had taken the trouble to go down
into the archive while they were at it . . .

Olga was sitting beside the only member of the Science Department who was there, Lyudochka. This Fifth-Level Other looked exactly like a woman who is known by the diminutive form of her
name ought to look—like a twenty-year-old young woman. She had
looked that way for ten years or so, even though in fact she was about
fifty. But then, Olga never looked anything like her hundreds of
years either.

The women were having an agreeable chat, surrounded by empty
desks with computer terminals and shelves of books and scrolls
(well, it wasn't the archive, but there were still plenty of those). They
looked like students gossiping in the library.

"And he likes to sleep on the pillow with me," Lyudochka was
saying. "Just imagine, he creeps under the blanket, sticks his head
out, and puts it on the pillow! Like a real person! Such a tiny little
thing, but he's smart . . ."

"Like a real person," Olga agreed, squinting at me. "Hi, Anton.
Only he's not an Other, or a person at all. He's a dog."

"Of course," said Lyudochka, slightly offended. "Naturally. Oh,
hello, Anton!"

"Mind if I sit with you for a while?" I asked, taking a chair.

"Sit down," said Olga. "Surprised?"

"By what?"

"The fact that I'm sitting here yacking. The end of the world is
nigh and I've just sat down with a friend."

"Maybe the end of the world is a standard sort of event for you," I
replied diplomatically.

"No, but the way life is arranged, there's always some small, local
end of the world happening somewhere. Trains run off the tracks,
airplanes crash, ships sink, oil depots explode. Epidemics wipe out

entire countries, people murder whole families, psychos torture children . . ."

Olga got up and sat on the desk, looking into my eyes. Lyudochka started to get up, apparently to leave, but Olga stopped her with a wave of her hand and kept talking.

"People who are dear to someone die. Wars blaze on for years and decades, crusaders kill Muslims, Muslims blow up Jews. Hutus slaughter Tutsis. But people live somehow. Some look up at the sky, calculating the movements of the planets. Some sow grain. Some are unfaithful to their wives. Some pick pockets. Some paint pictures. When soldiers were dying at Ypres, Balmont wrote: 'Exalted moment, framing her chord, streaming down pearly rain, setting hearts trembling.' Men were burning alive in tanks, children were weeping from hunger in cold beds, women blue from the cold were lugging sheets of armor plating about, building tanks—and somewhere nearby a composer was writing a bravura march for a triumphal procession, and somewhere someone was writing jolly little stories for children . . ."

"Oh come on, jolly little stories, during a war . . ." I began.

"Have you read Nosov, Watchman?" Olga asked, narrowing her eyes. "You must have read him as a child. And your daughter has probably read *Mishka's Porridge* and *The Market Gardeners*. He wrote them in 1942. When everything was hanging by a thread. Is there even a single word in them about war and death? No. Because if you can't give children bread, you have to give them hope at least. Yes I know, you'll tell me that I'm a Watch member, I'm a Light One, a Higher One, and I'm just sitting here chatting . . . Sit down! I haven't finished yet, Lyudmila! Yes, I'm chatting, because everyone who can deal with your case is dealing with it. And those who can't are dealing with their usual business. Their own bread, their own melody, their own pickpockets. Their own foolish little investigation. Even if the apocalypse is upon us. Because if it doesn't happen, the grain must not rot in the ground, and the song must still be sung.

And the thief must sit in jail. And abuses of office must be investi-
gated."

She turned toward Lyudochka, who looked at her with large,
round, frightened eyes.

"How old is your little dog?"

Lyudmila gulped and lowered her eyes.

"Twenty . . ."

"I can't hear you!"

"Twenty-seven . . . I don't . . . I feed him very strictly."

Olga didn't say anything.

"It's not even a seventh-level intervention!" Lyudmila exclaimed
with tears in her eyes. "When have I ever asked the Watch for anything?"

"The point is that you didn't ask!" Olga barked. "The point is
that you didn't warn us, you fool! Your rank entitles you to several
interventions a year, up to and including fifth level. Open the schedule of payments!"

"But what can—"

"Today I personally signed the license to prolong the life of a
witch's cat! And she's not some ordinary, petty, repulsive little witch,
she's the Grandmother of the Moscow section. And her cat is more
than seventy years old. And no way would we ever have granted
permission; we've been keeping an eye on that cat for ages—it's the
source of more than half her power! But since the witch was in pos-
session of the record of a Day Watch investigation into the two occasions when you extended the life of your pet, there wasn't a thing
I could do!"

Lyudochka turned white and gaped at Olga.

"Get up and get out," said Olga. "And don't let me set eyes on
you again today. Go and work at home—you know what's going on."

"But what . . . What will happen to . . ." Lyudmila said, and
gulped.

"Nothing will happen," Olga growled. "Your animal's not to
blame."

Lyudmila dashed to the door as if she was afraid Olga would change her mind.

"Next time submit an official request, you fool!" Olga shouted at her back, then sighed and shook her head. "Anton, how is it possible to work with people like that . . . What brings you here?"

"I need your help . . . as a woman," I said gruffly.

"Ah, what is it, has someone offended my little boysie-woysie, then?" Olga asked.

"Why do you have to be so mocking?" I asked.

"Well, if you remember I was a stuffed owl for a very long time." Olga chuckled. "And I didn't always stand in Gesar's office. For twenty years I stood in a school, in the biology laboratory."

"How horrible!" I exclaimed sincerely.

"To put it mildly. All the things I saw and heard . . . Well, what do you want?"

"Who is your husband's superior?" I asked point blank.

Olga thought for a moment.

"Is this connected with the investigation?"

"Directly. You've read my morning report . . ."

"Of course, no need to repeat yourself," Olga said flippantly.

"You remember the six Great Parties?"

"Yes, it's nonsense. I've lived in this world for quite a while, Anton. Been in the Watch all my life. No one has ever mentioned any Great Parties."

"I've been down in the archive. I asked Killoran to help me. She found an old document that mentions the six Great Parties. But very vaguely. Anyway, they are Light, Darkness, the Conclave, the Master of Masters, the Assumer of Appearance, and the Basis."

Olga rubbed her forehead and lowered her eyes. She jumped off the desk, took out a pack of cigarettes, and lit one. She narrowed her eyes and looked at me ironically.

"And, combining what the Tiger said with this . . . new information, you've decided that they're . . ."

"The Night Watch. The Day Watch. Witches. Vampires. Shape-shifters. And some unknown thingamajig, perhaps even the Twilight itself."

Olga blew out a stream of smoke and threw her head back, looking at the ceiling.

"So, Killoran . . . What's her name? Helen?"

"Yes."

"Six Great Parties . . ." Olga sighed. "Well look, I have two pieces of news for you."

"A good one and a bad one?"

"Yes, the usual thing," Olga said, but I didn't like the tone of her voice. "First, neither the Night Watch nor the Day Watch have any higher leadership. Even in Russia there isn't any, officially, although of course, Gesar's the number one."

"So it's the same for us as it is for the vampires? The master of the territory is the one who bit everyone in it."

"More or less. Or whoever initiated everyone. I don't know if you remember, but it was Gesar who initiated you, wasn't it? If you think about it, our lines of initiation all run back to him."

"And that's a bad start," I said with a nod.

"Everything seems clear enough with the witches," said Olga. "I don't know about any top-of-the-heap vampire. But shape-shifters definitely don't have any supreme leaders. You can ask Hena."

"Helen gave me the same advice," I replied disappointedly.

Olga gave me a sidelong glance before she went on.

"As for the Basis, I don't have a clue there either. And that, Anton, was the good news."

"Then what's the bad news?" I asked.

"Come on," Olga said, taking hold of my hand. "Come along . . . Higher One . . ."

I didn't ask any questions.

First, I enjoy setting up "moments of truth" like this myself.

Second, she wouldn't have answered.

Third, I sensed that I really wouldn't like this bad news.

We descended lower and lower. To the sixth underground level. To the archive.

I felt a twinge of alarm in my chest.

"Did Gorodetsky visit the archive today?" Olga asked the two guards.

They were obviously disconcerted.

"Yes . . ." the senior member of the duo, a Sixth-Level Other, finally managed to get out. "But . . . He doesn't have the right, does he?"

"He could have slipped in without us noticing him," added the other one. Only Seventh Level. Well, well, the very weakest had been put on guard duty; everyone was out "in the field."

"Of course," said Olga. "A Higher One can always addle the brains of someone on a lower level."

And with that kind phrase, she pulled me on after her as she pushed open the doors of the archive. Everything was as it had been an hour ago—darkness, with a cone of light above the desk.

Olga walked up to the desk without speaking. But, anticipating an unpleasant surprise, I looked at her through the Twilight.

To hell with all of Helen's precautions!

Olga was walking through the archive, completely covered in a scaly armor of spells. It looked like she must have activated a substantial part of her arsenal while we were on the way down. The Great One had bright rainbows of spells blazing on her fingers.

Olga stopped at the desk and looked around. She touched the kettle standing on the desk. She opened the box that Helen and I had found, took out the document, and gave it a brief glance.

"Aren't you going to say anything?" I said.

Olga was silent.

"Helen!" I called. "Helen!"

"Don't yell," said Olga. "She isn't here."

"But where is she?"

"How should I know? Maybe Dublin, for instance? Did you come to see her often?"

"Yesterday and the day before yesterday."

"And before that?"

"Well, I probably hadn't called in for a year," I muttered, feeling horror creeping up on me.

"She left more than a year ago. Finished making her notes and copied what she wanted, in exchange for other documents. And then, well, she left. She was sick of sitting in here. Were you away from Moscow then?"

I didn't answer.

"Who addled your brains?" Olga asked. "Higher One . . . You do realize that you've been duped, befuddled, enchanted? Whoever was here, it certainly wasn't Helen Killoran! The archive has been empty for a long time! If anyone needs something, they come down, switch on the light, rummage in the catalogues, and look for what they want!"

"You know what the worst thing is?" I asked.

Olga didn't answer.

"I can remember Helen leaving," I said. "She held a party, right here. We even danced together. I remember. *Now* I remember."

CHAPTER 2

IT WAS AN OLD PICTURE, POSSIBLY SOMETHING FROM THE seventeenth-century Italian school. Nothing special, a view of the canals in Venice. Gesar probably knew the artist, or perhaps that place had some special meaning for him.

I sat there, examining the little houses, bridges, and gondolas, and tried not to to notice the waves of coolness running across the back of my head. As if the shutters of an air conditioner were quivering right there beside me, breathing out a chilly wind . . .

"I think that will do," said Gesar. He lowered his hand heavily onto my shoulder and went back to his desk. Olga was sitting a little to one side, on a chair set there for her.

"So what's wrong with me?" I asked.

"Induced amnesia," said Gesar, looking at me in gentle surprise, as if I had said something stupid. "Nothing but induced amnesia. You were made to forget that Killoran left Moscow sixteen months ago. And so, when you went down into the archive and saw . . . Hmm . . . Saw someone there who looked like Helen, you quite calmly started talking to her."

"Gesar, I have all the required mental defenses in place."

"And even a few that aren't required, I noticed. The point is, Anton, that this is our oversight. Our common oversight. We're all well protected against the possibility of having false memories imposed on us or our existing ones distorted. At least by any Others who are weaker than us or our equals. Which means that no one but a Higher Other could have implanted an image of something that didn't exist in your memory. But . . ."

"We're not protected against erasure," I said.

"Against blocking. Erasing a memory would have provoked a defensive reaction too. But precise blocking wouldn't. You simply forgot that Killoran had left. That's all."

"But how did she"—I frowned—"if it is a 'she' and not a 'he,' get into our office?"

"With some difficulty, probably," Gesar said, and paused for a moment. "Our office's defenses are very secure. But if we assume certain factors, it is possible to sneak through."

"What factors?" Olga asked curiously. "I have my own theories, but I'd like to hear this."

"A Higher level of Power," said Gesar. "Color . . . Light or Gray. The absence of any malicious intentions. Under these conditions it is possible to bypass the spells that are in place. And with the ability to manipulate memory, it's possible to get past the guards too. Either by blocking their memories of Ms. Killoran's departure or by completely erasing their memories of an Other walking past them. I think that if we check everyone who has been on guard duty, we'll find these blocks, remove them, and discover the day and the hour when she arrived."

"And she's only just gone," I said. "I went to look for Olga immediately after our conversation. She had promised to pass on the document for translation herself. But obviously she left after me and cleared out. But who can it be, Boris Ignatievich? We know all the Higher Light Ones, there aren't so very many of us, even including those who are retired. Are Gray Ones Inquisitors?"

"Not necessarily," said Olga. "They could be Others in the process of changing their color. You know yourself that it happens only extremely rarely, and usually with Higher Ones. Sometimes the color changes all the way, sometimes it gets stuck in the middle, like with the Inquisitors."

"A Higher One who can be either color," I said. "Wonderful. I feel like an idiot."

"Don't," said Gesar. "If, in the course of my rather long life, I haven't thought about the danger of amnesic intervention, then I'm the biggest idiot of all."

"In any case, it must have been a Higher One who influenced you," said Olga. "And very, very professionally. Masterfully, in fact."

"I understand what you're driving at," Gesar said, nodding.

"So do I," I murmured. "Vampires. Even the very weakest vampire is a master of amnesia."

"And not only because of the secretion in their saliva," Olga said with a nod. "A Higher Vampire is a master of illusion . . . You didn't kiss her, did you, Anton? It might not have been a vampiress, but a male vampire."

"And yuck to you," I replied.

Olga laughed.

"All right, all right, I won't say anything to Sveta."

"And yuck again," I said with passion. "Thanks for trying to cheer me up, but I'm okay. Isn't there anything else, Boris Ignatievich? No other interventions?"

"No." Gesar shook his head. "It was all done with great finesse. Hard as it is for me to suggest it, quite possibly our uninvited guest's intentions were good."

"Even if he's the very Darkest of the Dark Ones, he doesn't want to die either," Olga said with a nod. A phone rang in her handbag, which was lying on the floor. Olga leaned down, took out the phone, and held it against her ear without speaking. She waited for a moment, listening to something, and then said, "I see. Carry on."

"From the archive?" I asked when Olga put the phone away again.

"Yes. Everything's clean. There are traces of the presence of an intruder, but no methods, neither human nor Other, can extract any information. We didn't really expect that they would. Anton, there was something you wanted to find out from Gesar when you came looking for me."

Gesar raised one eyebrow and looked at me.

"You wanted to find out from me, but you went to Olga?" he asked.

"It's a delicate matter," I explained. "Gesar, who stands above you?"

"I don't understand," said Gesar, frowning even more severely.

"You're the head of the Light Ones of Moscow. And of the whole of Russia, of course. And to some extent, of contiguous territories too, right?"

"To some extent," said Gesar. "It's all my Tibetan imperialism, you see. Well, and the fact that the Night Watch of Kirgizia, for instance, is headed up by a Second-Level Other."

"Who is the head of the Others of Europe? And of the whole world?"

"The answer's simple in both cases," said Gesar. "No one."

"That's not possible."

"Who is the head of all the people in the world?"

"We won't go into the UN," I said. "But even with my old-fashioned human patriotism . . . the USA is the most powerful country in the world."

"Of course," Gesar said dismissively. "But it doesn't lead the world, for one incredibly simple and funny reason, which I won't explain here. People don't have any absolute top leader. And it's the same for Others, Light or Dark."

"But what if one is needed?" I asked. "The document in the archives is dated 1215. And someone signed it in the name of the Light. If it suddenly becomes necessary to make some very important decisions . . ."

"It already is necessary," said Gesar. "And I've informed all the regional assemblies about it in a letter that was signed by myself and Zabulon and certified with the oath of the Light and the oath of the Darkness."

"And then what happens?" I asked tensely.

"Then things will happen as they already have several times in history. Zabulon and I will be granted the right to make a decision in the name of the Light and the Darkness. Formally speaking, we shall be the leaders. In the resolution of this matter."

"It's that simple?" I exclaimed.

"Democracy in its very highest manifestation," Gesar said, chuckling. "Although no, it's probably more like that communism we once wanted to build. Two rational and responsible human . . . hmm . . . former human beings who possess enough knowledge and experience of life and who happen to find themselves in the right place at the right time, are invested with the right to make a decision for everyone."

"Yefremov," I said.

"He was a good fellow, pity he was human," said Gesar, nodding. "But it's actually pure, simple practicality."

"So we've found two of the Parties," I said. "That's a pretty good start. Now for the witches, the shape-shifters, vampires, and whatever else."

"Provided, of course, that we have understood everything correctly," Gesar said skeptically. "The witches—yes. I'm not sure about all the rest of it."

"We're already working on it," Olga said. "Everyone's been briefed on the new information."

"What should I do?" I asked.

"Visit your family," Gesar advised me.

"I'll wait awhile," I replied. "Let them miss me."

"Then work," said Gesar. "Olga, what have we got on Ms. Yulia Khokhlenko?"

"We haven't got anything," Olga replied sourly. "Three pages of orientation material. She was born in 1890, in Little Russia. Later she lived in Kiev, Odessa, St. Petersburg, and Moscow. She settled here. And she was elected Grandmother twenty-five years ago."

"She's very young for a Grandmother." Gesar laughed. "It's a shame Arina left us. Now, she was good. Or Lemesheva. But this Khokhlova . . ."

"Khokhlenko," Olga corrected him.

Gesar just waved that aside.

"It's not important. That's not necessarily her real name. Probably a sobriquet from her place of birth. What's happening with that Herman of hers?"

"We were obliged to sanction another rejuvenation." Olga sighed. "I'll tell you about it later. Look, I was just about to send her the permit."

"She's not in the Watch?" asked Gesar, narrowing his eyes. "Look sharp then, Anton. You can take it, and have a word with her."

"What can I tell her?" I asked.

"Everything, within reason."

"What do we want?"

Gesar snorted.

"You should realize that yourself. The present Universal Grandmother. The head of the Conclave."

"And if she doesn't want to tell me?" I asked, getting up.

"Don't attempt to use force, that's for sure," said Gesar. "In that case, I'll go myself. But try to manage it somehow. And I'll go to see Hena right now."

"And I'll go to see the Moscow Master of Vampires," said Olga. "We still have some time, but there's no point in wasting it."

Yulia Khokhlenko, the head of Moscow's witches, the "Grandmother" in their terminology, didn't try too hard to look young. Maybe because of her position. Or maybe for some other reason.

Of course, she didn't look 125 years old. Sixty at most. She was lean and charming, with thick black hair; no doubt people thought she dyed it.

Granny Yulia worked in an ordinary municipal kindergarten called Little Sunshine in the southeast district of Moscow. As a simple teacher, not even the director.

The parents and the children all absolutely adored her.

At the entrance to the kindergarten I hung a simple, but very convenient spell on myself: Our Guy. After that I didn't have to worry about how to get past the security guard, or what the teachers and nurses I ran into would think—every one of them saw me as someone familiar, someone they knew, who had a right to be here. The security man shook my hand heartily, the teachers smiled, even the dour, tipsy electrician, standing on a ladder and fiddling with a fluorescent light tube, forced out a mangled greeting.

In the orientation information that Olga had given me, it said that Yulia Tarasovna Khokhlenko was now working as the class teacher of the preschool group. It was a small kindergarten. In the 1990s, when Muscovites almost stopped having children, half of it had been walled off and made into a private lycée. But times had changed, the lycée had been thrown out of the other half of the kindergarten, and now the Tajik *gastarbeiters* were working away in there, plastering, painting, and laying floors. All simultaneously, or so it seemed. The Little Sunshine kindergarten was about to expand.

I walked up a stairway with funny double banisters—one at the level of an adult hand and the other lower down, for the kids. I pushed open a door with a colored drawing cut out of some children's book hanging on it—Baba Yaga in her mortar, clutching her broom—and walked into the preschool group's classroom.

Thirty pairs of eyes stared at me. The senior group had just gotten back from a walk. Some of them had already removed their outdoor clothing, some were still tangled up in half-removed jumpsuits and trousers, some hadn't even taken their woolly hats off yet.

A moment later I was engulfed by a tidal wave of yelling, clamoring children.

If you think that a six-year-old child is nothing compared to an adult, then you've never been assaulted by thirty preschool children.

"What are you doing?" I howled as they toppled me over onto the floor, forcing my head down painfully against the shoe-drying rack. A wet felt boot tumbled onto my face. Thirty pairs of hands clutched at me.

Had the crazy old Grandmother turned her wards into security guards?

"Uncle Dima!" a little kid with light hair howled joyfully as he flung himself onto me.

"Uncle Pasha Uncle Pasha Uncle Pasha," chirruped a red-haired little girl.

"Daddy! Daddy!" howled a freckle-faced boy, so excited that he almost had tears in his eyes.

"Right, shoo, all of you!" a voice exclaimed somewhere above me, and the children retreated. Yulia Tarasovna had made her entrance—there's no other way to put it—from one of the other rooms that her group inhabited.

The children ran off, laughing.

"Everyone get changed, have a pee, and wash your hands!" Yulia Tarasovna commanded. And she held out her hand to help me up. I, however, disdained an old woman's help and got up myself, glancing warily at the children.

"Hello, Yulia Tarasovna," I said.

The witch was wearing a brightly colored dress and an abundance of beads, bracelets, and rings that could have rivaled any Gypsy. Well, what can I say—witches use the magic of artifacts . . .

"And hello to you, Anton Gorodetsky, Light Magician," Khokhlenko said in a low voice. "What were you thinking, Great One, hanging a 'charmer' on yourself on the way into a kindergarten? Don't you know that children react twelve times more powerfully to magic?"

"I never got around to testing that somehow," I confessed. "Are they your security guards?"

"Oh, come now, Anton!" said Yulia Tarasovna, offended. "How can you talk about little children like that? But even if they are guards, what's so bad about that? In a confined space thirty pre-schoolers are capable of cornering, maiming, and even killing an adult."

"You crack strange jokes, Grandmother," I said. "Where can we have a talk?"

"Come in." The witch sighed. "But take your shoes off. I observe sanitary and hygiene rules in here. They're children, after all!"

I had to wait about ten minutes for Khokhlenko to drive all her wards into the sleeping room, pack them into the beds, and come back out into the playroom. As she came out she did something, I felt a faint breath of Power, and a moment later the emotional atmosphere suddenly changed. The children fell asleep. All of them at once.

"Oh, tut-tut," I said.

"I don't usually do that," Yulia Tarasovna replied severely. "But you wanted to have a talk."

I nodded. To my delight the playroom contained a pair of normal, human-sized chairs. Otherwise I would have had to hunch up in a child's one or stand.

And the playroom also contained a cat.

Until the children went to bed, he sat on a cupboard, washing himself. A huge, orange tomcat, with such a good-natured face that it looked suspicious. This cat kept casting cute, welcoming glances my way.

When the children had gone out, the cat jumped down, walked across to me, and jumped up onto my knees. Then he immediately tumbled over onto his back and exposed his belly.

"What a rascal," I said.

But I scratched his belly anyway.

"Do you like animals?" asked Yulia Tarasovna, taking a seat facing me.

"I adore them," I said. I took a sheet of paper folded in four out of my pocket and held it out to the witch. "This is the official permission from the Night Watch for you to use magic to prolong the cat Herman's life."

"Oh, thank you," the witch said delightedly, carefully unfolding the document, smoothing it out, and examining it, then folding it and putting it away. "What joy for an old woman, what happiness!"

"Is the cat a German breed?" I asked, sitting Herman down on the floor and brushing the fine orange hairs off my trousers.

"No, no, he's ours, Russian, a mongrel. But he was named after the second cosmonaut of our planet, Herman Titov!"

I almost choked.

"I really liked him a lot," Yulia Tarasovna informed me confidentially. "Yuri Gagarin was charming of course; his smile alone was priceless! But I liked Herman more. A real man. A hero! And as well as that, he was second. Can you imagine how hard it is to be second, Light One? The same heroic feat, but you're the second one to do it. And you'll be second forever. It's not so hard to be the fifth. Or the tenth. But being second is a heavy burden forever."

"Mmm, yes," I mumbled. "Fascinating. Doesn't the director of the kindergarten object to the cat? Sanitary and hygiene rules . . ."

Khokhlenko trilled with laughter. The cat jumped onto her knees and curled up into a tight ball in habitual fashion. And the witch stroked him with a habitual movement.

"Oh, Anton, oh, that's hilarious . . . Who's ever going to object to me?"

"I'll pretend I didn't hear that," I said dourly. "Yulia Tarasovna, I haven't come to see you about this piece of paper."

"Yes, I understand that Higher Ones don't work as couriers," said Khokhlenko, immediately turning serious. "Allow me to guess? Is your visit connected with that Prophecy? Do you need the Grandmother of Grandmothers, the head of the Conclave?"

"I see that you earn a bit on the side from fortune-telling too," I said.

"No fortune-telling is required here, Anton. Only a head on your shoulders."

I nodded.

"By the way, Zabulon keeps me informed of how things are going," Khokhlenko said pensively. "So I do know . . . a thing or two."

I didn't ask if she knew about the archive and the way I had been duped.

"I need to meet with the head of the Conclave," I said. "With the Witch of Witches, the Grandmother of Grandmothers, the Great Grandmother, call her what you will. I know you don't give out that information to anyone, especially to Light Ones. But, as you understand, there's no evil intention involved here."

"Your good intentions are no great joy to us either," Yulia Tarasovna growled disdainfully.

"We could all die," I said. "The entire world. All the Others. All the people."

"Perhaps it's high time?" Khokhlenko asked in a quiet voice. "We all deserve it, to be quite honest. We absolutely deserve it. The humans and the Others."

She paused for a moment, then looked up at me with a grave, intent expression.

I wouldn't like to come face-to-face with her at night in a dark forest.

And not on a bright day in a bustling city either. If she decided I was her enemy.

"I understand," I said. "You're Ukrainian, aren't you? Yes, these days down there . . ."

"I'm a Little Russian," said the witch. "A khokhlushka. Don't call me Ukrainian, you'll offend me."

I nodded.

"I understand."

"What's going on down there now stinks, and in 1919 under Petlyura things were even worse," said Khokhlenko. "But where is it any better? Russian pigheadedness and drunkenness? American chauvinism and hypocrisy? European self-righteousness? Asiatic cruelty?"

"They're all people," I said.

"And are we any better?" asked the witch. "Our side or your side . . . Perhaps we should just let it happen, eh?"

I turned my eyes toward the half-open door of the sleeping

room, where the children were lying in their beds. Little arms and legs dangling out from under blankets, socks and sandals lying on the floor.

"Are they guilty too?" I asked. "Do they have to die too?"

"Everyone has to die sometime," the witch replied. "They might not be guilty of anything, but that's only for now . . . It will all happen sooner or later. A hundred years ago I'd definitely have turned a couple of them into piglets, to keep them out of mischief."

I permitted myself a smile.

"Can you really do that, Yulia Tarasovna?"

"Who knows?" she said, stroking the cat. "I don't have a good answer for your request, Light One."

"Yulia Tarasovna, Gesar will ask the Inquisition," I threw out on the off chance.

"He can ask until he's blue in the face," the witch snorted. "It's our women's business. The Inquisition doesn't know anything about that."

"I'll find out anyway," I said. "One way or another."

"Ah, phoo!" the old woman exclaimed, flapping her hand. "Why are you such a great fool, eh? You already know anyway. The Grandmother of Grandmothers is an old friend of yours!"

"What?" I exclaimed in confusion. "But how . . . she changed her color!"

"A witch doesn't have to be a Dark One," Khokhlenko snapped. "So she changed her color; that's her business, as long as she didn't break any laws."

"But she . . ."

"I know. You shut her in the Sarcophagus of Time. Until the end of the universe."

"She might as well not exist," I said. "You could say she's dead."

"You could, but you can't really! She isn't dead. She's in prison. The fact that the prison is eternal and magical doesn't change a thing. We Grandmothers convened in the Conclave. We discussed.

It's absolutely impossible to elect another Grandmother of Grandmothers as long as Arina is alive."

"She'll live for all eternity."

"So there'll be an eternal head of the Conclave."

"That's stupid!" I exclaimed. "Stupid! You have to change the
rules in a situation like this. If we don't have the head of the Conclave with us, there'll be nothing we can do."

Khokhlenko looked at me severely for a while before she spoke.

"Go home, Light One. Search for what you're seeking—I don't
think all your problems come down to one old witch. Tonight we
Grandmothers will gather to talk and thrash things out."

"And choose a new head?" I asked hopefully

Khokhlenko shrugged.

"Do *you* have a chance?" I asked for some reason.

"What's that to you?" the witch exclaimed in surprise, her eyes
glinting with long-standing resentment. "No, it's not our custom
to draw twice from the same region. Protectionism exists among
witches too, you know, though nobody likes it. Go, Anton. I'll give
you a call tomorrow morning."

"My number—"

"I know your number." She sighed. "Go on. You've tramped dirt
around the place, and I have to wash the floor now. There aren't
enough nurses, there aren't enough cleaners, they don't pay much in
a kindergarten. You won't set to work with a mop, will you? You've
got to save the world. So go and save it."

Halfway back to the office, I stopped and parked the car under a No
Parking sign. The sign made absolutely no sense; I wasn't in anyone's
way here.

I turned on the emergency lights, rummaged in the glove compartment, found a pack of cigarettes, and lit one. I turned the radio
up louder.

Arina . . .

How much simpler everything would be if I had her on my side. The old witch knew such a lot, she could do such a lot, and she had such a steely determination to reach her goal.

But I had shut her up in the Sarcophagus of Time. Then it had seemed like the only rational solution. So elegant . . . And self-sacrificing.

Only the Tiger had pulled me out. He was afraid Nadya would blow a fuse and rush into a mutually fatal duel with him. Arina had been left in the Sarcophagus.

But would it really be easier for me with her here? How did I know that she wouldn't find some positive meaning in the death of all living things, like her colleague and, apparently, onetime rival, Yulia Tarasovna?

Witches—there's no way to understand them. Dark ones or Light ones. They think differently anyway. Women . . .

I suddenly realized how much I wanted to see Svetlana and Nadya. To touch them. Or at least call and talk to them for a minute. Their cell phones were switched off and the batteries had been removed, all in the finest traditions of secret conspiracy. But I knew the number of the ordinary landline. And I had a SIM card that no one knew about, for a phone bought beside the Moscow mosque from a Tajik street trader (nothing really criminal, it was just that the SIM card was convenient for calls to Central Asia, and I didn't have to present any documents).

No, it was stupid. If I was being tracked seriously, they would trace the call. And I didn't want to give anyone that chance. After all, if there was some emergency, Svetlana would call my cell herself.

The witch situation wasn't clear yet. I could only hope that today they would get together at their Sabbath and choose a new Grand-mother of Grandmothers. I had to wait.

And I had to report.

I took out my phone and it rang in my hand. A photo of the boss appeared (don't ask me how I managed to photograph him; Gesar can't stand photos and videos) and rousing music started playing.

Ta ta-ta ta ta-ta-ta-ta, ta-ta ta-ta
Ta-ta ta-ta, ta-ta ta-ta ta-ta ta ta

All Higher Ones are posers in their own way. The Grandmother of Russian witches worked in a kindergarten and washed out dirty potties. The senior Light One of Moscow didn't like to be called on the phone—he preferred to call you, just a second before you decided to call.

"Hello, Gesar."

"How did the talk with your Grandmother go?" the boss asked.

"Hmm . . ." I wondered for a moment if the boss was trying to speak in conspiratorial fashion or if he hadn't noticed the vagueness of his own words.

"Grandmother says that her Grandmother, Arina, is alive and no one can take the place of a living Grandmother," I replied. "But today Grandmother is planning to spend the evening with her friends and they'll have a good talk about it."

"So it's Arina," said Gesar. "I was almost certain of it. I see."

"I can't hear you very well, boss," I said, dissembling shamelessly. "Are you far away?"

"In Prague, I told you."

So Gesar had traveled to Prague via a portal. Such a long distance and so quickly—the portal must have been prepared in advance. But why was I surprised by that? It would have been strange if it hadn't.

"How's the pussycat?" I asked.

"The pussycat? The Grandmother's pussycat?" I had unexpectedly managed to perplex Gesar. "You mean that fat-bellied Herman?"

"No, I meant the other pussycat," I said cautiously. "You know, the one with the congenital dental problems."

I heard mumbling and muttering in the background. Gesar said something brief in a language I didn't understand before he spoke to me again.

"Hena asked me to tell you that a pair of large fangs is no problem at all. Quite the opposite. And if you have any doubts, he politely invites you on a hunting trip."

"My apologies to the highly respected Hena," I said, then looked in the rearview mirror and stuck my tongue out at myself.

Damn, who could have known that Hena was right there?

"And did the highly respected Hena inform you if he is the undisputed leader of . . . Er . . . His own . . . His . . ."

"The supremely amiable Hena said that he is the most senior member of his kind," said Gesar. "He also said that they do not have, never have had, and never will have an overall leader, since that contradicts their very nature. He told me this firmly and clearly, in the language of mammoth hunters, which had absolutely no concept of untruth."

"I see," I said disappointedly.

"So the 'takers of form' aren't shape-shifters. Think, Anton."

The boss cut off the call.

I sat there for a few seconds, looking straight ahead stupidly. Not shape-shifters. That was a real bummer. Witches, yes; vampires, yes. But the shape-shifters weren't included; what a shame. No one loved the poor old shape-shifters. Even schoolgirls preferred the glamorous vampires.

Someone tapped gently on the glass at my side of the car. I turned to look. An overweight, middle-aged traffic cop smiled at me sweetly and gestured, inviting me to lower the window.

I hastily pressed the button and the glass slid down. A little column of ash dropped straight onto my trousers—the cigarette I'd lit five minutes earlier had burned out in my fingers.

"Dammit," I said, and flung the butt out at the traffic cop's feet in a reflex response.

"Hey there, don't push your luck too," the cop exclaimed excitedly. "Have you totally lost it? You're parked under a No Parking sign. So okay, with the emergency lights on . . . I can see you're talking on the phone . . . Well now, I'm not some kind of lunatic, am I? All sorts of things happen. Am I some kind of lunatic?"

"No, you're not," I agreed in embarrassment.

"I pull up behind you . . ." the traffic cop continued.

I glanced in the mirror, and there it was, a patrol car with its flashing light on, standing right behind me. It had obviously been there a long time.

"I sit there and wait," the cop went on. "And I think: this man's conscience will awaken any moment now! But no, it doesn't. You even stuck your tongue out at me in the mirror. Listen, you're a reasonable adult. Do you have a conscience?"

"I do, honestly I do!" I exclaimed.

"You finished talking," said the cop, continuing with the list of my transgressions. "And you kept sitting there! All right, I'm not proud. I got out of the car and knocked politely . . . And what do you do? You open the window and fling your cigarette butt at me!"

"I'm sorry," I said.

"Stopping under a sign. Littering from a car . . ." The cop hesitated for a moment. "I honestly don't know what the penalty for that is."

"Fine me," I said. "I'm guilty through and through, I won't argue. Fine me if you like, confiscate my license if you like."

"No reason to take the license," the cop said. "Not drunk, are you?"

"No."

"You've got a look on your mug as if you've been drinking."

"Check it," I said. "That's just the way my mug is. That's my life for you."

The traffic cop looked at me for a while. Then he leaned down and sniffed. I breathed out.

"What happened?" he asked with a sudden note of sympathy.

"My wife, my daughter . . ." I said, and then immediately corrected myself. "No, nothing like that, they're alive and well, only . . ."

"Only a long way away," said the traffic cop.

"Yes. Well, and . . ."

"Were you talking to them?"

"No. To my boss."

"Got a real earful, did you?"

"Something like that."

"Things bad at work?"

"A crisis."

The cop nodded and made a suggestion.

"Call your wife. Call her first."

"I can't," I said. "Her phone's switched off."

The traffic cop sighed.

"I see. But you can't stay here."

"I won't."

"And stop smoking," the cop added. "We've got a campaign against smokers in this country. Against smoking, that is. The prime minister gave up smoking, and he's got a pretty nerve-wracking job. So you can too."

"I can," I said with a nod. "I only smoke on rare occasions. I just got upset."

The traffic cop wagged a warning finger at me.

"And look in the mirror! It's not just there for decoration, is it?"

"No, the mirror's not just there for decoration," I agreed.

"That's right. It's not supposed to reflect your bruised and battered image, but something more important."

I didn't answer, just gaped stupidly at the traffic cop.

"Sure you haven't been drinking?" he asked.

"You can't even imagine what an important thing you just said," I declared. "You can't possibly understand. Thank you so much! Thank you!"

The traffic cop took a step back and shook his head.

"You get yourself home. Do you hear me? Drive home calmly and slowly. Your head's crammed full of other stuff, you shouldn't be driving right now. If you like, I'll drive in front and you follow me."

"You're a very light, radiant man," I said. "But don't worry, I won't have an accident. Everything will be fine."

The traffic cop shook his head again and set off back to his car.

I raised the window.

And looked in the mirror.

And I spoke out loud.

"What an idiot I am. The Mirror."

CHAPTER 3

I REACHED THE ECONOMIC ACHIEVEMENTS EXHIBITION DIS-
trict nineteen minutes later, which by Moscow standards is totally
unreal and, bearing in mind the state of the winter roads and the
fact that it was the afternoon, was absolutely inconceivable. If that
nice traffic cop had seen the way I drove after he let me go, he would
have cursed me.

I drove all the way with my car concealed by a Sphere of
Inattention—no one could see me, but they still gave way to
an empty space. And at the same time I viewed the lines of
probability—constantly.

Most of the lines ended with a totally shattered car, a pillar of
smoke, and a traffic jam several miles long. This wasn't exactly encouraging, but I extracted every scrap of information I could from
my prescient visions.

Change lane here, overtake, change lane again, skip into the opposite side of the road, overtake a beemer speeding along the outside
lane and then move back into the outside lane right under the nose
of a Kamaz truck hurtling down on me . . .

Brake here and plod along an empty road for two minutes, because some smart-ass has poured the wrong anti-icing agent on it
and the road has turned into a skating rink.

And step hard on the gas here. Along a narrow side street. Ignoring the No Entry sign.

Simply because I know that no one will come the other way and no one will dart out into the road.

Well okay, I drive this way because it's an emergency and I'm a Higher Other. But why the hell do ordinary people drive like this—like twenty-year-old kids whose dads have given them cars in a fit of stupidity?

And it was just when I reached the Exhibition district, as I was passing the old Cosmos Hotel, that my phone rang—fortunately I had already connected it to the car's music system.

"Hello," I said.

"Anton, this is Pasha," said the operations duty officer, whom I had phoned earlier.

"I'm listening."

"Egor Martynov, twenty-eight, uninitiated, works as an illusionist, winner of—"

"Keep it short!"

"He's not in Moscow," Pasha said resentfully; he liked thorough reports.

"Where is he?"

"At present he lives and works in Paris, he performs—"

"Is he there right now?" I demanded.

"Yes. If you only knew what an effort it cost me . . ."

I made a U-turn above the tunnel that runs under Galushkin Street. It would have been more dramatic to swing around across a double solid line, but I was out of luck—the normal U-turn was closer. I could have tried to get there around the Moscow Orbital Highway, but it was jammed solid right now—a truck had skidded and blocked off three lanes.

"Pasha, all the information about how to find him—e-mail it to me. And book a ticket on the next flight to Paris. When is it?"

"I already checked, in an hour and twenty minutes. From Sheremetievo."

"Get a ticket. That flight mustn't leave without me."

"Only business class," said Pasha. "Will Gesar sign your expenses? Will you come in to collect your travel allowance?"

I laughed.

"Pasha, get me the ticket. My passport details are in the database."

"I wish someone would send me on trips like this," Pavel grumbled. "I've already got the ticket. In fact I got it before I called."

"Thanks," I said. "I'll bring you a little magnet."

"A bottle of cognac," Pasha replied.

Paris isn't all that far from Moscow. Although the plane has to make a detour to fly around the long-suffering land of Ukraine. I sincerely hoped that Gesar, preoccupied with his own business in Prague, would only find out about my journey when I was already in France. Or perhaps even when I got back.

Unlike the packed economy-class cabin (Pavel hadn't been lying), business class was half empty. The seat beside me was free, and in the next row only the end seat, beside the window, was taken by a fat, respectable-looking man who had put on an eye mask even before we took off and was dozing. In contrast, I drank the complimentary champagne and had lunch (or dinner—it depends what you're used to calling it). I asked for a glass of cognac and wondered if I should doze for a couple of hours too.

It was a tempting thought. I couldn't expect any peace for the rest of the day, so . . .

I turned my head. Gesar was sitting in the seat beside me, gazing at me somberly.

"Boss," I exclaimed and prodded Gesar cautiously with my finger. To my amazement my hand didn't pass straight through him.

My finger sunk into the striped cardigan that Gesar had been sporting for a week. The cardigan was fancy schmancy, made of some kind of fine wool, with elongated wooden buttons, and it was a present to the boss from Olga—basically quite a recognizable item.

"Drunk, are you?" Gesar asked.

"Boss, that's not fair," I protested indignantly. "The traffic cop said the same thing, but you . . ."

"Ah, you've got a look on your face as if you've just been drinking," Gesar growled, and I decided that if everything worked out, I'd go to see a cosmetician. What was all this about my face?

"There," I said, holding out my glass. "That's all I was planning to drink."

Gesar sniffed the cognac and pressed the button to call the flight attendant. She appeared beside us straightaway—and immediately started gazing around wildly.

"This is business class, please go back to your place," she said imploringly.

"You're an intelligent woman, with a good memory, Raisa Alexeevna," said Gesar. "You remember all the passengers who walked past you and you know that I wasn't on the plane when it took off."

The flight attendant smiled in confusion.

"This is one of those cases the girls used to talk about in the training college," Gesar continued calmly. "The passenger from nowhere. No need to be afraid, it really is a good sign, the flight will go smoothly, without any incidents. In fifteen minutes I won't be here. Bring me a glass of cognac and sit in your cubbyhole for a bit."

The flight assistant nodded and dashed to the front of the cabin. There was a clinking of glass and she appeared beside us again—with a full glass of cognac.

"Everything will be all right," Gesar murmured. "And Darya Leonidovna has a benign tumor; don't worry about her. That's all, go now."

"Gesar, what's the point of all this posing?" I asked when Raisa Alexeevna had disappeared. "It would have been easier for you to convince her that you're a passenger. But you read her memory and checked someone's destiny . . . Whose?"

"Her aunt's. But she raised her. She's almost like her mother."

"But what for?"

"Why does the head of the witches of Moscow work as a common teacher in a kindergarten?" Gesar asked. "Swabbing the dirty floor with a mop and wiping the children's dirty bottoms? Why, in addition to the Inquisition, does Hena work as a volunteer?"

"In a society for the protection of animals?" I asked, unable to resist.

"In a hospital for the mentally ill. Anton, all of us, Light Ones and Dark Ones, need to show off to some extent. We all deny our human nature, but at the same time we fuss over people, we help them . . . Or harm them. And we show off to them."

"Even you, Boris Igatievich."

"Even me, Anton."

We said nothing for a moment, looking at each other. Then we brought our glasses together silently and drank a sip of cognac. The engines throbbed on a deep bass note. Gesar frowned and waved his hand; the sound retreated to the distant boundary of audibility.

"I'm getting old and deaf already, I don't like noise," Gesar explained.

"Trakh-tibidokh," I said.

"What do you mean by that?" Gesar asked with a frown.

"Nothing much . . . Watch the film *Old Khottabich* sometime."

Gesar didn't reply. He looked at me quizzically.

"Why did you come here?" I asked. "It must be hard to do that, straight into a flying plane . . ."

"That's putting it mildly," said Gesar. "But it was flying over Prague, it was in my field of vision, that made the job a lot easier."

"Boss, I'm planning to come back tomorrow."

"I realize that. Why didn't you report in to me?"

I shrugged.

"The Assumer of Appearance. The Mirror." Gesar nodded. "Yes, it's a possibility. We've been working on it since early this morning. It was the main working hypothesis, alongside the shape-shifters. But since the shape-shifters have now fallen away, we focused on the Mirror."

"And you didn't tell me?"

"What for?" Gesar asked in surprise. "Anton, you're not a solitary hero. You're working in a team. And the fact that your wife and daughter and you yourself are caught up in what is happening doesn't change a thing. You're part of a team! Do you understand? And you mustn't just go shooting off in the middle of the workday and fly to Paris on urgent business!"

"Gesar, Egor's in Paris."

Gesar sighed.

"I know, Anton."

"The boy that you . . . we exploited. Stabbed in the back."

"Anton, he's one of us. A low-level Other, potentially a Light One. And potentially a Mirror. In that situation, which, let me remind you, led to you marrying Svetlana and Nadezhda being born, we had to make use of someone."

"We should have used an adult."

"We needed an uninitiated Other with the potential of a Mirror Magician. You don't find those very often."

"Gesar, it's immoral!"

"It's immoral when there's a war going on and guns and planes bombard a city," Gesar barked. "It's immoral when people call other people subhuman and herd them into a concentration camp. To involve a minor in a police operation—in which, by the way, nothing happened to him—is perfectly permissible."

"As a result he refused to become an Other."

"On average, fifteen percent refuse," said Gesar. "He's not the first, he won't be the last."

"Is he still a potential Mirror?" I asked.

Gesar nodded.

"Yes, Anton. It's his destiny. Nothing can be done about that. If he becomes an Other, he'll forfeit that destiny. But he has refused."

"Are there any other uninitiated Others with an indefinite aura?" I asked. "Capable of becoming a Mirror?"

"We're searching," said Gesar. "We're searching all around the world."

"You mean we don't know if there are any?" I asked.

"I was certain that some Watch would already have one in its sights," said Gesar. "After all, there doesn't have to be just one Mirror. Egor was simply getting on with his life when Vitaly Rogoza came to Moscow."

"He came after Egor refused to become an Other," I pointed out. "Perhaps it's a 'floating' kind of ability. It jumped from Egor to Vitaly, then back from Vitaly back to Egor again."

"Hiccup, hiccup, go away, come again another day," Gesar muttered gruffly. He took a sip of cognac. "We're looking, Anton."

"But you haven't found anyone," I said.

"No. And since the Mirror hypothesis is now the main one, we need Egor."

I nodded.

"Anton, go home," Gesar told me gently. "You grasped the situation very quickly and very clearly. And you found him quickly too. But now let me have a word with the lad."

"Did you talk to him sixteen years ago?" I asked.

"Anton!"

"Gesar, it's my operation," I said. "You go to Moscow and think about the other points. Find out about the Two-in-One—who he is and what he is. But Egor's for me to deal with."

"Will you persuade him to come to us?" asked Gesar.

"No, I'll give him the choice."

"Anton, I order you . . ." Gesar began.

"Boris Ignatievich, you can't order me. First, I'm equal in Power to you and I'm conducting my own investigation on the basis of my own information and hypotheses. You have no right to take my case away from me."

"And second?"

"I can leave the Watch at any moment."

"And is there a 'third'?" Gesar asked.

"Just you try to stop me, Great One," I said.

Gesar sighed.

"Oh, it's so hard dealing with someone who hasn't been an Other for at least two hundred years! All right. Work away. But bear in mind, we don't need a Light Egor. We need Egor the potential Mirror."

He downed his cognac in one gulp and set the glass on the armrest between our seats.

And disappeared.

I sighed and closed my eyes.

Then I opened one eye and squinted at the armrest.

Gesar's glass, the one he had been drinking from, was still full.

It had been an illusion after all, not the boss in the flesh.

Simply a very, very convincing illusion.

I picked up Gesar's glass and took a small sip. After that I closed my eyes and fell asleep.

Customs control, border control, the control point for Others . . . I walked out of the Charles de Gaulle terminal, joined the end of a short queue for taxis, and called our duty officer.

Pavel was still on duty.

"What, already in Paris?" he asked with unconcealed envy. "Have you got warm weather there?"

"Oh yes, *they* do. About five degrees warmer than at home. Where's Egor?"

"You want the address?"

"No, I want to know where he is right now. Or rather, where he will be in an hour."

Pavel sighed ostentatiously.

"You could have warned me sooner . . . In an hour Egor will be dining near the Bourse. But remember that this is not precognition, it's from an intercepted conversation. He's meeting a friend and they're going to have dinner together."

"Well, well," I said. "Simple Russian conjurors live the good life! They settle in Paris, and dine in the center of town . . ."

"He has less than a hundred euros in his account," Pasha said skeptically. "So the magic trick didn't work."

My turn came, I got into a taxi, and spoke in French.

"Emmenez-moi à Bourse de Paris, s'il vous plaît."

I don't know if I looked like someone who had just rushed from Moscow to Paris in order to do something on the Stock Exchange. Sell a couple of oilfields, for instance, and buy an eau de cologne factory and a vineyard.

Probably not.

The dark-skinned driver made a couple of attempts to strike up a conversation with me. He asked if it was my first time in Paris, where I'd flown in from, and if I liked it in France. I answered in curt monosyllables, admitting that it wasn't my first time, that I'd flown in from Moscow, and that I liked it in France.

The last reply immediately sparked the driver's enthusiasm. So much so, that he started singing something about *"la belle France,"* obviously a classic, because even I had heard the song before.

A hundred years or so ago, this French patriotism from a man of dark skin would probably have been regarded ironically. Now it seems perfectly natural.

Maybe the Others ought to reveal themselves? Well, the fifteenth century was too early—they would have burned us at the stake. And in the nineteenth century it might not have been received too well. But why not in the twenty-first century? Differences in race and sexual orientation are tolerated now. So what's so special about the Others?

Well, there are a few things we can do. Certainly, the atom bomb will always be more powerful in any case, but when it comes to the secret services, things get a bit interesting.

The driver carried on prattling without a break. He sang the praises of Paris, expressed his pride in France, and told me that I should definitely drink wine and not vodka. Because Russians drink a lot of vodka, but what you should drink a lot of was wine. Only it had to be French. No one else in the world really knew how to make wine. Algeria was the only other place where they knew how. But nowhere else. The Russians made vodka, the Brits made whisky, the

Americans made bourbon. This was all bad, although vodka wasn't really too bad. But the French made wine, cognac, and calvados. Although he didn't drink any of it, because he was a Muslim. Except maybe a little bit of wine and a little bit of calvados. Only not during the fast. But he was always ready to tell a passenger about good drinks. Especially when he could see that the passenger enjoyed a drink or two.

"So you're in on this conspiracy too, are you," I said in a low voice. Taking out my smartphone, I opened the mirror app, chuckling ironically to myself at the associations of the word. And I looked at my face.

A rather battered face, it was true. Bags under eyes that were red from lack of sleep.

That visit to the school had taken a lot out of me.

Well yes, I could be taken for a burned-out alcoholic.

"Thanks for the advice," I said. We were already driving through the center of Paris; I had to pull myself together. "I'll definitely try everything you suggested."

Closing my eyes, I dragged up the image of Egor from the depths of my memory—the way he was at that moment when I first saw him. But the face, the figure, the clothes—none of that was important.

The aura stays with a person forever. Its development is completed by the age of two or thereabouts (sometimes a little earlier, sometimes a little later), and after that its form is more reliable than fingerprints. Yes, the colors change, depending on a person's mood and condition, but the overall pattern is invariable.

That's the way it is with everyone, except for individuals with an indeterminate destiny. At twelve years old, the age Egor was when I first met him, you very rarely come across auras like that. After the age of twenty, it's simply impossible to find any. But Egor, as far as I could recollect from a chance encounter several years earlier, still had an indeterminate aura.

His aura was multicolored, it shimmered and shifted constantly.

All the colors in it kept changing; for a long time. At one moment he could look like an out-and-out villain, at another like the kindest man in the whole world, and a minute later he blazed with the apparent intellect of a scientific genius, but only a moment after that there was nothing but a feeble intellectual glimmer.

Even for a human being this was way over the top.

But Egor was also a potential Other. And that changed everything. Of course, he could simply be initiated, and depending on his condition at the time, he would become either a Light One or Dark One. But the indeterminate aura made him also a potential Mirror. Egor could be initiated by the Twilight itself. He would partially lose his memory and acquire the ability to work at any level of Power, automatically matching the level and abilities of his opponent. And then, having fulfilled his purpose by living a short life as a Dark One or Light One and removing the "imbalance" in the forces of the two sides, he would be disembodied. Totally and completely.

Why the Twilight was so cruel in these cases and didn't allow its instrument to return to his former condition, either human or Other, I didn't know. But to judge from all previously known instances, the Mirror disappeared completely. When there's an Other, there's a problem; when there is no Other, there is no problem . . .

I relaxed. I imagined an immense, gray plain. I studded it thickly with the silhouettes of buildings. I tossed in a countless number of different-colored points of light.

That was more or less how Paris ought to look in the Twilight . . .

And then I imagined that a blinding light was shining down on me, that my shadow had acquired sharp outlines and I was sinking down into it, as if I was falling through a tear in reality . . .

And I was in the Twilight.

The crudely constructed, crooked wagon trundled smoothly along the country road. There were other carriages, wagons, and carts traveling in the same direction as us and coming toward us.

Without any horses.

The spectral silhouette of the driver—a wagoner in this world—

flashed a white-toothed smile at me from his box. He was holding the reins, but the far ends were just dangling in the air.

Of course, the Twilight isn't full of self-powered wagons.

But every level of the Twilight repeats our world in one way or another; the first level to the greatest degree. Sometimes it's like our world, only blurred and colorless. With the experience that comes from entering the first layer of the Twilight more frequently, it starts to look different, like a kind of projection, a certain "idea of things." So a modern car can look like a colorless modern car. Or it can look like an old carriage. Or it can look like a wagon. Possibly it could even look like a saddled dinosaur.

When I once asked Gesdar about this, he simply replied: "The visible in the Twilight is the result of an interaction between the external world and human consciousness. When the external world changes unpredictably and fantastically, the consciousness is filled with fantasies."

That's probably the way it is.

I'm still in the car, in an old but decent Renault that's driving through Paris. But on the first level of the Twilight the picture my eyes see has changed so much that I can't grasp it. So I see something else . . .

So okay. If it's a wagon, it's a wagon.

The important thing is that people don't change in the Twilight, they are just slowed down.

I ran my eye over the Parisian evening, deliberately registering the warm green light. It was peacefulness, calmness—the rarest feelings that people have in a big city. You only come across them in drug addicts and lovers whose bodies have only just separated from each other.

Right . . . We register that . . . Hold it . . . Remove the green . . .

Now the yellow. First a sunny yellow, bright and pure. An innocent, childish joy. A declaration of love and a first kiss. A wonderful book just read. I remove it too.

Now the blue. From transparent sky blue to a deep indigo. Intellectual work. Insights, conjectures, the joy of learning and discovery. Also not frequently encountered in large cities.

The white. Selflessness and self-sacrifice. A man signing a document to donate a kidney to his little nephew. A policeman advancing with reassuring words and open arms toward a psychopath with a gun at the ready as he holds his own son hostage. I remove that.

The red. From the dawn light to aventurine. From pastel pink to crimson, in case you have never been interested in the names of all that we see. Red is the most varied and brilliant color. Love and passion. Orgasm and pain. The righteous fury of the soldier and the base lust of the rapist.

I washed away the colors one after another. I sieved out and cast aside all the established, settled auras. All the people and all the Others within reach of my gaze. Only a few multicolored, trembling, childish auras remained, and I forced myself not to see the ones that were too small and weak.

The world became totally colorless, flickering between gray and sepia, as if it was trying to acquire color but failing.

There was just one single aura blazing ahead of me. Shimmering and multicolored. An indeterminate destiny.

"*Arrêtez ici,*" I said, emerging from the Twilight. I held out a fifty-euro note (the meter said forty-three). "*C'est pour vous.*"

The Bourse was a little bit farther on—a huge, beautiful building, already illuminated against the background of the dark sky. I walked about five yards and came to a wide opening in the wall, almost like a large garage with the doors standing open. Only in this garage there were tables with lamps and lighted candles standing on them. There were various people sitting at the tables, some dressed smartly, some simply. A strange sort of place, not out of the Michelin list of luxurious restaurants, but not exactly a cheap joint either.

I spotted Egor. He was sitting with his back to me, in the center of the space, discussing something with a respectable-looking middle-aged man who was kneading his steak tartar with leisurely movements of his fork.

Unfortunately there were no free tables. The little table behind Egor had just been taken by a young couple.

I felt very awkward about it, but I didn't hesitate. I looked at the couple and reached out through the Twilight.

They immediately stopped feeling hungry. They jumped up and fused together in a kiss. The waiter (who also seemed to be the owner of the little restaurant) applauded at the sight of such passion. Some of the customers supported him.

The couple tore themselves away from each other, gazing around in confusion at the other customers.

Perhaps they had come in here to clarify their relationship before they broke up. Or perhaps simply to chat before parting for a while.

But now everything had changed. The only thing they really wanted was to be alone together without any clothes on.

Apologizing in their embarrassment and turning away from curious glances, the couple slipped out of the little restaurant. I knew that they wouldn't go back to his place or to hers. They would take a room in the little hotel on the corner, right now, and the creaking of the bed would prevent their neighbors from sleeping and delight them at the same time.

Well then. At least they would have an absolutely magical night in Paris.

I sat down at the table that was now free. The man who apparently owned the place obviously wasn't expecting this, but he didn't try to argue. He came over to me with a smile on his face—a very professional kind of smile.

"Je voudrais une bouteille de vin rouge," I said. *"Je prends ce que vous recommandez."*

The waiter, or perhaps the owner, nodded and disappeared through a small door at the back of the room.

I looked for smokers and confirmed that there weren't any. Europe . . .

At that moment Egor started speaking. In Russian.

"It is certain to be popular, Monsieur Roman. As you can see, there are no free seats here."

"A couple has just run out," said "Monsieur Roman," chewing raw minced meat and washing it down with red wine. What a jerk this "Monsieur Roman" was—how could he possibly stand to be addressed like that? "And what's more," he went on, "the owner is a famous clown, even if he did retire a long time ago. It's a very convenient spot, but the rent is cheap. And it's only a small restaurant."

"The last point is a rather dubious advantage," Egor said tensely.

"My dear man," Roman responded condescendingly. "This little restaurant is not kept afloat by its elegant dishes—they are extremely ordinary—nor by its décor, or even the location. It all comes down to the owner. To the fact that he sits on the ladies' knees and drinks out of your glass of wine. He falls down, without anything slipping off the tray. He dances and sings "La Danse des Canards" as he brings you a duck breast with apples."

"But also . . ."

"Egor, you're a wonderful illusionist and prestidigitator," Roman said, sounding patronizing. "And I'll be happy to present your act in my restaurant. But I have to tell you straightaway that you won't be able to repeat what this clown has done. You won't be able to amuse all the customers in the restaurant at the same time. Your illusions are individual work. From five steps away there's nothing interesting to be seen. And if you go around to every customer, pulling coins out of their ears, you'll soon go crazy."

"I don't pull coins—"

"Egor! Let's drop the subject," Roman said gently. "If you find yourself a small space, like this one, and a good team, then I'm prepared to buy in. Fifty-fifty. A large hall's not for you."

The waiter came over and put down a bottle of red wine in front of me. He gave me a mysterious glance, flicked his finger against the bottom of the bottle, and the cork shot up into the ceiling like a bullet. Someone nearby laughed. I applauded theatrically. A glass of wine was poured for me, and then the waiter took a lighted cigarette out of his pocket. He took a drag, breathing the smoke up toward the ceiling, then handed the cigarette to me and I took a couple of drags. He took the cigarette back with a smile—and disappeared back through the service door.

"That's a shame, Roman," Egor was saying in the meantime. "But whatever you say. As for performing at your place, maybe we could discuss that now?"

Roman solemnly raised his hand and looked at his massive Patek Philippe watch. He shook his head.

"Sorry, I have business to deal with. I've got to run, my friend. Give me a call . . . The day after tomorrow would be best."

Everything seemed fine, except that the Patek Philippe was made in China and only cost fifty bucks—that is, if it was bought in a market in China. Or maybe one hundred if it was bought in the flea markets of Paris.

I suddenly felt furious.

"There's no point calling you the day after tomorrow," I said, picking up my glass and moving my table closer to theirs. "Tomorrow you'll spend the whole day with a small-time Russian oligarch, trying to persuade him to invest in your restaurant. You'll waste the last money you have on that, because he doesn't even like wine and he hates lobster. The day after tomorrow you'll ask the bank for an extension on your loan. So there's no point in Egor calling you tomorrow, or the day after tomorrow . . . Or calling you ever."

Roman looked at me with his mouth hanging open. He had a lump of bloody minced meat clinging to one perfectly white plastic tooth.

"Close your mouth," I advised him. "And get out of here."

I put just a tiny little bit of Power into the final words, not enough for it even to be considered an intervention, but enough to make this Russian-born Parisian restaurateur jump to his feet like a scalded cat.

"Gorodetsky, you cheeky rogue!" Egor said delightedly.

"Hello, by the way," I said.

"Hi!"

To my surprise, he actually sprang to his feet and grabbed me.

"Well now, Gorodetsky, if you tell me that we've met by chance . . ."

"Of course not," I said. "I was looking for you. Forgive me for that."

Egor gestured dismissively.

"I forgive you. Will you have some wine?"

"I've brought my own," I said, fetching the bottle from the other table. "We bring presents when we go visiting. And you've . . ." I began, and hesitated.

"Grown up?" Egor laughed.

"No, you grew up a long time ago. But now you're all pumped up. All that beefy muscle!"

Egor really did look like an athlete. From the back I'd thought it was just his jacket, but the jacket turned out to have nothing to do with it. It must have been his broad shoulders. Egor had taken swimming lessons as a child, and it looked like he hadn't spent the last few years lounging on the couch either.

"But you, you're exactly the same as you were," said Egor. "Only . . ."

"I'm drinking myself to death?" I asked forlornly. "I've been told several times recently . . ."

"You're tired. You're bruised, battered, and sad, somehow. Has something happened?"

I nodded.

"I'll tell you about it. Only let's sit and have a drink. Let's have something to eat. I'm straight off the plane. They fed me well, but . . ."

"What has happened?" Egor asked, looking into my eyes. "Maybe I can't read minds, but it's written on your face."

"It's a crisis," I said. "To keep it short. Some ancient thingamajig has come back to life and it wants to kill everyone."

"Chtulhu," Egor said with a nod.

"Who's Chtulhu?" I asked, puzzled. "Ah, Lovecraft."

"You're way behind the times," said Egor. "About twenty years behind. You don't even understand the hairy old jokes. Okay, so some mysterious thingamajig wants to kill everyone. Who is this everyone? The Others?"

"First the Others. Then the people. Maybe even the animals too. Basically everyone."

"He's probably some kind of botanist," Egor said. "His goal is to protect the world of plants."

"You ought to write comic books. You have a powerful imagination, and your nerves are even stronger."

"I had a difficult childhood." Egor chuckled. "Anton, what have you come for? Tell me."

"I want to initiate you," I said morosely.

"Of course, Paris is a broad-minded city," said Egor. "The very place for proposals like that."

"Egor, you have to become an Other. Believe me!"

"I can help somehow with the fight against your Chtulhu, is that it?" Egor said. "I haven't forgotten the way you lined me up for the very lowest level of Power for the rest of my life."

"Egor, it would still be great. You'd extend your lifespan very significantly. Become absolutely unrivaled in your profession. You could help your family and loved ones . . ."

"Anton, I'm fairly young and I'm already a very well-known illusionist," said Egor. "If my bank account's empty at the moment, that's no tragedy. I've got two offers, one from the Cirque du Soleil. If I accept it, I'll be paid a good advance immediately. You can tell I'm not lying, can't you? Then I'll go on. I have a wife, and I really love her. I've been unfaithful to her a few times, it's true, I've cursed and sworn at her sometimes, but I love her. I have a son, he's three years old."

"Congratulations," I said awkwardly. "That's—"

"Thanks. By the way, we called him Anton."

I snapped my mouth shut.

"Well, after all, those were the most vivid impressions of my childhood," Egor continued with a smile. "We couldn't call him Gesar, or Zabulon. Anton's a good name and it's quite common in France too; in the kindergarten they call him Antoine."

"That's very touching . . ." I began.

"And my wife's beloved grandfather is called Anton too," Egor said with an ironic smile. "Thanks for the concern, but I still don't want to become an Other."

"When you end up in the hospital with a heart attack, or your car skids on the road, you'll regret it," I warned him.

"No doubt. But for now, I don't want to do it."

I drained my glass. Good wine.

"Egor, you're not only a weak Other. You're a potential Mirror."

"And what does that mean?" he asked with a frown.

"If there's a serious imbalance between the Darkness and the Light, you'll change. You'll turn into a Mirror Magician, whose Power is unlimited and always equal to the Power of his opponent— Light or Dark, depending on the situation. It's extremely difficult to defeat someone like that."

"So far I don't see any cause for panic," said Egor.

"You'll change spontaneously. Without any initiation. You'll lose part of your memory and you'll act, consciously or otherwise, as the Twilight wishes."

"Now that does sound unpleasant," Egor admitted.

"And when you've performed your function—the one imposed on you by the Twilight—you'll disappear."

"I'll die?" Egor asked, twirling his glass in his fingers.

"I don't know. You'll simply disappear. Be disembodied."

Egor said nothing for a while. Then he nodded.

"Yes. That's certainly not good news."

"And it could happen," I said. "We have information. Basically, the group that can halt the apocalypse has to include a Mirror Magician. That's why I'm suggesting initiation. A Light One, a Dark One . . . What's the difference in the Twilight? If you become an Other, you can't turn into a Mirror Magician."

"And who'll become one instead of me?"

"I don't know," I muttered. "We'll find someone, I'm sure of it."

"You've changed, Anton," Egor said in a quiet voice. "Become more flexible. So in fact you don't have any other candidates, apart from me? But you're prepared to initiate me so that I won't be killed?"

"Yes. Because—" I stopped short.

"Because you're stuffed full of complexes and doubts, like a genuine member of the Russian intelligentsia," Egor blurted out. "In your mind I'm still the little boy who was set up by your wonderful boss. Sixteen years ago you had your face stuck in the fact that good isn't necessarily good, evil isn't always evil, and you weren't clad in white robes, but tattered jeans and a shirt with a dirty collar."

"You know where you can stick your psychoanalysis," I said, getting worked up and raising my voice.

"And although you've come to terms with it and gotten used to playing hide-and-seek with your conscience, you still don't feel completely at ease with it!" Egor shouted. "The way you all exploited me was the first dirty trick that you noticed. Not really much of a dirty trick, if you think about it. A mere trifle, really. But it obviously still rankles you. You want to put a final and complete end to that story. Rescue me triumphantly, for instance. And then you'll feel better. As though when that little compromise with your conscience disappears, it will erase all the others that followed. Right?"

For a moment I wanted to thump Egor in the face. Really wallop him. I even started getting up and something probably flickered in my eyes—Egor narrowed his own eyes slightly and tensed up.

"*Ne vous disputez, les filles!*" the owner said merrily, setting my food down in front of me. The two little medallions of veal were decorated with three slices of fried potato, a sprig of parsley, and intricate twirls of berry sauce. Then he leaned against my shoulder slightly. But he leaned hard. And glanced briefly into my face. His eyes were dark and heavy. Oh, these clowns, I never did trust them!

"Why don't you hit him with a fireball?" Egor suggested with a smile. He turned toward the owner and said, *"C'est de ma faute."* Then he glanced at me again and said, "Now look where we've gotten to. They all think we're pansies!" Then he spoke to the owner again: *"Désolé!"*

"Désolé," I echoed. People really were giving us disapproving sideways glances. Not, of course, because they'd taken us for a couple having an argument—it's simply not *comme il faut* to argue that loudly. Not proper.

The owner smiled—it was a broad smile, artificial through and through, like all clowns' smiles—and walked away.

I started fiddling with a veal medallion.

Egor took a sip of wine.

"I'm sorry," I said.

"I'm sorry," Egor said simultaneously.

We looked at each other and laughed. And a moment later the entire little restaurant turned toward us and started applauding.

"Oh, my sainted mother," I said. "They really do think—"

"Gorodetsky, here in Paris you must never disappoint the expectations of the audience," Egor said with a theatrical sigh. "Now we'll have to become genuine Europeans."

"Listen, I'm teleporting out of here right now . . ." I began.

"Where to, where to?" Egor inquired. "Are you abandoning me?"

And that triggered an absolutely idiotic fit of laughter from both of us. Surrounded by benevolent French smiles, it all really was very funny, but I could only hope that the story would never become known in the Watch.

They'd be sniggering at me for fifty years!

"So what about initiation?" I asked, chewing on a medallion. "Will you do it or not?"

"Of course. I'll go with you . . . Where do you need the Mirror?"

"I don't know yet. We're probably meeting in Moscow. Egor, do you realize what you're getting into?"

"Anton, you explained to me that the end of the world is expected in a week. And I—or someone like me—can prevent it. Even if it does cost my life. Do you think I really have any choice? Can any normal person have a choice in that situation?"

I shook my head.

"Of course I'll go," said Egor, chewing his veal. "And the food here *is* only middling. It's not bad, but . . . I had a much better chef in mind. It was a good idea—the Illusion Restaurant!"

"If we survive this, I'll find an investor for you," I said. "Only you have to make the restaurant 'Other-friendly.' That's a partnership program we have."

"Done," Egor said with a nod. "But I won't survive. Basically, I think I was supposed to be left back there in that passageway—white and drained of blood. You were just in too much of a hurry." He chuckled. "And you gave me sixteen extra years. Don't think I don't appreciate that. And you didn't even really know what to do; you had a look of absolute horror on your face."

"You remember?" I asked.

"Of course. I've never forgotten it for a moment. And I never doubted that sooner or later it would all end like this."

"All what?" I asked stupidly.

"Everything. It has all been . . . unreal. Borrowed time. A loan. Everything went wrong, but I'm still alive. It all feels like make-believe."

"I'm sorry, Egor," I said.

"Ah, come on, Watchman. I stopped feeling angry long ago."

"We all live on borrowed time," I said.

"Let's just say it's a term loan. That sounds more respectable." Egor looked around to find the owner, who kept glancing across at us, and gestured in the air with his finger, as if he was signing the bill. The owner nodded and leaned down over his cash register. "We can go straight to Moscow now."

"But don't you want to say good—" I said and broke off. "To see your wife and son before you leave?"

"My wife and son are in Nice," Egor said with a smile. "She's not expecting me to call."

"But you told me you loved her!"

"And I wasn't lying, Anton. Only I didn't say that she still loves me . . ."

My phone rang, sparing me the need to reply.

It was Pavel.

"Anton, I'm off duty now," he said, yawning. "But Gesar told me to call you at a quarter past eight and say that two tickets have been booked for the Paris-Moscow flight departing at ten thirty. For you and Egor."

"I see," I said. "Have you got the tickets?"

"Yes. Are you going to curse and swear at Gesar?"

"No."

"Then good night."

I put the phone in my pocket and nodded to Egor.

"You've convinced me, we'll go right now. Here in Paris, do you usually phone for a taxi, or stop one in the street?"

CHAPTER 4

I WALKED INTO GESAR'S OFFICE AT TEN THE NEXT MORNING. We had flown in from Paris that morning, and then I had taken Egor to the Economic Achievements Exhibition district, where his mother still lived. Only then did I go home and grab barely two hours' sleep.

There was something heroic about it.

As there was in the impervious, restrained expression on my face.

"Good morning, boss," I said. "Egor has come to Moscow, he's staying with his mother. He's prepared to take part in our operations if necessary."

"Good," said Gesar, studying my face curiously. "Well done, both of you. I'm glad."

"Can I go?" I asked.

"Hmm," Gesar said. "Is that all? No questions, arguments, or accusations?"

"No," I said. "Can I go?"

"Wait," said Gesar. "Sit down."

I obediently sat facing him.

"Anton, you have every right to be indignant," said Gesar. "But let me explain at the very start—there wasn't even any magic involved! Just psychology. An understanding of the motives that guide people and Others. Only you could have persuaded Egor to come to Moscow and agree to a suicide mission, and then only if you sincerely tried to talk him out of it."

"Boss, I understand."

"And so I—" Gesar broke off and frowned. "You really do understand? And you're not accusing me of anything? And you agree that we need Egor?"

"I feel really, really bad about it," I said. "We ruined the guy's life when he was still a child. But the stakes are too high. Neither his life, nor mine, nor yours is of any importance here."

Gesar said nothing for a moment, twirling a fountain pen in his fingers. For some reason he switched on the laptop on his desk—and immediately slammed the lid shut.

"So I'll be going then?" I asked. "Or is there some new information?"

"There is," Gesar said. "I won't keep you in the dark any longer. I'm sorry. I didn't notice that you really had grown up."

"Apology accepted," I said.

"Also, I'm not entirely sure that we do need a Mirror. The analysts set the odds at thirty percent for a Mirror, twenty for the shapeshifters, and fifty for something that we don't know yet. Don't get upset for the boy too soon, there might not be anything for him to do here after all."

"Thank you for that," I replied sincerely.

"Last, Olga's having some problems with our bloodsuckers," said Gesar. "Go and see her, she wanted to discuss it with you."

The text message caught me right outside the door of Olga's office. I took out my phone and glanced at it. I didn't recognize the number.

"The Grandmothers spent all night thrashing things out. No agreement. The next coven is tomorrow night. Yulia Tarasovna."

What the hell was this? The world was hurtling toward its end, and these old witches couldn't even choose themselves a new Great Grandmother! At least temporarily—there was a good chance that none of the Sixth Watch would survive the encounter with the Two-in-One in any case.

Oh no, they were going to gather again and again and argue about which of them was the oldest, most malign, and most repulsive!

I put the phone away and walked into Olga's office. The Great One was standing at the window, blowing cigarette smoke through a small open pane. It was drawn out into the frosty air in a vigorous stream of gray.

"That's bad for you and it's forbidden by government decree," I said.

Olga gave me a sour look.

"Have you been to Paris?" she asked.

"Uh-huh."

"I envy you. I once spent an absolutely wonderful year there . . ."

"I got five hours, but that wasn't too bad either," I agreed. "What's happening with the vampires?"

"What's happening with the witches?"

"They're discussing. They'll gather again tonight."

"As for the vampires . . . Everything's complicated with the vampires. The problem is that the Master of Masters was killed."

"So it was Lilith!" I exclaimed.

"No, Anton. You may be surprised, but it wasn't her at all. None of the vampires even knew anything about your Lilith. You ask Zabulon who she really was after all."

"Why me?"

"Zabulon's fond of you," Olga said without a trace of a smile. "No, the Master of Masters was only a three-hundred-year-old Polish Jew."

"A Jewish vampire?" I exclaimed in amazement. "Well, he certainly violated all the Talmudic prohibitions."

"I can't argue with that. Anyway, he was a genuinely powerful vampire, with only one weakness—alcoholism." Olga sent the cigarette butt flying out the window with a flick of her fingers, closed the small pane, and sat down at the desk.

I sat facing her.

"But that's nonsense! Strong spirits burn them."

"Strong spirits. He made do with the blood of extremely drunk people. That was partly what killed him."

"He got drunk and fell under a train?" I asked

"Worse. He quarreled with the head of the Warsaw Day Watch. With whom he had always been on friendly terms. It ended in a duel."

"Uh-oh," I said.

"The vampire lost, although he did have a chance. Higher One against Higher One, the magician is usually more powerful, only the vampire was more experienced. But he lost, I believe because he was drunk. He was caught by the Gray Prayer."

"Why didn't I hear about it?"

"Because it was in 1981. They fell out over politics, by the way— the head of the Dark Ones was a staunch communist and a supporter of Jaruzelski, while the vampire—"

"Olga, stop!" I said, raising my hands. "I'm not interested in the political views of vampires thirty years ago. Why haven't the vampires had a Master of Masters since then?"

"Well, because the new Master of Masters acquires the position by killing the previous one. And if the previous one died at the hands of someone who is not a vampire, then at least twelve Masters must fight for the title of the new Master of Masters—and only one must be left. From the technical point of view, they're already dead, of course, Anton. But they still want to live. Sooner or later one idiot can be found to challenge the Master of Masters. But so far they haven't been able to find twelve morons willing to launch into mortal combat. And they might not find them for another hundred years. The post has no real benefits, except that it's flattering to hold it. But the problems involved are overwhelming."

"*Matka Boska, jak mógł Wampir-Żyd zginąć od 'Szarego Nabożeństwa' Ciemnego komunisty? Jak w ogóle u ich w głowach to godziło się?*" I exclaimed.

Olga squinted at me quizzically.

"What's this, Anton, did you hang a 'Petrov' on yourself yesterday?"

"Well, yes," I said, embarrassed. "I don't know French, but to make it easier to get on with people . . . How did you know?"

"You just protested indignantly in Polish." Olga chuckled. "The Petrov crams the fifteen most widely used languages into your head, not just one. What a surprise, I never thought Polish was one of them."

"But anyway, what the hell was he thinking of?" I asked, slamming my fist down on the desk. "The Master of Masters—a Jew! That's an oxymoron! A Jew would not drink blood!"

"He wasn't religious," Olga said with a smile.

"And the head of the Dark Ones—a communist? How did he fit all this together with his scientific atheism?"

"He explained the abilities of Others exclusively from the materialist point of view. Anton, stop getting indignant. It's already happened, and a long time ago. The vampires weren't particularly keen to choose a new Master of Masters. And they don't want to now. They're convening another High Lodge in three days, but I wouldn't hold out any great hopes."

"Olga, why is it like this?" I asked. "The Watches have no overall leadership at all, only on the regional level. The shape-shifters have no leaders in principle. The vampires and witches apparently do . . . But in fact they don't, because the leaders are dead, and everyone only seems to be glad about it."

"Because we're solitaries, Anton," Olga replied. "We're not even wolves, they live in packs."

"Rubbish, rubbish, rubbish!" I said, sweeping my hand through the air. "Do you know what Egor told me yesterday? I warn him not to come. I offer to initiate him, so that he won't become a Mirror. And he says: 'Can any normal person have a choice in that situation?' "

"Well, he's a human being," said Olga. "A living, agonized soul. With ideals and delusions. But they are Others. Vampires. The Undead. And there's another thing you're forgetting, Anton. The vampires, as we now realize, believe that they were the very first Others. It was the vampires who concluded the agreement with the Two-in-One. So maybe they're not too happy to do battle with him?"

"No one loves the bloodsuckers," I said with a nod.

"You're behind the times," said Olga. "They ran a very powerful PR campaign that took in almost all the countries in the world. Show young girls a genuine vampire, and they'll squeal and make a dash for him, offering up their necks."

"I was talking to a young girl here quite recently—she wasn't over the moon about vampires."

"But it was a woman who sucked her." Olga chuckled. "If it had been a handsome young guy who could carry her in his arms for hours, things might have turned out differently."

She turned serious.

"I don't need any help yet, Anton. The vampires are huddled up in their nest in Manhattan."

"In New York?"

"Where else?" Olga asked in surprise. "It's their holy of holies! Their Mecca! Their Jerusalem! There are more of them per capita there than anywhere else. That's where the oldest lodges, clubs, and salons are. Both legal and illegal establishments. Now they're going to thrash things out and decide what's to their greatest advantage."

"And drink blood."

"Yes, of course." Olga sighed. "And what's more, since the gathering of the Masters was to some extent initiated by us, I'm almost certain that they've been given additional licenses."

I didn't say anything to that.

"Life is a dirty business," said Olga. "And life after death is absolutely vile. Go home, Anton, and go to bed. You look terrible."

"The witches will be making a decision tonight too," I said. "But I could rummage through the archive in the meantime . . ."

"Anton, you're working in a team," said Olga. "Calm down. Don't try to be everywhere. You got Egor here—well done! Now rest, at least until the evening. Everyone's thinking. Everyone's reading documents. Everyone's questioning the very oldest Others. You've earned a rest."

I stood up and nodded.

"All right. I won't even try to argue. But pay special attention to that vampiress who wrote me a message with the initials
of the people she bit. She managed to drive the Two-in-One away,
didn't she?"

"She's being looked at, have no doubt about it," Olga said with a
frown. "Every line's being followed up. But right now your line leads
to bed."

"Yes, sir," I said.

I could really have opened up a portal from the Watch office. Or
from the courtyard. But I got into Zabulon's car, drove around the
corner, and parked outside a "farmhouse products" and imported alcohol shop. It was a paid parking zone, but I decided the Great Dark
One's wallet could stand the strain.

In the shop I bought a bottle of wine (it wasn't the best of wine,
but I didn't feel like looking for a good wine shop), four pounds of
genuinely good beef, milk, butter, tvorog, eggs and sausage, a couple
of pounds of apples, some fresh bread, a few assorted olives, and some
hot peppers stuffed with cheese.

Then I walked out of the shop, took out my phone and hid it in
the glove compartment of the car, and slipped into a deserted alley.
I closed my eyes, pictured the place I needed to go to, pronounced
the words required, and leaned forward into the portal that opened
up in front of me.

"Daddy!" Nadya squealed joyfully. "Hoorah! Dad's come!"

"And he's brought presents," I said, opening my eyes. Nadya
immediately hung on my neck. "Hey, I'm wet and cold! Wait a
moment!"

"I missed you," my daughter replied. "I don't want to wait for
anything."

The portal to the refuge had been set up by Nadya. She had as-
sured us there was no way it could possibly be traced.

But I'd been determined not to abuse it.

I hugged my daughter. A moment later Svetlana came over.

"I was worried you would never bother to visit us," she said reproachfully.

"Olga sent me home and ordered me to catch up on my sleep. I decided that home is where you are."

"That's the right decision," my wife agreed, hugging us both.

"You'll knock over the bags!" I exclaimed.

"Put the bags in the kitchen!" Svetlana commanded. Nadya pouted resentfully and carried them into the "kitchen," that is, into the alcove behind the curtain.

"Bread, milk, meat," I said proudly.

"Did you bring any vegetables?" Svetlana asked briskly.

"Vegetables?" I echoed, disconcerted.

"Well, yes. Those things that grow in the ground, I put them in the soup. Carrots, onions, potatoes . . ."

"I didn't think about vegetables," I confessed. "But I got four pounds of good meat. I can grill steaks! And two pounds of apples."

"At least one tomato?" Svetlana asked.

"And I did get sausage, butter, eggs . . ."

"Basically, you remembered to get everything that contains cholesterol," Svetlana said with a smile. "You could at least have gotten tomatoes! And salad!"

"Who needs salad?" I exclaimed indignantly. "Why do you keep talking about food? Aren't you interested in the news?"

"Are you hungry?" Svetlana asked.

"Yes," I said. "Although the meal on the plane yesterday was good and I had a bite to eat in Paris as well."

A hint of something between admiration and indignation appeared in Svetlana's expression.

"I see you're leading a busy life! My dear, why don't you fly to Paris when I'm at home and I can ask you for something?"

"There," I said, unbuttoning my jacket and taking a little box out of my pocket. "What else can a poor man bring back from a business trip to Paris? Two bottles of authentic French perfume."

"This one's mine, it's mine, it's the most fashionable fragrance of the season!" Nadya exclaimed, grabbing the little box.

"How come?" Svetlana said indignantly. "I wanted that fragrance too."

"Keep calm, the other one's exactly the same!" I said triumphantly, taking out the second bottle.

My wife and daughter both turned toward me simultaneously. Then they looked at each other.

"Men!" My wife sighed.

"And this is Dad. He's one of the best!" said Nadya, backing her up.

"What is all this?" I asked indignantly. "You both wanted this perfume. And I brought a bottle for each of you! What's wrong with that?"

They exchanged glances again. Nadya shook her head.

"Come on," said Svetlana. "I'll feed you."

Dinner was delicious. Svetlana cooked what an Italian would have called spaghetti Bolognese, but there was too much meat in it, so it was more like Russian "sailors' macaroni." While I was eating, Svetlana looked at me.

"Olga's right," she said, "you need a rest. You look like . . ."

"An alcoholic?" I asked warily.

"No. One of Grebenshchikov's lyrical heroes. From the song 'Mama, I Can't Drink Anymore.' "

"Damn," I said. "Everyone's criticizing the way I look. I'm going to drink milk." I caught my daughter's expression. "Do you want to ask something?" I asked.

"Dad, do you know if Harry Styles's single has been released? They were supposed to announce it today?"

"Who's he?" I asked, puzzled.

"Oh, Dad, he's one of the boys in One Direction. The coolest one."

"Light, Darkness, and the Twilight!" I exclaimed. "How should I know? I only found out about Picnic's new album a month after it was released!"

"You could have asked Kesha," my daughter said sulkily. "You have seen him, haven't you?"

I snorted.

"Yes, I've seen him. Nadizhda, if you wanted to find out how your friend was getting on, all you had to do was ask, and not start inquiring about the Biebers and Timatis of this world."

Nadya rapidly blushed bright red.

"He's all right," I said after a pause to drive the lesson home. After all, Kesha was a very fine young lad, and I'd known him since he was a child, so to speak. By no means the worst friend for a young girl. An Other, a Light One, from a good family . . . Although what did his family have to do with this? He was a good lad, and that was it. "Let me tell you everything in the right order."

And I started telling my story.

About meeting Kesha. About the visit from Eve/Lilith. About the appearance of the Tiger. About my conversations with Killoran. About my memories being blocked. About the trip to Paris and Egor, who had come back to Moscow.

"That poor boy," Svetlana gasped. "Anton! Are you serious? You've got him involved in the Watches' operation? Knowing that he could become a Mirror and disappear?"

"The whole world could disappear," I said with a shrug. "I tried to talk him out of it. And he hasn't been a boy for a long time. Why don't you advise me what else I can do? All the Watches, not to mention the Inquisition, are digging in every possible direction at this very moment. But maybe there's something we're missing?"

"Look, Dad," said Nadya, who had gotten over her indignation. She picked up a sheet of paper. "I wrote this down here, while you were telling us everything. All the data that we have. Prophecies, the information from Killoran, the information from Lilith . . . Dad, did I get it right that the female vampire who pretended to be Killoran is the same one who wrote you a message with the initials of her victims?"

"Yes," I said, nodding. "Almost certainly."

"And you think she's the vampire that you once caught and who was disembodied?"

"I'm not sure about that any longer, little one. At first we thought the message in the bites that said 'Be ready' was a warning from the vampiress. But while 'Anton Go' really was the beginning of 'Anton Gorodetsky,' 'Be ready' was followed by 'He awaits.' But the vampire was female . . . after all, Killoran . . ."

I pondered for a moment and gestured in frustration.

"I don't know, Nadyusha. If it was a disguise, how do we really know who was behind it? We can't say anything. But I sense a strong kind of personal relationship there."

Nadya answered me very seriously.

"Even people should trust their presentiments, and we should especially. Dad, can you see that everything comes back to vampires?"

I nodded.

"How could I fail to see it? The Two-in-One is their god. He manifested himself through a Light One and Dark One—as I understand it, he incarnated himself in them, put them on like clothes. The Twilight uses the Mirror in pretty much the same way. The vampiress tried to pass on information to me, even before the Two-in-One appeared. And she was able to protect us from him—which is very strange, of course. Then she gave me a whole heap of information, while she was pretending to be Killoran. And Lilith told us a lot of things as well. And it seems like she was the oldest vampire on the planet."

"It all circles around vampires," Svetlana agreed. "We've got a clever daughter, Anton . . . A glass of wine?"

"No," I said firmly. "Milk."

Svetlana got up and went to the "kitchen." Nadka continued sitting there with her feet pulled up onto the chair and gnawing tentatively on a fingernail. She was pondering.

Dammit, what a clever, grown-up daughter I had!

And what a silly little child she was at the same time!

"Dad, I think the most useful thing to do right now is try to understand the various extra details of the Prophecy," said Nadya. "I think that's the most important thing."

"Why?" I asked her.

"Because the devil is always in the details," she replied seriously. "Dad! Does the devil really exist?"

"Why don't you ask me if God exists?" I said, trying to joke. But Nadya gave me a demanding kind of look and I replied reluctantly: "I don't know, but the old Others don't like to mention him. Or God either, come to think of it. Is that important right now?"

"I got distracted," Nadya declared. "Dad, what I wanted to say was . . . if we have to convene some kind of Sixth Watch, then the heads of all the Watches, and of the vampires, and all the others won't be any use to us at all."

"Why not?" I asked.

"Because the details haven't been observed. Have you forgotten, Dad? Say they work out now who's the most important of the vampires and the witches, they figure them all out and appoint them. So what? They all have to be tied together by blood, don't they?"

"That could be interpreted in a broad sense," I said. "Sveta, are you going to pour me that milk?"

"You mean you're serious?" my wife asked in surprise. "Just a moment."

"It probably can be interpreted in a broad sense," Nadya agreed. "Only there has to be blood. Now look . . . The most important Light One is me."

"How do you make that out?" I asked indignantly.

"Well, who else? Who has more right to represent the Light than an Absolute Light One?" Nadya asked.

"Don't get so high and mighty," I advised her. "Even if you do represent the Light, we'll ask you to appoint a representative."

Nadya snorted.

"The Dark One. Well, I don't know. A vampire, obviously. And a witch . . ."

"No one can understand the final point," I complained. "What kind of Party is that? 'The Basis, the Foundation' . . ."

"A Prophet," said Nadya.

I looked at her and froze.

"Remember that little book you read? *The Foundation: Incredible Stories about Prophets.*"

"About psychologists," I corrected her mechanically. "Well, or Seers, if you like."

"In short, a Prophet," Nadya said with a nod. "There aren't many of them anyway, and hardly any powerful ones at all. They're the basis of everything, they don't foretell the future, they shape it. And the bit about the blood is important too, right? Is Gesar somehow connected by blood with Glyba? No way. So they're no good."

"You're not connected with Glyba at all either," I said tensely.

"Not with him, of course. But I'm connected with Kesha now."

I felt an icy silence descend when Nadya finished what she was saying.

"By blood."

Something clinked behind me. I swung around and looked at Sveta. She put the glass full of milk down on the little table and looked intently at Nadya, half turning toward her.

"How . . . When?" I asked.

"A long time ago. Two months already."

"That's . . ." I refrained from using the absurd phrase "that's not possible" and concluded: "That's too early, Nadya."

"It just happened," she said perfectly calmly with a shrug. "We kind of decided spontaneously."

"Nadya, you're not old enough to do it spontaneously . . . Or unspontaneously!" I exclaimed, barely able to stop myself from shouting.

"Why aren't I?" Nadya asked, amazed. "I think even Tom Sawyer and Huck Finn, although they were younger than me . . ."

I thought I was losing my mind. And it seemed like I wasn't the only one.

"Tom Sawyer? With Huck Finn?" Svetlana exclaimed. "That's a very progressive kind of reading!"

"In the first place, Tom Sawyer and Huckleberry Finn are fictional characters," I said, trying to remain calm and collected. "And in the second place, nothing of the sort happened and it never could have!"

"What are you talking about?" asked Nadya, looking from her mother to me and back again.

"What are you talking about?" I asked.

"Blood brotherhood," said Nadya. "Innokentii and I swore an oath in blood and we signed our names in blood."

"Children's games," I said, and burst into laughter. "Nadya, what a child you are!"

There was a glugging sound behind me. I looked around again and saw Sveta pouring cognac into a glass.

"Me too!" I said.

"You wanted milk," Sveta said.

"Milk is for children!"

"Dad, Mum, did you think I was talking about sex?" Nadya asked in a cold voice. "That Innokentii and I had sex?"

"We didn't think anything," said Svetlana, handing me a glass. "We just didn't understand what you were saying."

"We've decided not to have sex for the time being," Nadya said reassuringly. "Kesha thinks it will retard the development of our magical potential."

I downed my cognac in one gulp.

"But I think he's wrong," Nadya continued pensively. "I think he's being a bit of a coward!"

I took the glass of milk out of Svetlana's hands and chased the cognac down with it.

"Well good for you. I'm very glad that you're both such rational young people."

I could have stopped there, but Nadya hadn't managed to hide the impish spite that was lingering in her eyes.

"But you're both still very young, after all," I went on. "So today your mother will have a talk with you about what a young girl ought to know."

"Definitely," Sveta said in a sweet voice. "We'll probably start with stamens and pistils, but then we'll talk about everything seriously."

"Mum!" Nadya exclaimed.

"And I'll have a word with Kesha," I added. "If, as you say, the boy is a bit of a coward . . . His father ought to have spoken to him on the subject, but since he doesn't live in a family, I'll talk to him. The poor boy probably wants to get it off his chest, find out what's happening to his body, and there's no one—"

"Dad!" Nadya howled. "Shut-up-shut-up-shut-up!"

"Are you going to troll your old parents again?" I asked.

Nadya pouted sulkily.

"I'll probably even buy him an encyclopedia for boys," I declared.

"I won't!" said Nadya. "I won't do it again! But it's your own fault, isn't it? For thinking that straightaway? And you talk about children's games!"

"And what else can the parents of a teenage girl think?" I asked. "A girl your age was on the way to spend the night with her boyfriend when a vampire attacked her."

"Then she's a fool," Nadya said sullenly. "And in any case, Kesha really does think it slows down magical development . . ."

"Is it true, about the blood?" I asked, trying to get away from this slippery subject.

"Yes. Kesha and I really did . . . Well, we swore this oath . . ." Nadya lowered her eyes.

"And you told me you cut yourself making a salad," I said, recalling Nadya with a plaster on her finger. "The Little Sunshine Madhouse."

"Maybe it is a madhouse," Svetlana said. "But our daughter's right,

Anton. The requirement for a blood tie is important. Perhaps it can be any kind of blood tie, but it has to be there."

"After the team gathers, they can swear an oath in blood," I suggested. "Like Nadya and Kesha."

"I don't think that will work," said Svetlana. "You know yourself, Anton, that requirements like this are a kind of fixed convention. A game. But with clear rules. 'Blood brotherhood' created so simply and crudely won't work."

I didn't argue with that.

Svetlana has a better sense of such subtle things than I do. She doesn't know, but she senses.

"Then I know absolutely nothing at all," I said wearily. "A tie of blood. Where does that get us? Mr. Glyba can adopt me and we'll go and do the job . . ."

"Go to bed," Svetlana said, putting her hand on my shoulder. "You need to rest."

"And are you going to rearrange your schedule to suit me?" I asked. "It's still the afternoon here."

"You won't bother us. Lie down and have a sleep; Nadya and I will watch TV."

And I didn't argue with that.

My sleep was sound and calm, and I had none of those dreams that are so misleading.

Simply sleep.

It was only just before I woke that it threw up a scrap of a dream that couldn't really be called either a nightmare or a vision.

At first I was standing in my Moscow apartment, and Gesar kept trying to climb in through the window. No, he wasn't levitating and he hadn't grown wings. A fire engine brought him on its extended ladder. Gesar clambered onto the cornice and waved to me with a grin.

In the dream it seemed perfectly natural that he should arrive that way and that his goal was to have a drink with me.

But while I was walking over to the window to let Gesar in, he slipped off the cornice somehow, and he was left dangling below the window, clinging on with his fingertips. I opened the window and tried to pull my boss in, but he was too heavy. I didn't even think about magic at all, as if there was no such thing. Then I went to get a rope to tie around Gesar so I could haul him into the apartment, but when I got back I saw my boss's gaping, frightened eyes and his fingers slipping off the ledge.

An instant later, following the laws of dreams, I was falling instead of Gesar, hurtling down past the wall of the high-rise building.

But even then I didn't feel any terror. I just looked into the windows curiously.

A woman putting on lipstick in a mirror. A beautiful woman, completely naked, apart from bright-red boots and a red bow tie.

Two elderly men playing cards. The cards were rather strange, with little colored pictures and text on them. On the table in front of the men, instead of cards, there were tiny creatures. Little monster-people in strange clothes with swords and knives—none of them more than four inches tall—jumping up and down and waving their arms, fighting and falling . . .

An elderly, cultured-looking man in professorial spectacles, feeding a swallow sitting on a kitchen chair with grasshoppers.

Two little girls sitting on the floor, swaying to and fro and swinging at each other moodily with dolls. The dolls were disheveled and so were the little girls. I thought they must be in pain and on the point of tears—but the children's expressions were determined and impassive.

A fat, bald man smoking a pipe, standing in front of a huge glass cabinet full of Karlsons. All different kinds of figures, in different colors and sizes and materials.

A teenage boy standing and talking to his mother. At one point he turned toward me and I saw that it was Egor, as he was the first time I met him.

After opening my eyes I lay there without moving for a while. I suppose I must have slept for two or three hours. A little bit more or less than that and I would still have felt short of sleep. But two or three hours was just the right amount of sleep to refresh my body and my mind. Not for long, unfortunately—only for half a day.

The room was dark, illuminated only by the feeble, glimmering colors of the television. There was a barely audible murmur of voices—Sveta and Nadya were watching something.

What strange things they are, our dreams!

Well, why would I dream of Gesar falling? Or of him climbing in through the window to have a drink with me?

And those strange people and events in the windows flying past me?

And young Egor?

Of course, if you try, you can find an explanation for everything. Gesar is trying to establish a normal human relationship with me, but things keep breaking down because of my weakness and reluctance to reach out to him in response.

The naked woman in the red boots and bow tie—that's banal, Freudian stuff. I want sex. With a dissolute stranger.

The men with the cards and the little monster-people . . . That's the Two-in-One, playing with us like puppets.

The professor feeding the swift with grasshoppers? That's . . . that's . . . well, let's say it's the futility of existence. He who is born to jump cannot fly. Except into someone else's stomach.

The little girls hitting each other—that's the Watches fighting.

The boy Egor is my guilt complex about him.

That only leaves unexplained the bald man with the pipe and the Karlsons. Well, we'll write that off as a joke of the subconscious.

For instance—it's a profoundly secret dream of mine to be bald, smoke a pipe, and collect Karlsons . . .

The television's murmuring was replaced by the lively music that plays over the credits. Then I heard a quiet woman's voice.

"A good film. My favorite film from my childhood."

"Only it's really, really ancient," Nadya replied skeptically. "It's not in 3-D."

"There wasn't any 3-D then," Svetlana said.

"But was there color? Or did they color it in afterward?"

"There was color," Svetlana said calmly. "And in those days children were better brought up and didn't try to show off by making cheap cracks in conversations with their parents."

"Oh, Mum . . . it was an honest question! That film we watched yesterday, about the children's camp, it was in black and white."

"Nadenka, don't ever think you're more cunning than your parents are. I was a little girl too, and I remember very well all the thoughts you have swarming around in your head right now. And believe me, not many of them are clever ones."

"Mum . . ."

"Why did you frighten your father and me like that?"

There was a brief pause.

"I . . . I did it for a joke."

"Well don't joke like that anymore. All right?"

"I'm at an awkward transitional age. I'm supposed to joke like that."

"You're only supposed to get covered in pimples. All the rest is optional. Surely you can understand that your father . . ."

I sighed noisily and stretched, then sat up on the bed.

My wife and daughter really were sitting in front of the television.

"Did I sleep for long?" I asked in fake alarm.

"Why, were you in a hurry to go somewhere?" Svetlana asked in surprise.

"No, but I'm cut off from everything here. Like you. What if Gesar's looking for me?"

Svetlana shook her head skeptically.

"Take it from me, Gesar would find a way to get through to you, no matter how cut off you might be. He would appear in your dreams if necessary."

"He would appear in my dreams," I echoed. "Aha."

I got up and went to the bathroom. I came out a minute later, drying my face with a towel.

Svetlana gave me a knowing look.

"Well, did he actually?"

"He appeared in my dreams," I confirmed. "I'll go and check right away. When should I come to visit you?"

"It's almost eight in the evening now," said Svetlana. "You'll come to us . . ."

She paused for a moment. Nadya and I glanced at each other. Svetlana didn't have moments of prescience all that often, but if they concerned family matters, her foresights were always unerringly accurate.

"You'll come to us at one in the afternoon," Svetlana said after her brief hesitation. Her face rapidly turned pale. "Yes. At one o'clock . . . in the afternoon. Tomorrow."

Svetlana and I had understood everything.

I would come the next day at one o'clock.

I would definitely come.

If I was still alive, of course.

But apparently that wasn't definite at all.

"Well, see you tomorrow," I said.

Sveta nodded and whispered with just her lips: "See you tomorrow."

" 'Bye, Dad!" Nadya called to me from in front of the television. "And I don't agree to spend the rest of my adolescence stuck in here!"

"All right, I'll bear that in mind," I called back, keeping my eyes fixed on Svetlana. "Shall I say hi to Kesha?"

"Oh, Dad!" my daughter said indignantly. "We've been through that already!"

"I'm serious."

"Then say hi, of course," Nadya answered warily.

I nodded to Svetlana.

"See you. I'll grab some potatoes tomorrow."

Sveta smiled. With an effort, but she smiled.

"And onions," she said.

"And even carrots," I promised. "Everything will be all right. I'm feeling great. Bursting with energy and ready for great deeds."

"That's because Mum and I pumped you full of Power," Nadya boasted. "I collected it and Mum poured it into you."

"Well, I've really got it made!" I exclaimed, opening the portal. "I even envy myself!"

I thought I heard the phone ring at the very moment I was stepping through the portal.

CHAPTER 5

AT NIGHT THE BUSINESS CENTER WAS AS WIDE AWAKE AS IT WAS in the daytime. The same kind of girls were sitting at the desk in the vestibule, I came across the same kind of security men along the way, and the same kind of inconspicuous Eastern-looking women in security service uniforms were washing the floors and scrubbing the panels of the walls.

"What an invigorating working atmosphere!" I said. "Eh?"

"You're really full of energy, I can see that," Olga muttered gruffly.

"Listen, you're the one who told me to take a rest!"

"I did," Olga admitted gloomily. "And I got a full-scale tongue-lashing for that from Gesar. Especially when he realized that he couldn't find you."

"Hidden better than anyone else," I said. "I'm proud of myself."

"Don't be. Gesar almost reached you. He said he could feel your dream. And if he had a few days, he would have gotten to you."

We walked into the elevator and I shook my head.

"That's bad. Very bad. So this . . . Double What's His Name . . ."

Olga snorted.

"Ah!" I said, slapping myself on the head. "The Two-in-One!"

"Oh yes, he's no weaker than Gesar is." Olga sighed. "But he doesn't know you, Sveta, and Nadya so well. It will be harder for those two to find them."

"You say that as if you're certain that they're not our friends and not our enemies, but something completely different."

"That's the way it is, Anton. The Twilight gutted them and filled them with something new. They're nothing but a facade."

"Then why not us? Why didn't Svetlana and I become the Twilight's instrument? Nadya wouldn't even have tried to resist, she wouldn't have understood what had happened."

As I said it, my blood ran cold. I imagined something pitiless, implacable, and irresistible erasing me and my personality. Or even worse, leaving it somewhere on the bottom of my soul, floundering and screaming in helpless horror. And then "I"—this gutted and altered "I"—go with an equally false Sveta to kill Nadezhda . . .

"There are rules for everything," Olga said. Her expression was severe and stubborn, as usual. "Apparently it can't do that."

"Why not?"

"Maybe it's beyond its power to embody itself in those it wants to kill. Maybe someone has to possess some particular feature in order to become the embodiment of the Twilight."

I nodded. She was probably right.

The elevator stopped and we walked out into a lobby. Straight toward the somber Day Watch security men—two battle magicians and a werewolf.

Apparently in order to save time, the werewolf was already in the form of an immense wolf.

"What if some casual passerby looks in?" I asked reproachfully, nodding at the wolf.

"We've got a permit for him," one of the magicians replied politely. "An Irish wolfhound, trained for security work."

"Although he actually failed the training course, couldn't understand it all." The other magician sighed.

The werewolf growled.

The magicians laughed.

Well, that's the way Dark Ones are.

Not very bright.

We were expected and no one even bothered to check our ID, fingerprints, auras, and the rest of it. Or rather, they probably did check them all, but not so that we would notice. Maybe it was in the elevator—it seemed to take a long time getting up here.

An Asian-looking girl magician (Japanese? Korean? Chinese?) led us from reception to Zabulon's office, opened the door, let us in, and stayed outside. She looked like a sweet, innocent girl, but I sensed that she was a Second-Level Battle Magician, and an old, experienced one at that, who had fought plenty of battles. I hadn't heard about her before. Zabulon had brought her in from somewhere far away.

"Anton," said the Great Dark One, smiling genially as he got up from behind his desk. "I'm so glad to see you! Olga! You're looking great!"

I looked around curiously.

While Zabulon had put his employees in a glass aquarium and chosen a somewhat calmer interior for the meeting room, he had kept his office in classical English style.

Wooden panels on the walls (with so many spells pumped into the wood that they were almost splitting apart from the Power trying to force its way out). The ceiling was also paneled in dark wood and old fabric wall covering. The furniture was very old, no doubt the work of some famous craftsman, but the only master craftsman I know is Chippendale, and only from the cartoon series.

The windows in the office were covered with sumptuous curtains of red velvet with tassels—probably the last thing you expect to find in a modern glass-and-metal business center.

Zabulon already had a visitor—a delightful, red-haired girl in severe round glasses. The girl was wearing a gray pantsuit that made her look like a businesswoman—but a very attractive and sexy businesswoman.

The only thing wrong was that this woman was over two hundred years old, and for two centuries of that time she had already been dead.

"Ekaterina," I said briefly, nodding to the Master of the vampires of Moscow.

"Anton," she replied, smiling with the corners of her lips. Then she frowned. She sniffed demonstratively, got up, and glided across (this word describes the process far more accurately than "walked over") to me.

"Careful now, my dear," Olga said in a voice as cold as ice.

"Don't treat me like a fool, Great One," Ekaterina replied without even looking at Olga. She leaned her head down to my neck and examined my skin closely for a few seconds.

"Have you seen everything?" I asked.

Ekaterina moved away from me to the desk and sat on the faded greenish-bronze leather of the desktop. There was total and absolute puzzlement in her eyes.

"Who?" she asked, and I imagined I heard envy and admiration in the voice of the Master of Vampires. "Who, Higher One?"

"It's not important," I replied. "Not important at all anymore."

"I see," Ekaterina said with a nod, keeping her eyes fixed on my neck. "But nonetheless, how . . . unusual."

I squinted at Zabulon. I still hadn't told the Dark One what had happened to his protégée. But the Great Magician's face remained impassive. Either he knew that the ancient vampire was dead, or he didn't give a damn. Or he was used to concealing any emotions.

"You don't like us," Ekaterina said with a note of sadness in her voice. "You don't respect us."

"Why do you say that? I've even had friends who were vampires," I replied.

"So I've heard," she said with a nod. "Only they all ended up the same way."

"We all end up the same way," I pointed out.

"Break!" Zabulon announced, clapping his hands. "I'd happily listen to your sparring, but we don't have that much time . . . how much do we have, by the way?"

Ekaterina raised her arm in an elegant movement and looked at something made of pink gold and diamonds running around her wrist that could just about have been mistaken for a watch.

"The gathering starts in ten hours. It's in New York, and all our important events are traditionally tied to midnight. If I'm going by plane, it's time I was on my way to the airport, Zabulon."

"I'll open a portal for both of you," the Dark One said.

"We still haven't agreed on 'both of us,'" said Ekaterina, glancing at me. "That wasn't simply taunting or sparring. All the vampires who have become involved with this young man have ended badly."

"It's your damned vampire god who tried to kill my family," I said. "I have a right to be annoyed."

Ekaterina snorted.

"I'm no supporter of old legends, wild gods, and ancient covenants. As far as I'm concerned, the Two-in-One can burn in hell. I'm happy with my"—she hesitated for a moment—"my afterlife. Beautiful young men, sweet blood, modern art. I haven't finished watching *Castle* yet, you know!"

Behind me Olga laughed quietly.

"Well, to stop the entire world going to hell, we have to choose a Master of Masters," I said.

"A Master of Masters," Ekaterina said with a frown.

"Yes," I confirmed. "A Master of Masters. We want to help with that."

"How?" the vampiress asked. "There'll be fifty of us Masters at the gathering. And let me tell you right away, I have no claims on the leading role. I couldn't handle it. But you know how our Master of Masters is chosen, don't you?"

"Yes, I do," I said.

"Then you understand that none of us are consumed with the desire to die . . . finally and completely."

"But then everyone will die," I said. "The people, the animals . . ."

"The little mousies, the birdies." Ekaterina snorted.

"You mean you don't believe it?"

"I believe it, Anton," said the vampiress, leaning forward slightly

219219

219219219

219219219219

and looking into my eyes. "These are our . . . fables. Our dark fables. We remember the god of Light and Darkness . . ."

"But if you're going to die anyway!"

"Even so, we want to live a few days longer," Ekaterina said with a smile. "And apart from that, misery loves company. Believe me, it's a lot easier to die, knowing that the whole world is dying with you."

"Seriously?" I asked.

The vampiress looked into my eyes, then looked away. And then she spoke in a peevish nagging voice, the illusion of youth had disappeared completely.

"Nothing will come of it. No one will agree. I can take you with me. The circumstances are exceptional, I'll find some explanation for my actions. But it won't get us anywhere!"

"Let's give it a try!" Olga said with a sudden note of warmth in her voice. "Come on, Katerina, keep your chin up!"

"Go to hell, you scheming . . ." The vampiress gestured with her hand and didn't finish what she was saying. "Everyone's flailing about, but it's pointless. Light One, I want three licenses."

"All right," Olga said calmly.

"A man about twenty-five years old, fit, pumped, and ripped," Ekaterina went on. "Only he mustn't use steroids; I'm careful with my health."

Zabulon looked at me curiously. I yawned and looked at Ekaterina.

"The second one. Make him a Caucasian type. Hot-blooded and young. Eighteen to twenty years old. And a boy too, fifteen or sixteen years old. Blond. He has to be a virgin."

Olga spoke again in the same calm voice.

"Do you have any other requests?"

"Well, you know my tastes," Ekaterina said with a shrug. "Except . . . make them all from the Central District; we haven't got much time."

"I know your tastes," Olga agreed.

She lowered her hand into her handbag and took out a bundle of forms. I think there were seven or eight of them. Olga separated out three and handed them to the vampiress.

"Agh, I was too modest!" Ekaterina sighed, watching the other sheets of paper disappear with a disappointed expression.

"As you quite rightly remarked, we don't have much time," Olga reminded her.

"Well, that's true," Ekaterina said with a nod. "Well then . . . see you soon."

"Eight hours from now, at this spot," Zabulon said in a quiet voice. "And bear in mind that if you're late, I'll drag you to New York myself, on time, but by a different route. One that you won't like at all."

"I won't be late," the vampiress said without looking back.

The door closed behind her. I looked around for a more comfortable chair and sat in the one that had been occupied by the vampiress.

"You've changed," Zabulon said, looking at me. "You've really changed."

I shrugged.

"I liked the old Gorodetsky more," Zabulon added. "So sincerely uncompromising."

"Oh come on," said Olga, sitting down and taking out a cigarette. "You liked him . . . Let's all burst into tears of tender emotion. Zabulon has fond feelings for Gorodetsky."

"Nonetheless, Anton, surely you were outraged by the vampire's behavior?" said Zabulon, continuing to probe. "She's going to kill two young men now. And then a boy as well!"

"I feel very sorry for the pure, organic beefcake, the passionate Caucasian, and the innocent blond boy," I said. "But in a few days all the beefcakes, Caucasians, and blond-haired boys in the world could die. And if the death of three innocents will save the world, then so be it."

"So you're no longer trying to solve the problem of a child's tears?" Zabulon asked merrily, slumping back in his chair. "So now you're looking at the problem of Omelas?"

"Stop talking gibberish, Dark One," Olga said in a tired voice. "Have you really been sniffing some kind of junk? You're garrulous and jittery, Dark One."

"Yes, Olga. I'm jittery and garrulous. I sense death ahead and I'm afraid. I don't want to die, Olga. So I'm keeping cheerful any way I can. And I haven't slept for two nights now. I close my eyes and see a void. It's waiting for me, Olga."

"The same thing's waiting for us," Olga replied. "Stop being hysterical. Let's think it through one more time. We only have one try."

"But why hasn't the wise Gesar come?" asked Zabulon, narrowing his eyes. "It's his idea—but we have to make it work?"

"He's at the Sabbath," Olga replied. "He's going to try to persuade the witches to choose a Great Grandmother."

"Oh! You took the risk of letting your husband go to a den of iniquity like that, full of lecherous old . . ." Zabulon began. He stopped and cleared his throat. "All right, I'll keep quiet."

"I'm here for Gesar. He told me everything he thought up," Olga said, after waiting for Zabulon to be quiet. "We have eight hours, right? I suggest working for four or five hours, then getting a bit of sleep. Can you come up with beds and a shower here?"

"I can come up with a Russian bathhouse and birch-twig brooms here," Zabulon replied peevishly.

He got up and turned toward the wall, and the wooden panels suddenly moved apart, revealing an immense plasma screen, a flip board, and a white board already covered with writing in felt-tip pen.

"So, forty-nine Masters will gather in New York . . ." Zabulon began.

"Get on with it," I said.

We really did work fruitfully for four hours without a break. I never thought I'd be able to say this, but working with Zabulon felt comfortable.

In some ways even more comfortable than working with Gesar.

They brought us tea and coffee, and once they brought sandwiches and a yogurt for Olga. Several times, when we needed to clarify some point, researchers and consultants appeared. The surprising thing was that most of them were human.

Of course, we had our own circle of human confidants. My old friend the polizei was by no means the only one. There were quite a few scientists, some of whom actually worked right there in the Night Watch office. As well as people in the government and in the security and military structures. Most of them couldn't reveal the facts—they were restrained by magic—but quite a lot of them worked on trust and collaborated with us out of ideological motives. Sometimes I think that if wolves and sheep were rational creatures, a significant percentage of the sheep would be found deliberately and voluntarily helping the wolves . . .

But in the Day Watch there were even more freelance humans. And if I read their reasons correctly, while some of them were also ideologically motivated, the majority was absolutely pragmatic. The nondescript little linguistic historian who gave us his advice after the first hour attracted surprisingly warm interest from Olga. I took a closer look—the philologist was sporting a masterfully executed lacework spell that attracted women to him. It was the work of a genuine master: It only worked on adults, and if the philologist failed to show any interest in a woman for several minutes, the effect completely disappeared. Otherwise the unfortunate ladies' man would have had all the women in the city trailing along behind him in a line several miles long.

It's the details that make magic complicated in the first instance. The classic example is King Midas, who turned everything he touched into gold. An example for children is Mickey Mouse as the sorcerer's apprentice, who tried to do the housekeeping by using magic. An example from folklore is the joke about the genie who grants three wishes and the family of a father, a mother, and a little son who dreams of having a hamster . . .

The simplest spells are the ones that have been in use for a very, very long time. They are formalized, precisely described, and constantly repeated. If we believe that it's the Twilight carrying out our wishes, responding to an order that is expressed through words or gestures or an impulse of the will (and I don't see any other alternative), then standard spells are routine work for the Twilight. It's just like someone pressing a key on a calculator and getting an answer. Of course, somewhere deep in the microcircuit invisible work is going on. Microcurrents scurry about, opening and closing p-n junctions, the calculator industriously plows through a mountain of information, and finally announces that two plus two equals four.

And everyone's happy.

But it's quite a different matter when someone wants something that a calculator, or even a supercomputer, simply hasn't been taught to do. Take the number X and multiply it by the number Z. If the result is greater than Y, add five to the result and print the answer. If the result is less than Y, draw a triangle on the screen.

Complicated?

Not at all, really. If you know even a tiny little bit of ancient Basic. We write the program and launch it . . .

It doesn't work.

We check the wiring, we check the power supply. We scratch our heads.

We drink a cup of coffee.

And then we catch on!

We write one more line: If the result is equal to Y, play the "Imperial March" from the film *Star Wars*.

There you go, now you can listen to the rousing, bravura music.

Spells are at the same time simpler (no need to know any programming languages, we "program" in normal human languages) and more difficult—because there are far more variants that have to be taken into account. And the consequences can be far more lamentable. Let's take the supersimple Fireball, for instance. If you don't set its size, point of appearance, speed and direction of movement, duration of stable existence, and parameters of stability precisely and unambiguously, you risk blowing yourself up.

Have you heard of ball lightning? That's what it is—fireballs created by novice Others, generally wild ones who haven't been tutored by anyone, who are full of enthusiasm and confidence in their own uniqueness. The Fireball has always been a popular spell, and in our age of fantasy and computer games, it's even more popular. So novice Others create Fireballs, forgetting to define exactly where they're supposed to arise.

And have you heard of spontaneous combustion? An ordinary person suddenly bursts into flames and is reduced to ashes! That's usually a Fireball too. Only in this case the Other imagined its point of appearance too near to himself. And he forgot to define its movement vectors and the duration of existence . . .

"Gorodetsky?"

I looked at Zabulon.

"Please favor us with your opinion," the Dark One said sarcastically. "You were absorbed in such profound and serious thoughts—what were they about, I wonder?"

"About the workings of the universe," I replied. "Zabulon, I think we've had enough repetition. We've planned everything. If it works, it works. Let's get a few hours' sleep."

"You're pumped right up to the gills with Power," Zabulon remarked casually. "You could go without sleep."

"I could. But I'd rather sleep for a while."

"Your wife?" Zabulon asked.

"My daughter. My wife channeled it."

"Take good care of her," Zabulon said with sudden seriousness. "Your daughter is unique—she's the only thing we have to put up against the Twilight. And apart from that, she's a remarkably intelligent and responsible girl for her age."

I cleared my throat in an attempt to conceal my confusion. Zabulon looked absolutely sincere and I couldn't see any ulterior motive in what he had said.

"I don't even know what to say, Dark One," I mumbled. "But you can be sure I'm taking good care of her."

*   *   *

They say that creating any portal, whether it's a hundred yards long or ten thousand miles long, requires the same amount of Power. I personally haven't created any portals yet; I don't have the skills for that, but I believe Nadya.

The difficulty with creating long-distance portals is making sure that they're accurate. No one wants to emerge into the subsoil deep below the surface of the road, or fall out of the air ten or twenty yards above the surface of the ground.

By the way, falling out of the air a hundred yards up is far less dangerous. Then you have time to put the brakes on with a spell. Magicians who don't have much experience quite often set up their portals to end high in the air.

The portal created by Zabulon was so precisely aligned to the surface that I didn't even feel change of level when I stepped into it. The only change was that my ears were blocked by the sudden difference in air pressure and my skin was instantly covered in sweat in response to the change in temperature, humidity, and all the other various factors that exist in nature.

After all, to be transported instantaneously from Moscow to New York isn't the most normal experience for the human body.

"I've always appreciated Zabulon's style," said Ekaterina. "He's set us down at the entrance to the Empire State Building. Right on Fifth Avenue!"

I nodded, gazing around. Zabulon's portal really was very fine. Not only was it perfectly aligned with the pavement, it was equipped with spells of invisibility and deterrence.

None of the people on the street saw us, but they all scrupulously walked around the small patch of ground where the portal had arisen. And although midnight was already approaching, there were lots and lots of people. New York, Manhattan, Fifth Avenue. No matter what you might think about the United States in general and this city in particular, it genuinely never sleeps.

There were people walking along, standing and staring at the building, talking on cell phones, smoking, speaking every possible language—my own ears, tormented by the Petrov, picked up English, French, German, Chinese, and Japanese speech. The air was cool, of course, but nothing to compare with our Russian winter. Around freezing, maybe . . .

"I haven't been here for a long time," Olga said pensively. "I remember when they'd just built it, the building was half empty, no one could afford to rent offices in it . . . They used to call it the Empty State Building then. Hey, Katerina, which way do we go?"

The vampiress looked around. She was exhilarated, agitated, and pink. Pumped full.

"Into the main entrance. It's very beautiful in there, by the way."

"The building's beautiful too," I agreed. "Somehow I thought the New York skyscrapers were uglier than this."

Olga laughed quietly.

"So this is your first time in New York? Don't worry, you're quite right, most of the skyscrapers are ugly. The Empire State is a rare exception, left over from an age when people put beauty above profit."

"And it is always bloodred like this?" I asked, looking up at the skyscraper receding into the sky.

The Empire State Building was lit up in dark maroon, illuminated richly and brightly—the bloody sheen even ran across the sidewalks, overlaying the bright colors of the advertisements.

"No, the lighting changes," said Olga. "According to events. Are your people responsible for this, Katerina?"

"Of course," the vampiress said contentedly. "When we gather for a coven, they light up the Empire State in the color of blood. The lodge used to meet in Oxford, but we moved here in the thirties. Where the power and the money are, where the night is alive, that's where we are."

"I'm not surprised," I growled.

The portal had already melted away and the effect of the spells was beginning to disperse. Most of the passersby walked around us, but a few people had almost crashed into me, and one barged gently into Olga, then apologized in embarrassment as he moved on.

"Don't you want to know how my fling went?" Ekaterina suddenly asked, looking at me intently. "What do you think, did I drink them dry? Or just amuse myself a bit and let them go?"

"It's all the same to me," I said.

"I drank one," the vampiress went on.

I sighed, reached out my hand, and set it on Ekaterina's shoulder. She peered at me delightedly and even leaned forward slightly.

Maybe she wanted to fight? Could she really be serious?

"Katerina," I said with feeling. "I couldn't care less how much of what you sucked out of whom. Did you drink the boy dry? Or the muscleman? Or the Caucasian? That's too bad, but it's your right, you were given the licenses. Now get on with your part of the bargain."

Ekaterina looked at me sullenly. Red glints twinkled on her glasses.

What would an Other need glasses for?

Especially a vampire?

Simply for show.

"I thought you had a serious psychological complex about us," said the Mistress of Vampires.

"I did. It passed," I replied curtly. "If you carry on jabbering and waffling, I'll catch a couple of your foster children and reduce them to dust. You know me, I'll find some reason. And if I can't, I'll invent one."

For a few moments we pitted gaze against gaze. I even got the impression that she was prepared to go for a duel of will—and that would be bad, very bad, because I would have to break her, and the other Masters would sense it . . .

But Ekaterina looked away.

"I won't provoke you anymore," she said. "Follow me. Don't talk. Try to let them take you for ordinary people."

Olga and I had concealed our auras earlier, and only Others like us, Higher Ones, could see through our disguise.

Naturally, there would be quite a lot of those among the Masters.

But they would also have to check us deliberately in order to discover our true nature.

"Who are we supposed to be here?" Olga asked as we moved toward the closest entrance of the Empire State Building.

"You're my lover," Ekaterina said. "And Anton is food."

"I thought it was the other way around," Olga said coolly.

"Anton has a fresh bite on his neck," Ekaterina explained. "Any Master will sense it. That's all right for a lover too, but you don't have any bites, and that's strange for food. I could . . ."

"Oh no," said Olga. "So I'm a lover, that's fine . . ."

I think Ekaterina even managed a gently mocking smile before Olga took her by the elbow, swung her around abruptly toward herself, and whispered in her face.

"Only bear in mind, you infant, that I was setting your kind on the stake before your great-grandmother had even been born. If you get abusive, your human lover will suddenly become your worst nightmare. Worse than Anton in a temper. Do you understand?"

Ekaterina nodded hastily.

"I know how vampires treat their human sexual partners," Olga explained with a glance at me. "Worse than their food. So, to avoid any unnecessary problems or bad feelings . . ."

"I understand," said Ekaterina.

Everyone goes out of their way to offend a vampire . . .

The vampire lodge had an abundance of human security guards. We walked through the foyer (luxurious) and took the elevator up to a floor somewhere in the eighties, then we were led through the corridors. Several times we walked up or down flights of stairs.

And all this time we were being passed from hand to hand by men and women in loose-fitting clothing, under which there was enough space for handguns and even machine guns. I didn't spot any magic on the people; they were evidently either mercenaries or were working for the promise of eternal life. Believe me, that's a very powerful stimulus—after all, only vampires and shape-shifters can pass on their abilities to anyone who wants them. As far as I was aware, intelligent vampires didn't break their promises and occasionally, for special services rendered, one of their human servants was accorded the dubious honor of becoming a living corpse. Their comrades had to know that their master wasn't lying. So that they would fight to the end for this great happiness.

Eventually, after yet another flight of stairs and another corridor, we came out into a small lobby with broad windows offering a view of Manhattan on one side and tall, double wooden doors on the other. The two black guards with machine guns standing by one of the doors didn't even think it necessary to conceal their weapons.

"Wait here, I have to arrange things," Ekaterina whispered, and walked quickly toward the door with the guards. They let her through without any questions, but they kept their eyes glued on us.

"Hey, bro!" I called cheerfully to one of the guards. "How you doin'?"

No reaction.

Slightly offended, I walked over to the other door, which was standing ajar, and glanced inside cautiously.

It was a spacious hall with numerous sofas, armchairs, and low tables set with bottles, plates, and warming trays heating food. People were wandering around the hall, talking, lounging on the sofas, and eating and drinking from the tables.

And there were quite a number of them. About fifty.

They were all different ages. I spotted a few handsome old men and several teenage boys and girls. The old men were watching CNN on a TV fixed to the wall; the teenagers were playing with game consoles of some kind.

But the general mass of them were twenty to twenty-five years old.

And all of them were beautiful or handsome, each in his or her own way. A tall, elegant black youth, a young girl in a white dress with her fair hair hanging loose, a statuesque woman with incredibly classical, regular facial features.

"What's in there?" Olga asked when I went back to her.

"The dining hall."

Olga looked at me for a few moments, then nodded.

"I see."

We didn't discuss anything else. We knew perfectly well that no vampire needed to feed every day. And certainly not on a live human being—in most cases packaged blood was enough for them.

Most vampires basically regard feeding as an intimate process and don't make a public display of it. At the very most, they make an exception for their clan.

But today there was a big gathering here. The global vampire lodge, represented by the most important Masters (currently there were forty-nine of those) simply had to arrange everything in what it regarded as appropriate style.

And that included the food. Most likely all the people gathered in the next hall were here voluntarily. Most likely they, like the security guards, had been promised that they would be turned into vampires—the beautiful, brilliant vampires eulogized by the deceitful books and the shameless movie industry.

And almost certainly no one would keep the promise that had been made to them. Licenses had been issued for them. They were food. The vampires could feed on them and let them go, or they could drink them dry.

"I wonder how Gesar's getting on." Olga sighed. "What do you think? Will he manage to sweet-talk the Grandmothers?"

"He could sweet-talk grandmothers," I said. "But those are witches."

Ekaterina came back to the lobby, but not alone. She was with a middle-aged blond woman. Or more precisely, with a vampiress whose age, naturally, I didn't know.

"It's not normal," the woman said after glancing at us.

"Greta, Vincello's sitting there in the hall with his own—"

"He was granted that right almost two centuries ago, and you know why," the woman snapped. "Katya, what you're asking is unreasonable."

"Everything has its price," replied the Mistress of the Vampires of Moscow. "What's yours? You're the marshal of this gathering, you can do anything."

The woman hesitated and glanced again at Olga and me. I suddenly thought that all the effort of masking our auras could come to nothing if Greta knew me by sight.

And she could. The vampires had heard about me.

"Have you got the belt with you?" the marshal suddenly asked, lowering her voice.

"Yes," Ekaterina said in an icy tone.

"That's my price."

Ekaterina glanced at us. Then she shook her head.

"No. You're out of your mind. That's completely out of the question."

"For ten years," said Greta.

"No."

"For a year."

What were they talking about? Yet again I regretted that somehow I managed to keep running into vampires all the time, but I knew so little about them. They were very secretive, of course, but a certain amount of information did exist . . .

"For a month," said Ekaterina.

"For three," Greta replied.

"Done."

The female vampires smiled at each other and embraced.

"Come through in two or three minutes," Greta said amiably. "Turn right straightaway and sit in the top row, so you won't stand out. And make sure your people sit quietly."

Greta walked away with that smooth vampire glide. The black security guards at the door stared straight ahead with stony faces. But what were they thinking as they guarded a gathering of vampires and saw the people destined for slaughter in the next hall? Did they feel glad that they wouldn't be touched? Were they dreaming of becoming immortal bloodsuckers?

Or were they not thinking of anything at all, which is most often the way of things.

"What kind of belt is that?" I asked in a low voice, moving closer to Ekaterina.

"None of your business," she replied, not looking at me.

"But really?"

"An artifact. An old magical object. A piece of scuffed pigskin with bronze clasps," the Mistress of Vampires replied reluctantly.

"And what does it give you?"

Ekaterina glanced at me and laughed.

"A sense of taste. Once a day it gives you a sense of taste and you can eat ordinary food. Eat it and taste it, like a human. It's only an illusion and you still need blood anyway. But you can eat it, and you won't have the taste of wet cotton wool in your mouth, but of strawberries and whipped cream, jamón with a slice of melon, pasta with Parmesan, buckwheat porridge with milk."

"Bloody steak," Olga added.

Ekaterina answered her perfectly seriously.

"Believe me, bloody steak is one thing we don't miss. But we could easily rip someone's throat out for a plate of semolina pudding with cherry jam."

"You should tell that to your . . . servants," I said, nodding toward the black enforcers. "So they wouldn't be so keen for promotion."

"They're warned, but they don't believe it," Ekaterina said dryly. "That's all now, let's go."

We followed her past the security guards.

The hall where the vampires were gathering looked like a university lecture theater—a semicircular amphitheater, rising up from a podium at the bottom. It could probably have accommodated a hundred or more people quite comfortably.

Or Others, of course.

We walked in through the upper entrance, beside the top row. We turned right and followed Ekaterina quickly in order to take our seats. The hall was in semidarkness; only the stage was brightly illuminated. There was a lectern with no one standing at it, but sitting at a small table beside the lectern were Greta, a handsome, youthful-looking individual, and a skinny, frail-looking old man. All vampires, naturally.

"Your attention for a moment, please," Greta announced.

Her voice was quiet, but the audience was already focused on business, and in any case vampires know how to speak so that you hear them, even if you don't want to.

"For worthy reasons," Greta continued, "Mistress Ekaterina of Moscow is accompanied by her attendants."

The audience looked around at us. But not all of them and only briefly. I was moving along beside the long bench with my head lowered, hoping that no one would get the idea of looking at the pitiful human being through the Twilight. Who was interested in me anyway? After all, we don't peek into the sandwich bag of the person sitting next to us on the commuter train . . .

They didn't look closely at me. And there were other humans in the auditorium apart from us. We reached the middle of the bench and sat down. I glanced around discreetly.

Delightful girls nestling against imposing-looking men. Handsome young men who couldn't take their eyes off their dead mistresses. Teenagers of both sexes—I had heard that in these cases it wasn't even a matter of perversion, but the strange urge felt by ancient vampires to create the illusion of a family for themselves. Vampires couldn't have children and, as far as I knew, for them sex had certain peculiarities. But some of them created surrogate families, adopting and raising children—basically leading some kind of simulacrum of a human life.

I remembered the mysterious "belt" that Ekaterina had loaned out for three months in order to get us into the session of the lodge. What a bad time they had of it, after all. How cold and joyless their life was!

Even though they were lucky, and didn't have to have semolina pudding with cherry jam. The vampires still showed no sign of getting started. They were clearly waiting for someone. I took out my earphones, leaned back on the bench, switched on the MP3 player, and it came up with "Picnic":

Nostradamus had his fill of pain and grief
And brought his visions forth into the light.
Had he but known that within easy reach
A world is hid that has no future time.

The world is but a hall of phantoms,
Learn to disappear.

Where, breathing in the gelid, peaceful air,
Time's serpent by the chains of sleep is bound
And cruel letters cannot be assembled into words
By the deliberate, unhasting hand.

The world is but a hall of phantoms,
Learn to disappear . . .

The door opened again and a slim little girl of about twelve walked in, wearing a checkered shirt that was one size larger than necessary, tattered jeans one size smaller than they should be, and with bare feet.

"Glad to see you, Ellie, but this is the third time we've had to wait just for you."

"Oh, I'm really sorry," Ellie replied in that sickly sweet teenage voice that drives adults into a frenzy. She sat down at the end of our bench and waved to Ekaterina, who nodded coldly. Ellie wasn't upset; she took a stick of gum out of her pocket, tossed it into her mouth, and started chewing. Pure swagger—she couldn't taste a thing . . .

It looked as if the underage vampire wasn't very popular around here—and she was used to that. I closed my eyes, remembering . . .

Aha. The Mistress of Stockholm. Yes indeed, an ancient and un-savory individual in a child's body.

"In my role as the marshal for today, I declare the meeting open," said Greta. "The Darkness, the Light, and the Twilight hear us."

"The Darkness, the Light, and the Twilight hear us . . ." all the Masters repeated in close chorus. Even the insolent "little girl," Ellie, who had already put her feet up on the long desktop and blown a bubble of gum, repeated it.

"By the Ancient Covenant, by the Ancient Law," Greta continued.

"By the Ancient Covenant, by the Ancient Law" the audience echoed.

"By Blood, Life, and Death," said Greta.

"By Blood, Life, and Death," the hall concluded.

Silence fell.

"Everyone knows the agenda," said Greta. "Since we are gathered here, I respectfully offer the floor first of all to Master Jack."

A black man got up out of the front row and walked toward the podium at a leisurely pace. He looked so much like the security guards at the door that I glanced in surprise at Olga. She shrugged, evidently having guessed what I was thinking.

But dammit, they didn't reproduce!

Then how . . .

Ah, but then, they might not be his children at all. They could be his great-great-great-grandchildren. His descendants from children conceived when he was still human. That was entirely possible.

"Brothers and sisters . . ." Master Jack began, spreading his arms out wide. He was wearing a sleek, imposing, snow-white suit. I could just imagine him in a normal human church, singing psalms or quoting the Bible. "I'm delighted to see you here! I've just called to mind a story that happened to a friend of mine in Texas, in the middle of the last century. He just happened to get all his teeth smashed out in a certain eatery down there! And they broke them out real good, so it would take more than a day to grow them back!

And then this acquaintance of his turned up at his place and said: 'Let's go to the dance, we'll pick up a few girls, have a dance and a good suck . . .'"

I sat there absolutely dumbstruck, with my jaw almost hanging open, listening to an ancient American vampire, addressing us in the finest traditions of Public Speaking for Beginners and telling us a vampire joke that was as old as smilodon shit.

The audience listened to this hoary, feeble, vulgar joke, which a final year schoolboy would have been embarrassed to laugh at. The audience laughed in chorus and applauded briefly.

Master Jack bowed.

I turned my eyes away in embarrassment. And I saw the little girl vampire blow a brownish-pink bubble of gum out of her mouth.

I realized that my world would never be the same again.

"Brothers and sisters," Master Jack continued. "We all know why we are gathered here. And none of us want to talk about it. But let's be quite frank. The Two-in-One has returned!"

A deathly silence—forgive the banal pun—fell in the hall. The vampires stopped breathing altogether and the humans seemed to hold their breath. At least I did.

"Were we expecting this?" asked Jack, moving out from behind the lectern and starting to walk to and fro. The attention of the audience had been won and now he started talking in all seriousness. "We realized that the equilibrium had been violated, that we had forgotten the ancient traditions and covenants . . ."

"If only a single bloodsucking rat had told someone about their rules and covenants . . ." Olga whispered in my ear. I gave her a grim look—vampires have very good hearing. But they were all absorbed in Jack's performance.

"And we all know that only one thing can stop the Two-in-One— the Sixth Watch. As it was of old. As it was at the beginning of our history, when the Twilight reached out to us with both hands, and we took hold of both and chose our paths."

I cursed to myself. Lilith, Ekaterina, the vampire who pretended to be Killoran and their entire kind . . .

They knew, after all. They knew something!

Not everything, but far more than they were telling!

The end of the world was nigh, and these puffed-up, self-important bloodsuckers were still hiding their secret. But who could have known that vampires, the very lowest of the Others, despised by Light Ones and Dark Ones alike, were really keepers of ancient knowledge? That they were actually the first Others?

But then, what was so surprising about it? The very simplest, the very "lowest" ought to be the first. Time had been needed for all the complex, subtle, specialized forms among Others to develop. The Twilight had needed to develop its self-awareness and its awareness of people. People had needed to learn to interact with the Twilight. To become Others entirely. To start working with Power at a subtle level.

But at the very beginning everything had been simple and clear.

Blood pouring out of a lacerated throat.

Life departing with it.

An increasing "magical temperature differential." The magical "temperature" falling in the dying man. Falling to zero. Like Nadya's. Or almost to zero . . .

And the absorption of this Power, flooding into the dying man—and immediately leaving him.

An inflow of Power.

An inflow of Blood, filled with Power.

And someone who drank that blood in their hunger, or in the fury of the victorious savage, had sensed it. And had managed to use it. To control it.

And then the Two-in-One came out to the campfires where the savages were holding their bloody funeral feast.

The Two-in-One concluded a covenant with them in the name of the Darkness, the Light, and the Twilight.

About what?

And for what purpose?

"Do you want to ask me if I'm willing to join the battle for the right to become the Master of Masters?" Jack pontificated. "Then I will answer: No, I am not willing. I am powerful, you know, I really, really am! But there are others more powerful than me."

He suddenly turned toward the old man sitting on the stage and bowed deeply. The little old man nodded benevolently

"If it was possible to simply hand over authority to someone," Jack exclaimed, reaching his hands up into the air. "If this was possible, I would hand it to Master Pyotr!"

A gentle murmur of approval ran through the auditorium. Apparently no one had any objections. All eyes were turned toward the old man sitting at the table. An expectant silence fell—and in that silence the bubble on the lips of the little girl vampire burst with a deafening pop.

Everyone turned toward the sound.

"Hey," said Ellie. "Sorry about that. I'm all for it! Master Pyotr, I'm for you!"

She waved to the little old man, smiling blithely (as monstrously inappropriate as that word sounds, applied to a child vampire). The old man waved back good-naturedly.

"My dear friends," he said in a quiet voice. "Thank you for these kind words; they are music to my ears, as they would be to anyone's. Thanks to you, Master Jack. And to you, my dear Greta. And to you, little Ellie, my sweetheart—thank you."

Pyotr spoke quietly. He smiled. And at the same time he radiated such an intense, sepulchral chill, such a mortally numbing aura of decay and deadly danger, that for a moment I caught my breath.

I wasn't the only one who sensed it. The handsome youth sitting between Pyotr and Greta squirmed. Until now he had seemed pleased to be on the stage, but now he really looked quite dejected.

"And thanks to you, Ekaterina," Pyotr suddenly said, looking up at the Mistress of Moscow. "Somehow today my glance keeps falling on you again and again."

If someone else's blood had not been pulsing through Ekaterina's veins, she would probably have turned white.

But in fact she gave a very dignified reply.

"I thank you, Master Pyotr. It is an honor for me."

The old man frowned, but he turned his eyes away from Ekaterina. He didn't look at us yet. We were not worthy of his glance.

"It is not permissible to hand on authority in that way, Master Jack," Pyotr said after a pause. "It is against the rules. And such authority would not be genuine authority. In order to acquire that authority, I have to drag a dozen of you down off the benches, knock you on the heads, and bite out your throats."

"With our consent," Ellie said in a quiet voice.

"Yes, little girl, with your consent," Pyotr agreed, nodding. "And I sense that will not be given. Of course, it is possible to be a little devious in one way or another."

The old vampire suddenly started giggling and nodding his head rapidly.

"What do you mean, Master Pyotr?" Greta asked nervously.

"It doesn't concern you, silly girl," Pyotr reassured her. "I could, I could . . . you could try to fight with me. And I could tear you to pieces. And become the Master of Masters."

The hall seemed to turn dark at his words. I felt the sudden tension in the vampires around me and a succession of odors surged past me: musk and ammonia, the sweet aroma of pheromones exuding from vampire skin and the sour stench of neurotoxin seeping out of fangs.

"Only I don't need that," said Pyotr. "And none of us need the Sixth Watch. And we won't fight against the Two-in-One, against him who gave us Power. If he decides to destroy the world, then he will destroy the world and that will be the end of us . . ."

His voice fell silent, as if the volume on a music player had been turned right down. Pyotr even lowered his head and stared at the table. Then he raised it abruptly and smiled cunningly.

"Only what I think is this, brothers and sisters. The Two-in-One has not come to punish us, the ones who have remained faithful. Oh no, not us! But those who have departed from the truth, from blood—it is their final hour that has arrived! It is the end of the Others! Of the Dark Ones and the Light Ones. The magicians and the enchantresses. They are finished, finished, finished. But we . . ."

He paused. The vampires listened. The vampires waited.

"But we shall remain," Pyotr said very confidently. "The herd will remain, and we shall remain to keep an eye on the herd. If the cattle are not slaughtered, there will be no order!"

He started chuckling.

And in response to his chuckling a wave of laughter from other vampires ran around the auditorium.

"As it was in the good old days!" Pyotr exclaimed. "With no humiliation, no documents! Choose a village or a town. Go there and feast. It will be that way again now, soon."

He's six hundred years old, I thought. That's really, really old. A really ancient beast. Eve/Lilith could laugh at six hundred years of life as a vampire. But I won't. It's a long time. Long enough to become powerful and terrible. Long enough to become the equal of a Higher Other in Power and to exceed him. Long enough to lose your mind, if you ever had one.

"He's very, very powerful," someone whispered in my left ear, and I caught a scent of strawberry. The little girl vampire screwed up her lips expressively. "And clever."

She slid back along the bench to her own place.

So.

There was at least one vampire who hadn't been fooled by my masquerade.

I started getting up and caught Ekaterina's frightened glance—yes, the Mistress of the vile nocturnal beasts of Moscow was genuinely frightened now.

"There's something I'd like to say to you, Master Pyotr, Mistress Greta, respected Masters," I said, squeezing past Ellie. Somehow I was sure that the little girl vampire wouldn't sink her teeth into the back of my neck. Not because she was a good girl, nothing like that.

She was simply more cunning and more intelligent than most of the others sitting in the hall.

"Then speak, since you wish to, Light One Anton Gorodetsky, Higher Other," Pyotr said with a smile. "You came to us uninvited, but we're not offended, are we now?"

Forty-nine vampires turned their eyes toward me. As well as a score of human minions: food, sexual partners, surrogate children . . .

Either our disguise had been really poor or the vampires had a much better intelligence and counterintelligence setup than we thought.

"Thank you, Master Pyotr," I said

"Not at all, Anton, not at all," the little old man said, and giggled. "How did he get in here, Greta? What was the pretext?"

"He was declared as food by Mistress Ekaterina," Greta replied

"And he didn't dispute it?" Pyotr asked.

"No."

"That's good," Pyotr said with a nod. And he fixed the gaze of his pale, unblinking eyes on me. "Let him speak. I enjoy talking to my food."

I walked all the way down to the lectern without speaking. Master Jack made no effort to move out from behind it. He stood there, dithering. This jolly vampire seemed genuinely confused and frightened.

Which was hardly surprising.

They did have a Master. A genuine Master—not formally confirmed in combat, but nonetheless genuine. Master Pyotr, who had spent decades lying in his tomb in Lvov, or so it had been thought, was perfectly hale and hearty. He simply hadn't stuck his nose out into the light, where he would have attracted the attention of the Watches.

And he was quite definitely not averse to drinking my blood. In a normal situation, he probably wouldn't have risked it. But now, on the verge of Armageddon, it was no problem. The old principle applied: "The war will cancel everything out."

"We are Others," I said, looking at the amphitheater looming up over me. At the vampires, both decrepit and youthful—and there really were both: some as ancient as the forgotten youth of humankind, some as youthful as the endless movement of passing time. "We are Others. We serve different forces. But in the Twilight there is no difference between the absence of Darkness and the absence of Light. The battle between us is capable of destroying the world . . ."

Pyotr laughed quietly.

"Drop that, Anton, drop it. The Great Treaty is not for us. We were here before it, and we shall be here after it. Are you trying to appeal to our sense of responsibility? Are you trying to remind us that we are a part of the world? We are a different world, Watchman. An eternal world, and not living mildew . . ."

"A dead world," I said, turning toward Pyotr. Everything had gone awry. My entire speech, invented by Gesar and polished to a high sheen by Zabulon. All the consultations with spies and analysts, all the phrases that should have hooked the Masters known to us—and persuaded them to launch into battle for the title of Master of Masters.

It was all down the tubes now.

"Dead," Pyotr agreed. "But only the dead is eternal. The living is doomed to become the dead, what lives is only fodder for eternity. We are eternal."

"No," I said. "Nothing dead is eternal. Mountains crumble to sand, deserts are flooded over, seas dry up. The dead are not eternal."

"Sand remains sand, water remains water," said Petya, shrugging his skinny little shoulders. "Where are the people who used to live on the slopes of the mountains and the shores of the sea? Not even their bones remain. Where are the languages that they used to speak? The wind has borne them away, not a trace remains."

"You are six hundred years old," I said. "Is that really so long?

Can you remember the mountains that have been worn away and the peoples who have disappeared? Lilith called you a mere suckling vampire."

To my surprise, Pyotr laughed.

"Lilith? Are you acquainted with the stupid, vain, naive Lilith? Ah . . . but of course." He threw his head back and sniffed in the air. "I see that she fed on you."

The vampire's eyes glinted.

"And how did she like you?"

"I don't know," I replied. "You can't ask ashes."

"Ah, that's bad," Pyotr said regretfully. "She was a funny little girl . . . once upon a time, very, very long ago. Yes, the very oldest Other—she was the very oldest Other. From human stock, naturally."

The features of his face slowly sharpened. The skin stretched and the bones showed through it. The forehead flattened out and crept backward. The brow ridges thrust forward. The nose became broader and larger and the cheekbones protruded. The chin almost disappeared, but the jaws moved out and grew larger. The sparse gray hair reddened—it didn't cover his bald spot properly, but a ragged bunch sprang up at the center of the crown of his head. The skin turned pale and chalky.

The body changed too. Pyotr's height didn't change—he remained short—but he seemed to be inflated somehow, becoming thickset and muscular.

"What kind of shit is this?" I said, taking a step back. Out of the corner of my eye I saw Master Jack backing away from the stage in total confusion, and Mistress Greta sitting there in a state of stupefaction entirely untypical of vampires. "Holy transcarpathian shit, you're a Neanderthal!"

"And what of it?" Pyotr asked coolly. "You all have our blood in you. There isn't a single person on earth whose line doesn't run back to us. And as long as the Earth keeps turning, our blood will never die out."

"I couldn't give a damn about your blood," I said. "You're more ancient than the mummies, Master Pyotr!"

"I am more ancient than human times," said the creature that only a moment earlier had looked like an old man, opening its jaws to reveal teeth too large to be human. If he was that well developed everywhere, I pitied the poor Cro-Magnon women who mated with the Neanderthals at the dawn of time . . . "No, I wasn't one of those who went out to meet the Two-in-One and concluded the Covenant of Blood, but even then I was already old enough and wise enough to keep a close eye on them . . ."

"Who are the members of the Sixth Watch?" I asked. "How can we drive away the Two-in-One? What agreements have the Others broken?"

Pyotr looked at me for a few seconds. Then he started laughing. Quietly, taking pleasure in it. He paused for a moment before asking me a question.

"Watchman, did you know that laughter is your invention? We didn't know how to laugh."

"How should I know?" I muttered.

"There were many things the hairless ones brought that I didn't like," said Pyotr. "But laughter is good. Laughter bonds and unites. The laughter of one is always the humiliation of another."

"Who says?" I asked, squinting at the hall. But they were all sitting there quietly. All looking at me and Pyotr. Hmmm. As the children's rhyme says: "and silence reigned, warmed by the breathing of the audience . . ." It was a pity that vampires' breath didn't warm anything.

"Just remember what you're laughing at," Pyotr replied with imperturbable confidence. "Laughter—if it's not physiological—is always humiliation. Humor is nothing more than the humiliation of one man by another. One man laughs at another when he is absurd and ridiculous, when he's in the wrong place at the wrong time. Charlie Chaplin is absurd with his cane and his flag at the head of a demonstration. Benny Hill is absurd in his role as a heroic lover.

Jim Carey is absurd when he brushes his teeth with a toilet brush. A lover hiding outside the window without his trousers is absurd, a husband who opens a closet, only to discover a lover, and believes that he's waiting for a bus, is absurd. I like human laughter, it's what distinguishes man from other cattle. It makes him worse than cattle. The Christian preachers sensed that there was evil in laughter—they were right not to bury comedians in their cemeteries."

"You've given me food for thought," I confessed after a moment. "But you're wrong. These are only specific instances. I'll find an example of a different laughter and different humor."

"What a shame you won't have time for that," said Pyotr. "Put it down to the humor of the situation, in which you're the one humiliated."

"Will you risk attacking a Light One? A Night Watchman?" I asked, stealing a quick glance at the other vampires. They weren't idiots, why would they want a war . . .

But if the Masters did want to object, they lacked the courage to do it.

"You called yourself food when you came in here," Pyotr replied. "The Inquisition will take our side. And anyway, in two days none of this will matter anymore . . ."

A long way behind me, right up beside the door, a bubble of gum burst with a loud pop. Pyotr looked up at the young vampiress with a stony stare.

"Oh, sorry, I won't do it again," Ellie jabbered. "It's rotten gum, and it caught on my fang, Uncle Pyotr!"

I wiggled my fingers, checking the spells that were hung on them. I had a whole heap of stuff in my arsenal, and at least one of the strikes ought to get through to the ancient monster.

But would I have enough time . . .

Pyotr gave me an ironic, stony stare and I realized that I wouldn't.

"Don't forget, I laid Lilith to rest."

He thought for a moment before he answered.

"I think you're lying. I think you had help. And that means . . ."

There was another pop from up by the door.

"Nothing to do with me!" Ellie exclaimed resentfully. "I'm not doing anything! I'm not saying a word and I'm not chewing!"

Pyotr breathed in noisily. He frowned.

And at last he got up from the table, flinging it aside. Greta and the handsome youth jumped up—vampires' reactions are fast, that can't be denied—and stepped out of the way.

Pyotr stood there, looking up at the door.

The door opened.

A black security guard staggered in slowly and unsteadily. He was holding his Uzi in one hand and pressing his other hand to his throat. He looked for Master Jack, spotted him, and tried to say something.

But his legs buckled and he fell, clattering down the steps, tumbling over and over and banging his head, but clinging stubbornly to his submachine gun.

The security guard landed right at my feet, with his head twisted to one side and almost separated from his body—his neck was sliced right across by a wound so deep it was amazing that he could have stayed standing at all.

One of the girls sitting in the hall sobbed convulsively. Her vampire master wrung her neck in a single movement—as if he had flapped his hand to drive away a fly.

Everyone looked at the door.

A slim, girlish figure appeared in the opening.

The one I had known as Helen Killoran walked into the auditorium, sucking on one bloody finger. She knocked on the door jamb with her left hand and took the finger out of her mouth.

"Knock, knock," she said.

She was a vampire. Now, when my brain wasn't clouded, I could see that quite clearly. And I could see that she was nothing like the Irishwoman who had once sorted out the mess in our archive. The illusions lay on her in layers, and beneath the illusions there was nonhuman flesh.

Unfortunately, I couldn't make out whose flesh it was.

"Who are you?" Pyotr asked.

Now it was absolutely clear that he was the most important one here.

"I'm a messenger," the vampiress replied.

Pyotr chewed on his lips. I sensed that he wanted to ask "From whom?" But he asked a different question.

"What do you want, messenger?"

"The Master of Masters," the vampiress replied. "And I think that's you."

I tensed up in anticipation.

"No," Pyotr replied. "I have no time for squabbling and brawling. Certainly, I do give advice to others and guide our young to the best of my ability. But I am not the Master of Masters and I have no intention of becoming him."

He was afraid!

This beast, who was older than human time itself, was afraid!

Maybe he could see something that I couldn't?

"That's very inconvenient and it will cost me extra time," the vampiress replied, strolling down the steps.

"There's nothing to be done about it," Pyotr replied coolly. "We have democracy here. No supreme rulers."

"It's a pity," the vampiress said. "A great pity that you didn't become the Master of Masters. It would have been simpler. And tidier. But perhaps I'll still take your blood anyway."

"If you can," said Pyotr.

"If I can," the vampiress agreed.

"That won't make you the Master of Masters!" Ellie suddenly shouted out from the back row.

"I know that, little girl," said the vampiress, nodding without looking around. "But I have a plan. I always have a backup plan. There was only one time I didn't."

She suddenly looked at me and spoke sadly.

"Sorry, Gorodetsky. You won't like this. But it has to be done."

There was something about those words. Something familiar . . .

"Yes, he really is completely out of place after all . . ." Pyotr said thoughtfully.

A moment later I went flying headfirst onto the bench in the third row. The vampires sitting there barely managed to dodge in time. In their place, I couldn't possibly have done that. Just as I failed to spot Pyotr's blow, which flung me dozens of yards through the air and smashed the stout wooden desktop with my head.

I was only saved by the defensive spells that were triggered—specifically by the Crystal Shield, a spell that young Others often disdain . . .

I clambered out of the heap of wreckage, feeling slightly stunned. The bench and the desktop had been reduced to planks of wood. That primeval bastard had ruined an antique—this auditorium must have been brought all the way from Oxford.

I got up, tugged a splinter out of my hand automatically, and stared in confusion at a teenage boy lying among the wreckage in a spreading pool of blood. The kid's body was shuddering in rapid convulsions; he was dying. His throat had been ripped out.

What was this . . . Had I caught him in passing? But I couldn't have.

The vampire with whom the teenager had come to the gathering was squatting down beside the body and gazing at it with a sadness that was obviously sincere. Then he heaved a deep sigh, lowered his head, and started lapping up the blood from the wound.

I felt sick. Perhaps for a vampire this was a perfectly natural and rational way to say farewell to someone who meant something to him.

But I wasn't a vampire.

I looked around, trying to gather my wits. There was a ringing sound in my ears and everything seemed slightly hazy somehow, out of focus.

But then, compared to what was going on around me, that was a minor detail.

All the humans who had been in the hall were dead. I saw mutilated bodies that only a moment ago were young, beautiful, and full
of life. In a mere few seconds they had all been killed—their throats
had been slashed open, their hearts had been ripped out, their arms
and legs had been torn off. Everything around me was awash with
blood. And the vampires were lapping up the blood as if they had
lost their wits, or bunching together in small groups, obviously ready
to fight anyone and everyone. To my amazement, I saw that one of
these groups involved Ekaterina, Ellie, and Olga.

The vampire beside me finished lapping up the teenage boy's
blood. He stroked the boy's head and cast an indifferent glance
at me . . .

And then he hurtled down onto the stage in a single bound.

There was a fight raging there. A whirling vortex of vampires, a
bundle of intertwined bodies and glinting fangs, with brief flashes
of arms and legs.

Pyotr wasn't involved in the fracas; he was standing a short distance away, gazing intently at the free-for-all. Greta and the handsome young guy had left the stage and made themselves scarce a
long time ago. Ah, but no . . . the handsome young guy suddenly
stood up in the center of the amphitheater, holding the body of a
young girl in his arms. He looked at her for a second, then gently set
her down and darted straight into the bloody battle like an arrow.

I suddenly understood what had happened.

Our mysterious ally among the vampires—if she could be called
an ally—was pursuing the position of Master of Masters. In the only
possible way that she could.

She had killed all the humans in the hall. And it was unlikely
that any of them were food. They were the vampires' lovers, male or
female, their surrogate children and their genuine descendants, their
great-great-grandchildren. People who were genuinely dear to the
bloodsuckers.

Yes, strange as that might sound, genuinely dear.

She had killed the people—and the vampires had rushed to

avenge them. And now, in this bloody, pitiless battle, she was earning herself the right to be a member of the Sixth Watch.

I jumped up on the desktop, ran along it to the aisle leading downward, jumped down, and walked toward the fighting vampires. I stopped when I caught Pyotr's expression.

We looked at each other over the tangle of fighting vampires.

Skirmishes started breaking out in the hall too, but they were short-lived and not fatal. Apparently, those who made no claim to the throne were taking advantage of the situation and trying to settle their scores with each other. But if anyone was killed, they were only isolated cases—the fights died down as instantaneously as they flared up.

And then the swirling melee on the stage started contracting. Fine gray ash started flying out of it in all directions. As the vampires, one by one, were reduced to dust, the battle only intensified even more. Perhaps because it was the weakest who had been killed first?

Pyotr's deep-set Neanderthal eyes bored into me malignly. Keeping my eyes fixed on him, I leaned down and took the automatic pistol out of the hands of the dead security guard. No one likes a hail of lead, not even vampires. And in this weapon the bullets easily could be enhanced with spells.

Pyotr bared his teeth balefully.

A vampire came flying out of the heap that had shrunk a lot at this stage—the same vampire who had lapped up blood beside me. He was clutching his head tight in both hands, as if he had a ferocious headache. Everyone in the hall went quiet, looking at him, but the fight—there were only two combatants still in it now—continued in total silence.

The vampire stared at me with insane eyes—and I saw that they were squinting in opposite directions. Then he took his hands away.

His head fell apart into two halves, as if it had been sliced through with a sword. He stood there for a moment while the monstrous processes of his body tried to heal even this wound.

Then the split head started smoking, giving off gray ash, and the vampire collapsed.

An instant later the final vampire still fighting the uninvited guest exploded and crumbled into dust.

The fake Killoran stood on the stage and looked around at the Masters. Apart from her torn clothes, she was uninjured, which wasn't really surprising for a vampire. Anything that doesn't kill them immediately heals very rapidly.

The vampiress reached out her clasped hand and opened it. Ash fell out of it in a thin trickle. Had she torn the heart out of that vampire, then? His main heart and his supplementary one?

"I assume authority over you, by the right of Blood and Power," the vampiress said. "Are there any who will dispute my word?"

I looked at Pyotr.

Come on now, my friend, I thought. *Come on, Ancient One. Dispute it. Somehow I have no doubt that you'll be torn to ribbons!*

Unfortunately, Pyotr had no doubt about that either.

"The Master of Masters has come," he said, bowing his head. "Word, Power and Blood . . ."

"The Master of Masters," all the vampires who were still alive repeated. I looked and found Jack, Greta, Ekaterina, and Ellie among them.

Olga was there too, of course. Staring intently at the fake Killoran.

"These people," the vampiress said, nodding toward me, "are my guests. Answer all their questions, give them every possible assistance, and do not harm them. Power and Blood."

"Power and Blood," the vampires echoed. I paid special attention to Pyotr—he repeated it too.

The old skunk certainly was a survivor!

"Wait!" I shouted to the new Mistress of Masters. "Answer me this . . ."

"I shall return when the hour comes, Anton," the vampiress re-

plied. "When the Others gather together. But in the meantime . . .
think. Decide what answer you will give."

"Then ask the question!" I shouted.

Killoran raised her eyebrows quizzically.

"Where will you stand when the hour comes? Among the six or
in front of the six? That's the question."

And she disappeared.

I wasn't trying to hide any longer. I looked through the Twilight
and tried to sense her, using every means that could.

There was nothing. There was no one. The vampiress had completely disappeared, but I couldn't see any traces left by a portal
either.

"I don't understand," said Olga, walking up to me. "I don't know
any ways to disappear like that, and I thought I knew everything."

Meanwhile the remnants of the vampires' forces—security guards,
human acolytes, and weak vampires—had all come running and
gathered in the hall.

"Who is going to answer my questions?" I asked.

"I can!" Ellie responded with the air of a diligent schoolgirl. "But
if you want the answers to more questions, then it's Pyotr."

I nodded to Pyotr, who was about to vanish into the crowd of
vampires.

"Hey, shaggy. Get over here!"

"As the guest of the Master of Masters wishes," Pyotr replied,
breaking into a broad smile. "Most willingly and with the greatest
of pleasure!"

"I never thought I'd say this; I'm generally in favor of preserving
endangered species," Olga said in disgust. "But it's probably a good
thing they died out."

PART THREE

MANDATORY MEASURES

CHAPTER 1

GESAR LOOKED TIRED AND SHORT OF SLEEP, AS DID I. TAKING part in a witches' Sabbath was probably just as stressful as visiting a vampires' convention.

"I asked Hena what the Neanderthals were like," Gesar growled, striding around his study. "He's probably the only Other we have who was around when they were."

"And what did he say?" I asked. The shape-shifter Inquisitor wasn't very talkative, but when he did speak, you could rely on what he said. He once told someone he had lived in a time before lies were invented.

"Hena said that basically they were almost like people," Gesar told me. "Only very large boned and very woolly. He used to cough up hairballs for weeks afterward."

"Hairballs?" I asked, puzzled.

"It's obvious you're not a cat lover, Anton," Olga sighed. "That's very enlightening, Gesar, but what about Pyotr? Did Hena know about him? And did Neanderthals often become Others anyway?"

"He didn't know about Pyotr. Neanderthals sometimes became vampires and shape-shifters, but he couldn't recall a single case of one becoming a magician. Hena believes their mode of thinking was very concrete. They could understand how Power was transmitted through blood or meat, but they couldn't control subtle energies."

I nodded. That sounded believable.

"But then they gradually became extinct," Gesar continued. "Most of them were eaten. Of course, they themselves had no objection to eating human flesh, like everyone else in those times. But first, they didn't have any magicians. And second, they were less aggressive."

"Then Pyotr isn't typically representative of his species," I said morosely. "He seemed aggressive and bloodthirsty to me. Although . . . when your evolutionary branch has been totally wiped out, literally gobbled up . . . that's not likely to fill you with the spirit of loving-kindness."

"Hena was reluctant to speak about the subject," said Gesar. "I think he feels very awkward. He was actively involved in thinning out the population of Neanderthals. Despite those hairballs. And I got the impression that he had Neanderthals in his family. Either his mother or his grandmother."

"It's like a Mexican soap opera," I said. "Maybe he and Pyotr are related? Maybe our transcarpathian friend is his daddy? We ought to introduce them."

"The usual thing," Olga snorted. "The best anticommunists were former Communist Party leaders. The most rabid anti-Semites are Jews, especially those of mixed blood. No, let's not get Hena and Pyotr together. Pyotr is a real piece of shit, but at least now we know all about him. But Hena might simply gobble him up, hair and all."

"Maybe that would be for the best?" Gesar suggested. He walked over to the window and looked out somberly into the courtyard. "What did Pyotr tell you? What do vampires know about the Two-in-One in general?"

"Unfortunately, pretty much what we already knew anyway. All the legends that we thought of as comforting vampire folklore are the absolute truth for them, no more to be doubted than the fact that the sun will rise in the morning. Vampires believe . . ." I thought for a moment and corrected myself. "Vampires *know* that they were the first Others. They learned to obtain Power by drinking the blood of their enemies. They learned to change themselves, change their bodies, and acquire new abilities. And the Two-in-

One came to them. The details of his appearance are debatable. Maybe two men walking beside each other, maybe Siamese twins. The vampires were told that henceforth they were the custodians of mankind."

"Oh really?" Gesar exclaimed, looking at me and raising his eyebrows. Then he stared out at the courtyard again.

"Yes, really. They were told that they were a special part of the human race, the best part. That they were being granted the right to kill people in order to feed themselves, since that gave them Power, but they had to follow some rules . . ." I cleared my throat. "Basically the same things that we demand from them now. Not to kill children or pregnant women, not to kill unnecessarily. The vampires accepted these conditions. As I understood it, there were some who didn't accept them, and the Two-in-One dealt with them very harshly and very persuasively. Yes, together with the right to feed on people, the vampires also inherited obligations. To protect the flock: against predators, against cataclysms, against epidemics. Against enemies who had not concluded a covenant with the Two-in-One."

"So basically, vampires aren't predators," said Olga. "They're shepherds. A shepherd eats the sheep, but he loves them, protects them against the wolves, tends the flock, and helps it multiply."

Gesar didn't say anything. And I knew why the Great One was so silent—all this sounded too much like the truth to question or argue with.

"And for many years, decades and centuries, there was a golden age on earth," I said sarcastically. "People lived in harmony with nature and themselves. The vampires held the top positions in the food chain and in the human hierarchy. Yes, everyone knew that the leader and, let's assume, the shaman, drank human blood. But so what? They didn't usually drink anyone to death. But they were always at the front in battle, and they could help out with their superhuman abilities. To be drunk completely dry, you had to make the leader really furious, or be captured by your enemies. I assume shape-shifters separated from the vampires at about this time, but

that didn't change the situation in any fundamental way. Big deal—
they didn't drink the blood, they devoured their victims completely:
six of one, half dozen of the other. This idyll continued for quite a
long time, until a couple of vampires violated the status quo."

"We could provisionally call them Adam and Eve," Olga said.

"Well, I don't know what apples they gorged themselves on," I
continued, "but they stopped drinking blood. Maybe they were the
first to learn how to work with power on a more subtle level? They
were still vampires, of course. Only they didn't suck blood; they
drank Power. Constantly, in background mode, so to speak. And
that certainly didn't limit their abilities. Perhaps at first they were
banished or, more likely, their entire tribe was banished by vampires
who were affronted by the breach of tradition. But their new abilities gave them an advantage. They started reproducing and multi-
plying. And people probably preferred the new order of things. No
one sucked blood, and if they sucked out Power—well an ordinary
person couldn't use it anyway . . ."

"And we have the feeling," said Olga, "that this was when the
Two-in-One made his second visit."

"We've been working hard," I boasted to Gesar.

"All these oral traditions are such a tangle, it's like a maze," Olga
complained. "All the Two-in-One's appearances are jumbled up together. But we think there were at least two. With a period of hundreds or even thousands of years between them."

"And the second one was a serious meeting at the highest level," I
said. "It was obviously attended by representatives of all the varieties
of Others who were organized then. Dark Magicians. Light Magicians. Witches—women's magic, which depends on artifacts and the
accumulation of energy, quickly separated off into a distinct variety.
And the vampires, of course, but they were no longer the most important group by then. I don't know about the shape-shifters—they
were probably yoked together with the vampires."

"There's not really any new information on that," Olga admitted.

"But the vampires know for certain about themselves, Light Ones, Dark Ones, and the witches."

"It sounds as though at this meeting there was serious friction between the negotiating parties," I said, chuckling. "The Two-in-One didn't like such a free interpretation of the initial agreement. But there was nothing he could do."

"We think there was an Absolute Other at that meeting," said Olga. "And the Two-in-One simply didn't want to risk a confrontation. We can say with reasonable confidence that the Two-in-One is another form of incarnation of the Twilight. Another type of stimulus response, let's say. The Tiger handles Prophets, since they mold a new reality and are most dangerous of all. The Two-in-One probably deals with large-scale, general problems . . . Anyway, he agreed to a new status quo and the appearance of Higher Others who didn't tear people to pieces or drink blood became a fait accompli."

"But it didn't all go off quite that simply," I added. "There was obviously some set of conditions under which the Two-in-One promised to return. For a bloody purge of the Others, let's say. And it looks like those conditions have come about."

"That's really bad," Gesar said with loathing. "This whole business is bad! Information that should have been preserved like the rarest of precious jewels was lost. No one in the Inquisition, with its bloated staff and its store of thousands of tons of manuscripts and artifacts, knows a single thing about the Two-in-One. The bungling oafs!"

"But you didn't know either, boss," I remarked. "Why blame anyone else, if you—"

"Of course I didn't know," Gesar agreed with surprising readiness. "And you, my young friend, do you know about the Dusty Granny? Or the Man-Candle? Or the Little Kizyak House?"

"The little what house?"

"Kizyak. Dried dung. If it's cow's dung, they call it *djepa* too, and if it's sheep's dung, they call it *kumalak*."

"I've never heard of it. It's something Eastern, right?" I muttered.

"Ah, but you should have heard of it. If that Granny hadn't been given a drink, the world would have come to an end. If that Man-Candle hadn't been put out, the world would have come to an end. If the right person hadn't entered that Little House . . ."

"The world would have come to an end," I sighed.

"No, but it would be filled with an appalling stench!"

"I get it," I confessed. "You had enough to deal with anyway."

"Precisely. You can criticize the territorial structure of the Watches as much as you like, but it's pretty flexible and it works. If we had some kind of central headquarters, it would be chaos; every emergency siren would go off there."

"Got it, got it, got it," I said with a nod. "Where's the Asian equivalent of the Inquisition? Beijing? Taipei? Tokyo?"

"Thimphu, you ignoramus. But unfortunately they don't have the information we need either. Or they were unable to dig it up out of their repositories."

"And in Africa and America?"

"There are no Inquisition centers in Africa, either of the Americas, the Antarctic, or the Arctic," said Gesar. "Although the North Americans will be establishing one in the next few years. There'll be problems with finding staff, of course, but they really want to do it."

Olga gestured in annoyance.

"Let them open three Inquisition centers for themselves. In North, Central, and South America! Those colonists, with their short history and inflated self-importance, all they ever dream of is outdoing old Mother Europe. How did things go with the witches, Gesar?"

"The Grandmothers fully appreciate the importance of what's going on," said Gesar. "But they're even worse off for information than the vampires are—they haven't got any information at all. But they believed everything we already know. They don't intend to try fishing in troubled waters and they're ready to do anything: provide any magical support, join the Sixth Watch, and even die in combat with the Two-in-One."

"At least there's some good news," Olga said with a nod.

"Not really. They said they're willing to help, but they can't."

"Why not?" Olga asked in a dry, businesslike voice.

"They want to discuss that at a meeting this evening. But only with a certain member of the Night Watch."

"But why?" I exclaimed, jumping to my feet. "What for? To what do I owe this honor?"

"You're way too photogenic," Gesar said mockingly. "Witches are always dreaming of feasting their eyes on a handsome youth . . . You mean you really don't understand what you owe it to?"

To my great regret, I did.

The cafeteria was empty.

I walked across to the serving counter and stared thoughtfully at the choice of salads. It was quiet, no one was rushing me, and the only sound was the clatter of cutlery in the kitchen: the staff was apparently taking advantage of the lack of customers to clean up.

Nowadays we work day and night. In the good old times dark deeds used to be committed by the light of the stars, not the sun, and the Night Watch went to work at night.

We still have the name, and a few customs and odd phrases that have endured (when a novice Night Watchman meets a Day Watchman during the night they still like to amuse themselves by asking: "What are you doing here? This isn't your shift!").

But of course we work around the clock. In shifts. Eight hours a day, with additional pay for overtime. With two days off. Saturday or Sunday shifts are accounted separately. With two periods of leave a year—a month in summer and two weeks in winter plus bank holidays, as well as a paid flight to a holiday destination of your choice. And health care (so that our healers won't have to treat every petty complaint like tooth decay and colds). Not to mention presents from the team on our birthdays and other significant dates.

If we had a trade union, it would be a very good trade union.

But we don't have a trade union, of course. We only mimic what the normal people do. Not consciously, but that's the way it turns out. In the olden days when people used to stay in their houses at night, with the doors and shutters locked, and only the town guards patrolled the streets warily, we would also live in wooden houses and gallop along the cobbled streets on our horses. When people built houses five stories high, dug out the first metro system, and invented a miraculous machine with a gas engine, we started wearing frock coats and neckties, strolling along the boulevards in the light of the newfangled gas lamps and searching for vampires in the cesspits of the big cities. When airplanes first took to the skies, and leather flying jackets and radios came into fashion, we also bought radios and started traveling between cities in planes, discussing the chances of class war among the shape-shifters. When paper books were transformed into electronic ones and "other" became an option for gender in questionnaires, we started using cell phones and tracking down vampires on the Internet, trading in shares, and researching the genome of witches.

We behave like people.

And not only because we disguise ourselves as them.

We Others haven't created anything different.

Perhaps we don't know how to create anything, except spells. And even our spells only work by the will of the Twilight. We're no more than qualified programmers who know how to set incredibly complex tasks for a supercomputer. The one who has the best connection to the Twilight, who formulates his request more precisely and more quickly, is the one who wins.

But otherwise we're surrounded by things that are human.

Offices. Clothes. Cell phones. Food. Movies. Roads. Music.

And the less material components of life too—behavior in relationships, the structure of organizations, moral principles, and work incentives.

When people set up neighborhood watches to patrol the street of their towns, our Watches appeared.

People set up their Inquisition—and we adapted the idea to our needs.

A benefits package for employees? We have all that too, including a staff cafeteria.

"You're looking a bit sad, Anton . . ."

I shook myself, realizing that I'd been standing in front of the salad counter for several minutes and the server, young Anya, was watching me with a smile. Anya was just over twenty and she had been studying at a catering college when one of us spotted that she was latent Other.

And after that something strange happened. Anya was told in the usual way how the world really worked and who she was, but she didn't accept initiation. She didn't refuse, as often happens with people of deep religious faith ("a wizard is cursed anyway, even if he does do good") or sometimes with members of the creative professions ("but what if I lose my gift for acting?").

Anya declared that she would like to take a look at the way Others lived. To figure out what we did and whether she wanted a life like that. And whom she felt closer to in general—the Light Ones or the Dark Ones.

It's important to make clear that she was a very positive, kind individual. She was an exemplary daughter, she'd been dating the same young man since she left school, and she worked as a volunteer in programs for the support of orphans, the protection of the natural environment, and the fight against Ebola in Africa.

Well, it all fit—she was clearly one of us. But surprisingly she took this stance: "I don't know, Light or Dark . . ."

Gesar handled Anya's case himself. He talked to her and tried to convince her. And then he took her to Zabulon, but he didn't manage to seduce the girl with the charms of the Dark side either. The result was that she had been working in our cafeteria for a year, but she intended to work with the Dark Ones for a while, and only then decide if she would become an Other, and if she did, which kind it would be.

I think that Gesar and Zabulon were both rather disconcerted by this rational approach. This was something new, coming from a human being.

"I've got a lot on my plate, Anya," I said with a smile. "And how are you, not made up your mind yet?"

"Not yet, Uncle Anton," the girl sighed.

"What's all this 'uncle' business?" I asked indignantly. "Why not call me granddad? You could be my daughter, of course, but for Others a laughable age difference like twenty-five years doesn't really count."

"It doesn't count anywhere anymore, Uncle Anton," she replied with a shy smile. "A daughter, a granddaughter, a lover . . . As long as it's a good person, then the age, the skin color, the sex—they're mere details."

"Hmmm," I said. "Anyway, make your mind up quick, and I'll initiate you myself. In person."

"Oh, Uncle Anton, it's such a great responsibility," Anya cried. "You! In person! I'm just a normal girl, really. I can't believe my luck."

"Enough of that," I said with a wave of my hand. "What salad would you recommend?"

"The Caesar," Anya said. "I made the right dressing and toasted the croutons myself. Not like in the restaurants—fling in some mayonnaise, tip the croutons out of the packet, slice up the chicken— and your Caesar salad's ready!"

"You've persuaded an old man," I said. "Give me a double portion of the salad and a bowl of soup. Any kind, you choose."

"The borscht turned out well today," Anya said as she served my salad. "And the pea soup is great, if there's any left . . . Just a moment, Granddad Anton!"

"Now that's really going too far," I growled as Anya walked away. I knew the girl made fun of everyone, including Gesar, and she needled each one of us on our own weak spot. Not maliciously of course; in fact it was even rather enjoyable to be treated like an individual and given this personal attention. And on the other hand, it also made it a bit clearer why Anya couldn't make up her mind if she was with the Light Ones or the Dark Ones.

I ought to advise Las to take a look at her. They might get along well . . .

I was still watching Anya walk away when my phone rang in my pocket. I took it out and saw there was no caller ID.

"Hello."

I heard my wife's alarmed voice.

"Anton, it's me, Svetlana. Come quickly!"

I didn't even think for a second, I simply opened the portal—demolishing part of the serving counter in the process. And I didn't even put the tray down, I just stepped forward, still holding it.

And stopped when I heard Nadya laughing.

My wife and daughter were sitting with their arms around each other, discussing something. The TV was switched off, the wall lamp was glowing gently, there were half-empty cups of tea and a plate of sandwiches on the low table in front of them. Everything was completely and absolutely peaceful and innocent. Well, not quite! There was also a tiny little glass standing in front of Svetlana. Cognac, judging from the color.

"I'm a moron," I said, and my wife and daughter turned around.

"Well look at that! Dad's brought the salad!" Still laughing, Nadya took the fork off the tray and picked up a bit of food. "Delicious!"

Svetlana looked at me in alarm.

"What is it? What's happened?" she asked.

"I came because you called me," I said. "You just called and ask me to come immediately in a very frightened-sounding voice."

"Mum didn't call!" said Nadya, telling me the obvious. Her smile still lingered.

"That's the problem, little one," I said. "That's the problem!"

"Keep calm," said Svetlana. "Nobody hitched a ride with you. Where did you open the portal from?"

"From our cafeteria," I said, nodding at the tray. "From the office."

"That's a safe place," said Svetlana, as if she were trying to convince herself. "Maybe it's Gesar being clever, trying to find out where we are?"

"If it's Gesar, he's not just being clever, he's being devious!" I said, annoyed. "Nadya, can you sense anything?"

But my daughter was already standing there with her arms flung out, peering into the Twilight. Every Other naturally develops their own individual stance to launch a particular spell. For instance, when I look hard into the Twilight, I lean forward slightly, pull my elbows in, lower my chin, and sort of glower from under my eyebrows. But Nadya does the opposite—she opens her arms, throws her head back, and closes her eyes.

"Nothing, Dad," she said, shaking herself and opening her eyes. "Everything . . . everything's blocked off. Everything's as usual. On all the levels."

Our refuge really was isolated on all levels of the Twilight. Only the portal, which had to be opened by one of us, could bring someone here. Of course, we couldn't see anything from the refuge either; the only thing Nadya could do was check that the defenses were intact.

"What could anyone tell from watching me teleport?" I asked. I picked up the glass of cognac off the table and drank it. Svetlana, feeling a bit calmer now, wagged her finger at me. "Someone tricked me. But what for? Just for a joke?"

"The most anyone could discover is the vector of displacement," said Nadya. "I've just realized that if you monitor all the levels of the Twilight simultaneously, you can determine the direction. Like a line, a shadow, across the surface of the earth."

Svetlana and I looked at Nadya.

"I couldn't watch all the levels like that," our daughter confessed. "And even if you figure out the direction, you still can't tell where to look next, what the distance is."

"But of course you can!" said Svetlana. "It's where the line runs into an invisible barrier in the Twilight. You just follow it until you bang your head against a wall. Smack! You can't see the wall, but you'll run right into it."

"And the barrier's impenetrable," Nadya sighed. "Stupid, right?"

"We're leaving," Svetlana said with a nod, getting up off the sofa. "Nadya, open a portal. To the Watch office."

"Which one?" our daughter asked briskly.

"It doesn't matter. Wherever's easier. Day Watch, Night Watch, that's not important right now!"

Nadya nodded. She wrinkled up her face, frowned, and smiled guiltily.

"It's not working. Everything's drifting . . . I can't take aim . . ."

I suddenly remembered I was still holding the tray in my hands.

"This is a tray from the Watch cafeteria," I said. "Can you pick up the trail?"

Svetlana looked at me indignantly and twirled her finger beside her temple.

"Are you talking to your daughter or a dog?"

But Nadya wasn't concerned about such subtle points. She took the tray and stared at it.

Objects preserve memories. About where and when they were made and about people they have belonged to. In this particular tray there was a memory of a factory that produced polyvinylchloride resin, and of the location of the cafeteria in the Watch building.

"Yes, that's easier," Nadya said delightedly. "Just a moment . . ."

She ran her palm across the tray, catching a drop of dressing that had fallen off the salad. She looked at her hand, frowned, took out a paper handkerchief, and wiped off the dressing. Then she put her hand back on the tray . . .

Looking at my daughter, I thought about how some things have to be learned. And how your genetic background, individual aptitudes, and unique abilities are no help at all in such cases.

You might find that everything in life comes easily. You might have the fingers of a Paganini, the looks of a Marlon Brando, add perfect pitch and a Stradivarius violin into the bargain. But show up late for your first solo concert at the Santori Hall in Tokyo or the Golden Hall in Vienna and the disappointed critics will vilify and revile you.

It's not because you're an idiot. It's because, for instance, you didn't build enough time into your plans for the traffic jams in Tokyo, or you didn't set your watch forward to Viennese time. The mistake will be petty, absurd, and disastrous.

When you're at war and the enemy is close at hand, you don't fiddle with tissues in your pocket. If the dirt on your fingers bothers you so much, if you really have to wipe your hand, you wipe it on your clothes. A few seconds can decide everything, or almost everything.

This is something you only learn from life.

I sensed the final moments that we had been granted to escape draining away. I couldn't even shout to make Nadya hurry—she needed to maintain her concentration. If she couldn't open the portal, then things were very, very bad indeed . . .

"Just a moment, Dad," Nadya whispered. "Just a moment . . ."

The air darkened, forming the aperture of a portal. I caught Svetlana's joyful glance and I felt really delighted myself.

And then the building was shaken by a heavy blow.

The TV pitched forward and fell off the table, the dishes started jangling in the cupboard, cracks ran across the walls. Nadya staggered and dropped the tray. The portal that had almost taken shape disappeared.

She cried out as if she was in pain and went limp—I caught her by the shoulders and froze, gazing around. Whatever was happening, it didn't seem like a magical attack. Or even like an earthquake—and anyway, what kind of earthquake could there be in St. Petersburg?

"Nadya, what's wrong with you?" asked Svetlana. My daughter started moving and straightened up awkwardly.

"They broke off the portal so abruptly I wasn't expecting it."

She seemed more bewildered than hurt. I tried to imagine what it was like to have your spell suddenly broken off like that. And I couldn't. I'd never had that experience.

"Let's go," I said.

We started moving toward the door—and then there was another blow.

A more powerful one.

The wall with the bricked-up window in it cracked and bulged inward like a blister. The air was filled with mortar and brick dust. Some of the bricks poked out into the room.

"Quickly!" I shouted.

It was a solid door, very strong, made of steel, with the old wooden one neatly attached to it on the outside. And two strong locks— CISA locks might be common in Russia, but the "Banham" would have confounded any burglar. And three bolt bars as well—not just little bolts, but bars running right across the door.

I opened both locks and pulled back one of the bolt bars, and then the third blow struck. This time the old bricks gave way and came flying into the room.

They were followed by a cast-iron wrecking ball—a huge lump of metal on a cable. It burst in and hung there in the middle of the room for a moment. Time seemed to stand still; I saw broken bricks frozen in midair (the mortar had taken such a strong grip that the bricks broke in half, instead of parting at the joints). The battered sphere had once been painted in cheerful blue and yellow tones, but now the paint had flaked away, exposing dirty-gray metal. It was bathed in surprisingly bright sunlight from the enclosed inner courtyard, and standing there in the courtyard, almost completely filling it, was a crane . . .

I could just make out two figures in the cabin.

I didn't waste any time thinking, just swung my hand and severed the cable on which the lump of iron was suspended. It worked. The ball started swinging back, but deprived of support, it slammed down into the floor, smashing halfway through it and blocking the hole in the wall. To add to the fun for our attackers, I flung a Sha'ab's

Ring over it—that's a spell from the arsenal of the Higher Dark Ones. Now it would be very, very difficult to get in through the hole.

If we hadn't been dealing with the Two-in-One, I would have said it was impossible.

I was encouraged by the fact that the vampire god hadn't yet tried to attack our magical defenses, but had set about breaking into the apartment by human means. His powers weren't unlimited after all.

"Anton!"

The door was already open—for the first time in many years—and I darted out into the stairwell after my wife and daughter. Just as I was pulling the door closed behind me, there was a sudden flash; a bright glow surged out through gap around the door and it was slammed hard against the frame.

The Two-in-One hadn't gone for anything fancy, but had just tossed a Fireball into the gap. If the apartment hadn't been an absolutely isolated "box," protected by magic, the entire stairwell would have been set ablaze.

"I left my handbag behind!" Svetlana shouted indignantly, without looking back as she ran down the steep steps. She was holding Nadya by the hand. I dashed after them, but the door of the next-door apartment opened in front of me so suddenly that I wouldn't have been surprised to see the smirking faces of the Two-in-One.

But instead it was an old lady, with a hooked nose, cataracts in her eyes, and long, tangled gray hair. At a witches' Sabbath or a convention of fantasy fiction fans, she would have been harangued mercilessly for sticking too closely to the traditional image of a witch.

But then the way the old woman was dressed would never have done as a costume for a role-playing convention. No one ever dresses up as a witch in bright-yellow Bermuda shorts down to the knees and a T-shirt bearing a picture of a cat waving its paw. I got the feeling that this granny had either robbed her great-grandson or gone gaga and imagined that she was a young girl again.

But despite everything—the frightening, senile appearance and the inappropriate clothes— she had an incredibly respectable, even aristocratic air about her. St. Petersburg is probably the only place where you'll see that, in the old buildings in the center, where the most stubborn apartment owners live, the ones who stood up against the bandits in the nineties and the nouveau riche in the aughts . . .

"Young man!" the old woman exclaimed in a surprisingly loud voice. "We don't slam doors around here!"

"I won't do it again," I promised as I ran by.

"Are you Vera Savvovna's grandnephew?"

"No," I shouted up from the next floor down.

"It's three years since you attended a Landlord's Future Cooperative meeting," the old woman shouted after me reproachfully.

But we were on the ground floor already.

We looked at each other for a few seconds, gathering ourselves. Then Svetlana nodded. I swung open the door and walked out of the hallway.

Or rather, out of the front entrance, as they say in St. Petersburg.

Svetlana maintained the shields as usual, and I prepared to attack, although the failure of my previous attempt didn't exactly fill me with confidence. But this time we had Nadya with us—an inexhaustible source of Power . . .

Only there weren't any enemies.

It was an ordinary street in St. Petersburg, covered in snow, enveloped in a light, frosty mist, but also bathed with sunlight for a change. It was incredibly beautiful—the high, clear sky, the blinding sunlight, the powdery snow swirling in the air. A tram went clanking past along its rails. A respectable four-door sedan followed it cautiously, the driver obviously wary of ice. The street was narrow here, with only two lanes, and even the tram line was one way.

"Something's not right," I said, shuddering from the cold. We could really have done with our coats; it was at least five degrees below freezing out in the street, and the air in St. Petersburg is very damp.

"No one's around," said Svetlana. "It looks like someone has set up a Sphere of Inattention here. Or something like that . . ."

"That's bad news," I said. "Let's go!"

I walked off the pavement into the road and raised my hand to stop the rather chic French family car that was struggling to force its way along the snowbound street. Some metropolitan capital this city was, with the snow still uncleared at midday!

The woman driving the car stared at me with obvious suspicion, swung the wheel to move away from me, and sped up.

"Stop her!" Svetlana exclaimed.

"She's got two children in the backseat," I protested.

But it was too late. My wife made an abrupt gesture, as if she was jerking on something invisible, and the car halted with a squeal of brakes.

"I've got a child here too," Svetlana declared, and ran toward the car.

The woman had obviously made an intuitive connection between us and her engine cutting out. She grabbed her cell phone and shouted something like: "Go away, I'm calling the police!"

But Svetlana had no intention of discussing anything. She opened the door, which was fortunately unlocked, and a moment later she had dragged the woman out from behind the wheel. To say the woman was dumbfounded would be a gross understatement. It would be fair to assume that this attractive young woman, pampered, well dressed with long legs, clearly wasn't used to situations like this.

But all credit to her, she got her bearings quickly.

"Give me the children!" she howled, "Give me the children, you bastards!"

Svetlana was already in the driver's seat. Nadya ran around the car and flopped into the seat beside her. In any other situation I would have been scandalized, but there was no time for that right now. I opened one of the rear doors: a boy and a girl, both about five years old, were sitting in their car seats. They were frightened, but at least they weren't bawling. They could have been twins.

"Out we get," I said cheerfully. "Mummy said you have to get out."

And at that moment a rain of fire descended upon the car.

We all know that comparisons are odious, but this really did look like rain made of fire. The drops appeared somewhere high up in the sky, then fell, almost invisible in the sunlight, until they plunged into the snow with a hiss. As if someone had tipped over a tank of gas up there and set it alight.

The Magician's Shield protected me from above as well as from the sides, but the shield was only two yards wide, and the rest of the street was already ablaze.

"Into the car," I shouted to the woman before doubling up in order to squeeze through and sit between the two children. Drops of fire drummed loudly on the shield above my head.

The woman dashed around the car, keeping her hands on the hood, as if to prevent it from moving, and sat beside Nadya. My daughter didn't try to argue, she just moved over. It was lucky that she and the woman were both thin.

"Let's move!" I shouted, but Svetlana had already stepped on the accelerator. The car jerked forward with a squeal—it seemed to move even before the engine cut in.

"Cover me!" Svetlana snapped over her shoulder. "Nadya, give your father backup!"

Defense had always been her job. But then, she hadn't coped the last time—so why not swap roles?

I summoned the Clear Gaze and the car around me turned colorless and blurred—its contours became vague and hard to focus on. The woman and the children froze, like dummies. The buildings towering above us were empty and abandoned. The sky glimmered dully, with the transparent belt of dust and asteroids that takes the place of the moon on the first level stretching out across it. My eyes felt cold—not from the cold of the weather, but from the icy chill of the Twilight.

Svetlana was less affected by the changes; her skin simply turned slightly paler and her hair took on an ash-gray tint. Nadya didn't change at all; her movements didn't even slow down like everyone else's do when you look at them from the Twilight. She turned around and nodded to me.

I looked deeper—the car changed shape, becoming something with a high roof, like a London cab, but semitransparent, as if it were made of glass. The sensation of cold grew even more intense, and it was joined by a feeling of pressure on my eyes—even just to look at, the second level of the Twilight wasn't the most comfortable of places. The world changed too. The buildings were rapidly transformed into cliffs. The colors faded away completely and everything was veiled in thick, gray fog.

But three moons suddenly appeared in the sky—a small white one, a large yellow one, and an absolutely tiny one, blazing bright crimson, with faintly visible fountains of lava.

The woman who owned the car disappeared completely and the spectral glow of auras quivered where the children were sitting. Oho, it looked like the little girl had Other potential . . . yes, and the boy had a glimmer of something too . . .

Nadya waved to me. She was as quick and lively as in the real world.

I started looking deeper. The cliffs morphed into gray hills that were covered with streams of monochrome mud. Everything finally turned completely flat and muted, with only occasional weak glimmers of color, hinting at the blueness of the sky, the yellowness of the sun, and the blackness of the earth. Then the process reversed itself, the colors started showing through again, until they became really vivid.

Just looking at the sixth level of the Twilight was hard work. But now I could feel the constant stream of Power flowing into me from my daughter.

"No," I said. "I don't see anyone!"

"What about the rain?" I heard Svetlana's voice ask from the place where she would have been sitting.

There wasn't any fiery rain either. It took me a moment to realize what that meant.

The Two-in-One wasn't attacking us with magic in its pure form. Maybe he wasn't sure that magic would work, or maybe there was some other reason. The rain of of fire falling on us was actual fiery rain—a suspension of gasoline or some other combustible substance that had been ignited in the air above our heads.

And he had destroyed our refuge in the same convoluted way, hadn't he—by transporting a demolition crane into a tiny enclosed courtyard.

What did that mean?

In the school he had fought us with magic and he was winning. You could say that he actually won. Only the vampiress had scared him off with a straightforward physical attack.

Maybe that was why he had changed his tactics?

Or had he decided that now, when the three of us were together, he might not have the advantage in a battle of magic?

But the most important question was: Where was the Two-in-One? He wasn't on any of the six levels of the Twilight.

But of course.

He was on the seventh level. In our world.

I canceled my Twilight vision and found myself back in the car. A frightened little boy was sitting in the seat on my right. A terrified little girl was sitting in the seat on my left.

"Stop the car, I'll get out and take the children," the young mother said quickly. "Take the car, take everything. Give me—"

"Don't you see what's happening?" I asked.

Strangely enough, she stopped talking and looked around.

The Renault—I'd finally figured out the car's make—was driving through fiery rain. From above we were protected by the shield, but as we moved along, the fire drifted against the windshield. Svetlana had even switched on the wipers, and they were sweeping off the drops of burning gas. In combination with the powdery snow, which glinted in the sunshine, this produced an enchanting, fairy-tale effect.

We overtook the tram that had rumbled past us earlier. Svetlana honked the horn to attract the driver's attention and, once she had passed the tram, she turned sharp right directly in front of it.

"What do you think you're doing?" I shouted as we darted past right under the nose of the lumbering heap of metal.

"Taking evasive action!" Svetlana replied.

"Can you see any pursuers?"

"No!"

The boy beside me suddenly broke into merry laughter. There's just no understanding children—they start bawling or laughing at the strangest of times.

"I'll have to customize your car a little bit," I told the woman. "Did you deliberately buy the model without a sunroof?"

"It's cheaper," the woman muttered. Her eyes were completely wild.

"We'll fix that right now," I said.

I raised my hand and pictured an invisible blade growing out of my fingers. Just a little bit of pure Power . . .

Then I traced out a circle above my head.

The woman started howling when I punched out a section of the roof with a single blow. The young boy cheered, "Hooray!"

I pulled myself up and stuck my head out through the hole, raising the Shield above me. The wind lashed at my face with all its might, but it was often worse on the second level of the Twilight.

We were driving along a different street, but there was still almost nobody around. Even though the weather was nice—for St. Petersburg. Even though we were almost in the center of the city. I thought I saw some people hurrying away from us in a small side street that we passed. The few cars that we encountered hurtled past us, gathering speed, and turned off at the first opportunity.

"They're somewhere nearby," I said. "They're keeping this lousy gas drizzle falling on us, and frightening the people away."

"Well at least they're doing that," Svetlana replied. "Forgive us in the name of all that's holy," she said to the woman, "but they're trying to kill us and we're hiding. There's no way we can stop right now and let you out. You can see what's going on."

"Yes," the woman replied. "Some kind of mystical nonsense . . . No, I don't want to know anything, I don't want to hear it. I've got children! Just let us out!"

"As soon as possible," said Svetlana.

"Fine, as soon as possible," the woman agreed meekly.

As I listened to this surreal dialogue I gazed around. The Two-in-One was nowhere to be seen. He wasn't chasing after the car, he wasn't running along the pavement beside it.

"Dad, check the roofs," my daughter suddenly said.

It wasn't the most beautiful or touristy area of St. Petersburg, but the buildings weren't new either. They were old, dating back at least to the early twentieth century. They were all of different heights, with a variety of weird and whimsical roofs—some were almost flat, some were steep, mansard roofs with dormer windows, and some had little towers and ornamental gables.

"No," I said. "They're not chasing us."

"That's not possible!" Svetlana exclaimed, making another sharp turn into a narrow side street. "They're here, they must be here!"

I agreed with that completely. The Two-in-One was somewhere close by. But he wasn't chasing us.

Was he moving ahead of us, luring us on somewhere?

Was he influencing Svetlana, making her follow the right direction?

That was possible too.

Anything was possible, but if you discarded the improbable, the answer was obvious.

I dived back into the car and rubbed my finger over the leather surface under one of the child seats with my finger. I smiled at the boy, who was following my actions closely.

And then I flung out my arms—the doors flew open and my little neighbors went flying out of the car, together with their seats.

The side street we were driving along really was very, very narrow and both seats slammed into the walls of the buildings.

"Dad!" Nadya yelled in horror.

Svetlana braked sharply and stared blankly at me.

I looked at the woman. She was frowning and rubbing her forehead with two fingers. It didn't look at all like the behavior of a mother whose two children have just been thrown out of a moving car.

"The car's not new, and neither are the child seats," I said. "But there aren't any marks from the seats on the leather; they've only just been put in. Step on it!"

Svetlana shook her head, looking in horror from me to the scene behind us and back. I looked back too—the seats were lying in the snow and a red patch was spreading out beside one of them.

"Anton . . . Anton, I think you made a mistake," Svetlana said in a quiet voice.

"No I didn't," I said stubbornly. "Are those your children?" I asked the woman.

The woman's chin dropped and she slumped onto the dashboard.

"She's passed out!" Svetlana exclaimed.

"It's the shock of the control being broken off!" I replied. "She's a puppet! They were controlling her!"

"Who?" Svetlana shouted.

"Those . . . children!" I said with a nod toward the car seats in the road. "It's them, the Two-in-One!"

Svetlana killed the engine.

"I can't leave it like this! I've got to check!"

"The fiery rain has stopped," Nadya said pensively.

"The gas could just have run out," said Svetlana, getting out of the car. "I'll check . . ."

"Stop!" I shouted, jumping out after her and grabbing her hand.

We stood beside the car that blocked off the entire side street. On either side of the road lay two child seats, with a motionless little arm protruding from one of them.

"You killed those children," Svetlana said in a low voice. "You . . ."

I raised my hand and a wave of Power surged down the street. Crude, untargeted energy. The very simplest spell, the Press.

And the most important thing was that it could only be stopped by the same simple method. By a discharge of pure Power.

Svetlana looked at me, biting on her lip. I could tell that she didn't believe me. That she desperately wanted to stop the Press and go dashing to those child seats, to see how the children were, to try to help them . . .

She didn't believe me.

But she waited.

The Press crept along the side street in a hazy, murky tidal wave—it's quite a sluggish spell, not too spectacular. The snow it had passed over was left shiny and glittering, polished to mirror smoothness. Flattened beer cans lay here and there, looking like line drawings. After a slight crunch, the two-dimensional projection of a trash can appeared on the surface of the pavement, pressed down into the asphalt.

I thought in an abstract kind of way that if I really had made a mistake, in a moment the street would look like a horror movie. And this was my last chance to stop the Press.

But I realized that I wasn't going to stop it.

And at the very second when the Press was about to grind down the seats and the children's bodies, a vague form suddenly shot up in front of the wave of Power, changing its shape and dimensions as it rose. There was a sudden, opposing impulse of Power—and my spell disappeared.

And so did the seats with the children in them. Standing in their place were the Light Magician Denis and the Dark Magician Alexei.

Or would it be more correct to say their shells?

"How did you guess?" Denis asked. His voice was the same as it always used to be. He used to say "Hello Anton" to me in exactly the same tone at the office. He was a polite young man, but he preferred to address everyone by their first name.

"From a whole set of things!" I shouted.

I could see my breath in the cold, puffs of vapor Nothing came out of Denis's mouth.

"Denis, if you can hear me," I said. "If you're still alive somewhere inside there . . . try to resist! It's the Twilight. It's another of its manifestations. You can fight it . . ."

Denis laughed.

"Gorodetsky, you're acting as if an evil magician had deprived me of my will. That's not the way it is at all, Gorodetsky. I let him in myself."

He turned to Alexei, who stepped off the pavement into the road. The two magicians took each other by the hand.

"Now we are united in a single whole!" Alexei added.

It was clear enough. The usual verbal diarrhea of someone possessed: "I let *this* in myself!" "Now I'm stronger and wiser, and I don't sweat!" "When I allowed the Dark One to think for me, the world became simple and clear!"

"I'm so glad, Anton," said Svetlana, taking me by the hand. "I'm so glad that you were right!"

Now there was a ludicrous kind of parallel between the Two-in-One and the two of us, with both pairs holding hands.

Except that our daughter was standing behind us, and she promptly repeated Denis's question.

"But, Dad, how did you really guess?"

"It's all very simple, little daughter. They didn't look at their Mum even once. A genuine magician may be fascinating for a child, but Mum's even more important than that."

Nadya laughed.

We stood there looking at each other, waiting to see who would make the first move. Making the first move isn't always a winning strategy.

"Do we have any grounds for compromise?" Svetlana suddenly asked. "Any possibility of negotiations? After all, there was a time, Two-in-One, when you used to deal with Others without dashing straight into combat."

Denis and Alexei shook their heads simultaneously.

"Compromises are made with the strong," Denis replied.

"And that's not you," Alexei added.

"But you're dragging things out," I said. "Maybe we're not so very weak after all. Maybe we'll lose, but what if we manage to kill one of you in the process? How would you like being the One-in-One?"

Alexei opened his mouth as if he was about to say something . . . But he didn't. He and Denis swung around in a strange way—their entwined arms swiveled unnaturally at the shoulder—and the former Light One and Dark One walked away along the narrow street.

"Looks like I gave them something to think about," I said. "Or him. Which is right? Christ, I had no idea I was so eloquent."

I turned around.

The Tiger was standing beside Nadya, holding a paper cup of coffee and sipping it through a straw.

"Hello, Anton," he said. "Hello, Svetlana. Yes, I probably put them off. Sorry if I interfered, today really is a splendid day to die."

CHAPTER 2

THE COFFEE BAR WAS SMALL AND HOT, THE TINY LITTLE tables were packed close together, and the lamps on them had plush red shades. As well as coffee the place served cognac and whisky, canapés, and tiny little cakes. It was a pretty niche venue, a place where you could sit for a while with a good coffee and eat something strictly symbolic.

And the coffee here really was good; there were varieties from at least a dozen different places—Nicaragua, Brazil, Kenya, Cuba, Costa Rica . . .

"Do you like this place?" I asked the Tiger.

He nodded and took a drag on his cigarette.

"Yes."

"I feel guilty," I said. "Didn't you pick up that terrible habit from me?"

"Yes, I did," the Tiger agreed. "And the coffee too."

I wrinkled up my brow, remembering.

"I wasn't drinking coffee then."

"Not right then. But you were thinking how much you would like a cup of coffee . . ."

"Dealing with you gods is hard work," I said with a forced laugh. I looked at my daughter, who seemed to be the calmest of all of us. She looked completely at home in this coffee shop, where the crowd mostly consisted of young people between fifteen and thirty. I noticed that almost no one here was drinking alcohol, only coffee. It was strange, the way one generation differed from another. The old ways disappeared, and the old myths went with them . . . Not many people outside our country knew that modern-day Russia no longer guzzled vodka at the slightest possible excuse. There was no one smoking in the coffee bar either—except the Tiger of course.

"Like one?" the Tiger asked.

"It's against the law here to smoke in public buildings," I replied gloomily. "We're civilized people and this is the twenty-first century."

"Here," said the Tiger, handing me the pack. "No one will notice that you're smoking. And the smoke won't harm anyone. Not even you. And they'll be the most delicious cigarettes you've ever smoked."

"You should work in the tobacco business," I murmured, taking the pack. I'd never seen one like it before—the cigarettes were called Twilight. The nicotine content was shown as zero and the tar content was -0.6.

"They clean out your lungs as you smoke them," said the Tiger. "A good marketing idea?"

"I think you've become dangerously humanized," I remarked as I opened the pack. "And I don't mean the coffee and the cigarettes, I mean your sense of humor."

"That's your fault too," the Tiger told me.

"How come? I'm not funny at all, except maybe when I fall face-down in the salad."

"Yes, you're as serious as a tombstone," the Tiger admitted. "You reduced that situation to a stalemate. I couldn't kill the boy-Prophet. But there was still a risk that the prophecy would be proclaimed. So I was obliged to remain here, among people, indefinitely, until Innokentii Tolkov dies, and preferably until you, your wife, and your daughter die too."

"Well thanks for being so candid," Svetlana sighed.

"I abandoned the idea of accelerating the process," the Tiger said resentfully. "I had to wait for the natural course of events. But that meant I had to stay here. Indefinitely."

"And you started living a human life," I said, taking out a cigarette and sniffing it. It smelled of tobacco. A pleasant smell, to the nostrils of a smoker. No, I wasn't going to break the law by smoking in a coffee shop! I regretfully jammed the cigarette back into the pack. "Let me guess . . . you have an apartment?"

"Not just one, I have homes in several different cities," the Tiger replied. "You should see my bungalow in the Dominican Republic!"

"And you probably have a girlfriend too?" I said. "And maybe not just one?"

The Tiger smiled modestly.

"The mind boggles," I said. "And then the children will be born with superpowers."

"No, no," the Tiger replied hastily. "That's a very serious step, I'm not ready for that yet."

"So were you incarnated in a human being then?" I asked, lowering my voice for some reason.

"I don't understand," the Tiger said with a frown.

"He means the Twilight," said Nadya. "Right, Dad?"

I nodded.

"I am not the Twilight," the Tiger said with a sigh of annoyance. "The Twilight doesn't have . . ." He pondered for a moment. "A personality? A mind in the human sense? An incarnation? Essentially, I'm a certain part of it. A functional organism. Or mechanism. I exist in my own right."

"That's what you've become," I remarked. "You've been corrupted by human life. With all its little joys."

The Tiger nodded.

"Well, good. I've got nothing at all against that. You don't go around killing poor Prophets left and right—and that's just great! So tell me, who is the Two-in-One?"

"I don't have any more information than you do," said the Tiger, slightly offended. "Another part of the Twilight."

"That is, part of you?" Sveta asked.

"Of the Twilight!" the Tiger replied insistently. "Does your left hand know what your right hand is doing?"

"My head does," Svetlana told him.

"Unfortunately, I'm not the head," said the Tiger, taking a sip of coffee. "I had a mission. I came to this world to carry it out . . ."

"And in between visits?" Nadya asked.

"I didn't have any 'in between.'" The Tiger laughed. "And I stayed here. I've been thinking things over. And I realized I don't like the Two-in-One."

"Why not?"

"First, because if he kills you, I'll have to go back," the Tiger said irritably. "And I happen to be waiting for the next *Star Wars* to be released."

"If only Lucas could hear that," Nadya exclaimed in delight.

"Second, I don't like the very little that I do know about the Two-in-One," the Tiger went on. "If he thinks that the Covenant of the Twilight has been violated, then he has no other option but to exterminate all the Others. And the disappearance of the Others will result in the death of all life on the planet."

"Why?" I asked.

The Tiger shrugged.

"I only know the result. And I don't like it. Perhaps the Two-in-One doesn't care if he's left on a lifeless planet. Perhaps the Twilight doesn't care . . . or it isn't aware of what's happening. But I'm against it."

"What a stroke of luck for us that you've been humanized." I chuckled. "Tell me, can you stop him?"

"The ancient god of Light and Darkness? The vampire god? Who has appeared in the world to stage the apocalypse?" The Tiger shook his head. "No chance."

"But he walked away today!"

"Perhaps because I appeared so unexpectedly," the Tiger suggested. "Or perhaps because the prophecy says 'three victims the fourth time.' How many times has he tried to kill you so far?"

"Once," I replied gloomily.

"Now it's twice. I'm pretty sure that when he attacks the third time, he'll back off again. Perhaps he'll justify his retreat to himself by some weighty considerations of logic, but the real reason is different. Whether he's knows it or not, the Two-in-One is following the prophecy. The first and second times he withdrew when a new opponent appeared. He'll find a reason to withdraw one more time . . ."

"And the fourth time he'll kill us."

"If you don't kill him," the Tiger said with a nod. "Nadezhda Antonovna is an Absolute Enchantress. Her Power is unlimited. But as you know perfectly well, skill is required to use Power properly. So if there's a duel, my money would be on the Two-in-One."

"But what about the Sixth Watch?"

The Tiger thought about that.

"Would it be stronger than the Two-in-One?" I asked.

"The Sixth Watch would be the right opponent," the Tiger said eventually. "Thousands of years ago, six Others concluded some kind of agreement with the Twilight in the person of the Two-in-One. Now the agreement has been violated, and the Two-in-One has been incarnated to punish all the Others as renegades. But if the Sixth Watch is resurrected, a dialogue will probably be possible. The Treaty could be renewed, mistakes could be put right, and so on."

"But you don't know what the Treaty was, what the mistakes were, what the Sixth Watch was?"

"I told you, no!" the Tiger replied peevishly. "I'm on your side. I'm for the Others and the people, because I like being an Other-person. And I'm ready to help, but don't expect answers to any of your questions. I don't have them."

"But can you guess at any?" Svetlana asked. "After all, you're closest of all to the Twilight."

The Tiger laughed.

"Yes, I can guess . . . the Sixth Watch wasn't forgotten immediately, right? You found out about the occasion when it discussed collaboration with the human Inquisition. Why?"

"Why did it reject the idea?" I said.

"No, not that! Why did it discuss the question at all? Why did it even exist, if the Two-in-One hadn't appeared for hundreds or thousands of years?" the Tiger replied.

"The Sixth Watch was the most ancient of all our Night and Day Watches," I said morosely. "At the dawn of time the Two-in-One appeared to the Cro-Magnons and the Neanderthals. And they decided something. Let's assume they discussed things without any formal structure, at the shaman level . . . Some kind of group got together and they decided something. And then the Two-in-One showed up again a lot later, when he had some grievances to settle. Civilization already existed, with its ancient cities . . ."

"Ur, Shang, Egypt, Atlantis," the Tiger said without a trace of irony.

"Our Watches didn't exist yet," I said, thinking out loud. "But some kind of Sixth Watch was chosen for the meeting with him. Were they the same Others who gathered at the dawn of time? Or their successors? And why Sixth?"

"More likely it was called The Watch of Six," the Tiger suggested. "Or The Six Watchmen. Something like that."

"What you could call 'the six supervisors' in Russian thieves' jargon," Svetlana said wryly.

"You could put it like that," I said, watching as the Tiger pensively blew smoke out of his mouth. I gave in and took a cigarette from the pack. As I lit it I caressed it with my finger.

"You poser," Svetlana said derisively.

"You could put it like that," I repeated, taking a drag.

The cigarette really did taste superb—if you can say that about poison.

"The question is, why did the Sixth Watch disappear?" Nadya

said. "At the beginning, the Two-in-One came to the vampires and shape-shifters. There weren't any specialized differentiations yet. But by the time he made his second visit, there were—and they appeared as six forces united in the Sixth Watch. But why did it exist for centuries before and after the Two-in-One's second coming, and then disappear?"

"It didn't just disappear, the very memory of it was lost," Svetlana added.

I shrugged, and the Tiger repeated my gesture. "I don't know," he said, "but that's what I would advise you to think about: What was the Sixth Watch needed for, and why did it disappear? Perhaps then you can work out how to defeat the Two-in-One. And who the members of the Watch are."

He got up, and I realized our conversation was over.

"Are you tracking us?" I asked.

The Tiger shook his head.

"But you appeared at just the right moment . . ."

"I appeared when I sensed someone was using Power—you were using it, and so was the Two-in-One. I realized you were dueling, and so I came."

"It's a good thing you used the Press when you did, Dad," said Nadya. "Bye-bye, Tiger!"

"Bye-bye, Absolute Little Girl," the Tiger said absolutely seriously. "I hope everything will be all right. Although there isn't much chance of that."

I was expecting the Tiger simply to disappear. But first he took some money out of his pocket and put two thousand-ruble notes on the table. Then he walked out through the door of the bathroom.

"He's become completely humanized," I said in amazement. "It's unbelievable."

"Nadya, open a portal to the Watch office," Svetlana said. "I realize that's the place where you couldn't defend yourself against the Tiger. But it's still safer."

"Maybe Gesar has some kind of refuge in mind?" I sighed, taking a drag on my cigarette.

A young waitress walked up to our table. I thought she had come to take the money, but she stopped beside us and glared at me indignantly.

"Is something wrong?" I asked

"Well, what do you think?" the girl asked. "You're smoking! Shall I call the police and get them to charge you?"

"Yes . . . er . . ." I said in embarrassment, stubbing out the cigarette in the coffee that was left in my cup and flapping my hand in the air. "I'm sorry. It was stupid of me."

"Don't be angry with my dad," said Nadya. "He was lost in thought. He's just got some bad news."

"Has something happened?" the waitress asked suspiciously, but her expression softened as she watched me taking money out of my pocket.

"Yes," said Nadya. "We're all going to die."

"Well, that is news. What a comedian." The waitress snorted, raking up the money.

One day, in a casual conversation, Olga had told me that she almost became a witch. Not in the metaphorical sense, like "that woman is a witch," and not even in the pseudoscientific sense that any female Other is inclined to use the magical techniques of witchcraft. But in the absolutely literal sense. There was a time when if things had gone differently, Olga would have started boiling up potions in a cauldron, charging amulets with magic, hexing people, and making "medicinal ointments" to drive virgins wild.

But everything turned out differently and Olga became a Light Other.

Things are actually more complicated than that. Yes, there are certain essential signs of a witch—the use of artifacts and vegetable or animal extracts, the frequent use of magic that is only accessible to women (there's nothing sexist in this, it's just that male physiology doesn't allow you to work certain spells, like the Bottomless Pit or brew the potion Mummy's Rat-a-Tat, which includes three drops of breast milk).

In fact, witches often use physiological fluids—which is one reason they're not liked. In this respect they're a bit like vampires and werewolves, with their craving for blood and flesh. However, despite all the rumors, these "virgins' tears" and "drops of baby's blood" are usually gathered without whipping innocent young maidens or chopping children into pieces. But there are some straightforward sadists among witches too, and if a young girl hears a witch say, "I want your tears," she'll probably be too frightened to respond rationally.

That was why people used to burn witches, whenever they could catch them. And at one point the Inquisition got so annoyed about it all that the Conclave took a real hammering. And after that the witches, who had been quite powerful and independent, started keeping a lower profile.

But I had no doubt that witches were among the very first Others. Originally they were probably vampires who had learned to do a lot with a little and extract Power from a few drops of blood, instead of quarts of it.

But there is another far more interesting question. Did the witches start storing Power in beads, rings, and earrings because they already wore them, or did they start wearing jewelry so they had a place to store Power? I was inclined to believe the latter. Which, by the way, would explain the universal female passion for jewelry—human women wore it to disguise themselves as Others, as witches. In less enlightened times a woman could find it useful to be regarded as a witch.

In fact, even nowadays it can be pretty handy . . .

"How are you?" I asked Nadya.

"Fine, Dad," my daughter answered.

That's the only answer she's ever given me in the last couple of years: "Fine," "Okay," "Cool." It's her awkward age, I suppose. At ten she used to ask me about everything, and when she was twelve I could still ask her about absolutely anything.

"An unusual spot for a witches' Sabbath, isn't it?" I asked.

My daughter shrugged.

"Why do you say that? I think it's a very good spot. They can't keep on meeting in Kiev all the time, up on Bald Hill, can they?"

"There's the Brocken in Germany too," I reminded her.

"Everywhere has its own Bald Hill," Nadya said with a shrug. "In Moscow the witches meet on the Sparrow Hills . . . Try to catch me!"

She pushed off with her ski poles and glided down the slope.

We were standing on the crest of a hill. One side of the slope was wild and unkempt, with a scattering of boulders. In some places the wind had blown away the snow to expose the dark underlying rock, and in others it had piled up huge snowdrifts.

On the other side the slope had been cleared and it was covered with a smooth layer of snow. There were snow cannons, long lines of ski-lift pylons, and the diminutive figures of skiers and snowboarders slithering down the slope in their bright-colored outfits. The sun was sinking in the west and the ski lifts were only carrying people down now. It gets dark quickly up in the mountains, and in half an hour all these tourists would be taking showers and getting changed, and an hour or so after that they'd be eating dinner and drinking beer.

It was a small ski resort on the border between Austria and Italy, set in the narrow valley of a mountain pass, with a host of hotels, boarding houses, and restaurants, huddled along the road that ran through the valley. There were ski lifts everywhere, on the west and east sides of the valley. This place probably lived a different life in the summer, based on ecological tourism, with long hikes along the slopes to collect edelweiss flowers and admire the cows.

But the resort only really came alive in the winter.

And when the witches held a convention here.

I had been planning to go to the meeting alone, as Gesar had told me to. But at the very last moment, when Nadya and Svetlana had already been allocated a room on one of the basement levels of the Night Watch building, the plans were changed. Zabulon showed up, saying that he had been contacted by one of the senior witches in the Conclave, and the witches "wanted Gorodetsky to bring his daughter with him." Half an hour was spent arguing about security, until the Inquisition guaranteed Nadya's safety (although, to be quite honest, I wasn't sure that the entire might of the Inquisition, including all its spells of prohibition and the artifacts in its special repositories, would be capable of destroying the Two-in-One). Then it took another half hour for Nadya and me to persuade Svetlana. She responded to the suggestion of letting Nadya accompany me to the Conclave with the same suspicion she had shown fifteen years earlier, when I offered to feed Nadya from the bottle. Women just don't believe that men know how to take care of children.

But the invitation from the Conclave was very specific and it couldn't be interpreted in any other way. Anton Gorodetsky and his daughter, Nadezhda. No more, no less.

In the end there wasn't enough time to get to Austria by using any human form of transport. And the area immediately surrounding the hotel where the witches had gathered for their Conclave had been securely closed against magical portals. I had never seen Gesar and Zabulon so annoyed and embarrassed as when I asked them to open a portal directly into the hotel.

They couldn't do it.

And neither could the Inquisition.

The witches had used some special spells and artifacts of their own, making it impossible to travel directly to their Sabbath. Our journey acquired the surreal air of a James Bond adventure as ski suits and equipment were brought for Nadya and me.

We had been on skiing trips before, and this was a simple piste, only "light-red" in the local classification, well tended, and clearly marked. Even so, I took precautions on the descent, using magic to calculate the probabilities as I followed Nadya down. I was slightly alarmed to realize that my body had begun forgetting its downhill-skiing skills. There was one spot where I would have gone tumbling head over heels, another where a wild young snowboarder would have cut in on my slow, clumsy advance and knocked me over, and a third spot where I would have become overconfident as I started remembering a thing or two, increased my speed, and gone rolling down the slope again . . .

So I followed Nadya down without hurrying, like a novice, slowing myself by doing a snowplow, meandering across the slope, and gradually piecing back together what I had forgotten. I thought what a shame it was that we hadn't been to the mountains for a couple of years. It was really great up here . . . and how wonderful it was when little Nadya used to ski down behind me, looking so funny and concentrating so hard . . .

We reached the bottom of the slope right beside the hotel where the Conclave was taking place. I hadn't taken a close look until then, or maybe the hotel had been protected with some kind of witches' spell of darkness, but down here the display of auras was dazzling.

Others.

Mostly Dark Ones.

Witches.

The hotel was called Winter Hexerei, a name with an old-fashioned charm and air of menace about it. The Dark Ones are fond of provocative, revealing little jokes like that—vampires tell funny stories about blood, teeth, and sucking; shape-shifters make wisecracks about wolves, fur, and midnight. And witches just adore talking about sorcery.

The poster at the entrance was equally impish and provocative.

"Welcome to the delegates of the DCLXV traditional convention of feminist gerontologists, cosmetologists, botanists, and personal relationship consultants."

It was a bit longwinded, of course, especially in the German version, but it conveyed rather well the essence of what witches do. I would have added zoologists too—lots of witches' spells use substances of animal origin. But then that would have sounded really ponderous.

"How did I do?" Nadya asked as she slowed to a halt.

"Really good," I said sincerely, stopping beside her. "Did you check the probabilities through the Twilight?"

Nadya hesitated for a second before she confessed.

"Well . . . just a bit. I got frightened halfway down and took a look. It was a good job I did, if I hadn't slowed down, I'd have fallen. Are we going in here?"

I nodded. We were standing beside the hotel entrance, with a leisurely stream of people flowing past us. Most of them were witches, most of them were old and most of them were wearing ski suits and holding skis.

"Where shall we put the skis?" Nadya asked as she took hers off.

I pointed to a rack beside the restaurant's open-air patio. During the day people left their skis there while they ate, but now, with night coming on and the air turning colder, the patio was empty except for a few people smoking by the door. The sky had turned dark very early and lights were coming on all over the valley—beside the hotels, along the road, on the ski trails.

"Let's dump them here," I said. "It would be rather absurd to lug them in with us, wouldn't it?"

"They're good skis," Nadya said. But she obediently put her pair beside mine. "It was so fantastic to go skiing again . . ."

"When this crisis is all over, we'll take a trip into the mountains," I said. "I promise."

Nadya flashed a quick glance at me and nodded. But I could see she didn't believe it. I didn't even believe it myself.

"Herr Gorodetsky? Young Fräulein Gorodetsky?" a plump, middle-aged woman in a luminous white and orange jumpsuit asked, walking up to us.

"Yes, yes, of course," I replied.

The question was rhetorical, naturally, since we could see each other's auras. The woman was a witch. A Higher Other.

"Etta Sabina Waldvogel," said the witch, holding out her hand. "I've heard a lot about you, Herr Gorodetsky."

I struggled frantically to recall an old memory.

"Frau Waldvogel . . ." I said, nodding, and asked: "Would I be correct in assuming that you are the author of *Guidance on Journeying and Journeyers?*"

Etta Sabina's eyes glinted with curiosity.

"Have you read it, Herr Gorodetsky?"

"No, I was unable to obtain a copy."

"It is rather rare," Waldvogel said offhandedly. "And I'm not sure that I can release the *Guidance* to anyone outside our own community . . . or that such highly specialized literature would be of any help to you. But I can let you have *Frau Etta's Brief Trasology*. It's more popular and easier to follow."

"I'd be glad to read it," said Nadya.

"And I'd be glad to give it to you, sweetheart," Etta cooed. "Come on, let's go somewhere a bit warmer!"

We followed Etta into the foyer of the hotel. There were no normal people there, only witches, including at the reception desk. Even the waitress carrying little jugs of mulled wine around the foyer was a rather high-ranking witch. Unlike our escort, they were all disguised as young, beautiful women.

"What a pleasure it is for me to see an Absolute One, my child!" Etta said sweetly, putting her arm round Nadya's shoulders and hugging her. After the cold, frosty air she looked exactly like a charming, ruddy-cheeked, genial middle-aged woman.

The owner of the little gingerbread house that Hansel and Gretel visited probably looked exactly the same.

Or maybe she and Etta had actually been acquainted and used to visit each other for supper?

"Thank you, Grandma," Nadya replied, lowering her eyes modestly. "It's such a pleasure for a foolish and thoughtless girl like me to be invited by such wise women and given an opportunity to improve my mind . . ."

Waldvogel laughed.

"Oh, what a sharp little tongue!" she exclaimed, patting Nadya on the neck. "Why, you're a witch, little girl!"

"I'm not a witch," Nadya objected. "You're mistaken, Grandma."

"A witch, a witch!" Etta repeated cheerfully. "All genuine sorceresses are witches . . ."

Nadya jerked her shoulder out from under Etta's arm. I looked at my daughter curiously—she had tolerated the embrace for a long time, although ever since she was a child she had always hated this kind of physical contact from genial strangers who stroked her hair or patted her on the cheek. She didn't actually suspect that people's intentions were bad. She just didn't like undue familiarity.

"I'm not a witch, Etta Sabina Waldvogel," Nadya said in a low voice that resonated strangely, filling the small foyer. The witches froze. "I'm not a witch, I'm not a werewolf, or a vampire, or a sorceress. I'm something more than that. I'm an Absolute One. Remember that, Mother of These Mountains."

For a brief instant Waldvogel changed, as if someone had run a damp rag over her, wiping away her magical makeup. The charming woman standing beside us was replaced by a bloated, ancient crone, with beady eyes drowning in loose folds of skin covered with a cobweb of fine red veins. Her half-open mouth was absolutely toothless, and I suddenly recalled that one of the traditional sins of witches in the Middle Ages was drinking a mother's breast milk. Apart from sucking out Power—probably at least much as vampires sucked out—there could have been another reason for doing that . . .

Then "normal vision" was restored, and the cheery, red-cheeked lady was there beside us again.

"And all with just the voice," Waldvogel said admiringly. "I haven't removed that appearance for thirty years, I'd almost forgotten how to do it. I'm impressed, little girl. Well, come along now, come along!"

The bustle in the foyer resumed, with witches scurrying to and fro. Some came in and sat at the bar in their ski suits and boots, drinking hot wine, while others went off to their rooms.

Witches certainly know how to throw a good party for their Sabbath!

"Everyone has come, absolutely all the rooms are taken," Waldvogel murmured as she led us to the elevator. "I hope you don't mind that I booked you a very basic one; after all you won't be staying overnight, it's only so that you have somewhere to tidy yourselves up . . . Was the skiing good? How's the snow?"

"It was really great, thanks," I replied.

"Excellent, excellent. Come and ski here more often, it's a good spot, and I asked the mountain to remember you, so you won't crash or break any bones—unless you do something really stupid, of course . . ."

How much of what she said was true and how much of it was the kind of bluster that witches all excel in? Could a witch really ask a mountain to do something? And if she could, what did that mean?

I didn't ask.

Our heavy boots clattered on the floor of the elevator as we got in and rode up a few floors. Waldvogel opened the door of the room right beside the elevator (I knew from personal experience that these rooms were the very smallest, which were usually given to solitary, unassuming travelers and guests who smoked and looked like alcoholics—the ones most likely to get the urge to go out during the night).

But we didn't have to spend the night here.

The room was cramped, but clean and tidy. Lying on the bed, which was too wide for a single and too narrow for a double, was a magnificent suit of dark-blue woolen fabric, a white shirt, a tie, socks, boxer shorts, and a pair of fashionable men's shoes. And lying beside them was a long black dress (which, to my surprise, looked slightly worn), a pair of black tights, black pants, a black bra, and black shoes.

Nadya turned to the witch with an indignant air.

"I'm sorry, Fräulein," the witch said imperturbably. "I didn't wish to embarrass you. But you are with your dad, after all, not some young man, and your father is hardly going to be shocked by the sight of your underwear."

Nadya blushed violently, raked up the clothes, and disappeared into the bathroom.

"Ah, children," Waldvogel sighed. "But I'm afraid there's nothing I can do. A girl attending a Sabbath for the first time is obliged to dress in the traditional style. Everything black. Some believe that the underwear can be white, but I consider that an impermissible liberty. They start by blowing their noses in paper handkerchiefs, then they stop shaving their armpits, and they end up with white lingerie under a black dress—and look where it all leads: states crumble, morals decline, and they hold exhibitions in the churches."

"How very politically correct you are, Frau," I said, pulling off my heavy boots and starting to unzip my ski suit.

"Yes, that's the way I am," the witch said. "Kinder, Küche, Kirche, as we say in Germany. A healthy society starts with a healthy family and good taste! Do you need any help, Herr Anton?"

"I'll manage," I said, pulling off the ski suit. "I hope you won't mind if I don't take a shower, but just rub myself down with the throw from the bed and change into the clean clothes?"

"I don't mind," said the witch. "A man's sweat is the finest aroma a woman can smell. You won't feel embarrassed getting changed with me here?"

"Not in the slightest," I replied, taking off my sweat-soaked underclothes.

"What a pity," Etta said. "I adore my craft, I love being a witch, and I'm a good witch, believe me, Anton. But it's a shame that our appearance is so . . . unattractive."

"But no one can see that," I said, getting dressed quickly. "And it doesn't seem to affect your health at all."

"I can see it," the witch complained. "And you can see it."

"Oh come on, what's the problem, really?" I protested. "We Others aren't the only fish in the sea, and it's not as if we're so macho that all the men in the world pale in comparison."

"Should I knot your tie for you?" Etta asked. "Men sometimes don't know how to tie a tie."

I nodded, holding out the tie—it was dark-blue silk that matched the tone of the suit, with gold stars embroidered on it.

"I used to knot all my husbands' ties," Etta murmured, examining my tie somberly and holding it up against the jacket. "Hans, may he rest in peace, and Wolfgang, and Alfred, good riddance to him, and Otto, and Conrad, and Ludwig, and Basil . . . He was one of you, by the way, a Russian. And Antonio as well, and Horst . . ."

"How many husbands have you had?" I asked.

"About a hundred," Etta said with a casual wave of her hand. "Don't get the idea that I saw them all to their graves, Gorodetsky, we usually lived together for two or three years, then I got a bit bored, and men get this yearning for heroic deeds—I don't like that sort of thing . . . So I got divorced, or I simply left. It was only Hans that I lived with right to the end of his life, and Alfred, of course, and Ludwig . . ."

The door of the bathroom opened and Nadya came out with a rather embarrassed air.

"How do I look?"

I examined my daughter critically and was surprised.

"You know, you look pretty good. The dress could have been made for you . . . although I don't think it's new."

Etta giggled.

"You guessed! It isn't new. Girls have been going to their first Sabbath in it for three centuries. But we had it taken in for Fräulein Nadya; the dressmaker worked all day on it . . ."

"You look magnificent too, Dad," said Nadya. "You ought to wear a suit and tie. It's so . . . charmingly old-fashioned."

"Thank you, my dear," I said with a nod. "You certainly know how to make your father feel good. Frau Waldvogel, how are we doing for time?"

"You have a quarter of an hour," said the witch. "You can have a glass of beer or wine in the bar. Or vodka, if you like. What do you usually drink in the evenings?"

"No, I can't have vodka, I promised my bear that I wouldn't drink any without him," I replied. Nadya giggled. "Frau Waldvogel," I continued, "can you satisfy my curiosity on one point . . . Is this really your six hundred and sixty-fifth gathering?"

I think the witch was actually embarrassed by my question.

"In a certain sense it is," she replied evasively. "You see, Anton, we witches are rather superstitious. So we've been holding the six hundred and sixty-fifth session of our Conclave for almost a century now. It has become a tradition."

"An interesting solution," I said.

"That's what I think too," the witch replied without a trace of irony. "After all, the most important things in life are peace of mind and a positive attitude."

I couldn't think of anything to say to that.

But Nadya could.

"That's a good one, Dad," she said in a quiet voice.

CHAPTER 3

THE CONCLAVE OF WITCHES WAS ASSEMBLED IN THE HOTEL restaurant. A decision had been made "to combine duty and pleasure," as they say. Fortunately, there weren't mountains of food—the sight of two hundred munching witches would have been just too much. Most of them really love eating, and copious hors d'oeuvres easily could have distracted them from the beginning of the end of the world.

The tables were set with only tea, coffee, wine, beer, and cognac (which was the preferred tipple of many of the ladies), canapés with red and black caviar, foie gras on small pieces of toast, various little fancy cakes, and slices of gateau (there is no limit to the amount of sweet things that witches can eat).

Most of the delegates had already taken their seats when we got there. For the most part, they had chosen to look young and were dressed brightly, but even the appearance of those who looked middle-aged or older was an improvement on reality, designed to deceive. The Power that witches possess drains them of beauty and youth. They can live for a very, very long time, almost forever in fact, like the rest of the Others. But we live our long lives in bodies that are young, while witches live theirs in the bodies of old crones.

Frau Waldvogel, who was dolled up in a luxurious evening dress and modern jewelry (which was obviously very expensive), led us to a table where the most highly respected witches were sitting. As far as I could see, they were all Higher Ones. Khokhlenko was among them, but even she seemed rather surprised to be there. The Grand-mother of Moscow probably had been been seated at the top table out of respect for us . . . *For Nadezhda, that is,* I thought to myself. *Not for us. For Nadya. She's the one they're interested in.*

As we made our way between the tables, I heard snippets of con-versation.

"Jack was a fine young fellow, very fine. But you know, my dear, a childhood like that is simply bound to scramble a person's brains. There weren't any psychologists back then, so he took it out on those poor prostitutes . . ."

"No, no! You've got it all wrong! Physical chastity is absolutely unimportant. I mean, it is desirable, but it isn't the main criterion! What is important is spiritual innocence; you could even call it spiri-tual naïveté, a purity that comes from the bottom of the heart, an innocence of the mind! And given the right treatment, the heart of a chaste girl like that . . ."

"How disgusting," Nadya said in a low voice, taking hold of my hand—she was listening to the conversations too. "At least I know I could never be taken for that kind of virgin."

I pretended as though I hadn't heard that.

However, there were less disturbing conversations too.

"Early in the morning! The very moment the edge of the sun ap-pears over the horizon, you go out into the fields and start collecting the buds, thinking good thoughts, with a smile on your lips, and you can sing a quiet little song . . ."

Maybe if we'd kept listening it would have turned out that the flowers were being collected for some gross, abominable purpose, but we moved on to our table and didn't hear the end of the story.

In contrast with the vampires' gathering, everything here really was very pleasant indeed—especially if you didn't listen too closely or try to look through the cosmetic spells.

The room was full of smiling women, young and old, all eager to give Nadya a peck on the cheek and give me a hug. There was an abundance of pink clothing on display—my daughter was almost the only one wearing black. There were little jokes and quips, bright smiles, pieces of cake floating from one table to another on saucers, tea being poured—as well as wine, beer, and cognac. The Conclave of Witches was like a flock of pink, fluffy animals, all chewing intently and wagging their little tails.

But the first rule in dealing with cute, fluffy animals is not to poke them with your finger—unless you happen to be wearing thick gloves.

"Sisters!" one of the witches sitting at our table called, getting to her feet. Her voice sounded strong and steady, and it filled the entire space—the same trick that Nadya had used a little earlier. "Our modest community is honored today by the presence of Nadezhda Gorodetsky and her father, Anton Gorodetsky."

I winced. Yes of course, it's very flattering when your children are well known and highly thought of. But it's still rather sad to know that you're nothing more than an appendage to your own daughter.

"We all know what is happening," the witch continued. She was slim, with olive skin, black eyes, and hair "the color of a raven's wing" as the poets loved to say. "I, Ernesta, greet our guests on behalf of everyone and promise them all the help that we can give."

That sounded very encouraging. A bit of help, for a change.

"Thank you, Ernesta," I replied, getting to my feet. I had heard about the speaker before; she was a Spanish witch, one of the most revered in the community. But there was something strange here . . . "May I ask a personal question?"

Ernesta smiled and nodded.

"I thought that you had been in the Inquisition for many years now."

"Since 1891," the witch responded politely. "Are you surprised that I am at the Conclave?"

"Yes."

"The Conclave as an organization is not involved at all in the opposition between the Watches. We have Light Ones among us. And in general, the Conclave is rather like a special-interest club for girls."

I permitted myself a smile, since that was what was expected of me.

"So I am able to serve in the Inquisition, while remaining a witch and participating in the Conclave."

"Good," I said with a nod. "Then tell me this: As both a member of the Conclave and a serving Inquisitor, do you know how the information on the Two-in-One came to be lost? Such important information about a god, engendered by the Twilight? The Sixth Watch was still remembered in the Middle Ages. What happened after that? Why are we still floundering about, scrabbling for crumbs of information and unsure of how to interpret it correctly?"

Silence descended—the witches even stopped chewing.

"I cannot answer that," said Ernesta. She wasn't embarrassed—there isn't any way to embarrass a witch—but she clearly did not like the question. "Information of such great importance should not have been lost. But it really is missing. There are certain secondary documents of some importance, hints, references in books . . . If you would like to know my opinion . . ."

"I would," I said, nodding.

"The information was deliberately destroyed. And a number of Others must have been involved in destroying it. Light Ones, Dark Ones, Inquisitors, magicians, witches, vampires . . ."

"The Sixth Watch must have been involved," Nadya exclaimed. "Isn't that it?"

"Bravo, little girl," said Ernesta. "That's exactly it. We came to the conclusion that the members of the Sixth Watch had intentionally obliterated the memory of it."

"We?" the plump, light-haired witch sitting beside Ernesta asked in surprise.

"*We* as in the Inquisition," Ernesta explained. "Anton, unfortunately we are unable to give you any more information. None of our sisters know anything about the Two-in-One and the Sixth Watch."

"We too have terrifying stories that we try to forget," a witch at the next table said in a squeaky voice. She was one of the few who were not disguising their age with sorcery, and by human standards she looked about a hundred years old. "And the story of the Two-in-One, sweetheart, is one of those."

"Do you know something, Mary?" Ernesta asked.

"About the Two-in-One?" Mary shook her head sharply, disturbing the sparse bunches of gray hair that had been arranged like curls to decorate her bald cranium. "No, no, sister . . . I know about Thomas with the Matches, about the Little Spindle and . . ."

"Don't tell us about that in the presence of outsiders, sister," Ernesta told her gently but firmly. "We value your stories, sister. But tell us later."

Mary nodded and even put her wrinkled hand over her mouth in a comical gesture. I actually felt a strange respect for this ancient witch who made no attempt to conceal her age.

"By the way, sister, have you not forgotten something?" Ernesta asked. "And I don't mean about the Two-in-One."

"What could I have forgotten?" Mary asked indignantly.

"Well . . . to take a look at yourself in the mirror before you left your room," Ernesta said, twitching her shoulders. "To powder your nose . . . Or splash some water from an onyx chalice on your face."

Mary frowned at first. And then she turned as white as chalk. She lowered her eyes and peered into the polished silverware on the table.

The witches around her started giggling quietly. They might all be sisters, but first and foremost they were women.

Mary raised her hands to her face and stood up. She took her hands away.

She was no longer an old crone, but a blindingly beautiful young woman, with blond hair and blue eyes.

"Thank you, my sisters," Mary said in an icy voice. "Thanks to all of you who smiled at me this evening . . ."

"Sit down, Mary," said Ernesta. "Everyone knows how eccentric you are. I thought you had deliberately come to the meeting looking like that. Sit down and don't disgrace yourself."

Mary sat down, casting a dark glance at Ernesta.

I seized the opportunity to speak.

"To get back to the question of help. We need your representative, either appointed or approved by the head of the Conclave. By the Grandmother of Grandmothers."

"And there we have a problem, for which you are directly responsible," said Ernesta.

"Arina," I said with a nod. "Yes, that's right. I shut your Great Grandmother away in the Sarcophagus of Time. In my defense, I can only say that I intended to while away eternity together with her."

"You joker," Ernesta snorted. "I won't lie and say that I'm grieving for Arina. As you have probably noticed, we're rather cool with each other."

"How could I not notice?" I asked, twirling a little silver spoon in my fingers.

"And therefore we reacted positively to the request from Gesar and Zabulon," the witch said with a smile.

"But?" I asked. "You have the word 'but' stuck on the tip of your tongue. Spit it out quickly, before you choke on it."

"But we cannot choose a new Great Grandmother," Ernesta sighed. "Since the previous one is still alive."

"Remove her," I said. "Can you not demonstrate some flexibility here?"

"Can *we* not demonstrate flexibility?" Ernesta queried, raising her left eyebrow and gazing at me intently. "*We* can. Flexibility is our middle name. How else could we have survived in a world full of coarse, bloodthirsty men? But do you know how we choose the Great Grandmother?"

I shook my head, sensing that I wouldn't like what I was about to learn.

"The Grandmother of Grandmothers must be acknowledged by the Shoot," said Ernesta.

"Hooray!" I exclaimed sincerely. "I was afraid it might be something rather more . . . exotic."

"No, Anton. It's nothing more than the Shoot. Here it is."

She casually lifted up the napkin lying over a pot that was on the table in front of her. I half rose to examine what the napkin had been covering.

I had noticed the pot before and had assumed that it contained some kind of food. But it turned out to be a flowerpot. With a wooden thing sticking out of it.

"What's that?" I asked.

"The Shoot," Ernesta said with a smile.

"But from the look of it, I'd say it was a wooden—"

"The Shoot," she repeated emphatically. "The symbol of the eternal life and vigor of our community."

"From the way the Shoot looks, I'd say your community is a little withered."

"Do not judge on appearances," the witch parried. "In the hands of the Grandmother of Grandmothers the Shoot starts to blossom. And that is the uniquely clear and evident confirmation of her position. In combination, of course, with a certain degree of authority and Power."

"All right," I said. "So have you chosen someone?"

"The Shoot did not blossom," Ernesta said. "According to tradition, this has happened several times—when a clearly unworthy Grandmother of Grandmothers was selected, when the voting was carried out under duress, and once when an attempt was made to choose a leader while the previous incumbent was still alive."

"Is there no way you can remove someone from the position?"

"Only by poisoning the jam," Mary said ominously. "Good old arsenic . . ."

"While Arina is still alive, we cannot elect anyone to replace her," Ernesta said with a shrug.

"Then what do you want me to do?" I asked. "Why did you invite us here?"

"We hope that the Shoot *will* allow us to choose a leader," Ernesta said. "If the candidate is—"

"Oh no!" I interrupted. "Don't even think about it!"

"Then the world will perish," the witch retorted. "We are not joking, Gorodetsky. We are offering your daughter the position of Grandmother of Grandmothers."

"Nonsense," I said. "Total and absolute rubbish."

"Why?"

"I know a little bit about your rules," I said spitefully. "A future witch has to receive a gift, an initiation from a genuine witch, and it has to happen in early childhood, even adolescence is already too late . . ."

I stopped, looking at Ernesta's smile. I'd suddenly remembered something.

After Arina kidnapped Nadya, Sveta and I had fought to get our daughter back. And then Arina had given Nadya a gift, supposedly as an apology . . .

"But the initiation has already begun, Anton," said Ernesta. "Ten years ago Arina, the Great Grandmother herself, granted Nadya the ability to work with plants—the very cornerstone of witchcraft."

"You're insane!" I exclaimed. "She's only fifteen!"

"Is it really a matter of age?" Ernesta asked in surprise. "Arina is not the oldest among us."

"My daughter is a Light One," I reminded her, though I knew I had already lost.

"Almost fifteen percent of witches are Light Ones," Ernesta told me obligingly.

"She'll age rapidly and become . . . become ugly," I said in a quiet voice.

"Like us," Ernesta said with a nod. "She will have to live behind a mask, and if the men she loves are Others, they will know that they are not kissing a young woman, but an old, withered one. All that is true. This is the price. But I thought we wanted to save the world."

I looked at my daughter.

"Dad, of course I agree," Nadya said.

She was very calm, her face set in an expression of imperturbable benevolence.

"Nadya, the process is irreversible," I said. "And very rapid. You'll grow old in just a few years. Well, ten or twenty at the most. Right now that seems like an eternity to you, but it isn't. You'll see that ten years fly past in an instant. I don't know of course, maybe Kesha or someone else . . . but after all it's easier for Others to live with Others . . . and only witches live with ordinary people, because they don't know who they're really kissing . . ."

The hall was silent. And the silence was deafening.

My daughter looked at me as if she was waiting for me to finish.

"You won't even be able to have a child," I said. "No, that's not right, you will be able to, but only in the first few years after you become a witch . . . Dammit, you're still only a child yourself!"

"Dad, I realized immediately why the witches had invited us to the Conclave," Nadya told me in a soothing voice, as if she were the grown-up and I were a frightened little child. "I called Innokentii and we discussed everything. We'll get married as soon as the Two-in-One has been dealt with. Of course, I'll have to have a child as soon as I can. We might even have time to have two children. I know we're not mature enough, especially in the psychological sense, but I discussed everything with Mum too, and she said you two would raise your grandchildren, so that we could continue with our education . . ."

I stood there with my mouth wide open, gulping in air, looking so pitiful that not even the witches could gloat.

"Everything will be all right, Dad," Nadya said, getting up. She stood on tiptoe and kissed me on the cheek, then walked out from behind the table and stood in front of Ernesta. "I'm ready," she said. "What do I have to do?"

My daughter was going to become a witch.

My daughter, an Absolute Enchantress, a clever, beautiful young girl, was going to become a twisted old crone.

Before she even reached thirty, she would be a repulsive old woman, constantly hiding behind spells of disguise.

And there was nothing I could do about it. Ernesta was right and Nadya was right—the fate of the entire world was at stake . . .

"Sisters, are we willing to accept Nadya Gorodetsky as one of us?" Ernesta asked.

The witches replied with a drone of approval.

"Do we agree to the Absolute Enchantress Nadya Gorodetsky becoming the Grandmother of Grandmothers, our leader and commander?" she continued.

"This is out of order," Mary suddenly declared. Despite the enchanting appearance she had assumed, her voice was still squeaky and senile. "Arina was Russian and Nadya is Russian. It's not correct to appoint a leader from the same region twice in succession!"

"There has only ever been one Great Grandmother from Africa!" shouted a dark-skinned woman at the back of the hall.

"As if we get treated any better . . ." another indignant voice called out.

"Belgium has never . . ."

"Quiet!" Ernesta exclaimed, raising her voice. "There are many of us and we all have ambitions, grievances, and aspirations. But understand this—if Nadya Gorodetsky does not become the Great Grandmother now, then Arina will remain the Great Grandmother forever. Until the end of time. And the entire world will perish!"

The witches fell silent.

"Arina has hung on too long as it is," Mary croaked.

"And so I propose as an exception, that Nadya Gorodetsky be elected Great Grandmother," Ernesta declared solemnly. "Do you support this proposal?"

This time there were no protests.

There was something surprisingly simpleminded, almost primi-

tive about this procedure. Like the election of an ataman by the
Cossacks, when they used to ask everyone to shout if they liked the
ataman or if they didn't.

"Nadya, hold out your hand and place it on the Shoot," Ernesta
said.

I watched this obscene and insane spectacle—my daughter setting
her hand on an ancient wooden dildo. And I said nothing.

"Hold it tight . . ." Ernesta said in a surprisingly hesitant voice.

She closed her hand around the wooden Shoot.

Nothing happened.

"In the old days they didn't bother with half measures," Mary
muttered, but stopped when she caught Nadya's eye. Nadya snatched
her hand away from the Shoot and wiped it on her dress.

"You did hold it, didn't you?" Ernesta asked, as if she hadn't wit-
nessed the entire process with her own eyes. "But then . . ."

She turned toward me.

"I understand," I said. "There's nothing you can do."

Ernesta shook her head.

"I'm sorry, señor. Very sorry. We wanted to help. We . . . we love
life."

I looked at the gathering. At two hundred witches, cloaked in
magical disguises, concealed behind veils of enchantment, pretending to be the beautiful women they once were, or perhaps had never
been.

But kind or malicious, they really did love life. In all its manifestations.

This love of life drove them to commit monstrous atrocities. They
indulged in depraved, lewd debauchery; they dissected infants and
copulated with animals; they poisoned cattle and sucked out mothers' milk; they pounced on solitary travelers at night and forced them
to gallop across the fields and run wildly along the roads. They were
only slightly less mad than March hares. They were the very essence
of Mother Nature, of the planet Earth itself—nature is also pitiless
and remorseless, capricious and derisive, guileful and bloodthirsty.

They were witches. Naive and cruel children, trapped in old women's bodies. There is no male equivalent of the witch; the warlock of old folk tales is quite different. To be a witch, you have to be able to give life. Without that you can never learn how to take life away so lightly.

"I'm really sorry too," I said. "But don't distress yourselves, ladies. We'll think of something."

Nadya came back to me and I hugged her.

"Sorry, Dad," she whispered. "I looked pretty stupid, right?"

"Not stupid, but funny," I replied.

"You used that word instead of 'absurd,'" Nadya said. "I can tell."

Ernesta clinked a spoon against a wineglass—in the silence the sound was as alarming as a phone call in the middle of the night.

"Is there anything else we can do for you, Señor Gorodetsky?" she asked. "We could partially lower our defenses, so that you can open a portal from here."

"Are you throwing us out already?" I asked, holding out my hand and imagining its shadow on the table. It had to be there, didn't it, the shadow cast by the crystal chandeliers? And it didn't matter if I couldn't see it. It existed. The shadow of my fingers, reaching down into the Twilight . . .

"No, but . . ." Ernesta replied, sounding rather bewildered and looking at my hand.

I shuffled my fingers, feeling the chill of the Twilight at their tips.

"Dad, what are you doing?" Nadya asked in a whisper.

"Hitting switches, fixing glitches," I said, tapping my fingers on the table. "Never mind the baffled witches."

"I don't understand."

"That's okay," I said, tapping out the rhythm with my fingers. Three short beats, three long ones and another three short ones. Impulses of Power surging into space, into the Twilight.

"Who are you?" Ernesta suddenly asked, frowning and looking past me. "This is a private event."

Her voice gradually became quieter and quieter, as if someone was turning down the volume on a music player, and her eyes opened wider and wider. She was obviously staring at someone standing behind me.

I looked around and nodded to the Tiger.

"Sorry for bothering you. We didn't agree on the signal, but I thought you'd understand."

"Witches," the Tiger said in a low voice, running a thoughtful glance over the geriatric gathering. As the witches recovered their wits (ah, what a shame I hadn't seen how he appeared) the atmosphere in the restaurant turned . . . well, not to panic, but more to tense anticipation. "I've never liked witches."

"Why not?" I asked in surprise.

"They . . ." The Tiger pondered for a moment, as if trying to find the words for something he had always known, but had never needed to express. "They harass. Badger. Pester. Hassle."

"I admire your range of vocabulary," I said. "What exactly do they harass?"

"The Twilight," the Tiger replied simply. "Ordinary Others ask. Witches demand."

He frowned and gestured with his hand, as if he regretted what he had just blurted out.

"I need your help," I said.

"Yes," said the Tiger, nodding. "I'm very surprised that you didn't ask sooner."

"You didn't suggest it so I decided it must be too difficult. Or impossible."

Perhaps I imagined it, but I thought I saw an expression of entirely human anguish cross the Tiger's face.

"Not impossible. Difficult."

"They can't choose a leader," I said. "They can't even elect Nadya, as long as Arina is alive in the Sarcophagus of Time."

"There are two things I can do," the Tiger declared, looking me in the eye. "I can destroy the Sarcophagus. Dissolve it in eternity. That probably means Arina will be killed."

"And the second thing?" I asked.

"We can try to get her out," said the Tiger. "Only it will be up to you to talk to her. I can only bring someone out of the Sarcophagus if they wish to come out. But in this case . . . in this case there may be unforeseen consequences."

"Such as?" I asked.

"I'm not sure," the Tiger said with a frown. "I . . . I can't see the future clearly. Both situations are vague, but the one in which we bring Arina back is extremely hazy."

"Anton, if I understand the position correctly," Ernesta added quickly, "we are quite happy with the first option. Arina will be handled peacefully and we can choose a Grandmother of Grand-mothers, who will not be your daughter. It all works out perfectly!"

"Dad!" Nadya exclaimed, looking at me indignantly. "Will you . . . will you agree to that?"

I sighed, and stepped toward the Tiger.

"Just as I thought," he remarked sadly. "Gorodetsky, why don't you like simple solutions?"

"They usually have complicated consequences," I replied.

Traveling in the grip of the Tiger was no fun.

Only a moment ago we were in an Alpine restaurant with two hundred witches, whose combined ages probably amounted to about a hundred thousand years.

But the Tiger had simply grabbed me by the collar, and sud-denly here we were, surrounded by swirling gray glop. It looked like foam made of little soap bubbles, illuminated weakly by a dim white light from some indefinite source. The bubbles parted as we moved through them, yielded springily underfoot, and retreated when I reached my hand out toward them.

"What is this?" I asked. The Tiger was still grasping my collar, holding me out at arm's length. "And would you kindly let go of me, please?"

"This is the space between the levels of the Twilight," the Tiger replied. "These are the reverberations of emotions and echoes of feelings. This is everything that has ever existed in the world. The squeak of the first mouse as it was caught by the first cat. The purring of a cat, curled up on a woman's knees. The shriek of a new mother who has sensed that her child will be an evil man. The weeping of a criminal on the night before he mounts the scaffold. All the sounds of the world. All the colors of the world. All the feelings of the world."

"Thank you," I said, "very poetic. But . . ."

"If I let go of you, you'll disintegrate into . . ." the Tiger thought for a moment. "Into tiny bubbles."

"But Zabulon told me he hid between the levels of the Twilight."

"Your Zabulon can do many things, Gorodetsky. Be patient. We need to talk. I don't get any pleasure out of holding you up by the scruff of your neck."

"By the scruff of my neck," I laughed. "You really have got a grip on the language! Okay, let's talk."

"At this very moment we are passing the point of no return, Gorodetsky," said the Tiger. In the feeble, grayish light his face looked like a plaster mask. His lips barely even moved, and his eyes were blank gaps, openings into nothingness. "Are you sure you want to get Arina out of there? Perhaps we should just lay her to rest?"

"What's wrong, Tiger?" I asked. "Do you think the old witch will confound me once and for all?"

"No, Anton. That's not it at all."

I caught on. I was getting smarter every day—it was frightening to think how shrewd I would be when I reached Gesar's age.

"So, on the contrary, she'll explain everything?"

"Yes, Anton, Arina knows everything. About the Sixth Watch, about the Two-in-One. She even knows a lot more about the Twilight than she lets on. Perhaps more than I know myself."

"What makes you think that?"

"I can foresee it. If you talk to her, everything will change. Everything will be absolutely different, Anton."

"For instance?"

"It's quite possible that you will die," said the Tiger.

"Well, unpleasant things like that happen to people."

"You're not an ordinary person, you're an Other. You don't have to die."

"What else?"

"I'll die," the Tiger said simply. "In this version of the future I die."

"And in the other version?" I asked after a moment's pause.

"I die in that one too."

"I see," I said with a nod. "Then tell me the most important thing, Tiger . . ."

"Nadya dies in the reality where you decide to destroy the Sarcophagus," said the Tiger. "In the alternative reality, she doesn't necessarily die."

"Then why are you even bothering to ask my opinion?" I laughed.

"Because the reality in which Nadya doesn't die will bring you greater suffering," said the Tiger, turning his eyes away. "You could come to regret that we didn't shatter the Sarcophagus in eternity."

"That's impossible!" I shouted. "That couldn't happen. Why would it?"

"I don't know," replied the Tiger. "I'm not certain. I'm not the Twilight, after all. And I'm sick, Anton. I'm infected with humanity, that's why I'm talking to you now. And even if I were well, reading the destinies of Great Ones and an Absolute Enchantress is fiendishly difficult."

I groaned. I wanted to shrug the Tiger's hand off my neck and dissolve into little bubbles.

I'd never imagined I could possibly consider such a simple, cowardly way out.

"Take me to the witch," I said. "Maybe I'll regret this, but there's nothing else I can say right now. I can't choose a future in which Nadya is killed. Let's go to the Sarcophagus."

"All right," said the Tiger. "I knew that already, but I had to make sure. So let's go, you who was begotten of the Darkness. I'll take you to Arina . . ."

"What?" I shouted, then the gray gloom dissipated and I went tumbling across a cold marble floor. "Who?"

The only reply I heard was the Tiger's quiet whisper in the distance.

"Now it's up to you to persuade her."

I got up and looked around. The Tiger wasn't there. There was only a dimly lit stone hall with a high dome above it. Arina was nowhere to be seen. I took a few steps. The air was still as fresh and cool as I remembered it.

"Arina," I called. "It's me! Anton! Anton Gorodetsky!"

"I already guessed it wasn't Chekhov. He was a cultured man, who didn't yell like that when other people were sleeping . . ."

The witch's voice was coming from somewhere above me. I stopped and looked up.

There was a gray cocoon, twisted together out of rags and threads, nestling crookedly against the domed ceiling about three yards above my head. The cocoon trembled and a hand appeared, making a gap in the wall, and then another. Finally a head was thrust out through the gap.

"Good morning, Arina," I said, looking at the witch. "I'm sorry I woke you."

"You won't get away with just apologies," said the witch. "Are you alone?"

"Yes," I said, and paused before asking: "What's that . . . thing made of?"

"You don't need to know that," said Arina. "Just turn away for a moment."

I turned away and moved toward the center of the Sarcophagus, hearing rustling and crackling sounds behind me, as if Arina was rolling up her cocoon.

It was really disgusting.

Maybe it was very rational, ecologically sound, and natural to weave a cocoon and sink into hibernation. But that's what you expect from an insect, not a human being.

Witches . . .

"I'm glad to see you, Anton," Arina said. "You're looking good. Only a bit tired somehow . . ."

I looked around. The witch was standing behind me and the cocoon on the ceiling had disappeared. Her face was calm and peaceful. She was wearing a smart business suit with slacks (I vaguely recalled that she had arrived here in different clothes).

"How's the Minoan Sphere?" I asked. "I kept thinking about it, wondering if it would get you out of here."

Arina ran her hand over her clothes and a little ball glinted in her hand.

"That's absurd," she said. "Very little Power flows in here. It would have taken another twenty or thirty years for the Sphere to charge."

"Is that why you went into hibernation?"

"Yes. But when you entered, a lot of Power burst in with you. The Sphere is charged now."

"Don't be in any hurry to use it," I said. "Maybe we'll leave here some other way."

"Well now," Arina said with a smile. "Tell me about it!"

"We've got problems."

Arina nodded.

"So what's new?" she asked.

"What do you know about the Sixth Watch and the Two-in-One?" I asked.

Arina's face suddenly went tense and her eyes glinted viciously.

"The Sixth Watch is dead! The Two-in-One no longer exists!"

"The Watch is dead all right," I said, nodding. "But the Two-in-One has just tried to kill my daughter twice."

Arina stood there, shifting from one foot to the other and staring daggers at me. Then she sighed and sank down onto the floor.

"Sit down, Gorodetsky, there's no point in standing. Let's talk."

"Haven't you done enough sitting?" I asked in amazement. "Don't you want to get out of here?"

"Yes, I do. But I don't know if I ought to," she replied. "Sit down, will you? An hour or two won't make any difference, and I've spent years in here."

I nodded and sat down facing her.

"What's happened? Tell me everything from the beginning," Arina demanded.

"First a vampiress appeared. Gesar believes she's one that I once laid to rest, who has been resurrected. She bit a series of people, and the initials of their names spelled out a message: 'Anton Gorodetsky, be ready, he awaits, it's your decision.'"

"What nonsense," Arina muttered. "Like some Agatha Christie detective story. That's not the Two-in-One. It's not his style."

"I didn't say it was. Whoever this vampiress might be, she turned out to be on our side. My daughter was attacked at school. Two Others who were guarding her, a Light One and a Dark One, killed the third guard, and an Inquisitor. It looked like they were possessed."

"How did they kill him? Fire and ice?"

I nodded in relief. Arina really did know about the Two-in-One!

"Are they together?" Arina asked.

"They try to hold hands all the time," I said cautiously

She nodded.

"Svetlana and I couldn't beat them," I went on. "But the vampiress showed up and drove them away. It was just like an ordinary fight, only very fast . . ."

"Go on," Arina said.

"A prophecy occurred. All the Prophets and all the Seers proclaimed the same thing at the same time: 'It was not spilled in vain, nor burned to no purpose. The first time has come. The Two shall arise in the flesh and open the doors. Three victims, the fourth time. Five days are left to the Others. Six days are left to people. To those who stand in the way, nothing will be left. The Sixth Watch is dead, the Fifth Power has disappeared. The Fourth has come too late. The Third Power does not believe, the Second Power is afraid, the First Power is exhausted . . .' After that we started searching for the Sixth Watch and its members."

Arina nodded and closed her eyes.

"Do you understand what it's about?" I asked.

"How long ago was the prophecy proclaimed?"

"Four days ago."

"So this is the last day," said Arina. "Yes . . . I understand everything. What's happening in the world right now, Anton? What's happening to the people?"

"Everything's the same as usual," I said. "War in the Middle East. War in Ukraine."

"That's trivial," said Arina, shaking her head. "But then, the balance doesn't have to be disrupted so obviously. The world can appear normal until the very last day."

"What balance?"

"Between good and evil, of course."

"I wouldn't say the Day Watch has gotten completely out of hand . . ."

"Good and evil have got nothing to do with the Watches!" she snapped. "You of all people should understand that. The Night Watch maintains a stance of altruism, or more precisely, active altruism by Others toward people. The Day Watch regards the welfare of people and their requirements as insignificant in comparison with the requirements of Others."

"But that still comes down to good and evil in the end. On the day-to-day level," I said.

"Tell that to the people who die for the exalted ideas of the Night Watch," Arina said dismissively. "People and Others have rather different ideas about good and evil."

"All right," I said, "so the balance has shifted. I believe you. The world really does seem to have gone insane. But this is human business, even if people decide to start World War III."

"What is the Twilight?" Arina asked.

"A certain rational force," I said. "A superforce."

Arina continued looking at me expectantly.

"Generated by human thoughts, emotions, dreams . . ."

"The Twilight doesn't have a physical body," Arina said. "It doesn't even have a mind in the human sense of the word; it's something quite different. The consciousness of people who are alive now is the pattern of its will. The memory of people who have died is the pattern of the Twilight's memory. If the world tends toward evil, the Twilight becomes harsher. If the world tends toward good, the Twilight becomes kinder. But the Twilight doesn't like to change; homeostasis is fundamental to every living thing."

"You mean to say there's more evil in the world now than, let's say, during World War II?" I asked, shaking my head. "I don't believe it!"

"It's not a matter of there being more. It's a matter of the balance. World wars are a monstrous atrocity, a boundless ocean of pain and fear. But they also involve great hopes, self-sacrifice, acts of mercy! A war doesn't alter the balance, it merely raises the stakes. But if the Two-in-One has come, it means the balance has shifted. It means there is evil everywhere. Quiet, calm, indifferent evil. In men and women, children and adults. When the balance changes, the Twilights starts feeling uncomfortable, it begins to resist the change. And it manifests an entity of some kind in the human world. In the simplest cases, it's Mirror Magicians, who restore the balance at a local level. If it's something more serious, then it's Absolute Others, who can give the world a new truth and change people's nature. If prophecies capable of disrupting the balance are proclaimed, the Tiger comes. But if the balance is disrupted fundamentally, then the Two-in-One appears."

"Who is he?" I asked. "I had meetings with vampires, I know he's an ancient vampire god . . ."

"Ah, he's not the vampires' god," Arina said with a frown. "Those ancient, toothy bloodsuckers are too ambitious. The Two-in-One is the great balancer, the eraser, the purger. If human civilization goes off the rails, he comes and destroys it. He reduces life to the most basic, banal truths. Eating, drinking, killing, reproducing. That's what the Two-in-One does, he simplifies."

"Well he hasn't managed it yet," I said.

"Who told you that?" Arina asked in surprise. "He has come many times before."

"But we're alive. People are alive. And he—"

"The Two-in-One doesn't kill all the people!" she exclaimed, gesturing abruptly. "He kills the Others, or almost all of them—to be honest I don't know exactly. 'Five days are left to Others, six days to the people,' right? Where does it say that everyone will die?"

"Well . . ." I said embarrassed. "From the context it—"

"Not everyone," Arina said calmly. "The overwhelming majority. Ninety-nine percent. Or 99.9 percent. And a large number of animals will die too, especially the more complex ones. Do you know why?"

I shook my head.

"Because Power will come gushing into the world. Because the Twilight can't recycle it all, it doesn't need that much. And if the Others, who use Power, who control it through the Twilight and bleed off the excess, are killed, then people will be swamped by Power. One by one, they will all acquire the ability to work magic. And then it will start. It's not even like giving a man a machine gun—this is an atom bomb. Imagine you're an ordinary man. And suddenly you find that you're able to work miracles. Only simple ones to begin with. But what are the simplest things? Burning. Blasting. Freezing. Shredding."

"Everyone has enemies," I said.

"Of course. And even if you don't want to harm anyone, you'll feel frightened that they want to harm you. And you'll start flinging magic about wildly, simply in order to defend yourself and your loved ones. Some will learn to do certain things, some will try to introduce rules and new laws, but people won't have enough time to learn how to handle this gift, there won't be any teachers to help them to understand how to live as Others. There won't be any Watches. And the world will collapse."

She paused for a moment and then went on.

"Yes, and don't forget about the animals. They generate Power too. And when magic is accessible to everyone, when there's an excess of it, the Twilight will start fulfilling *their* wishes. And animals have very simple wishes, Anton. Even simpler than people's."

"The world will come to an end," I said.

"Almost. It will go on until very few people are left and the survivors learn how to cope with their new powers. Until homeostasis is restored and people lose their magical abilities . . . But new Others will appear among them. They'll be primitive and weak by our standards, but in the changed world *they* will be the kings and rulers. And history will embark on a new cycle. Yet again."

"Which brings us back to the Sixth Watch," I said. "To how you happen to know about it and what we can do."

Arina nodded.

"All right, only I don't want to tell the same story a hundred times. Call the Tiger."

"What Tiger?" I asked in an unnatural voice.

"The one who brought you here. It's not possible for an Other to enter the Sarcophagus of Time. I'm not a fool, Anton."

CHAPTER 4

THE WITCHES WERE EATING. IT WAS PROBABLY A NERVOUS RE-
sponse. I had assumed that after I disappeared with the Tiger they
would start discussing the situation or all go to their rooms. But
they had decided to continue with their meal.

The hors d'oeuvres and the cognac had disappeared from the
tables, and entrées of every description had appeared. The meat
dishes included roasted piglets, saddles of lamb, and roast beef.
There were all kinds of poultry, from quails to grouse and turkeys.
And the fish ran from filleted trout to immense sturgeon carved
into slices. The only alcohol left now was wine, but there was an
incredible amount of it. The pretty young witches acting as wait-
resses kept bringing out dishes of oysters and prawns, which were
eaten raw.

"I've arrived at a good moment," Arina said in a quiet voice.

We walked back to the same spot from which I had left, right
beside the top table. Nadya was sitting in her place, having a friendly
conversation about something with the witches beside her.

"After you," I said quietly to Arina. "I think it's you they've been
waiting for."

Arina snorted and walked up to the table. She reached her hand
over Ernesta's shoulder and took a quail off her plate.

Silence fell in the hall. All the jaws that had been eagerly grinding up food stopped moving and all eyes were fixed on the Great Grandmother who had returned from oblivion. Only Nadya looked pleased to see me. I forced myself to smile at her in return.

"Too spicy," Arina said, breaking the silence. She crunched up the whole quail, including the bones, like a wolf. "I see you're gorging yourselves, sisters."

"Arina!" Ernesta exclaimed, jumping up and hugging the other witch.

"And hello to you, you old pest," Arina replied good-naturedly. "So in a tight corner you remembered me, did you?"

"Well, as you know, my dear, we don't have any procedure for removing Great Grandmothers from their position if they disappear without a trace . . . or if they desert . . ." Ernesta purred.

"You should try deserting to where I've been," Arina retorted sarcastically. "So the Shoot hasn't acknowledged another mistress then?"

Arina reached out her hand, and the pot with the wooden phallus crept across the table toward her. She gave the Shoot a gentle slap and the dry wood seemed to explode, throwing up green sprigs that transformed it into a bush, which was instantly covered in white blossoms. Arina waited a few moments while the flowers dropped their petals and shrank, setting into strange fruits that looked like tiny white apples.

Arina casually picked one, tossed it into her mouth, and chewed it.

Ernesta lowered her head and squatted down in a deep, old-fashioned curtsy. Chairs scraped back as the witches got up and bowed to Arina, some curtsying or going down on their knees.

"Enough, enough," Arina said with a wave of her hand. "I have returned, sisters. No need for applause."

"She's amusing," the Tiger said quietly behind my back. "A good thing I didn't kill her."

"And it's lucky for us that we didn't kill you," I added.

The Tiger smiled.

Then he leaned his head to one side, listening to something.

He frowned.

"Daddy!" Nadya exclaimed, jumping up and nestling against me.

Arina wiped her hand on her hip.

"Ernesta, did you secure the Conclave?" she asked.

"Arina!" the other witch replied indignantly.

"Easy now, I'm not blaming you," said Arina.

The windows in the restaurant looked out onto a mountainside with the glittering threads of ski tracks running down it and Sno-Cats creeping across the surface on their caterpillar tracks. Suddenly the glass in one window started jangling and the witches sitting close to it all jumped up and moved away. The panes first bent inward and then bulged outward like sheets of polythene.

"You have to leave," said the Tiger. "Anton, do you hear me?"

The glass gave a final rattle and then shattered into a spray of daggerlike splinters. Some of the pieces were motionless, suspended in midair; other pieces were thrown back and some simply disappeared. Every one of the witches who had come to the Conclave must have been wearing dozens of protective amulets.

Cold air blew in through the broken window.

And then the Two-in-One jumped up into the restaurant, soaring over the windowsill. He landed gently on the floor and froze.

In the few hours that had passed, he had changed fundamentally: I realized what Arina had meant when she asked if the two Others were "together."

The former Light Magician Denis and the former Dark Magician Alexei had fused and they weren't wearing any clothes. The bare sides of their bodies had grown together, as if they were Siamese twins, their pelvises and shoulders had turned outward to the sides, and they were now a single contorted creature with four legs and four arms. There was one leg at each side and two in the middle, which looked as if they were starting to fuse together—the genitals had receded, leaving barely a trace. There was a pair of arms above each side leg and the two heads were leaning inward, pressing against each other. It was an insane hybrid, worthy of the insane Dr. Moreau.

A spider-man, but nothing like the hero from the American comics: This was a repulsive monster.

"A real charmer," Nadya said in a quiet voice.

"Sir, this is a private function," Arina said loudly. "Kindly leave the premises."

The Two-in-One laughed in two voices and flung out his arms, as if he was about to embrace the entire hall.

"I like that!" Alexei's head said.

"How sweet!" Denis's head added.

"Stall him," Arina told Ernesta, swinging around and taking Nadya and myself by the hand.

It was very telling that even here, surrounded by the two hundred most powerful witches in the world, at a venue protected by countless spells and amulets, it never occurred to Arina to say "kill him."

We set off at a run toward the doors of the service area at the far end of the restaurant, leaving a crowd of frightened and infuriated witches between us and the Two-in-One.

But I must admit that frightened as they were, they obeyed their Great Grandmother's order. When I reached the doors I looked around, letting Nadya and Arina go on ahead, and saw a genuine battle beginning.

The floor of the restaurant cracked open, sending parquet blocks flying in all directions. Prickly, flowing vines grew up through the hole, encircling the Two-in-One, before immediately crumbling to dust. Chairs and tables started advancing on the spiderlike monster, as if this were a children's cartoon. I watched a table run (its legs even bent at the knees!) and crash into the Two-in-One's belly, shattering into splinters. All the cutlery on the tables flew to one spot, meshed, and stood up as a skeletal figure that was two yards tall, with knives for fingers and a jaws made from lobster crackers. This metal monster fought the Two-in-One longer than anything else, lashing him with its knives and trying to thrust them into his body, until it was melted.

The Two-in-One's choice of spells wasn't very fancy. Fire and ice, heat and cold. He only used pure Power a few times, to fling witches aside and deflect magical blows.

"Anton!" the Tiger shouted, grabbing me by the shoulder and shoving me through the doorway. His face was contorted in fury—something I had never expected to see. "Wake up! They won't stop him!"

"What if we all try?"

"You won't stop him either!"

"What about you?"

The Tiger pushed me forward and I accepted the inevitable and ran. He didn't want to fight. Neither did Arina, and she seemed to know even more than the Tiger did.

We were in the kitchen, where pretty young witches were working away, evidently very proud of their assignment. Food was boiling and steaming in large pans, filling the air with delicious aromas, timers were beeping, and sliced meat and diced vegetables were lying on chopping boards.

"*Was sollen wir jetzt tun? Was sollen wir jetzt bloß tun?*" asked a young witch, grabbing me by the shoulder. She was genuinely young, not concealing her real appearance. And she was curious; she wanted to know what was going on, didn't want to hide from the magical bloodbath.

"*Flieht!*" I shouted. "Run!"

"*Aber wir können Ihnen helfen!*" the young witch suggested bravely, spreading out her hands. Blue sparks started flickering between her fingers. A great help she would be . . .

"*Flieht!*" I barked, looking around for Arina and Nadya. They were already at the far end of the kitchen. I noticed a boy about three years old sitting on a table. He was bawling and rubbing his eyes with his little fists. What I was thinking must have shown in my face, because the young witch grabbed the boy and hugged him tightly.

"*Das ist mein Sohn!*" she shouted. "*Mein Sohn—nicht das, was Sie denken!*"

She wasn't lying, it really was her son and not a snack for the witches.

"*Dann solltest du erst recht von hier verschwinden, du Närrin! Bring dich in Sicherheit!*" I shouted and ran on. The Tiger was covering our retreat, moving through the chaos and uproar with his typical grace.

I don't know if the little witch took my advice, or if a sense of duty to her "sisters" outweighed her fear for her son and she joined the battle against the Two-in-One.

I didn't look back.

We ran out of the kitchen into a space that was cool and airy. Some kind of utility room or pantry . . . Arina was already fiddling with the lock on the tall metal doors. First she tried to open it, then she simply smashed it off with a blow of her hand (I spotted a tiny, economical discharge of Power). The doors swung open and she dashed out into the night and the swirling snow. Nadya paused for a moment, waiting for me, and then we all ran out after Arina. I slammed the door shut and sealed it with the Absolute Lock.

"This is bad," the Tiger gasped behind me. "Very bad . . . The Twilight is closed off."

"Open it, you *are* the Twilight!" I told him.

"I can't," the Tiger answered, "*He's* the Twilight now. I don't have the right!"

We were standing on a snowy road at the foot of a shallow slope. A Sno-Cat with blinking blue lights was slowly creeping up the slope, making mournful sounds. I didn't feel the cold at all.

"We'll have to fight," I said. "We'll have to—"

The Absolute Lock can't be removed, it just dissipates spontaneously after a while. So the Two-in-One simply smashed the door to tatters. For a moment the metal was covered by a bluish crust of ice, and then it shattered like glass. Had he cooled it all the way down to absolute zero, then?

The Two-in-One ran out after us, and I realized that his duel with the witches had taken a serious toll: One of his central legs had been torn off at the knee and black liquid was spurting out of the stump. But that didn't seem to bother him. And neither did the massive kitchen knife thrust into Denis's eye right up to the handle, or the huge orange tomcat clinging to Alexei's neck and methodically scraping the former Black Magician's face with its claws.

"You've come too soon, Two-in-One!" I shouted. "This is only the third time!"

Denis's remaining eye glared at me.

"This one counts double," the Two-in-One replied.

The monster's four arms reached out toward us and I mentally activated my Shields, moving back and protecting Nadya and Arina with my own body.

"Dad!" Nadya shouted, and I felt a stream of Power flowing from her to me. I glanced around briefly at my daughter and saw that Arina was no longer there beside her. The old witch had gone. She had abandoned us!

"Stop!" said the Tiger, stepping between me and the Two-in-One. "You're breaking the rules here. The time hasn't come yet! The prophecy said three victims the fourth time, on the fifth day!"

"Out of my way, you brat," said the Two-in-One, striking the Tiger with a boiling jet of fire from his right hands and a swirling stream of blue-black smoke from his left hands. "I don't give a rotten damn for your prophecies!"

The Tiger shook himself and crimson flames and blue chunks of ice fell off him onto the ground. The asphalt under his feet started boiling and swelled up into humps. The snow and ice evaporated into clouds of heavy, bluish mist.

"No one has any right to violate prophecies!" the Tiger exclaimed almost joyfully.

He stepped forward, tugging his feet out of the molten asphalt. I could feel the heat, even behind the Shields I had put up.

"And now I have the right to act," the Tiger said, moving toward the Two-in-One.

The Two-in-One dashed at him and the two creatures of the Twilight merged into a single, tangled knot.

They rolled across the ground, embroiled in an ordinary, straight-forward fight, not a battle of magic. But perhaps sorcery was involved after all. When the embodiments of two laws of nature—two functions that have acquired human form—fight each other, it has to be magic, even if the battle is fought with teeth and nails, fangs and talons.

The Two-in-One didn't change; he fought in his "human spider" form. But the Tiger's shape shifted. Sometimes I could see flashes of paws and ferociously bared teeth. And sometimes I saw bloodied hands and a human face with an equally ferocious grin.

It all seemed to be happening at the same time, as if he were man and beast simultaneously.

The orange tomcat came flying out of the tangle with its legs splayed and dashed across the snow toward the doors of the restaurant, meowing wildly.

I started backing away toward Nadya. There was nothing I could do to help the Tiger. If I struck any kind of blow I risked hitting our only protector.

"Open a portal!" I shouted to my daughter.

"I can't! The Twilight's boiling!" she exclaimed despairingly. "Everything's swirling about . . ."

I could also sense that something was wrong with the Twilight, without having to glance into it. The ground under my feet started shuddering. Ghostly purple lights appeared on the mountaintops. A low, intense humming sound filled the air.

The Twilight was fighting with itself. Its two incarnations were grappling in mortal combat: the Two-in-One, the ancient destroyer of civilizations, and the Tiger, their ancient protector. Both immensely powerful. Both remorseless.

But the Tiger had only one indisputable right—to ensure that we didn't die today. To protect the prophecy that had been proclaimed.

"Let's run for it, Nadya," I said. "Come on . . . this wrestling is bound to end badly."

"Dad, we won't get away," my daughter said, taking hold of my hand. And then she said something I had never heard her say, even when she was a child: "Dad, I'm afraid . . ."

There was a blinding flash, a bright streak of fire and ice, as if something had exploded deep in the tangle of fighting bodies. They fell apart, with the Two-in-One flying off in one direction and the Tiger in the other.

But the Two-in-One got up, and the Tiger just lay there.

The Two-in-One looked at me with his only remaining eye—one of Denis's. The knife was still protruding from the eye socket beside it. Alexei's face had been reduced to bloody mush and his head was spinning about wildly.

"You're all—" wheezed the Two-in-One.

At that very moment a Sno-Cat came rumbling across the road on its caterpillar tracks. Its blinking lights and beepers had been switched off and its scoop was lowered.

The vehicle crashed into the Two-in-One, toppling him over and crushing him. It then started spinning around on the spot, pulping the human flesh with its tracks. The Two-in-One howled in two voices and fell silent.

Nadya and I just stood there, dumbstruck.

The Sno-Cat came to a halt and its engine cut out. The door of the cabin opened and Arina clambered out and jumped down onto the snow.

"I thought you'd run away," I said.

"You can't run away from destiny, silly," Arina replied.

I walked up to the Sno-Cat and looked at a hand protruding from under a caterpillar track. The hand twitched, as if it could sense my gaze, and it grabbed at the frozen ground. The vehicle jerked upward and the maimed, half-crushed Two-in-One started creeping out from under a machine that weighed tons.

"You never know when to stop, you brute," said Arina, leaning down over the Two-in-One, who had already crept halfway out. She was holding the Shoot—no longer a flowering bush, but a wooden

phallus again. Only now, without its pot, the Shoot looked less obscene, at least from one side—and from that side it looked like a
wooden dagger.

Arina raised it over her head and swung it down hard and fast,
piercing the body of the Two-in-One. The mutilated monster suddenly disappeared without a trace and the dagger, stuck in the
ground, darkened as it clad itself in bark and grew a single, thin
sprout.

"You killed him!" I said. "You killed him!"

"The Two-in-One's not that easy to kill," Arina said regretfully. "I
stopped him for a while."

"And where is he?"

"He withdrew into the Twilight," said Arina. "To lick his wounds."

"Dad!" Nadya shrieked.

I went dashing to my daughter. She was kneeling beside the Tiger,
who was stirring feebly, trying to sit up. I leaned down and held out
my hand to help him to his feet.

"How does it look?" the Tiger asked, turning toward me.

It looked appalling—half of the Tiger's head was missing. It had
been sliced off neatly from the top down to one ear, leaving a surface
with a smooth, glassy crust. Or perhaps the wound was filled with
glass.

"I'd say you're dead."

"What a good thing I'm not human," said the Tiger, thrusting
his hand into the gap for a moment. Then he shrugged and asked:
"Have you got any cigarettes?"

"Won't that be bad for you?" I asked, trying not to look at the
fearsome wound. I rummaged in my pockets—I'd put those cigarettes that the Tiger gave me in one of them . . .

"Nothing's bad for me any longer," the Tiger replied calmly. "I've
only got two minutes left to live."

"And what then?" asked Nadya, bewildered.

"Then I'll withdraw into the Twilight, little girl," said the Tiger.
"I broke the rules."

"No you didn't!" I said. "You were protecting the prophecy! Performing your own function!"

"That's splitting hairs," the Tiger said. Taking the pack from me, he pulled out a cigarette, stuck it in his mouth, and it lit up. "It worked though," he said. "Unfortunately, midnight arrived while we were fighting. After that I didn't have any right to stop the Two-in-One from killing you."

"But you stopped him anyway!" Nadya exclaimed.

"That's right," the Tiger said with a nod. "Let's just say I got carried away."

"Is there anything we can do?" I asked. "Can we help? You're not a human being . . ."

"That's just the problem. The Twilight has cut me off. Turned off the Power, if you like."

The Tiger blew out a jet of smoke and looked up at the clear night sky. "You're lucky. You have the stars. Someday human beings will stop killing each other with the Two-in-One's help and reach the stars."

"I can give you Power!" Nadya shouted. "I'm an Absolute Other! How much do you need, Tiger?"

The Tiger looked at my daughter and I thought I sensed a rapid, unspoken dialogue between them. Nadya lowered her eyes.

"Don't be sad," said the Tiger. "I told you, I'm not human at all. I won't even die like you do. Don't be sad. You have to cope with *him*. And you have Arina now; she seems to know what to do."

"Tiger," I said. The final seconds of his life were draining away, but I had to ask this. "Remember what you called me at the Sarcophagus? You were wrong. I'm a Light One."

"I didn't say you were a Dark One." The Tiger laughed. "Ask Zabulon. He'll explain."

The Tiger stretched, dropped his cigarette, and ground it out thoroughly with his foot. He raised his head and looked up at the sky again with a smile.

Then he sank down and sat on the ground.

Of course he wasn't human, but he died like a man, in every sense of the word. Unlike the Two-in-One, his body remained lying there. The glassy flesh darkened and started bleeding.

I hugged Nadya and held her close, then looked at Arina, who had come over to us.

"Take out the Minoan Sphere," I told her.

"Where to?" the witch asked in a quiet voice.

"The Day Watch office. To Zabulon."

Arina froze with the Sphere in her hands.

"Are you sure?"

"Absolutely. And don't try to run away, you'll be ashamed for the rest of your life."

"As if there was much of that life left . . ." Arina muttered.

Oh, how they gaped at her!

Our two Great Higher Ones: Gesar and Zabulon. The Son of Tibet and the Son of Judea. The Light One and the Dark One.

She sat there modestly, opposite them, wearing a business suit that looked surprisingly appropriate in Zabulon's office. The witch Arina: the head of the Conclave of Witches.

Zabulon was still in his incredibly maniacal mood. It wasn't obvious at first glance, but then he kissed Arina ceremoniously on the hand and complimented her in French.

"Comme vous êtes charmante!"

"Ah, you old rogue," Arina replied flirtatiously.

Gesar said nothing, but sat there glaring at the witch, while she studiously ignored him.

Olga sat in the corner of the office, breathing smoke from her cigarette into an expensive Japanese air purifier and watching Gesar intently. Arina cast a fleeting glance at her before speaking again.

"Stop that now, Boris. I forgave you a long time ago."

Gesar turned as red as if he was about to have an apoplectic fit, but still didn't say anything.

Svetlana simply sat at one side with her arms around Nadya. She hadn't asked any questions when we appeared in Zabulon's office; she'd just taken her daughter and hugged her.

Maybe she already knew everything anyway. Maybe they'd been tracking us and had seen it all.

I couldn't care less if they had.

"I promised Arina that she wouldn't be harmed, that her freedom would not be restricted, and that she would not be forced to do anything she found offensive," I said. "She has promised to tell us everything she knows about the Two-in-One and the Sixth Watch."

"We've discovered a thing or two as well," Gesar said reluctantly. "A thing or two . . . Go on, Arina."

"The Two-in-One is the purger of human civilization," said Arina. "To be more precise, when the human race violates the age-old balance between good and evil, the Twilight starts suffering. So when the equilibrium is disrupted, the Twilight tries to restore it. And since the Twilight reflects the moral and ethical condition of humankind, it is biased toward evil and the methods it uses are not the kindest. It sends the Two-in-One, who purges."

"How?" Gesar asked.

"In the simplest way possible, from the Twilight's point of view. The Two-in-One kills the Others. Either all of them or at least the overwhelming majority—I don't think he really needs to drag the final vampire out of his coffin or the final shape-shifter out of his burrow. In normal circumstances, we Others maintain the balance of Power; we use up the excess. Which means that people aren't able to make use of magic, which spares them the temptation of dangerous toys."

"If we die, then the people will kill each other," Gesar said pensively.

"Yes. The vestiges of civilization that remain are very simple, but strangely enough the balance between good and evil is restored."

"What's so strange about that?" Zabulon exclaimed gleefully. "It's not evil to smack your neighbor over the head with a club, make him work in your field, and make his wife warm your bed. That's normal, natural behavior. Basic practicality. Animals are also beyond good and evil—when a wolf kills a hare, it doesn't feel any hatred. Evil is when you convince your neighbor that he ought to work in your field, give his wife to you, and sing your praises at the same time."

"Thank you, we get the idea," Gesar told him in an icy voice.

"The Two-in-One was the first emanation of the Twilight, the first agent of its will," Arina continued. "He concluded the very first, most ancient covenant between the Twilight and the Others. We Others maintain the equilibrium between good and evil, allowing the Twilight to lead a calm and comfortable existence. But if evil becomes dominant, the Two-in-One comes and makes us pay the bill. And now that time has arrived."

"And what if good becomes dominant?" Nadya asked quietly.

"Unfortunately, my girl, that has never happened," Arina replied. I thought I caught a note of genuine compassion in her voice. "At least, it has never happened on a global scale. Although we have tried to make it happen, of course. Throughout history, new religions have been invented, new ethical principles, new variations on the social contract . . ."

"Communism was a stupid idea though," said Zabulon, keeping his voice low to avoid an unnecessary argument.

"Are you sure the time is here?" Gesar asked Arina, ignoring Zabulon. "But why am I asking? He wouldn't have appeared otherwise . . . Why do you know about this? Why don't we know? Why is there nothing in the archives of the Inquisition? Who cleaned out every last mention of the Sixth Watch and the Two-in-One?"

"Do you really not understand, Gesar?" Arina asked. "Honestly and truly?"

Olga stubbed out her cigarette with an abrupt movement and got up.

"We cleaned it all out. Isn't that right, witch?"

"Of course," said Arina. "It was a secret, naturally, but there was the Watch of Six, which kept the secret, and there were documents in the archives. And the Higher Ones knew, including you and Zabulon."

"I have already reached that conclusion by logical deduction!" Zabulon added. "If there is information that I am obliged to know, but I don't know it, then the only possible explanation is that I made myself forget it. I couldn't have been influenced from the outside. Discard the impossible and the improbable must be true."

"Thank you, we appreciate your opinion," said Gesar. "When did this happen? Who was involved?"

"The full membership of the Sixth Watch. And all the Higher Others knew."

"Why was it done?" Gesar asked.

"It was 1914," Arina stated simply. "A hundred years ago. You began an experiment, with a world war and a revolution in Russia. We all know that the scientist influences the results of the experiment, if he knows basically what is happening. You wanted to turn humankind toward the good and you were afraid that your knowledge of the Two-in-One would prevent you from doing what . . . what was necessary."

"Who is 'you'?" Gesar asked indignantly. "Is that me? Or Zabulon?"

"You and Zabulon, among others. Essentially all the Great Ones were involved, but it was you and Zabulon who insisted on holding the experiment in Russia. And at the very last moment, by the way! France was the favorite, with Germany and Great Britain hot on its heels. The United States was excluded from the start—their previous experiment with the Civil War was considered a failure. But you insisted that Russia must be the guinea pig."

"Me and my patriotism," Gesar grunted.

"Well, you could call it that," Arina replied sarcastically. "What you actually said was: 'It's a savage country, it won't be any great loss.'"

Zabulon laughed and slapped his hands down on the desk.

"That's excellent, Gesar! That's wonderful. How very like a Light One."

"And you . . ." Arina began.

"Stop! I don't wish to know!" Zabulon cried. "It has no bearing on the business at hand, and I don't want to know."

"Whatever you say," Arina agreed amiably. "We purged everything. All the data in the archives. All the records in the chronicles. Nothing was left but the scraps of vampire legends and references in secondary documents that everyone had forgotten about. And then we wiped our own memories clean. We took a very thorough approach."

"But why can you remember it?" Gesar asked.

"I took a different view from the very start," she said. "I sensed that neither of the experiments would turn out well. Neither the world war nor the revolution. You can't coerce human nature like that. And you can't make good out of evil. No one can manage that."

"But you remember!" Gesar persisted.

"I kept my memory in a separate place." Arina laughed. "We witches have an artifact that stores the memories of all the Great Grandmothers. I didn't even have to do anything special, so you didn't spot any cunning on my part. The moment I picked up that artifact, I remembered . . . And I realized what we had done. But it was too late. All I could do was watch what was happening to Russia. Keep an eye on you idiots. And follow instructions . . . Until I got too sick of it all."

Gesar and Zabulon sat there looking miserable and wretched. The grin of maniacal glee had even disappeared from Zabulon's face.

And I must say I really enjoyed that.

"So you know everything, then?" Olga asked in a businesslike tone. "Who the members of the Sixth Watch are and how to defeat the Two-in-One? There's no point in going over old grudges now."

"No, there isn't," Arina concurred. "Yes, I know. That's why I was so distraught. I could see the way everything was going. I was searching for a solution. A way to save myself and all of us, to save the country and the entire human race. But I didn't find it . . . Didn't you ever even wonder why in Russia the subtle world suddenly started warping and cracking? An Inferno breaks through, an Absolute Enchantress is born, the *Fuaran* is found, the Tiger appears . . . What do you make of all that? Things come apart when they're botched."

"Well," said Gesar, looking at me and Svetlana, then averting his gaze. "The Absolute Enchantress was my initiative."

"Ours," Zabulon said unexpectedly, and I looked at him in amazement.

"Ours," Gesar agreed. "We saw that the Twilight was unsettled. Certain fragments of knowledge kept resurfacing . . ."

"So we carried out certain work," said Zabulon. "To prepare for the appearance of an Absolute Enchantress. As a weapon against the Twilight."

"There was something the Tiger told me before he died," I said, staring at Zabulon. "He said I was 'begotten of the Darkness.' And he told me you would explain what that meant."

"Yes, I can explain that," Zabulon said glibly.

"Please don't," Gesar said to him. "Let's get on with business."

"This has to do with our business," I said. "Tell me."

"You could say it's all a matter of genetics," Zabulon began. "Or even—"

"Don't," said Gesar, raising his voice.

"Or even eugenics," Zabulon continued. "The abilities of an Other are not necessarily inherited by offspring, but there is a definite correlation, which is easiest to calculate after several generations. We don't study the genes, but we calculate the lines of probability."

Gesar didn't protest anymore. He just sat there, looking at me.

"The Absolute Enchantress had to be born from two lines," said Zabulon, keeping his eyes fixed on me. "One of them had to be Light—and that was quite easy, there was a very wide choice. The other line had to be Dark, and it had to pass through me. That was mandatory."

I swallowed the lump that had risen in my throat.

"But I'm a Light One," I said.

"Boris Ignatievich was convinced that a Light One and Dark One wouldn't be able to get on together," said Zabulon. "So he waited for the right moment and initiated you in a Light state of mind. I was very offended by that for a long time, and to be honest, I was angry with you too, although it wasn't your fault in any way."

"My father was an ordinary human being," I said firmly. "A normal, ordinary human being!"

"Yes," Zabulon agreed readily. "It's an unfortunate fact that children rarely inherit the abilities of Others; they usually skip a generation. Gesar and Olga actually had a candidate of their own, but they managed to lose the boy somehow and only found him again when it was too late. And my last four granddaughters actually have no Other abilities whatsoever. But things went a bit better with my three grandsons—and you were the lucky one."

"Dad is your grandson?" Nadya asked in the silence that had fallen.

Zabulon gave an embarrassed shrug.

"So that makes me your great-granddaughter?" Nadya went on.

"And what about me? Gesar, who are you to me?" Svetlana exclaimed.

She jumped to her feet and dashed across to Gesar, who pulled back, raising his hands in a gesture of appeasement.

"Who are you to me? My father? My grandfather? What sort of Bollywood epic is this? Maybe I should start dancing and break into a song about the long-lost daughter who has been found?"

"You're not related to me," Gesar said in a loud, emphatic voice. "There were Light Ones in your family line, you had the potential of a Great Enchantress, and that was enough! Yes, we exploited you, we put you in contact with . . . suitable candidates. And we wrote Nadezhda's birth into your destiny! But that's all. I'm not your relative!"

"What a pleasure it is to hear that!" Svetlana exclaimed, and slapped Gesar hard on the cheek.

The Great Light One put his hand to his face and gaped at her in confusion.

"I've been dreaming about doing that for a long time," Svetlana declared joyfully.

"Give him another for me," I said.

"Gladly!" said Svetlana, and she did. Then she turned to Nadya and said. "That's all, we're leaving."

"It will mean the end of the world, little girl," said Arina.

"I couldn't give a damn," Svetlana replied. "Don't order me around, you old witch. Or are you my mother, or granny, or great granny?"

"Now leave me out of that!" Arina exclaimed, throwing up her hands. "All we women are sisters! And no matter what kind of mess the men might make, we have to answer for life, don't we? And you're a doctor, you swore the Hippocratic oath."

"The Soviet doctor's oath," Svetlana replied morosely, but she sat down again beside Nadya and pulled her daughter close.

"Everyone calm down," Arina continued in a conciliatory tone. "This is no reason for a quarrel. As if you didn't know, Sveta, that you were prepared for Nadya's birth and led toward it. So what? You have an intelligent, beautiful daughter. Do you really regret that? And you, Anton? This old fogey had a little fling with your grandmother. You can barely even remember her, and did you ever even think about your grandfather? You didn't care who he was. Well there he is now, your biological grandfather. It makes no difference to anything."

"Yes it does!" Nadya protested. "The kids asked me in school: 'Gorodetsky, are you a Jew?' And I said there weren't any Jews in my family. But there are. I lied to them all!"

And that suddenly relieved the tension. Zabulon started laughing first, grunting and hammering his fists on the table. Gesar started smiling, still holding his hand over the cheek that had been slapped first. Olga smiled and shook her head, and even Svetlana couldn't suppress a chuckle.

"Feeling better now?" Arina asked amicably, and I suddenly suspected that our merriment had been prompted by one of her subtle, inconspicuous witch's spells. She was very good at doing that sort of thing. "Now, let's get back to business. The Watch of Six consisted of representatives of the Six Great Parties . . ."

"What a surprise," said Svetlana.

"First, a vampire," Arina continued. "A representative of the most ancient Others. The college of vampires was represented in the Watch of Six by Viteslav."

"May his dust rest in peace," said Zabulon. "Ah, Kostya, you creep—just look who you killed!"

"In fact, none of them are still alive, apart from me," Arina told us. "Second, the witches. As you already realize, I represented the Conclave. Third, a representative of the Light magicians: Alfred Klaus Lange."

"He was killed in 1040, in a duel with the Black Magician Christophe Gautier," Gesar chimed in.

"To be more precise, they killed each other," Zabulon added. "For some reason they suddenly developed very strong feelings about the relations between Germany and France. A strange business, they seemed to be drawn to each other . . . Ah! I understand!"

"That's right," said Arina. "Gauthier represented the Dark Magicians. Obviously there really was some kind of morbid, subconscious attraction between them; they got along very well together in the Sixth Watch." She squinted sideways at Nadya.

"I'm only a little girl and I don't understand any of your innuendoes," Nadya declared.

"Fifth, there was a Prophet," Arina continued.

"A Prophet," I said with satisfaction. "So there *was* a prophet. And I think I know that prophet, don't I, Arina?"

"You did know him." Arina said with a nod. "Erasmus Darwin. A good kind of fellow, but unfortunately he drank to excess. Especially after he purged his own memory . . . He suddenly seemed to run wild."

"His life lost its meaning," Gesar said softly.

I looked at Zabulon, but he didn't say anything. Erasmus had once been his pupil, but the Dark Magician's face was like a mask of stone.

"And the sixth party . . ." Arina paused for a moment. "In fact this party is not represented by an Other in the literal sense of the word."

"An uninitiated Other," I said. "A Mirror Magician. Right?"

Arina nodded.

"You almost figured it all out. A Mirror. A wonderful young girl by the name of Maria Montessori. When she forgot about serving on the Watch of Six, she forgot all about the world of the Others. But she had a well-rounded personality and she lived an interesting life. A human life."

"Gesar and I can appoint the representatives from the Parties of Darkness and Light," said Zabulon. "We have that right. You can appoint a representative for the witches . . ."

"That's no problem," said Arina, shaking her head. "I'll go myself."

"The vampires have acquired a new leader," Zabulon continued. "And in view of her direct involvement in recent events, I think she will soon present herself to us. That leaves a Prophet and the Mirror Magician."

"The Mirror Magician is in Moscow, we both know him," Gesar said coldly.

"Ah, everything is knotted together so tightly." Zabulon sighed. "Who brought him here?"

"I asked him to come," I said.

"Oh, well done, Antoshka," Zabulon said with a nod.

I pretended not to have heard him use the diminutive form of my name.

"And a Prophet," Gesar added. "I suppose that Glyba . . ."

"Not Glyba," I said. "Innokentii Tolkov."

"Justify that remark," Gesar told me.

"Everything here is interconnected," I said. "And there are also additional conditions, which mean that the representatives have to be the following: Innokentii Tolkov for the Prophets, Zabulon for the Dark Ones, and Nadya for the Light Ones."

CHAPTER 5

THE DAY WATCH OFFICE WAS EMPTY. ZABULON HAD SENT ALL his colleagues home, even the operational duty officers, before we appeared. They wouldn't have been a help in any case.

So the tea and sandwiches were brought by Sveta and Nadya.

"There was something else in the Prophecy too, remember?" I began. 'The Sixth Watch is dead'—well that's clear enough. Prophets are obliged to maintain the rhythm of prophecy, so the six parties had to be listed. But Prophets can't prophesy about themselves. For instance, the prophecy said 'The Fifth Power has disappeared.' I think that's about the witches, and specifically about Arina."

Arina nodded.

" 'The Fourth Power has come too late,' " I continued. "That's about Egor. If the Mirror Magician had already been embodied . . . or if Vitalii Rogoza had been able to carry out his function to the end, then everything would have gone differently. Svetlana would have been killed. Nadya wouldn't have been born. Maybe I would have died too."

Sveta hugged Nadya without saying a word. That was the way they sat almost all the time now, huddled up against each other.

"The Mirror wasn't trying to liquidate a banal imbalance of force in the Moscow Watches," I said. "He was trying to deal with the global problem. But he didn't have time . . . 'The Third Power does not believe'—that's about us, the Light Ones. About you, Gesar. We've lost our sense of purpose, we've lost our belief and our hope."

Gesar looked away.

" 'The Second Power is afraid,' " I said, nodding to Zabulon. "Sorry, Granddad, but that's about you."

Zabulon bared his teeth in a white smile.

" 'The First Power is exhausted,' " I concluded. "The vampires. They were the first force of Others. They are exhausted. Worn out. They have degenerated. We have proved to be better predators than the undead who drink blood."

"All right, but what does all this have to do with the composition of the Sixth Watch?" asked Olga.

"I'll go on in a moment," I said. "But in the meantime it would be a good idea to send for Egor and Innokentii."

"I already have," said Gesar. "I don't agree with what you're saying, but they're on the way. Carry on."

"There's also the thing that Lilith said," I added, looking at Zabulon. "But first I'd like to know who she was and what was her relationship to you."

"She was one of the first," said Zabulon. "And once, a very long time ago, she . . . took me under her wing."

I waited for more.

"I think the blood that runs in my veins was in hers too," Zabulon continued reluctantly. "Her life began in the most ancient of times and she hid from everyone. But she owed me a few favors. And I owed her some too. Perhaps she was one of the group that met the Two-in-One. I was hoping that Lilith would tell you more. For the same reason that she maintained contact with me."

"Blood," I said.

"Yes, blood."

I recalled the ancient beast who had crumbled to dust in my home. Could my line of descent really run back to her? Could Nadya really be descended from her?

Anything was possible. We don't choose our ancestors.

And we're not obliged to live up to their expectations.

"Some of what she said simply confirms other information," I went on. "She listed the parties, in her own way. The one born of the Light is a Light One."

No one argued with that.

"Then one born of the Darkness is a Dark Magician."

Or with that.

"The one who took another's Power is a vampire."

Gesar nodded.

"The one who has no Power of his own is a Mirror Magician."

Zabulon nodded.

"The one who sees is a Prophet."

Svetlana sighed.

"The one who senses is a witch."

Arina raised her hand to attract attention before adding: "But the most important thing she said was very . . . vampirish. Ancient. All of the Six must be bound by the primary power. The first power. Blood."

"Pyotr, the Neanderthal vampire, said that his blood is in every living person on earth." Olga reminded us. "And in principle he's right. We are all of the same blood."

"Yes, but I don't think that that kind of homeopathic dilution is what is meant here," I said. "If I'm right, it's all very simple. Nadya has to be one of our group—she's an Absolute Enchantress, the only force capable of beating the Twilight, whatever form it's incarnated in."

"But I couldn't beat it," said Nadya. "Dad, I'm not afraid, but I simply couldn't do it."

"You were alone that time," I said. "This time you'll be the Watch member from the forces of Light. With you, Zabulon, from the forces of Darkness. You and only you, because you're connected with Nadya, through me. The Prophet can only be Innokentii. He and Nadya swore blood brotherhood. They're connected."

"They cut their fingers with a little knife and signed their names in blood?" Zabulon asked mistrustfully. "Why, that's absurd! Games for children!"

"It depends on how you look at things," Gesar said softly. "All right. Innokentii Tolkov."

"Egor. The Mirror Magician."

"What about him?" Zabulon asked suddenly. "Perhaps he's your son, Gorodetsky. That would be a surprise!"

"I once rescued him from a vampiress who lured him with the Call. They are tied together by blood. And by the way, I am connected to them by that same Call, and through me so is Nadya, and so are you, Zabulon."

"If it really is the same vampiress, returned from her death after death," the Dark One remarked.

"Who else could it be?" I asked.

"But where is she?" Zabulon countered.

"She said she would come when the time was right. She has come before this, there are no grounds for disbelieving her."

"Let's accept that," Gesar agreed. "But what blood connects Arina with any of you?"

"Maybe you can answer that?" I said to the witch.

Arina flung her hands up in the air.

"Why are you all so obsessed with this idea of blood? There weren't any blood ties in our Watch of Six . . ." She paused and thought for a moment. "Perhaps there were—trifling indiscretions of youth . . . But nobody demanded anything of the kind. Why have you decided you need to pay attention to what Lilith said? It's a vile name anyway, satanic! You shouldn't set any store by what she told you!"

"Tell us, Arina," I said.

"Maybe I'm Zabulon's long-lost grandmother?" Arina suggested. "I don't know, stop pestering me about it! I don't have any children, my only daughter died in infancy, and then I couldn't have another child, like all witches. I've never bitten anyone, and I haven't been bitten by any vampires either . . ."

She stopped and chewed on her lip.

"What?" I asked.

"It's nonsense," Arina replied firmly. "It's got nothing to do with all the others you've listed. If you're so certain you need a tie of blood with a witch, then look for another one."

For the first time I felt my confidence falter.

"No, there has to be a connection," I muttered. "Everything fits."

"Anton," Svetlana said softly. "There's something I don't understand here. Do you mean to say that our daughter is a member of the Sixth Watch, along with Zabulon, Arina, Egor, Kesha, and that vampiress—the one whose name you can't even remember?"

I nodded.

"Without you or me . . ."

"Yes."

"You've lost your mind," Svetlana said in an icy voice. "You've gone crazy, Gorodetsky. You want to send our daughter into a deadly dangerous battle, accompanied by a Dark Magician who laughs for no reason at all, a vampiress who has returned from the next world, an overweight little boy, an uninitiated Other who works as a conjurer, and an old witch?"

"I changed my color, by the way," Arina reminded her. "Now I'm a pure Light Healer, just like you."

"A leopard never changes his spots!" Svetlana exclaimed furiously.

"And that's a fact," Arina agreed. "But I am a Light One. And you know, Svetlana . . . Anton's right after all!"

I looked at Arina and she looked back.

"Shut up, witch," I said. "Shut up."

"Everyone's always so rude to me," Arina sighed.

We looked into each other's eyes, and it felt as if we were talking— it wasn't the magical kind of conversation that Others can have; we were simply thinking about the same thing.

"So that's it then," Arina thought. *"How did you guess, Gorodetsky?"*

"I just did," I thought, looking at the witch's face. Either she had removed her camouflage, or I had started seeing right through her—

her beauty had evaporated, but it hadn't been replaced by her genuine, pitiful appearance. Arina was simply a sad old woman. *"That's
the way it is, isn't it? Always and everywhere."*

*"You're right about that, Gorodetsky. But it would be better to tell. Be-
lieve this witch."*

"No. Not right now."

Svetlana looked at us in alarm.

"I like what's happening here less and less," she said. "Gesar . . .
Zabulon . . . Don't you get the feeling that these two are holding
something back?"

"You should know best," Zabulon replied diplomatically.

"Anton Gorodetsky, I request you to answer," Gesar said. "As your
superior, as your teacher . . ."

"As the one who defied what was foreordained and made you a
Light One," Zabulon added vengefully.

"What are you hiding?" Gesar asked. "I know you, Anton. You
would never send your daughter on such a dangerous mission without yourself or your wife. Regardless of any prophecies!"

"I'm certain that the members of the Sixth Watch are in no danger
in their encounter with the Two-in-One," I said.

Gesar peered at me intently, then shrugged and announced his
opinion: "He seems to be confident about what he says. Bearing in
mind Anton's ability to find nonstandard solutions, I'm willing to
trust him."

Svetlana wasn't reassured. But fortunately, just then the door of
the office opened and four people came in: Egor and the old battle
magician Mark Jermenson, who were discussing something excitedly; Kesha, who was looking disgruntled; and the Prophet Sergei
Glyba, who had his arm around Kesha's shoulders.

"I took extra precautions with the boy anyway," Gesar explained.

"And quite right too," Glyba declared loudly. "I've already explained everything to Kesha and he has agreed, right, Kesha? Saturn
is in Libra, the year is on the turn. Last night the moon was obscured
by clouds."

"It was a new moon," Arina informed him.

"Really?" Glyba asked in surprise. "But all the same, there were clouds. So Kesha agrees that I should be the one in the Sixth Watch . . ."

"I don't agree at all," Kesha said angrily, shrugging Glyba's arm off his shoulder. He saw Nadya and his eyes flashed; he immediately straightened up and even pulled in his stomach.

He was a good boy. Even if he was clumsy and overweight.

"Thank you for coming," said Gesar. He got up and stepped forward, assuming the role of the host without being invited to. Zabulon spread his arms out theatrically and shook his head, but didn't say anything. "Almost all of us know each other . . . do you remember me, Egor?"

"Yes," Egor replied. "You haven't changed."

Gesar nodded.

"And you look better than you did back then on the roof, Zabulon."

Egor was very calm. Even tranquil.

"Hello, Egor," said Svetlana. "I'm Svetlana, Anton's wife. And this is Nadya, our daughter."

"And I'm a witch," said Arina. "Just a witch."

"Hello there," Egor said with a nod. "Pleased to meet you."

He walked over to Arina, reached out his hand, took a tiny scarlet flower out of her hair, and presented it to her. Then he smoothly did the same thing with Svetlana and Nadya.

"I didn't feel any magic," Nadya said in a surprised voice, examining the flower.

"It isn't magic, it's sleight of hand," said Egor, bowing politely. "I understand you have a team that is about to do battle with a monster in order to save the entire world. And I have an important function to perform in it."

"You could put it like that," Zabulon agreed.

"I'm ready and willing," Egor said with a nod. "I've been warned about the possible consequences and I have no problems with that.

I accept responsibility for the risks involved. Do I need to sign anything?"

"We work without bureaucracy," said Gesar. "Sit down. Would you like some tea or coffee? A sandwich?"

"Coffee," said Egor, walking over to the table. He shook my hand. Zabulon also reached out to him across the table and, after a moment's hesitation, Egor shook hands with him too.

"Olga," Gesar commanded. "Bring Egor a coffee and a latte for me."

Olga shrugged in exactly the same way as Zabulon had when Gesar started giving orders. My wonderful boss not only regarded himself as the most important person in any situation, he also treated any woman, even his own beloved, in the simple manner of the bygone times of his youth. It was the woman's job to bring tea or coffee for a guest, and that was that. Olga accepted the situation and didn't say a word, but just walked out into the reception area, where the secretary's coffee machine stood.

"And I'll have water; still, not fizzy!" Jermenson shouted after her as he walked across to Gesar and sat down beside him.

"Are we still waiting for someone?" Egor asked.

"Yes, the sixth member of the team isn't here yet," Gesar said evasively.

"That sounds a bit vague," said Egor, looking at me.

"I'm sorry, I should have told you," I explained. "It's a vampiress. The one who attacked you that time."

To my surprise not a single muscle even twitched in Egor's face. He just scratched the spot above his eyebrow with the tip of one finger.

"She was laid to rest. They told me."

"Sometimes they come back. But she seems to be on our side, Egor. She helped us to fight off the Two-in-One when he showed up the first time. And then she became the vampires' Master of Masters by fighting for the title at their assembly."

Egor looked at me in amazement and started reciting something—

it took me a moment to realize that it was the words of one of Grebenshchikov's old songs.

" 'She's so smart and she's so fine, she's read all the books she should have read, for sure; she goes out hunting dressed in bright-colored silk . . .' " Anton, you told me she was an inexperienced young vampire. Do they suddenly become so powerful when they're resurrected?"

"There," Zabulon said in a loud voice. "Even a callow boy can see that it's nonsense! I told you so, Gesar. It can't be her. It can't be. There's no way that regenerating a deceased vampire can make him more powerful than he was before. And he can't even be regenerated if his ashes have been scattered at sea; there's nothing left to regenerate!"

Gesar shrugged.

"Then who is it? She wrote Anton messages, she sneaked into our offices and gave him advice, she defended the entire Gorodetsky family in front of our very eyes."

"It wasn't her," Zabulon said firmly. "I don't know. Any other vampiresses, they're all mistresses of illusion."

"Now boys, stop quarreling!" Olga shouted from the reception area. "We're expecting a guest, aren't we?"

Gesar and Zabulon shut up.

"Someone's knocking," said Olga. "I'll get it."

Sergei Glyba darted over to the window with surprising agility, grabbing Kesha by the hand and dragging him away from his conversation with Nadya. Jermenson, on the contrary, stood up and moved closer to the door. The old battle magician's face lit up in eager anticipation.

I got up too and positioned myself between the door and my family.

"Ah, so that's it," we heard Olga say. "Very interesting. Come in."

"She's certainly making the most of her entrance," Zabulon remarked as Olga walked in through the door first and cast a mysterious, thoughtful glance at me.

Then Olga stepped aside and a young girl dressed in jeans and a nylon jacket walked in. The snow was still dusting her collar in a way it never does with living people—that only happens with vampires, who are as cold as ice. And I remembered this vampiress. A thin face with high cheekbones and dark, sunken eyes. When a vampire's organism has stabilized, this stigma of eternal hunger is hidden, it retreats deep within. But this vampiress had never developed into a mature individual. She had been disembodied for unlicensed hunting and attacking members of the Night Watch.

"Didn't I tell you? I was right!" Gesar exclaimed triumphantly.

"Hi there," I said to the vampiress. What else can you say to a dead enemy who has just risen from hell? Especially to an enemy who once seemed terrifying and dangerous, but proved to be no more than a weak and lowly pawn in someone else's game. And then all of a sudden turned into an incredibly powerful friend.

The vampiress looked at me. A shadow of recognition flickered across her face, followed by powerless malevolence. No, a vampiress who looked at me like that could never have rescued me . . . Then suddenly her face blurred, changing its shape, her body started stretching upward, and her figure changed into a man's. It was one of those illusions that vampires are so fond of, but it was also the kind of full-on morphing that only a Higher Vampire can perform.

"No," I said, watching as the faces appeared, one after another. "No!"

First came the vampire Vitieslav from the Inquisition. There was recognition in his expression too, and even a hint of affection. Then he saw Arina and obviously wanted to say something to her. But his place was taken by another face and I winced in pain when I recognized Gennadii Saushkin, whom I had disembodied in Edinburgh. He was once a good-natured, law-abiding citizen—insofar as that's possible for a vampire—and then he became an insane killer.

Somehow I could tell that none of them were real. The vampiress, Vitieslav, and Saushkin hadn't come back to life, all squeezed into a single body. It was something else. Some kind of disguise, but so perfect, so profound, that the masks were almost alive, almost real.

Almost. But they were still masks. Someone was wearing
them . . .

Gennadii Saushkin recognized me too, and lowered his eyes in
embarrassment, as if he felt ashamed to see me, his executioner.
And then another face surfaced, one that looked like his, but a lot
younger.

"But that's not . . ." I began.

Kostya shrugged with a guilty expression.

"Sorry, but here I am. All those dolls inside one another, and I'm
the one in the middle."

"I killed you," I said. "Twice. You burned up in space . . ."

Kostya nodded, then frowned and corrected me.

"Fortunately, I froze first."

"And then I disembodied all of you on the sixth level of the Twilight," I went on. "With Merlin's spell . . . Are you telling me that
Merlin got it wrong?"

"Merlin didn't get it wrong," said Kostya, shaking his head. "But
the Twilight took a special view of my case. It . . ." Kostya paused,
trying to find the right words. "It raised me up."

"Why would it do that, I wonder?" Zabulon said.

"Hello, boss." It looked ridiculous, but Kostya addressed Zabulon
very politely, almost fearfully. "Sorry for dropping in out of the blue
like this."

"Why would it do that?" Zabulon repeated.

Kostya unzipped the jacket, which had become too small for him.

"For the sake of the Sixth Watch, apparently. So that it could be
convened. I'm sorry, but you couldn't have done it on your own."

"Because we had forgotten everything?" Zabulon asked.

"No," Kostya replied after a moment's pause. "Because if I wasn't
here, the Sixth Watch couldn't possibly defeat the Two-in-One, even
theoretically. And the Twilight plays fair."

"So the Twilight is on our side, then?" Gesar asked eagerly.

"It's on its own side," Kostya said. "But there are rules, you see,
and it abides by them. An agreement was concluded between the

Others and the Two-in-One. That agreement must be implemented or rescinded. For that there have to be two sides. And both sides must have a chance."

"Strangely enough, I'm glad to see you," I said.

Kostya nodded seriously.

"Strangely enough, I'm glad to see you too," he replied. "The existence I have now is a very odd one. But it's better than nothing."

"Why did it do this to you?" I asked.

"I haven't talked to it about that," Kostya said with a shrug. "But I have thought about it. I think one or two vampires more or less doesn't matter all that much to the Twilight. It could return any vampire it wanted to the world, but it happened to choose me. Maybe because I killed Vitieslav, the vampire who used to be in the Sixth Watch, and from the Twilight's point of view I became his successor? But the Twilight also gave me a little part of other vampires. Even my father, for some reason."

"I gave Gennadii Saushkin my blood," Arina said in a low voice. "He was trying to copy your formula and increase his level of Power. He hoped that a witch's blood would help."

"There's the tie of blood," I said. "It all started because of the vampires, and everything has kept circling around them. The Twilight has used them to link us all together."

"And now it will force us to make a choice," Kostya said. "Sorry, but I have to ask this. I'm not trying to give orders, but we have very little time left . . . The Power that has come is almost at the door. You have to choose. Who are the members of the Sixth Watch?"

I looked at Gesar. He nodded.

"You decide . . . You're the one being asked."

He seemed to have hunched over and gone limp. As if all the air had been let out of him.

"In the Sixth Watch you will represent the vampires," I said. "Arina will represent the Conclave of Witches. Innokentii will represent the Prophets."

"As the head of the Association of Seers and Prophets, I do not—"

Glyba began, but stopped short, looking at me. Or maybe he was looking at something else? Into the future? "I have no objections," he concluded, sounding bewildered.

"The Mirror Magicians will be represented in the Sixth Watch by Egor," I continued. "Since there is never more than one Mirror Magician in the world at one time, his appointment is automatic. The forces of Darkness will be represented in the Sixth Watch by Zabulon, by virtue of the right granted to him by the Inquisition, the heads of the Day Watches, and the blood of Lilith, the oldest of the Dark Others. The forces of Light will be represented in the Sixth Watch"—I looked at Svetlana and shook my head—"by my daughter, Nadezhda Gorodetsky, by virtue of her right as an Absolute Light Enchantress."

"The Sixth Watch has been convened," said Kostya. He paused for a moment and added: "Since this is so important to all of you, I'll give you a little hint. The Sixth Watch has been convened correctly. We have a chance of overturning the agreement with the Two-in-One."

"You mean we can beat him?" Nadya exclaimed joyfully, taking a step forward. "Thanks, Dad."

I smiled at my daughter, but shook my head.

"No, of course not. You've seen him. He's not the Tiger, he crushed the Tiger. And the entire Conclave of Witches couldn't stop him. Perhaps you could, you're his equal in Power. But he's more cunning and he's used to killing. And if you killed him, you'd kill the entire Twilight, but we need that, don't we?"

Nadya frowned.

"There won't be any duel, little girl," Arina said quietly, walking up to Nadya. "I've just realized that, old fool that I am. All we can do is revoke the agreement. Declare it null and void."

"He's coming," said Kesha. "He's coming and he—"

The boy suddenly fixed his eyes on me. This time I had no doubt that he had seen the future. And he shook his head at what he had seen.

"What options do we have?" I asked. "You know there aren't any."

We heard the sound of steps in the reception area and the new members of the Sixth Watch spontaneously bunched together. Even Zabulon sighed, got up from behind his desk, and moved across to them.

I stayed where I was, close to the door.

"Anton!" Svetlana shouted.

"Stay where you are!" I ordered her.

The Two-in-One appeared in the doorway.

He had changed again. The Light Magician Denis and the Dark Magician Alexei had been finally and completely transformed and fused into a single creature, a man at least two and a half yards tall, with massively thick arms and legs and a disproportionately large head, even for a giant like that. His eyes bulged and his half-open mouth was full of sharp teeth. He was naked and had absolutely no sexual features.

Little children sometimes draw monsters like this, and then their concerned parents start thinking about a visit to the psychologist.

Little children sometimes remember what the old folks have forgotten and foresee what the grown-ups don't want to think about.

The Two-in-One lowered his head and stepped into the room— and I felt the Twilight shudder.

In distant parts of the world, in the special-access collections of the Inquisition in Prague and the witches' secret vaults under Madrid; in the regional branches of the Night and Day Watches; in the vampire catacombs of London, in Berlin and Taipei, Kiev and San Francisco, Tokyo and Warsaw; all the amulets and artifacts that had accumulated Power over hundreds and thousands of years were discharged simultaneously.

An Icelandic volcano with an unpronounceable name erupted, flinging up a pillar of ash and flame, as a torrent of energy poured through its base. In the Atlantic Ocean an American submarine broke in half when it was caught on a line of Power, a streak of boiling water at a depth of a hundred yards. In the air above Spain a single-engine plane was transformed into a swan five yards long, with the panic-stricken pilot clinging to its neck. Moscow, which had never known any serious earthquakes, was hit by a tremor measuring six on the Richter scale, which destroyed a newly elevated road. The air was filled with a reverberating hum.

And the Two-in-One was enmeshed in a web of green fire.

He howled and flung out his arms, trying to tear apart the magical bonds. But they didn't yield. The amount of Power in them was very great—more than even the Twilight could withstand.

A murky, whitish Shield appeared, dividing the office in two, but even through the Shield the blazing web threatened to burn out our retinas. The Two-in-One staggered, trying to stay on his feet, but the web glowed even more brightly, biting into his flesh.

"Now then!" Gesar shouted with the wild abandon of a hunter finishing off a wounded animal.

The green flames soaked into the body of the Two-in-One and the glow faded. The Shield was extinguished and the Two-in-One stood there as if he was listening carefully to something in his grotesquely huge body.

He burped, releasing a cloud of foul-smelling green smoke.

Everything went quiet, apart from the cups and saucers rattling on the desk. And then a small cup split in two, spilling out an unfinished espresso

The Two-in-One raised his head and growled quietly.

"Well, we had to try it, didn't we?" Zabulon said in an apologetic tone of voice.

The Two-in-One took a step forward.

"The Sixth Watch has been reestablished!" Arina announced, stepping forward and standing beside me. "Two-in-One, the Sixth Watch has been reestablished. By virtue of the right of the Covenant of Blood, we demand negotiations!"

The giant fixed his gaze on her and paused for a moment before speaking.

"Who are the members of the Watch of Six?" he asked

"I, Arina, for the witches. Zabulon for the Dark Ones. Nadezhda for the Light Ones. Egor for the Mirror Magicians. Innokentii for the Prophets. And . . ." Arina hesitated for a moment. "Konstantin for the vampires."

"I shall talk to him first," the Two-in-One announced. "By virtue of the right of the first Others, he speaks first."

Kostya stepped out to join Arina.

"I am the Dark Other Konstantin Saushkin, the Master of Masters."

"This is deception!" the Two-in-One declared. "You are dead."

"I have been dead for a long time," Kostya said coolly. "I am thrice dead. I died when I became a vampire, initiated by my own father. I died far from the earth, isolated from Power. I died on the sixth level of the Twilight, killed by Anton Gorodetsky. I am undead. What right have you to be indignant that someone who is dead has joined the Watch?"

"You hindered me."

"I corrected your error. You had no right to attack a future member of the Watch of Six."

The Two-in-One hesitated again before he replied.

"Speak."

"By virtue of the right of vampires, the first Others, who concluded the Covenant of Blood with you, I hereby annul that covenant henceforth and forever. Not everything should be resolved in the simple manner to which you are accustomed. I declare the Covenant of Blood abrogated."

"Whom do you offer in sacrifice as confirmation of your words?" the Two-in-One asked. "You know the rules. Bound by blood. Love and hate. Nobility and treachery. Strength and weakness."

"I offer in sacrifice Anton Gorodetsky," Kostya said, and I heard Svetlana screech behind me. "I loved him as my oldest friend. I hate him as my killer. He acted nobly in becoming my friend, defying the rules of the Watches. He acted treacherously in sending me to my death. Because of him I have become strong and because of him I have become weak."

The Two-in-One didn't react in any way to Kostya's words. "Now you speak, witch," he said.

"I am a Dar— A Light Other, the head of the Conclave of Witches," Arina declared. "By virtue of the right of witches, who stole their right to Power from the vampires and shape-shifters, by virtue of the women who concluded the Covenant of Blood with you, I annul it henceforth and forever. There is too much blood and much evil, even for us witches. The Covenant of Blood is abrogated."

"Who is to be sacrificed for your words?"

"Anton Gorodetsky," Arina said with a nod. "I loved him . . ." Suddenly she laughed. "Even a decrepit old witch has the right to fall in love with a man. I hate him because he did not notice my love, he loves another, and could never be mine. He acted nobly in not noticing my love and he acted treacherously in failing to notice it. I would have given him my strength, but he has no need even of my weakness."

"The Mirror," said the Two-in-One.

Egor sighed.

"Now, how does it go . . . I am Egor Martynov, an uninitiated Other and a Mirror Magician . . . probably. By virtue of the right—" he said, and stopped for a moment. "By virtue of the right of the party that preserves equilibrium, by virtue of the right of the party that realizes its purpose only in death, I annul the Covenant of Blood, because the balance must be maintained in some other manner. Without destroying everything. I abrogate it forever and all the rest of it, blah-blah-blah."

"Your sacrifice?"

"Anton Gorodetsky," Igor said. "I love him, he saved me. And I hate him, he deceived me. He acted nobly in defending my right to a destiny of my own, but he acted treacherously, because his own destiny was more important to him. He showed me strength and I chose weakness. There. That's about it."

"The Prophet?" the Two-in-One asked.

"I am Innokentii Tolkov," Kesha said. "A Prophet. A Light One. First Level. I represent all Prophets, because I am the only one who suits in this case. I annul the Covenant of Blood, because there is no future in it. And I wish to see the future. Henceforth and forever."

"The sacrifice?"

"Anton Gorodetsky," Kesha said in a faint voice. "He saved me too, kind of. But that's not the important thing. I love him because he is Nadya's father. And I . . . I hate him. Because I have to name him, and he knew that I was going to name him. And he behaved nobly, he never tried to stop me being friends with Nadya, although I know that he doesn't like me, he thinks I'm a clumsy, namby-pamby weakling. And I'm a traitor . . . because Nadya and I deceived him. And I have strength, which I know not only foretells the future, but also changes it, only I am weak . . . and I cannot change the future so that I could name someone else."

"The Dark One," said the Two-in-One.

"That's me," said Zabulon, without making the slightest attempt to move from the spot. "Zabulon, a Higher Dark One, representing the Dark Ones, obviously. I annul the Covenant of Blood; it is an archaic and irrational use of material. Henceforth and until the end of time. My sacrifice is Anton Gorodetsky. I love him—he is the most successful of my descendants. I hate him, he became a Light One and he likes it—I hate him especially because he likes it. He is a fine and noble enemy, but he is prepared to use treacherous means, and that makes me especially furious, because he would have been a truly great Dark One. And I am stronger than him, and would probably always have been stronger, but I could not do what he is doing now. In that way I am weaker. I have tried to do something of the kind sometimes, and I always stopped in time . . . but he does not know how to stop."

"The Light One," the Two-in-One announced.

I couldn't stop myself—I turned and looked at Nadya. And I nodded to her, because right then she was feeling really, really bad, and there was nothing I could do to support and protect her.

"I am a Higher Light One, Nadezhda Gorodetsky," said Nadya. Her voice was matter-of-fact—the very sound of it made my blood run cold. "I annul the Covenant of Blood. I hate it; perhaps there was a time when it was the best answer, the correct solution, but that time was long ago. I abrogate it forever. Let there be nothing but good or nothing but evil, if that's what people deserve. But we've had enough of this balance. A balance of good is always a balance of evil too. I . . . I . . ."

"You must name a sacrifice," the Two-in-One said.

"My sacrifice . . ." Nadezhda began, and stopped, looking at me. I nodded to her encouragingly. There was nothing that she could do about this. Absolutely nothing. "My sacrifice is Anton Gorodetsky, my father. I . . . I love him because he is my father and that's a good enough reason. And I hate him! I hate him because I should be standing where he is and he should be standing where I am, but he understood everything before I did and did as he wanted! And that's probably awfully noble of him, only it's terribly, terribly, treacherous. And I'd give away my Power, I don't need it. I'd be willing to live as an ordinary person, but I'm too weak to kill you . . . But I'll get stronger and I'll totally pulverize you. I'll go right through the Twilight and burn you out completely, or I'll invent special Twilight defoliants and poison every one of its levels. Do you think I'm a fool and I don't realize where you hide and what you're made of, you trashy, creeping blue garbage?"

Silence fell, broken only by Nadya's heavy breathing.

"The Watch of Six has spoken," the Two-in-One declared. "The Covenant of Blood is abrogated. No longer will anyone preserve the balance of good and evil among people. Henceforth your destiny is in your own hands."

For just a tiny, fleeting moment I thought he would turn and walk away. As the Tiger had once done.

For just a fleeting moment I thought my daughter's name was a magic talisman that would save me even on the brink of the abyss.

"I accept your sacrifice," the Two-in-One said.

Out of the corner of my eye, I saw him raise his immense hand and hold it out toward me. But I didn't want to look around. I looked at my daughter and my wife, who was being held firmly by Olga. And somewhere nearby was Gesar, who had made me the person I was; and my newly acquired Dark granddad, Zabulon; and the sharp-tongued old witch Arina, with her misplaced love; and the young Prophet Kesha, with his arms round Nadya's heaving shoulders; and the brave, good man who had grown out of the frightened boy Egor; and those battle-hardened old stagers Jermenson and Glyba . . .

But I looked at my daughter and my wife, trying to smile as sincerely as I could, so they would remember that smile and know that I was proud of them.

And then something icy blue and fiery red struck me in the back.

EPILOGUE

A GRAVEYARD IS A JOYLESS PLACE AT ANY TIME OF THE YEAR. In spring, when the air is cool and fresh and the trees are hazy with new green leaves, thinking about death is especially distressing. In the heat of summer, when the smell of the hot earth rises up into the air, a graveyard seems like a lurking predator, biding its time before it pounces on you. In autumn, under the gray, rainy sky, a graveyard is dreary and repulsive.

But the worst time of all is winter. The hard ground refuses to yield to the spades, and the thought that someone is about to be left in that frozen earth sends chilly shivers up and down your spine.

It was an old cemetery, right in the center of Moscow. Funerals were only held here very, very rarely, and always for people who were either very famous or very rich. Of course, it didn't have the prestige of the famous Vagankovo and Novodevichy cemeteries, but anywhere in the center of Moscow is pricey for the living and the dead.

"We don't often bury one of our colleagues," said Zabulon. "Usually there's nothing left to bury . . . and we don't get together with the Light Ones very often either."

He simply stood there for a while, wrapped up in his warm coat, then removed his gloves, took a wreath with the inscription FROM THE DAY WATCH OF MOSCOW from the shivering assistant who was standing behind him, placed it on the fresh grave, and stood back again with his head lowered.

"Farewell. You served loyally," he said.

Gesar never wore gloves. Maybe he had been used to the cold since the long-gone days of his youth in Tibet, or maybe he liked flaunting his folksy simplicity. The wreath FROM THE NIGHT WATCH OF MOSCOW was handed to him by Olga.

"A hard destiny," he said. "And a hard death. But . . . you were one of us and you always will be."

He lingered on the spot for a while, then looked at Zabulon, took a flask out of his pocket, and held it out to the Dark One.

"Here . . . let's see them off in the Russian style."

"A fine old Russian custom," Svetlana remarked in a low voice, "swigging French cognac in a graveyard . . ."

She took hold of my hand.

Zabulon let Gesar take a mouthful first, took one himself, and then held the flask out to me.

"Anton?"

"I won't, if you don't mind," I said. "I have to take care of my health now. Good health is the most precious thing a human being has."

"Anton, stop that," Zabulon said, looking at me reproachfully. "We'll take care of your health. And if you need treatment, we'll use all the resources of both Watches. You've earned it."

"I don't want to drink to them," I said, nodding at the grave where the monstrous body of the Two-in-One—the former Light Magician Denis and former Dark Magician Alexei—lay in an immense coffin. "He killed me, after all. One side of me."

"We all reach the end of the road sometime," Gesar replied. "Others are immortal, but . . ."

"And people are simply mortal," I said. "Sorry, but I won't drink. They're not to blame. But people don't drink to their own killers."

"You could say he took it easy on you," Gesar reminded me. "He could simply have killed you. Finally and completely. Disembodied you. Incinerated you. Extracted every last drop of your Power."

"He did kill me," I said. "By making me a man, he killed me. Maybe not right now, but in twenty years . . . Or thirty. And that's it."

"That's the way people live, Dad," said Nadya.

She was standing beside me, holding Innokentii's hand.

"Okay," I said, and took the flask from Zabulon.

The cognac seared my throat.

I closed my eyes, focusing on my inner sensations, and tried to look through my eyelids, into the Twilight.

But of course I couldn't do it.

"Rest in peace, may the Twilight be gentle," I muttered, handing back the flask.

Everyone was gradually drifting away. It was a joint funeral, held by both Watches, but the Light and Dark Watchmen were going to separate wakes. The two minibuses standing at the gates of the cemetery would take them in different directions.

Kostya Saushkin waved to me, but he didn't come over. And I think he was right. The Twilight had left him here on earth and given back to him what takes the place of life for vampires. We had been friends once, but that didn't alter the fact that I had killed him and he had killed me.

"Come on," said Semyon, walking up to me. "We have to go. It's the custom. Don't feel angry with Denis. He got wiped out in the line of duty."

"I'll drop around later," I said.

Semyon stuck his hands into the pockets of his jacket. He was embarrassed.

"But Anton . . . You can't . . . The restaurant's blocked off with a Sphere of Negation . . . You won't get through on your own."

He was right, of course.

"I'll bring him in," Svetlana said. "You guys go on. We'll follow."

Svetlana, Nadya, and I deliberately walked at a leisurely pace. And Kesha, of course. He was right there. Maybe he and Nadya would go their separate ways in a couple of months . . . or a couple of hundred years. But Kesha obviously saw something more optimistic in their future.

I'd have to put up with him.

"There are famous people here," Nadya said in a quiet voice. "Look, there's a famous film director, he made cartoons! And there's a writer . . . Oh, I've read his books!"

"Yes, a very respectable gathering," I said. "The Two-in-One should be pleased."

"Stop it, Dad!" my daughter told me. "He didn't kill you, that's all that matters!"

I remembered how Svetlana had sobbed as she hugged me. I sat there on the floor, pawing at the icy remnants of my shirt on one arm and the singed tatters on the other. Compared with the Two-in-One's usual blow, it was no more than a goodbye kiss.

But it was a genuine goodbye, because at that moment the Two-in-One was lying dead on the floor. And the former Watchmen of the Light and the Darkness had died in his gruesome body.

I didn't even understand straightaway what had happened. I was too glad just to be alive. Not even Gesar's embarrassed stare and the crestfallen look in Zabulon's eyes alerted me.

Or even the way that Svetlana suddenly stopped sobbing, drew back, and peered at me . . .

Then Nadya told me, with the ruthless frankness of youth: "Dad, you're human!"

Yes, I had become a human being. A perfectly ordinary person. Without even a hint of Other powers. With a "magical temperature" far higher than the threshold at which premonitions and the ability to perform paltry magic tricks are manifested.

I hadn't run out of steam, the way Others can do sometimes. I wasn't squeezed dry, the way Svetlana was after she fought the Mirror Magician.

I had irrevocably become a human being.

"I think part of the Two-in-One kind of felt sorry for you," said Nadya. "That's the reason, isn't it?"

I didn't want to offend my daughter. She's a clever girl. But she's also an Absolute Enchantress and it would be useful for her to be wise too.

"No, Nadya," I said. "That part of the Two-in-One was cruel and was very angry with me. That's why I'm still alive."

Nadya didn't say anything to that.

The minibuses had already left by the time we got into the car— Zabulon hadn't asked for his present to be returned. Svetlana took the wheel and I didn't object—without the ability to read the lines of probability, I would have been like a blind man on the road.

"You're not entirely right, you know, Anton," Svetlana said. "You didn't become human because someone felt sorry for you or hated you. You became a human being because you *were* human. You remained a human being, even after living as an Other for a quarter of a century. That's a very rare thing. And that's why you're still alive, even after the Two-in-One killed the magician in you."

I nodded. She was probably right. That was probably the way it was. But not even my wise wife could tell me how to live now.

I'd just have to learn.

People manage it, don't they?

ABOUT THE AUTHOR

Sergei Lukyanenko was born in Kazakhstan and educated as a psychiatrist. He began publishing science fiction in the 1980s and has published more than twenty-five books.

Andrew Bromfield (translator) is a founding editor of the Russian literature journal *Glas*. He is known for his acclaimed translations of Victor Pelevin and Boris Akunin, and his work has been short-listed for numerous translation prizes.

THE NIGHT WATCH SERIES BY
SERGEI LUKYANENKO

NIGHT WATCH   **DAY WATCH**   **TWILIGHT WATCH**

NEW WATCH   **SIXTH WATCH**